NEW SCIENCE FICTION AND FANTASY
eclipse
THREE

Also Edited by Jonathan Strahan:

Best Short Novels (2004 through 2007)
Fantasy: The Very Best of 2005
Science Fiction: The Very Best of 2005
The Best Science Fiction and Fantasy of the Year: Volume 1
The Best Science Fiction and Fantasy of the Year: Volume 2
The Best Science Fiction and Fantasy of the Year: Volume 3
Eclipse One: New Science Fiction and Fantasy
Eclipse Two: New Science Fiction and Fantasy
The Starry Rift: Tales of New Tomorrows

With Charles N. Brown
*The Locus Awards: Thirty Years of the Best in Fantasy and Science
    Fiction*

With Jeremy G. Byrne
The Year's Best Australian Science Fiction and Fantasy: Volume 1
The Year's Best Australian Science Fiction and Fantasy: Volume 2
Eidolon 1

With Terry Dowling
The Jack Vance Treasury
The Jack Vance Reader

With Gardner Dozois
The New Space Opera
The New Space Opera 2

With Karen Haber
Science Fiction: Best of 2003
Science Fiction: Best of 2004
Fantasy: Best of 2004

NEW SCIENCE FICTION AND FANTASY

Eclipse THREE

EDITED BY JONATHAN STRAHAN

NIGHT SHADE BOOKS
SAN FRANCISCO

For the late, great Charles N. Brown, last of science fiction's great lions, dear friend, and tireless supporter.

Acknowledgements

Eclipse Three is, as always, more than just the product of one person: it's the creative output from a small village of people. Once again, Jeremy, Jason, and Ross at the Shade have stood tall and provided me with the support I needed to do the book that I wanted to do; something for which I'm incredibly grateful. I'd also like to thank all of the contributors to the book. This book evolved much more naturally than it's predecessors, with stories coming from unexpected places at unexpected times, so I'm very grateful to everyone who has sent me stories this time. I'd like to thank Peter Watts for his understanding, and the Richard Powers Estate for the fabulous cover.

Finally, two special thanks. This book may not have been completed without the support of my good friend Gary Wolfe, who has never ceased to remind me of its value, and it certainly wouldn't have been done without the support and hard work of Marianne Jablon, who was both in-house editor on this book for me and tireless supporter. I'm very lucky indeed.

CONTENTS

INTRODUCTION

JONATHAN STRAHAN

A good book cover attracts the eye of a potential reader. It makes a book pleasing to behold, and makes you eager to pick it up and look further. A *great* book cover does more. It encapsulates the essence of the book and communicates that essence clearly and simply to anyone who might be interested.

When I first saw the cover for *Eclipse One*, the opening volume in this series, I could immediately see that it was a *good* cover, but I wasn't sure that it was a *great* one. It certainly had all of the right ingredients. Designer Michael Fusco had created a clean, simple series design that could be used with almost any piece of art. Multiple award-winning artist Michael Whelan's pre-existing art provided an appropriate air of ambiguity. What the cover didn't do, though, was "fit" the book that I felt I had in my mind's eye. It didn't have quite the same feel; represent the essence of the stories completely.

Now, creating a cover that fits an anthology is always difficult, and it is especially difficult when you are talking about a book such as *Eclipse*, which is unthemed and intended to be as varied as possible. Still that fit is something an art editor strives for, and that a designer works to achieve. It's also something that has become enormously important to me as an anthologist over the last year or two.

Increasingly I've felt that it's essential to create a total package that is, for want of a better word, "honest." I want the cover, the blurbs, the cover quotes, the introduction, and the stories to tell the same story, to deliver the same message to anyone who picks the book up so that they have a clear idea of what it is they're going to get. It's an ideal, but it's one that I think is worth working towards.

Because of that I was much more confident about the cover for *Eclipse Two*, which came out last year. I had decided, in consultation with my publisher, to make the second volume in the series a much more science fiction oriented book. I approached more science fiction writers than fantasy writers for the book. I chose stories that had robots and space-ships and vast empires. And art editor Jeremy Lassen provided a peach of a cover, taking a well-known piece of art by Hugo Award-winning artist Donato Giancola and nudging it into Michael Fusco's design in such a way that it was bright and shiny and new. I remember the excitement I felt when I opened the email that had the cover attached, and how I felt that it was just exactly *right* for the book. Even now, I think it's one of the best covers to appear on any of my books.

I was, however, frankly nervous about what kind of cover would be found for *Eclipse Three*. Like the first volume of the series, it's a varied volume featuring stories that range from straight fantasy to swords and sorcery to eloquent social science fiction. What could possibly, I wondered, honestly represent that variety? I needn't have worried.

When I first saw the cover art for *Eclipse Three* I knew immediately it was *right*. Following his own passion for great science fiction art, Jeremy Lassen had searched out and found something special: an unpublished piece of art by the late Richard Powers. Powers was possibly the greatest artist ever to work in the science fiction field, producing more than eight hundred science fiction paintings during a long and distinguished career that saw him produce iconic covers for Robert Heinlein, Isaac Asimov, Arthur C. Clarke, and many, many more. Although when Powers started his career his work fit the conventional pulp paperback style of the day, he quickly evolved a Surrealist style that was influenced by the likes of Picasso and Yves Tanguy, but was highly personal and very much his own.

The painting was perfect for *Eclipse* because it was vibrant, rich, and evocative. It suggested something hip and cool, but it didn't prescribe anything. It spoke directly to the essence of what I thought an *Eclipse* volume should be—varied, engaging, and ever changing. It also had connections to the science fiction world that I couldn't resist. The first volume of Damon Knight's classic *Orbit* series of anthologies had a Powers cover, as did the first volume of Pohl's *Star* and one of Robert Silverberg's *New Dimensions*. He'd also done some classic covers for books that had meant an enormous amount to me, like R. A. Lafferty's *Nine Hundred Grandmothers*.

I was sufficiently thrilled by the cover that I wanted to know more.

After all, how likely is it that unpublished Powers art of this caliber still existed? As it turns out the provenance of the art is as mysterious as the image Powers created. His agent Jane Frank told me that information on the work was severely limited. It is signed "Powers Laz/org," as he signed all of his commercial work, which suggests it was done for publication. But there's no information on it having been published. It has the hallmarks of a Powers book cover—layout, collage style, signature, etc.—but no other information. It is a mystery. And for me, that makes it perfect. A mysterious cover—bright and filled with energy—for a mysterious book. It's my hope that, when you've read the group of stories that make up this latest *Eclipse* you'll think it's perfect too.

Before I hand you over to the stories, though, a few thanks. *Eclipse Three* exists because of the generosity and dedication of Jeremy Lassen, Jason Williams, Ross Lockhart, and John Joseph Adams at "the Shade." Without them this book literally wouldn't and couldn't exist. I'd also like to thank the contributors to the book who have let me publish such wonderful work, and Jane Frank at the Powers Estate. As always, though, my greatest thanks goes to my wife Marianne, who has been there for every difficult moment I went through getting us here.

And last, thanks goes to you, the reader, for picking up this book and being willing to enter the worlds contained within it. Whether you were there for *Eclipse One* and *Eclipse Two*, or this is your first time under its darkling skies, welcome, and I hope to see you here again next year.

Jonathan Strahan
Perth, Western Australia
July 2009

THE PELICAN BAR

KAREN JOY FOWLER

For her birthday, Norah got a Pink cd from the twins, a book about vampires from her grown-up sister, *High School Musical 2* from her grandma (which Norah might have liked if she'd been turning ten instead of fifteen) and an iPod shuffle plus an Ecko Red t-shirt and two hundred-dollar darkwash 7 jeans—the most expensive clothes Norah had ever owned—from her mother and father.

Not a week earlier, her mother had said it was a shame birthdays came whether you deserved them or not. She'd said she was dog-tired of Norah's disrespect, her ingratitude, her filthy language—as if fucking was just another word for very—fucking this and fucking that, fucking hot and fucking unfair and you have to be fucking kidding me.

And then there were a handful of nights when Norah didn't come home and turned off her phone so they all thought she was in the city in the apartment of some man she'd probably met on the internet and was probably dead.

And then there were the horrible things she'd written about both her mother and father on facebook.

And now they had to buy her presents?

I don't see that happening, Norah's mother had said.

So it was all a big surprise and there was even a party. Her parents didn't approve of Norah's friends (and mostly didn't know who they were) so the party was just family. Norah's big sister brought the new baby who yawned and hiccoughed and whose scalp was scaly with cradle-cap. There was barbecued chicken and ears of corn cooked in milk, an ice-cream cake with pralines and roses, and everyone, even Norah, was really careful and nice except for Norah's grandma who had a fight in the

5

kitchen with Norah's mother that stopped the minute Norah entered. Her grandmother gave Norah a kiss, wished her a happy birthday, and left before the food was served.

The party went late and Norah's mother said they'd clean up in the morning. Everyone left or went to bed. Norah made a show of brushing her teeth, but she didn't undress, because Enoch and Kayla had said they'd come by, which they did, just before midnight. Enoch climbed through Norah's bedroom window and then he tiptoed downstairs to the front door to let Kayla in, because she was already too trashed for the window. "Your birthday's not over yet!" Enoch said, and he'd brought Norah some special birthday shrooms called hawk's eyes. Half an hour later, the whole bedroom took a little skip sideways and broke open like an egg. Blue light poured over everything and Norah's Care Bear Milo had a luminous blue aura, as if he were Yoda or something. Milo told Norah to tell Enoch she loved him, which made Enoch laugh.

They took more of the hawk's eyes so Norah was still tripping the next morning when a man and a woman came into her bedroom, pulled her from her bed and forced her onto her feet while her mother and father watched. The woman had a hooked nose and slightly protuberant eyeballs. Norah looked into her face just in time to see the fast retraction of a nictitating membrane. "Look at her eyes," she said, only the words came out of the woman's mouth instead of Norah's. "Look at her eyes," the woman said. "She's high as a kite."

Norah's mother collected clothes from the floor and the chair in the bedroom. "Put these on," she told Norah, but Norah couldn't find the sleeves so the men left the room while her mother dressed her. Then the man and woman took her down the stairs and out the front door to a car so clean and black that clouds rolled across the hood. Norah's father put a suitcase in the trunk and when he slammed it shut the noise Norah heard was the last note in a Sunday school choir; the *men* part of *Amen*, sung in many voices.

The music was calming. Her parents had been threatening to ship her off to boarding school for so long she'd stopped hearing it. Even now she thought that they were maybe all just trying to scare her, would drive her around for a bit and then bring her back, lesson learned, and this helped for a minute or two. Then she thought her mother wouldn't be crying in quite the way she was crying if it was all for show. Norah tried to grab her mother's arm, but missed. "Please," she started, "don't make me," but before she got the words out the man had leaned in to take them. "Don't make me hurt you," he said in a tiny whisper that echoed in her skull. He handcuffed Norah to the seatbelt because she was struggling. His mouth looked like something drawn onto his face with a charcoal pen.

"This is only because we love you," Norah's father said. "You were on a really dangerous path."

"This is the most difficult thing we've ever done," said Norah's mother. "Please be a good girl and then you can come right home."

The man with the charcoal mouth and woman with the nictitating eyelids drove Norah to an airport. They showed the woman at the ticket counter Norah's passport, and then they all got on a plane together, the woman in the window seat, the man the aisle, and Norah in the middle. Sometime during the flight Norah came down and the man beside her had an ordinary face and the woman had ordinary eyes, but Norah was still on a plane with nothing beneath her but ocean.

While this was happening, Norah's mother drove to the mall. She had cried all morning and now she was returning the iPod shuffle to the Apple store and the expensive clothes to Nordstrom's. She had all her receipts and everything still had the tags, plus she was sobbing intermittently, but uncontrollably, so there was no problem getting her money back.

Norah's new home was an old motel. She arrived after dark, the sky above pinned with stars and the road so quiet she could hear a bubbling chorus of frogs and crickets. The man held her arm and walked just fast enough to make Norah stumble. He let her fall onto one knee. The ground was asphalt covered with a grit that stuck in her skin and couldn't be brushed off. She was having trouble believing she was here. She was having trouble remembering the plane. It was a bad trip, a bad dream, as if she'd gone to bed in her bedroom as usual and awakened here. Her drugged-up visions of eyelids and mouths were forgotten; she was left with only a nagging suspicion she couldn't track back. But she didn't feel like a person being punished for bad behavior. She felt like an abductee.

An elderly woman in a flowered caftan met them at a chainlink gate. She unlocked it and the man pushed Norah through without a word. "My suitcase," Norah said to the man, but he was already gone.

"Now I am your mother," the woman told Norah. She was very old, face like a crumpled leaf. "But not like your other mother. Two things different. One: I don't love you. Two: when I tell you what to do, you do it. You call me Mama Strong." Mama Strong stooped a little so she and Norah were eye to eye. Her pupils were tiny black beads. "You sleep now. We talk tomorrow."

They climbed an outside stairway and Norah had just a glimpse of the moon-streaked ocean on the other side of the chainlink. Mama Strong took Norah to room 217. Inside, ten girls were already in bed, the floor nearly covered with mattresses, only narrow channels of brown rug between. The light in the ceiling was on, but the girls' eyes were shut. A second old woman sat on a stool in the corner. She was sucking loudly on a red lollipop. "I don't have my toothbrush," Norah said.

"I didn't say brush your teeth," said Mama Strong. She gave Norah a yellow t-shirt, gray sweatpants and plastic flip flops, took her to the bathroom and waited for Norah to use the toilet, wash her face with tap water and change. Then she took the clothes Norah had arrived in and went away.

The old woman pointed with her lollipop to an empty mattress, thin wool blanket folded at the foot. Norah lay down, covered herself with the blanket. The room was stuffy, warm, and smelled of the bodies in it. The mattress closest to Norah's belonged to a skinny black girl with a scabbed nose and a bad cough. Norah knew she was awake because of the coughing. "I'm Norah," she whispered, but the old woman in the corner hissed and clapped her hands. It took Norah a long time to realize that no one was ever going to turn off the light.

Three times during the night she heard someone screaming. Other times she thought she heard the ocean, but she was never sure; it could have been a furnace or a fan.

In the morning, the skinny girl told Mama Strong that Norah had talked to her. The girl earned five points for this, which was enough to be given her hairbrush.

"I said no talking," Mama Strong told Norah.

"No, you didn't," said Norah.

"Who is telling the truth? You or me?" asked Mama Strong.

Norah, who hadn't eaten since the airplane or brushed her teeth in twenty four hours, had a foul taste in her mouth like rotting eggs. Even so she could smell the onions on Mama Strong's breath. "Me," said Norah.

She lost ten points for the talking and thirty for the talking back. This put her, on her first day, at minus forty. At plus ten she would have earned her toothbrush; at plus twenty, her hairbrush.

Mama Strong said that no talking was allowed anywhere—points deducted for talking—except at group sessions, where talking was required—points deducted for no talking. Breakfast was cold hard toast with canned peaches—points deducted for not eating—after which Norah had her first group session.

Mama Strong was her group leader. Norah's group was the girls from room 217. They were, Norah was told, her new family. Her family name was Power. Other families in the hotel were named Dignity, Consideration, Serenity, and Respect. These were, Mama Strong said, not so good as family names. Power was the best.

There were boys in the west wings of the motel, but they wouldn't ever be in the yard at the same time as the girls. Everyone ate together, but there was no talking while eating so they wouldn't be getting to know each other; anyway they were all very bad boys. There was no reason to think about them at all, Mama Strong said.

She passed each of the Power girls a piece of paper and a pencil. She told them to write down five things about themselves that were true.

Norah thought about Enoch and Kayla, whether they knew where she had gone, what they might try to do about it. What she would do if it were them. She wrote: *I am a good friend. I am fun to be with.* Initially that was a single entry. Later when time ran out, she came back and made it two. She thought about her parents. *I am a picky eater*, she wrote on their behalf. She couldn't afford to be angry with them, not until she was home again. A mistake had been made. When her parents realized the kind of place this was, they would come and get her.

I am honest. I am stubborn, she wrote, because her mother had always said so. How many times had Norah heard how her mother spent eighteen hours in labor and finally had a c-section just because fetal Norah wouldn't tuck her chin to clear the pubic bone. "If I'd known her then like I know her now," Norah's mother used to say, "I'd have gone straight to the c-section and spared myself the labor. 'This child is never going to tuck her chin,' I'd have said."

And then Norah scratched out the part about being stubborn, because she had never been so angry at her parents and she didn't want to give her mother the satisfaction. Instead she wrote, *nobody knows who I really am.*

They were all to read their lists aloud. Norah was made to go first. Mama Strong sucked loudly through her teeth at number four. "Already this morning, Norah has lied to me two times," she told the group. "'I am honest' is the third lie today."

The girls were invited to comment. They did so immediately and with vigor. Norah seemed very stuck on herself, said a white girl with severe acne on her cheeks and chin. A red-haired girl with a freckled neck and freckled arms said that there was no evidence of Norah taking responsibility for anything. She agreed with the first girl. Norah was very stuck-up. The skinny girl with the cough said that no one honest ended up here. None of them were honest, but at least she was honest enough to admit it.

"I'm here by mistake," said Norah.

"Lie number four." Mama Strong reached over and took the paper, her eyes like stones. "*I* know who you really are," she said. "*I* know how you think. You think, how do I get out of here?

"*You* never will. The only way out is to be different. Change. Grow." She tore up Norah's list. "Only way is to be someone else completely. As long as some tiny place inside is still you, you will never leave."

The other girls took turns reading from their lists. "I am ungrateful," one of them had written. "I am a liar," read another. "I am still carrying around my bullshit," read the girl with the cough. "I am a bad person." "I am a bad daughter."

It took Norah three months to earn enough points to spend an afternoon outside. She stood blinking in the sun, watching a line of birds thread the sky above her. She couldn't see the ocean, but there was a breeze that brought the smell of salt.

Later she got to play kickball with the other Power girls in the old, drained motel pool. No talking, so they played with a silent ferocity, slamming each other into the pool walls until every girl was bleeding from the nose or the knee or somewhere.

After group there were classes. Norah would be given a lesson with a multiple choice exercise. Some days it was math, some days history, geography, literature. At the end of an hour someone on staff would check her answers against a key. There was no instruction and points were deducted for wrong answers. One day the lesson was the Frost poem "The Road Not Taken," which was not a hard lesson, but Norah got almost everything wrong because the staff member was using the wrong key. Norah said so and she lost points for her poor score, but also for the talking.

It took eleven months for Norah to earn enough points to write her parents. She'd known Mama Strong or someone else on staff would read the letter so she wrote it carefully. "Please let me come home. I promise to do whatever you ask and I think you can't know much about this place. I am sick a lot from the terrible food and have a rash on my legs from bug bites that keeps getting worse. I've lost weight. Please come and get me. I love you. Norah."

"So manipulative," Mama Strong had said. "So dishonest and manipulative." But she put the letter into an envelope and stamped it.

If the letter was dishonest, it was only by omission. The food here was not only terrible, it was unhealthy, often rotting, and there was never enough of it. Meat was served infrequently, so the students, hungry enough to eat anything, were always sick after. No more than three minutes every three hours could be spent on the toilet; there were always students whose legs were streaked with diarrhea. There was no medical care. The bug bites came from her mattress.

Sometimes someone would vanish. This happened to two girls in the Power family. One of them was the girl with the acne, her name was Kelsey. One of them was Jetta, a relatively new arrival. There was no explanation; since no one was allowed to talk, there was no speculation. Mama Strong had said if they earned a hundred points they could leave. Norah tried to remember how many points she'd seen Kelsey get; was it possible she'd had a hundred? Not possible that Jetta did.

The night Jetta disappeared there was a bloody towel in the corner of the shower. Not just stained with blood, soaked with it. It stayed in the corner for three days until someone finally took it away.

A few weeks before her birthday, Norah lost all her accumulated points, forty-five of them, for not going deep in group session. By then Norah had no deep left. She was all surface—skin rashes, eye infections, aching teeth, constant hunger, stomach cramps. The people in her life—the ones Mama Strong wanted to know everything about—had dimmed in her memory along with everything else—school, childhood, all the fights with her parents, all the Christmases, the winters, the summers, her fifteenth birthday. Her friends went first and then her family.

The only things she could remember clearly were those things she'd shared in group. Group session demanded ever more intimate, more humiliating, more secret stories. Soon it seemed as if nothing had ever happened to Norah that wasn't shameful and painful. Worse, her most secret shit was still found wanting, not sufficiently revealing, dishonest.

Norah turned to vaguely remembered plots from after-school specials until one day the story she was telling was recognized by the freckled girl, Emilene was her name, who got twenty whole points for calling Norah on it.

There was a punishment called the TAP, the Think Again Position.

Room 303 was the TAP room. It smelled of unwashed bodies and was crawling with ants. A student sent to TAP was forced to lie face down on the bare floor. Every three hours, a shift in position was allowed. A student who moved at any other time was put in restraint. Restraint meant that one staff member would set a knee on the student's spine. Others would pull the student's arms and legs back and up as far as they could go and then just a little bit farther. Many times a day, screaming could be heard in Room 303.

For lying in group session, Norah was sent to the TAP. She would be released, Mama Strong said, when she was finally ready to admit that she was here as a result of her own decisions. Mama Strong was sick of Norah's games. Norah lasted two weeks.

"You have something to say?" Mama Strong was smoking a small hand-rolled cigarette that smelled of cinnamon. Smoke curled from her nostrils, and her fingers were stained with tobacco or coffee or dirt or blood.

"I belong here," Norah said.

"No mistake?"

"No."

"Just what you deserve?"

"Yes,"

"Say it."

"Just what I deserve."

"Two weeks is nothing," Mama Strong said. "We had a girl three years ago, did eighteen."

Although it was the most painful, the TAP was not, to Norah's mind, the worst part. The worst part was the light that stayed on all night. Norah had not been in the dark for one single second since she arrived. The no dark was making Norah crazy. Her voice in group no longer sounded like her voice. It hurt to use it, hurt to hear it.

Her voice had betrayed her, telling Mama Strong everything until there was nothing left inside Norah that Mama Strong hadn't pawed through, like a shopper at a flea market. Mama Strong knew exactly who Norah was, because Norah had told her. What Norah needed was a new secret.

For her sixteenth birthday, she got two postcards. "We came all this way only to learn you're being disciplined and we can't see you. We don't want to be harsh on your birthday of all days, but honest to Pete, Norah, when are you going to have a change of attitude? Just imagine how disappointed we are." The handwriting was her father's, but the card had been signed by her mother and father both.

The other was written by her mother. "Your father said as long as we're here we might as well play tourist. So now we're at a restaurant in the middle of the ocean. Well, maybe not the exact middle, but a long ways out! The restaurant is up on stilts on a sandbar and you can only get here by boat! We're eating a fish right off the line! All the food is so good, we envy you living here! Happy birthday, darling! Maybe next year we can celebrate your birthday here together. I will pray for that!" Both postcards had a picture of the ocean restaurant. It was called the Pelican Bar.

Her parents had spent five days only a few miles away. They'd swum in the ocean, drunk mai tais and mojitos under the stars, fed bits of bread to the gulls. They'd gone up the river to see the crocodiles and shopped for presents to take home. They were genuinely sorry about Norah; her mother had cried the whole first day and often after. But this sadness was heightened by guilt. There was no denying that they were happier at home without her. Norah had been a constant drain, a constant source of tension and despair. Norah left and peace arrived. The twins had never been difficult, but Norah's instructive disappearance had improved even their good behavior.

Norah is on her mattress in room 217 under the overhead light, but she is also at a restaurant on stilts off the coast. She is drinking something made with rum. The sun is shining. The water is blue and rocking like a cradle. There is a breeze on her face.

Around the restaurant, nets and posts have been sunk into the sandbar. Pelicans sit on these or fly or sometimes drop into the water with their wings closed, heavy as stones. Norah wonders if she could swim all the way back into shore. She's a good swimmer, or used to be, but this is merely hypothetical. She came by motorboat, trailing her hand in the water, and will leave the same way. Norah wipes her mouth with her hand and her fingers taste of salt.

She buys a postcard. *Dear Norah,* she writes. *You could do the TAP better now. Maybe not for eighteen weeks, but probably more than two. Don't ever tell Mama Strong about the Pelican Bar, no matter what.*

For her sixteenth birthday what Norah got was the Pelican Bar.

Norah's seventeenth birthday passed without her noticing. She'd lost track of the date; there was just a morning when she suddenly thought that she must be seventeen by now. There'd been no card from her parents, which might have meant they hadn't sent one, but probably didn't. Their letters were frequent, if peculiar. They seemed to think there was water in the pool, fresh fruit at lunchtime. They seemed to think she had counselors and teachers and friends. They'd even made reference to college prep. Norah knew that someone on staff was writing and signing her name. It didn't matter. She could hardly remember her parents, didn't expect to ever see them again. Since "come and get me" hadn't worked, she had nothing further to say to them. Fine with her if someone else did.

One of the night women, one of the women who sat in the corner and watched while they slept, was younger than the others, with her hair in many braids. She took a sudden dislike to Norah. Norah had no idea why; there'd been no incident, no exchange, just an evening when the woman's eyes locked onto Norah's face and filled with poison. The next day she followed Norah through the halls and lobby, mewing at her like a cat. This went on until everyone on staff was mewing at Norah. Norah lost twenty points for it. Worse, she found it impossible to get to the Pelican Bar while everyone was mewing at her.

But even without Norah going there, Mama Strong could tell that she had a secret. Mama Strong paid less attention to the other girls and more to Norah, pushing and prodding in group, allowing the mewing even from the other girls, and sending Norah to the TAP again and again. Norah dipped back into minus points. Her hairbrush and her toothbrush were taken away. Her time in the shower was cut from five minutes to three. She had bruises on her thighs and a painful spot on her back where the knee went during restraint.

After several months without, she menstruated. The blood came in clots, gushes that soaked into her sweatpants. She was allowed to get up long enough to wash her clothes, but the blood didn't come completely out and the sweatpants weren't replaced. A man came and mopped the floor where Norah had to lie. It smelled strongly of piss when he was done.

More girls disappeared until Norah noticed that she'd been there longer than almost anyone in the Power family. A new girl arrived and took the mattress and blanket Kimberly had occupied. The new girl's name was Chloe. The night she arrived, she spoke to Norah. "How long have you been here?" she asked. Her eyes were red and swollen and she had a squashed kind of nose. She wasn't able to hold still; she jabbered about her meds which she hadn't taken and needed to; she rocked on the mattress from side to side.

"The new girl talked to me last night," Norah told Mama Strong in the morning. Chloe was a born victim, gave off the victim vibe. She was so weak it was like a superpower. The kids at her school had bullied her, she said in group session, like this would be news to anyone.

"Maybe you ask for it," Emilene suggested.

"Why don't you take responsibility?" Norah said. "Instead of blaming everyone else."

"You will learn to hold still," Mama Strong told her and had the girls put her in restraint themselves. Norah's was the knee in her back.

Then Mama Strong told them all to make a list of five reasons they'd been sent here. "I am a bad daughter," Norah wrote. "I am still carrying around my bullshit. I am ungrateful." And then her brain snapped shut like a clamshell so she couldn't continue.

"There is something else you want to say." Mama Strong stood in front of her, holding the incriminating paper, two reasons short of the assignment, in her hand.

She was asking for Norah's secret. She was asking about the Pelican Bar. "No," said Norah. "It's just that I can't think."

"Tell me." The black beads of Mama Strong's eyes became pinpricks. "Tell me. Tell me." She stepped around Norah's shoulder so that Norah could smell onion and feel a cold breath on her neck, but couldn't see her face.

"I don't belong here," Norah said. She was trying to keep the Pelican Bar. To do that, she had to give Mama Strong something else. There was probably a smarter plan, but Norah couldn't think of anything. "Nobody belongs here," she said. "This isn't a place where humans belong."

"You are human, but not me?" Mama Strong said. Mama Strong had never touched Norah. But her voice coiled like a spring; she made Norah flinch. Norah felt her own piss on her thighs.

"Maybe so," Mama Strong said. "Maybe I'll send you somewhere else then. Say you want that. Ask me for it. Say it and I'll do it."

Norah held her breath. In that instant, her brain produced the two missing reasons. "I am a liar," she said. She heard her own desperation. "I am a bad person."

There was a silence and then Norah heard Chloe saying she wanted to go home. Chloe clapped her hands over her mouth. Her talking continued, only now no one could make out the words. Her head nodded like a bobblehead dog on a dashboard.

Mama Strong turned to Chloe. Norah got sent to the TAP, but not to

Mama Strong's someplace else.

After that, Mama Strong never again seemed as interested in Norah. Chloe hadn't learned yet to hold still, but Mama Strong was up to the challenge. When Norah was seventeen, the gift she got was Chloe.

One day, Mama Strong stopped Norah on her way to breakfast. "Follow me," she said, and led Norah to the chainlink fence. She unlocked the gate and swung it open. "You can go now." She counted out fifty dollars. "You can take this and go. Or you can stay until your mother and father come for you. Maybe tomorrow. Maybe next week. You go now, you get only as far as you get with fifty dollars."

Norah began to shake. This, she thought, was the worst thing done to her yet. She took a step toward the gate, took another. She didn't look at Mama Strong. She saw that the open gate was a trick, which made her shaking stop. She was not fooled. Norah would never be allowed to walk out. She took a third step and a fourth. "You don't belong here," Mama Strong said, with contempt as if there'd been a test and Norah had flunked it. Norah didn't know if this was because she'd been too compliant or not compliant enough.

And then Norah was outside and Mama Strong was closing and locking the gate behind her.

Norah walked in the sunlight down a paved road dotted with potholes and the smashed skins of frogs. The road curved between weeds taller than Norah's head, bushes with bright orange flowers. Occasionally a car went by, driven very fast.

Norah kept going. She passed stucco homes, some small stores. She saw cigarettes and muumuus for sale, large avocados, bunches of small bananas, liquor bottles filled with dish soap, posters for British ale. She thought about buying something to eat, but it seemed too hard, would require her to talk. She was afraid to stop walking. It was very hot on the road in the sun. A pack of small dogs followed her briefly and then ran back to wherever they'd come from.

She reached the ocean and walked into the water. The salt stung the rashes on her legs, the sores on her arms and then it stopped stinging. The sand was brown, the water blue and warm. She'd forgotten about the fifty dollars though she was still holding them in her hand, now soaked and salty.

There were tourists everywhere on the beach, swimming, lying in the sun with daiquiris and ice cream sandwiches and salted oranges. She wanted to tell them that, not four miles away, children were being starved and terrified. She couldn't remember enough about people to know if they'd care. Probably no one would believe her. Probably they already knew.

She waded into shore and walked farther. It was so hot, her clothes dried quickly. She came to a river and an open air market. A young man with a scar on his cheek approached her. She recognized him. On two occasions, he'd put her in restraint. Her heart began to knock against her lungs. The air around her went black.

"Happy birthday," he said.

He came swimming back into focus, wearing a bright plaid shirt, smiling so his lip rose like a curtain over his teeth. He stepped toward her; she stepped away. "Your birthday, yes?" he said. "Eighteen?" He bought her some bananas, but she didn't take them.

A woman behind her was selling beaded bracelets, peanuts and puppies. She waved Norah over. "True," she said to Norah. "At eighteen, they have to let you go. The law says." She tied a bracelet onto Norah's wrist. How skinny Norah's arm looked in it. "A present for your birthday," the woman said. "How long were you there?"

Instead of answering, Norah asked for directions to the Pelican Bar. She bought a t-shirt, a skirt, and a cola. She drank the cola, dressed in the new clothes and threw away the old. She bought a ticket on a boat—ten dollars it cost her to go, ten more to come back. There were tourists, but no one sat anywhere near her.

The boat dropped her, along with the others, twenty feet or so out on the sandbar, so that she walked the last bit through waist-high water. She was encircled by the straight, clean line of the horizon, the whole world spinning around her, flat as a plate. The water was a brilliant, sundazzled blue in every direction. She twirled slowly, her hands floating, her mind flying until it was her turn on the makeshift ladder of planks and branches and her grip on the wood suddenly anchored her. She climbed into the restaurant in her dripping dress.

She bought a postcard for Chloe. "On your eighteenth birthday, come here," she wrote, "and eat a fish right off the line. I'm sorry about everything. I'm a bad person."

She ordered a fish for herself, but couldn't finish it. She sat for hours, feeling the floor of the bar rocking beneath her, climbing down the ladder into the water, and up again to dry in the warm air. She never wanted to leave this place that was the best place in the world, even more beautiful than she'd imagined. She fell asleep on the restaurant bench and didn't wake up until the last boat was going to shore and someone shook her arm to make sure she was on it.

When Norah returned to shore, she saw Mama Strong seated in an outdoor bar at the edge of the market on the end of the dock. The sun was setting and dark coming on. Mama Strong was drinking something that could have been water or could have been whiskey. The glass was colored blue so there was no way to be sure. She saw Norah getting off the boat. There was no way back that didn't take Norah towards her.

"You have so much money, you're a tourist?" Mama Strong asked. "Next time you want to eat, the money is gone. What then?"

Two men were playing the drums behind her. One of them began to sing. Norah recognized the tune—something old that her mother had liked—but not the words.

"Do you think I'm afraid to go hungry?" Norah said.

"So. We made you tougher. Better than you were. But not tough enough. Not what we're looking for. You go be whatever you want now. Have whatever you want. We don't care."

What did Norah want to be? Clean. Not hungry. Not hurting. What did she want to have? She wanted to sleep in the dark. Already there was one bright star in the sky over the ocean.

What else? She couldn't think of a thing. Mama Strong had said Norah would have to change, but Norah felt that she'd vanished instead. She didn't know who she was anymore. She didn't know anything at all. She fingered the beaded bracelet on her wrist. "When I run out of money," she said, "I'll ask someone to help me. And someone will. Maybe not the first person I ask. But someone." Maybe it was true.

"Very pretty." Mama Strong looked into her blue glass, swirled whatever was left in it, tipped it down her throat. "You're wrong about humans, you know," she said. Her tone was conversational. "Humans do everything we did. Humans do more."

Two men came up behind Norah. She whirled, sure that they were here for her, sure that she'd be taken, maybe back, maybe to Mama Strong's more horrible someplace else. But the men walked right past her toward the drummers. They walked right past her and as they walked, they began to sing. Maybe they were human and maybe not.

"Very pretty world," said Mama Strong.

A PRACTICAL GIRL

ELLEN KLAGES

"**C**an I watch *Howdy Doody* when we get home?" Carolyn Sullivan asked. She pushed the cart down the canned foods aisle of the Shop-Rite while her mother added creamed corn and green beans to the basket.

"*May* I. And what's the magic word?"

"May I *please* watch *Howdy Doody?*"

"All right, if there's time after we make the beds. We have guests coming."

Carolyn sighed. The Institute for Advanced Study was holding a conference over the weekend, and they were expecting a visiting professor to arrive the next day. The house on Mercer Street had been in the family since the end of the Civil War. When Ensign William Sullivan's ship was torpedoed late in 1943, all hands lost, his widow transformed it into a guest house, to support herself and her baby daughter.

Einstein lived a block away.

Mrs. Sullivan wheeled the cart into a check-out line. "Would you like to play the register game?" she asked. "It'll be good practice. School starts next week."

Carolyn nodded. Her mother thought the game was a kind of homework—good for her—but she liked trying to add up all the groceries in her head as fast as the check-out girl could use the keys. She was the best in her class at arithmetic.

She put the cans of corn on the belt and watched as the white tabs jumped up at the back of the machine with a soft *ka-ching*, like ducks in a shooting gallery. Twelve cents, four times, which was easy. Then the beans. The first one was 13 cents, and she smiled, because there were four of them too, and that was 52 cents, which made the dollar rectangle in her head whole again. 48 + 52 = 100.

It made her happy when the numbers meshed together with nice, even edges.

The girl was fast, and Carolyn lost track, a little, when the roast went through—$2.37—because it was a big number and it ended with a seven. They were the hardest because they almost never made nice shapes. But when the girl hit TOTAL, Carolyn was only 68 cents off.

"Pretty good," her mother said as they loaded the bags into the back of the station wagon. She pulled a Tootsie Pop out of her purse. "I think that deserves a reward."

Carolyn made the candy last, sucking, not biting, and still had a tiny nub left when all the groceries had been put away. But by the time the last pillowcase had been fluffed and placed just-so, it was too late for *Howdy Doody*, so she went out to the backyard with her book. Newly cut grass clippings clung to her bare legs like jimmies on an ice cream cone, and her hair hung damp on the back of her neck in the August heat, but discomfort was the price of freedom. Next week it was back to plaid uniforms, memorizing and eagle-eyed nuns.

She sat against the stone wall that separated their yard from the woods, grateful for the shade of the elm. Four pages into *Johnny Tremain*, she heard the solid *thwack* of a bat hitting a baseball, and a second later a white missile whizzed over her head and landed in the underbrush beyond with a swishing of leaves and a soft thud.

Silence, for a moment, then a babble of boys' voices. She stood up and looked across the manicured lawn of the Taylors' house next door. On the far side, she saw a trio of crew cut heads above the wooden fence. New kids, moved in last week.

"Do you have our baseball?" one of them yelled.

Carolyn cupped her hands around her mouth and called back. "It's in the woods."

"Okay."

He headed for the chain-link fence at the back of his own yard, and had one sneaker wedged a foot up before she could warn him, "You won't get through from there. Blackberry bushes. Big thorns."

She watched him shrug and leap the fence anyway.

"Ow! Shit!" came through loud and clear a moment later.

The urge to yell, "I told you so," was strong, but she hadn't met that boy yet. He swore, so he might try for payback. She watched him climb back into his yard, rubbing his knee, then made a bold decision.

"I'll get it."

Her mother always warned her about the woods. Besides the black-berries, it would be easy to get lost among the acres of trees. "You're all I have," she'd say. So Carolyn had never explored beyond the wall, mostly because, up until this summer, she hadn't been tall enough to climb over. But she was now.

She looked behind her to see if she was being watched, then scaled it and surveyed the ground on the other side. A soft verge of grass and dandelions grew at the base, and the blackberries seemed to peter out midway behind the Taylors'. She jumped down.

The ball had left a trail through the undergrowth, and she found it soon enough, too pale and too perfectly round to be part of the natural chaos. She recovered it from underneath a clump of damp leaves, dis-turbing a legion of rolly bugs and one fat salamander.

She'd planned to walk down the verge to the Wallers' house, on the corner, and return the ball from the sidewalk side. Then she saw three flat stones, piled one on the other, the topmost painted with a faded red crosshatch, like a tic-tac-toe game waiting to happen. That wasn't nature, either. She squatted down. The stones marked what looked like a path leading deeper into the trees. It might be nothing, and it might end in more blackberries, but, except for the market, she'd been cooped up inside all day. Chores and more chores. Everything had to be tidied up, "neat as a pin," when guests were coming.

Carolyn scuffed her feet in the leaves as she walked back to the stone wall, leaving her own trail, and threw the baseball as hard as she could across the Taylors' yard, shouting, "Ball!" It landed next to the birdbath and knocked over a garden gnome. She headed away from the sudden clamor.

No one had used the path in a while. Saplings blocked her way and sprang back, hard, across her arms as she pushed through. Twigs snagged at her ankles, and her white socks were soon covered with a carpet of tiny green burrs that would take forever to pick out. But it *was* a path, and every hundred yards or so she found another pile of rocks. Some of them had tumbled over, but one stone always had the same mysteri-ous crosshatch.

The woods were cool and shady. Carolyn could smell the earth, almost sweet from decomposing logs, with a bitter undertaste of autumn after autumn of fallen leaves. No breeze, and except for the sound of her feet crunching along, all she heard were birdcalls and the occasional rhythmic *knock-knock-knock* of an unseen woodpecker.

The path paralleled Stony Brook for a little while, then veered off to the left and ended at an old wooden fence with a narrow stile, its boards warped and moss-covered. Carolyn put one careful foot on the bottom step. It creaked, but held her weight, and she climbed up and sat at the top, looking into the ruins of what had once been a large and elaborate garden, not just a backyard.

Rosebushes taller than her surrounded stone benches and a sundial. The edges of a gravel walkway were blurred with weeds, and wildflowers grew knee-high. A dozen bees droned lazily in midair.

The walkway led to the back of an old barn. A huge maple tree, still thick-leafed with summer, blocked her view of all but one wing of the house—a single story with a bay window below a magnificent stained-glass peacock. She sat on the stile for a few minutes, savoring the discovery of a new place and debating about exploring further.

She had come this far, and didn't want to turn back now, but entering the garden wasn't just being in the woods. It was trespassing. If anyone still lived in the house—which didn't look too likely—she'd get caught. They'd call her mother and *then* she'd really be in trouble. She'd spend the last week of summer doing laundry and dishes and ironing. Inside.

After several go-rounds with herself, curiosity won and she clambered into the garden. Gravel skittered and the bees flew off to a safer distance, but nothing else happened.

The walkway continued around the barn. She turned the corner and barely stopped an out-loud gasp. The house on the other side of the wide drive was enormous, with gabled windows and a cupola, every inch covered in ornate Victorian gingerbread that needed painting.

She still thought the place was deserted—until she saw the round-fendered Buick, parked with its nose just inside the "barn," which turned out to be a four-car garage. The Buick had a Princeton sticker on its bumper, and New Jersey plates, 1952, just like her mother's car, all legal and up-to-date.

Carolyn stepped into the shadows and scrunched down. She eased around the corner of the house, planting each foot carefully so her Keds were almost silent. The wide porch held a line of peeling Adirondack chairs and wrapped all the way around to the front. That was even grander—stone pillars and more stained glass, green-limned copper letters over the entrance that said THE BRAMBLES.

It was a mansion, the biggest house she'd ever seen outside a magazine. But, except for the Buick, it would be easy to believe no one had been here for years.

"Hullo. Have you ever seen a giant turtle?"

Carolyn gave a little yelp and jumped back, whacking her elbow on a drainpipe. Cradling her arm, she looked around to see who had spoken.

It took her a moment to notice that the massive front door was open, just a crack, a foot in a leather oxford wedged into the gap.

"How giant?" she asked. Her brain was full of other questions, but that was the one that came out of her mouth.

The oxford moved and the door opened to reveal a boy about her age, sitting cross-legged on the floor. He made a circle with his arms, wider than his body. "Like this."

"Wow." Carolyn climbed the steps and stood on the porch.

"He's very old," the boy said. "Grandaddy sent him from China for my daddy's birthday. He's magic."

"Sure he is." Carolyn tried not to laugh, because the boy sounded serious, but she was a practical girl. She didn't believe in magic and fairy tales and all that baloney. Her family? Not so happily ever after.

The boy shook his head. "Not Daddy. Lotion."

"*Lotion?*" Was that what he'd said?

"My turtle."

"Funny name for a turtle." Even an imaginary one.

"He's Chinese." The boy stood up and pushed the door all the way open. He had short brown hair and was taller than Carolyn, by a couple of inches, but she could tell right away that there was something wrong with him. One side of his head was shaped funny, and his eyes didn't look straight at her, just a little beyond.

Real. Imaginary. Didn't look like it'd make much difference to him.

"Who're you?" he asked.

"I'm Carolyn. I live on Mercer Street, on the other side of the woods," she said, slowly, the way she talked to the little kids she babysat.

"I'm Bibber." He stopped and shook his head again. "No. The man from the bank says I'm too old. Now I have to be Robert." He looked from side to side, as if someone might be hiding on the porch, then whispered, "*You* can call me Bibber."

"How old *are* you?"

"Eleven. Last month."

"Oh. Me too. But not until December." She leaned against one of the pillars. "Do you live here?"

Bibber nodded.

"You must have a really big family."

"No. Just Higgins and Cook and Mrs. Addison, the housekeeper. But she's having a Day Off."

"How 'bout your mom and dad?"

"Mommy died having me and Daddy's in the war hospital. He's sleeping and he won't wake up."

"I'm sorry," Carolyn said. She wondered if it was Korea, or the last war.

"I know. That's why the bank man makes the rules for me." Bibber pointed at the doorway. "You wanna come in?"

"I guess so." He didn't look dangerous, and Carolyn felt sorry for him. Not just because he was—slow, but because she knew how it felt to have a war steal your father.

The inside of the house was cool and dark, darker than the woods. Heavy velvet curtains covered the windows, and massive furniture loomed around her. The walls were encrusted with big, gilt-framed paintings of dead birds and fruit.

"I don't play in here," Bibber said. "But Lotion sometimes hides under the sofa."

They walked through three rooms with high ceilings and fireplaces tall enough to stand up in. A long table with twelve chairs around it was bigger than her whole dining room at home; another eight chairs lined the walls. Twenty people could have dinner, she counted without really thinking.

The next room was one she didn't know a name for. Her house had a living room and a dining room, a kitchen and a utility porch, but this room was none of those. It had high-backed leather armchairs and small side tables and cabinets full of foreign-looking objects: curved knives, lacquered boxes, intricately carved figurines. On the walls were animal heads, stuffed and mounted, their glass eyes glinting in the dim light as she walked by.

"What did your grandfather do?" she asked.

"He went far away on boats. He bought things for museums." Bibber pointed to a cabinet. "He kept some of them."

"Yeah. I can see."

"I like *this* room," Bibber said, opening the double doors.

It was a library, floor-to-ceiling bookcases with rails that held two wooden ladders. At the far end, beneath the stained-glass window she had seen from the stile, was a bay window with a cushioned seat. The curtains were tied back, and in the sunlight, the leather spines of the books—brown, maroon, deep green—felt like an extension of the woods.

A table with two glass-shaded lamps sat in the center of the room, chairs on either side; a thick carpet with ornate dragons and flowers covered most of the parquet floor.

"I do too," Carolyn said. It was exactly the sort of room she had read about and always longed for, a place to sit and read for hours and hours. Cozy and enclosing, a world of its own, the perfect place to get lost in a story. "Have you read all these?" she asked. She looked around, wondering where she'd start, if it was hers.

Bibber didn't answer. He looked down at the carpet, staring at the head of a curled green dragon.

"Bibber?"

"I can't read by myself," he mumbled. "I know all my letters, but—"

"Oh." Carolyn couldn't imagine not being able to read. "Where do you go to school?"

"I don't. Nanny taught me lessons." Bibber sat down and wrapped his arms around his knees. "But she went away."

Carolyn hesitated, then sat down near him. "Well, I bet the bank man will get you another Nanny real soon."

"No." Bibber began to rock back and forth. "The bank man says I am too old. Mr. Winkle has hair now, and I have to go to Vineland."

"He can't send you *there!*" Carolyn blurted, before she could stop herself. Vineland was the state school for the feeble-minded. Going there was so bad that the nuns used it as their last-resort threat when someone didn't do their homework, or failed a test.

"He says I have to. And I can't take Lotion."

How could they forbid an imaginary animal? Carolyn traced a finger along the plush wool of the dragon's tail. "When do you go?"

"Next week," Bibber said. He wiped his eyes with the edge of his wrist. "I wanna stay here."

"I would too," said Carolyn.

They sat in silence for a few minutes before Bibber stood up. "Wanna see my picture book?"

"I guess."

He went over to a bookshelf, pulled out a pebbled black volume, opened it, shook his head, took out another. "There he is!" he said, suddenly sounding very happy.

Bibber laid the book on the long table and motioned for Carolyn to come see. When she stood up, she saw that it wasn't a real book, but a scrapbook, the pages filled with snapshots and postcards and ticket stubs. Someone had written names and dates and notes under each photo.

"That's my daddy, on his birthday." Bibber pointed to a photo of a boy kneeling with his hand on the edge of what really did look like a large turtle shell. The rest had been cut off by the camera. The caption underneath read: *Bobby with a gift from Father, all the way from Nanking China!* A card next to it said: *A puzzler for you, son. Can you find the secret?*

"Wanna see another one?"

"Sure."

Pinching the bottom corner between his fingers, Bibber carefully flipped the page to reveal a single, larger photo. Two boys in knickers sat cross-legged on either side of a huge tortoise, its shell painted with a complicated design, groups of connected dots.

"See. That's him and Lotion."

The caption read: *Bobby and friend Bill admire the new addition.*

Carolyn gasped, out loud this time.

The turtle was real.

And the other boy was her father.

Bibber wanted her to stay longer, but Carolyn needed to go home. She promised she'd return, then walked back through the woods, her mind racing with questions she doubted Bibber could answer. When she reached the stone wall at the edge of her own backyard, she felt like she'd been far away for a very long time. But next to the Taylors' a group of boys were still playing ball, and when she went in the back door, her burr-covered socks hidden in the pocket of her shorts, her mother had just begun peeling potatoes for supper.

"There you are," her mother said. "Where did you disappear to?"

"I was hot, so I took a walk," Carolyn said, which was true enough. She got a tumbler from the cupboard and drank a glass of water. "I'm going to go upstairs and read for a while, okay?"

"Dinner in an hour," her mother said.

Carolyn went upstairs, but not to her room. She opened the door to the attic—slowly, so it wouldn't squeak—and climbed the stairs in her bare feet. Way back under the eaves was a trunk with bits and pieces of her father's life before the war. She'd found it two summers ago, and had looked through most of the stuff, but she'd never mentioned it. She figured it wasn't against any rules—he *was* her father—but it made Mom sad to talk about him, so mostly they didn't.

The trunk was wood and brass with a rounded top. Carolyn had to move three cartons of winter clothes and Christmas ornaments before she could slide it out far enough to open the lid.

A flat box held wedding pictures, official papers and Navy medals. She set it aside, along with a Princeton High yearbook and pennant. She thought there was a folder from when he was her age—school essays and a science-fair project—and she was hoping that somewhere in it she'd find the answer to why *Bibber* had a picture of him. Because anything about her father was important, and Bibber would be lost to Vineland soon.

Carolyn opened a school composition book. Homework, math or science, with doodles and games of tic-tac-toe among the equations, some in pencil, some in blue or black ink. She leafed through a couple of pages and was about to throw it on the "other" pile when one of the doodles caught her eye—a sketch of a pile of rocks with a cross-hatch pattern. Below it, in a kid's handwriting, it said: *Secret Passage of the Lo-Shu Club.*

Excited, she turned a few more pages, but the attic was too hot to sit still, and sweat had begun to drip between her shoulders. She pulled out the next layer of papers in the trunk; they were crayon drawings—too young—so she carefully replaced everything except the composition book and shut the lid. She hid her find under the mattress in her bedroom and had her hand on the railing when "Honey? Supper," came from downstairs.

"Where did you go on your walk?" Her mother asked after a sip of iced tea. They were eating cold chicken and potato salad at the kitchen table, because there were no guests.

"Just down to the library." That was more or less true.

"Sounds lovely. It was too hot to bake anything, so I made an icebox cake for dinner tomorrow night. But if you want a snack, have an Oreo. The cake's for company. Don't cut into it."

"I won't." Carolyn was used to FHB—family hold back.

After dinner she washed their dishes and put them in the drainer, and only missed a few minutes of *Mr. Wizard*, her favorite show. When *Arthur Godfrey* came on, she left her mother knitting a new throw for the easy chair, and stole up to her room to find out more about the Lo-Shu Club.

Page after page of the composition book was covered with what looked like parts of tic-tac-toe games, some with the usual **X**s and **O**s, and some with numbers in the squares instead. She could see that two people had written in it, because the 4s and 8s were different. The diagrams were surrounded by dozens of addition problems, like the drills Sister Liguori gave for practice, but all really easy—just the counting numbers, in batches of three: 4+9+2, 3+5+7, 8+1+6, 4+5+6….

She liked puzzles and story problems because the answers made sense in real life. If Sister Liguori gave them one about cooking eggs, Carolyn could be sure the answer wasn't going to be a fraction, because who would take a third of an egg to a picnic? It was harder trying to figure out what the *story* was when all she had was numbers, but these were starting to make interesting patterns in her head. She was at her desk, chewing on the end of a pencil, deep in thought, when her mother called from the hall. "Lights out. Sweet dreams."

Rats. "'Night, Mom," she called back. She turned off her desk lamp, but took her flashlight under the covers and lay on her side. She had to use one hand to hold the light and the other to hold the notebook open flat, so she couldn't write anything down, but she was determined to get all the way to the end.

Half an hour later, her neck had a crick, and she was fighting back yawns. Uncle. She was too tired to think any more. She riffled through the remaining pages, about a dozen, then stopped and sat bolt upright, sheltering the book and the light in her lap.

Inside the back cover of the composition book, in capital letters and bright red ink, it said:

THE OATH OF THE LO-SHU CLUB.
ANY MEMBER IS MY BROTHER, AND I WILL RESCUE HIM FROM DANGER, NO MATTER WHAT, NO MATTER WHERE.
I HEREBY SWEAR BY THE SIGN OF THE MAGIC TURTLE.

Underneath were two crosshatches and two signatures—William A. Sullivan and Robert M. Wilkins.

Bill and Bobby.

Carolyn woke up with her arms wrapped around the composition book, the flashlight down by her feet. She stashed both under her pillow and went down to breakfast, racing through corn flakes and orange juice so that she could return to her quest. Then her mother got out the vacuum cleaner.

"You can do the downstairs first," she said, as if it were some kind of treat. "I'll tackle the linens. I don't want to be ironing in the heat of the day. Holler when you've finished the living room and I'll carry the

Hoover up so you can do the bedrooms—it's still a little heavy for you."
She patted Carolyn on the arm.

So it wasn't until after lunch, when her mother went off to the cleaners
and the bank and the drugstore, that Carolyn had a chance to get back
to the notebook. She sat at the dining room table with a pile of scratch
paper, going over her own sums for the third time, checking her work,
when the doorbell rang.

The professor was early.

She put down her pencil and went to the screen door. An older lady
with blond hair and glasses stood on the front porch in a plain blue dress,
a cardigan sweater folded over one arm. Someone from the women's
club, raising money for the March of Dimes again?

"Can I help you?" Carolyn asked.

"I'm Dr. Hopper. I believe I'm expected?"

Holy moley. Most of their guests were scientists. Only big brains got
invited to the Institute's conferences. But none of them had ever been
a lady before.

"Oh. Sure. Please come in," Carolyn said, in her most polite, talking-
to-guests voice. "My mother will be home in a few minutes." She held
the door open, saw a suitcase, and remembered to ask, "Do you need
help with that?" Dr. Hopper was on the skinny side.

"No, thank you. I can manage." She picked up the small Samsonite
case and walked into the front hall. "What a lovely home."

"Thanks." Carolyn thought hard. She'd watched her mother check
guests in, but had never done it by herself. "Have a seat," she said, gesturing to the dining room table. "Would you like some iced tea?"

"I would. It's rather warm today."

Carolyn went into the kitchen and stood on a chair to get down one
of the nice glasses. The lever on the ice-cube tray stuck, and the pieces
came out broken, but she didn't think it would matter. She took the
sweating glass and a napkin out to the table.

Dr. Hopper had a pencil in her hand, tapping it on the pile of scrap
paper. She looked up when Carolyn came in. "I see you're working on
the Lo-Shu problem."

Carolyn caught the glass before she dropped it all the way, but it
splashed enough to soak the napkin. She set the tea onto the table. "How
do *you* know about that?"

"I'm a mathematician." Dr. Hopper took a sip. "Legend says it was
first discovered by a Chinese emperor who noticed the pattern on the
shell of a divine turtle, and thought it was an omen."

"A *turtle?*" Lo-Shu. The light bulb finally went on. *Lotion!*

"That's the story." She smiled at Carolyn. "Mystical poppycock, of course. But it *is* the most common variation of an order-three magic square."

"Magic? It isn't math?"

"It's both." She laid the papers flat on the table. "Why don't you sit down, show me what you've found." She was a guest, but she sounded like a teacher.

"It's a square, three across, three up and down, with all the counting numbers, no repeats." Carolyn pointed to one of the diagrams.

$$\begin{matrix} 4 & 9 & 2 \\ 3 & 5 & 7 \\ 8 & 1 & 6 \end{matrix}$$

"Do you see a pattern in the digits?" Dr. Hopper asked.

"I think so. The top row adds up to 15. So do the others."

"Very good. In this configuration, the sum of every row, column, and diagonal is the same 'magic' number—15."

"What can you do with it?" Sister Liguori was big on using math in real life.

"Not a thing. It has no practical application." Dr. Hopper laughed. "But that's a plus to many of my colleagues. *Pure* mathematics is about truth, unconnected to everyday life. They create their own perfect worlds, happily—" She turned. "Oh, hello."

"Hello. Welcome." Mrs. Sullivan stepped through the doorway from the kitchen and held out her hand. "I'm Eileen Sullivan. We spoke on the phone." She looked down at the stack of papers. "I see you've met my daughter, Carolyn."

"Oh yes. We've been discussing higher mathematics."

"Really?" Mrs. Sullivan raised an eyebrow. "I hope she hasn't been—"

"Not at all. I'm enjoying myself." Dr. Hopper stood up.

"Well, we try to make our guests feel at home here. Why don't I show you to your room?" Mrs. Sullivan headed toward the stairs. "You're at the back, on the right. A lovely view of the woods this time of year." She looked down at the suitcase. "May I take that for you?"

"No, thank you, I can manage."

Carolyn's mind kept wandering off to a place Sister Liguori had never mentioned—a perfect world where numbers could be magic. But her hands helped make dinner, set the table with the good china, and serve while her mother chatted with Dr. Hopper, who was one of the less boring guests they'd had. She'd been in the Navy during the war, a WAVE, but in a laboratory, not on a boat, working on something called a computer—a machine that could do arithmetic. Now she had a job with an important company, building an even bigger one.

"They're the first machines man has built to serve his brains, not his brawn," she said. "One day children will use something like UNIVAC for their homework, instead of memorizing multiplication tables."

Mrs. Sullivan frowned. "But then they won't *learn* anything."

"They will. They'll learn how to *use* numbers, see the patterns and connections. That's what mathematics is all about." She reached into the pocket of her sweater and took out a pack of Luckies. "Do you mind?"

"Not at all. Let me get you an ashtray." She went into the kitchen.

"What's your conference about?" Carolyn asked, leaning forward. She had never told her mother about the numbers making shapes, when they played the cash-register game, because it would sound kind of weird, but she thought Dr. Hopper probably understood.

"Let me see. Tomorrow morning's schedule has papers on combinatorics, twin primes, set theory, and imaginary numbers."

"What, like a make-believe one—fifty blibbity-blips?"

Her mother put the ashtray and a book of matches by Dr. Hopper's plate. "Carolyn! That's no way to—"

Their guest held up her hand. "It's a reasonable conjecture," she said, lighting her cigarette. "But no. Numbers like this." She took a mechanical pencil from the same pocket and drew a figure on the inside cover of the matchbook: $\sqrt{-1}$. "The square root of negative one."

Mrs. Sullivan stared. "I was an English major, and I only got through algebra, so forgive me, but if you multiply two negatives, isn't the answer always positive?"

"Yes. Every time."

"So the square root of negative one is impossible."

"No, only imaginary." Dr. Hopper smiled. "I know it sounds like mathematical fiction, but it's quite useful in understanding electromagnetics and quantum mechanics."

"I see," Mrs. Sullivan said.

Carolyn could tell that her mother was only being polite, but *she* wanted to know more about how numbers could be magic and how imaginary things could be useful. Because if the numbers in story problems were about real life, then—

"Is that your topic at the conference?" Mrs. Sullivan asked.

"No, Dr. von Neumann and I are part of a symposium on recent developments in electronic data coding. Among other things, we're going to be discussing one of *your* favorite games." She turned to Carolyn.

Huh? "Which one?"

"Tic-tac-toe." She tapped her ash into the small glass dish. "A bright young man at Cambridge—England—has programmed a computer called EDSAC to play. The **X**s and **O**s are on a cathode ray display—like the picture tube in your TV."

"It's a pretty easy game," Carolyn said. Why would the brains talk about *that?*

"Exactly. It's finite, with perfect information."

"What?"

"Sorry. Mathematically, that means there's no luck involved. You can know every possible move, and there are only a limited number."

Carolyn nodded. "Yeah. Nine."

"Not even close. Try 362,880."

"Uh-*uh!*"

Dr. Hopper smiled again and drew a small tic-tac-toe board on the matchbook. "First move you have nine choices where to put an **X**, right?"

"Sure. That's what I said."

"Ah, but then the next player has *eight* choices of where to put an **O**. Seven choices for the second **X**, and so on until someone wins. Or ties." She stubbed out her cigarette. "That big number is nine times eight times seven times six—" She waved her hand in the air. "Etcetera, etcetera."

"Why on earth would anyone want to build a machine that plays games?" Mrs. Sullivan asked.

"Programming a computer to make logical decisions is the first step in replicating human intelligence. If all goes well, Tic-tac-toe is going to help create a better future." Dr. Hopper stood up. "May I use your phone? It's a local call. Dr. von Neumann."

Carolyn's mother seemed to be in a bit of a daze. Guests usually talked about the weather, or how the Phillies were doing that season. "Of course," she said after a moment. "On the table, in the hall. I'll get dessert. Coffee?"

"Please. Two sugars. I'll only be a minute." Dr. Hopper put her napkin down beside her plate and left the room. Carolyn heard her dial, then say, "Johnny? It's Grace. Are we still on for breakfast tomorrow?"

All night, Carolyn tossed and turned, thinking about numbers and Tic-tac-toe—and Vineland. Even though she had never met her father, only seen pictures, she felt like she almost knew the boy in the notebook, who had sworn to rescue his best friend if Bobby was ever in danger. Too late for that.

But now *she* could rescue Bibber.

The next morning, while her mother was getting ready for a Women's Club meeting and Dr. Hopper was waiting for her taxi, she filled the pockets of her shorts with chalk and pencils and a pen. She tucked a dozen sheets of scrap paper into the composition book that held the secrets of the Lo-Shu Club. She was ready.

By 9:30, the house was empty. Carolyn left a note—*Gone to the library.*—and headed into the woods. When she reached the stile, she slipped over into the garden. She crept along the far edge until she could see in through the library's bay window.

Good. Bibber was there. He lay on his stomach, moving a line of toy soldiers around a fort made of blocks. She duck-walked along the base of the porch to the front door and tiptoed through to the room of cabinets and animal heads, then quietly opened the double doors to the library.

Bibber looked up, and his whole face filled with a smile. Carolyn put her finger to her lips—*Shh.*

Bibber nodded. "Why are we being very quiet?" he whispered.

"I don't want your housekeeper to hear us."

"Oh. She won't," Bibber said. "Mrs. Addison is in the kitchen with Cook. She leaves me alone until my lunch." He shrugged. "Unless I make a big noise."

"What time do you eat?" Carolyn asked in her normal voice.

"Lunchtime."

That wasn't much help. But Carolyn figured it'd be at least noon, and that gave her plenty of time. "Do you know how to play Tic-tac-toe?" she asked.

"Uh-huh. I'm pretty good."

"Great." She laid the composition book and two pencils on the table. When she drew the grid on a piece of scratch paper she said, under her breath, "By the sign of the magic turtle."

Carolyn knew how to use numbers for a lot of useful things, but she hadn't known they could be magic until she met Dr. Hopper. If *she* said that was real, Carolyn believed it. She was at the Institute, with Einstein, the smartest man in the world, so she ought to know.

"You go first," she said.

Bibber drew a tiny **X** in the top right corner, and she followed with an **O** next to it. She wanted to put her **O** in the center—it was the best move—but she also wanted Bibber to win the first game. When he drew his third **X** in a row, he smiled in triumph. "I told you. I am good at this."

"Yep. So you get to draw the next one."

He did, his tongue in the corner of his mouth, concentrating on making the four lines as straight as he could.

There. They had both drawn the sign that made them members of the Lo-Shu Club. "You are my brother," Carolyn whispered. "I will rescue you from danger." She made an **O** in the center square, but let Bibber win again.

"Where do you keep Lotion?" she asked.

"He crawls all over the house. The downstairs part. Right now he's under the table."

"Here?" Carolyn moved one of the chairs and squatted down. On the carpet was the biggest tortoise she had ever seen—even bigger than the one in the Bronx Zoo. At her movement, he turned his head and looked at her with a yellow, reptilian eye. "How do you get him to come out?" They couldn't lift him, not even the two of them. He was the size of an ottoman.

"I wait until he's hungry," Bibber said. "We could try and feed him now."

"What does he eat?" He looked as prehistoric as a dinosaur, with scaly front feet the size of salad plates. He might eat *anything*.

"Fruit and stuff. Leftover salad. Watch." Bibber pulled a cluster of blue-black grapes from his pocket and lay them in a pile a foot away from the edge of the table.

In real-life slow motion, the tortoise rose up and lumbered forward, one leg at a time, until he stood over the grapes. He extended his surprisingly long neck, lowered his head, and mashed the grapes into his mouth in three pulpy bites.

"It's bad to feed him on the rug," Bibber said, pointing to a purple stain that was almost invisible against the elaborate floral design. "Mrs. Addison says."

"I can see why." Carolyn stared at Lotion's back. She'd planned to draw the Lo-Shu numbers onto the turtle with chalk, but she didn't need to. The pattern was carved into nine plates on his shell, the center square marked with five dots arranged like the pips on Monopoly dice, faint traces of red paint in the deepest grooves.

Lotion was already magic.

Now for the tricky part. Carolyn circled the room, chalking $\sqrt{-1}$ on the four walls, the window frame, the doors, and a side or shelf of each bookcase.

"What are you doing?" Bibber asked.

"Making things imaginary." It was pure math, and would be unconnected to the real world, where Vineland waited.

When she had marked all the openings, she made one more circuit, checking her work, then turned to Bibber. "Can you sit on Lotion?" The tortoise had eased back down to the floor, and lay with his eyes shut. He *looked* sturdy enough.

"Sure. I ride him around, sometimes." Bibber straddled the carved shell and scratched the tortoise on the top of his leathery head. "How long do I hafta sit here?"

"You'll know." Carolyn hoped that was true. She circled the room again, taking a few books from the shelves: *Huckleberry Finn, Treasure Island, The Wind in the Willows, Peter Pan, The Jungle Book, The Wizard of Oz.* She added a dictionary and the scrapbook with the picture of their fathers to the stack. Then, stepping around Bibber, she arranged the eight books in a square, three on a side, with Lotion at the center to make nine.

"What are those?"

"Books I think you'll like."

"I can't read." Bibber frowned. "I told you."

"You will. Pure math creates its own perfect world." She wrote nine blue numbers in ink on the soft skin on the back of Bibber's neck:

$$4 \quad 9 \quad 2$$
$$3 \quad 5 \quad 7$$
$$8 \quad 1 \quad 6$$

Magic turtle, magic boy.

"That tickles." Bibber laughed.

"Sorry." She patted his hair. "But now you can live happily ever after." She turned toward the door.

Bibber frowned. "Are you leaving?"

"Uh-huh."

"No. I want you to stay." He sounded sad.

Carolyn looked around at the room full of books and light and comfortable chairs, a room she'd always dreamed of. It was so tempting—a lifetime to sit and read, uninterrupted, no chores, no nuns—she bit her lip—no Mom. *You're all I have,* she heard in her mind, and shook her head. "I can't, Bibber. I have to go home."

"But you'll come visit?"

She opened the double doors. "I'll try." She stepped into the next room and closed them behind her, then marked each one with $\sqrt{-1}$.

"Keep Bibber away from Vineland," she said aloud, then added, "Please."

There. That was all the magic she knew.

She tiptoed back through the house, holding her hand tight on her pocket so the pen and pencils wouldn't make a noise. She was in the room with the paintings of fruit before she noticed that her other hand was empty. Her father's composition book, with all the notes and secrets of the Lo-Shu Club—she'd left it on the library table.

In a quiet hurry, she went back for it. Through the dining room, into the room she had no name for, to the double doors that—

Carolyn stared.

There were no doors.

Stuffed and mounted animal heads stared out glassily from above the wide rosewood cabinet that now filled the wall. And among them hung the empty shell of an enormous tortoise, its carved and polished surface glinting in the dim light.

DON'T MENTION MADAGASCAR

PAT CADIGAN

For Allen Varney

I don't actually remember meeting Suzette. It's like we were heading in the same general direction and fell into step together. She knew everybody I knew and vice versa, but amazingly enough we had no ex-boyfriends in common. But we'd never have let a guy come between us. "No penis between us," Suzette used to say with her big old grin. Girlfriend had a *great* grin.

Suzette was about five-four, five-five, and proportioned like a dancer. I think she had trained as one once but she never said and I never asked. I've never asked a lot of questions; still don't. It's not that I don't care or I'm not interested. I've just always figured that if there's anything I need to know about anyone, they'll tell me, no need to interrogate. Not that I mind answering questions as I also figure if anyone wants to know something, they'll ask; no need to admit to anything prematurely.

Suzette was more forthcoming. She'd drop tantalizing little tidbits into a conversation in an offhand way—like, "Hey, I used to have shoes like those but someone stole them while I was getting defibrillated. I swear, you gotta keep an eye on your stuff *every minute* in Mongolian emergency rooms." Anyone else, it would have been showing off; Suzette just knew how to take things in stride. I like that in a person.

The only time I ever saw her ruffled was on this one occasion. At the time, she was an office manager for a real estate agency and coming in regularly to the coffee bar. By day I made soy lattés and iced half-caff mochaccinos with a twist, and I studied computer engineering at night school. About 11 o'clock on a Tuesday morning, she showed up looking like a woman who'd just been caught in a high wind—rumpled, dreadlocks practically standing on end, eyes too wide and too bright, and a little out of breath.

I said, "Jeez, what happened?"

"I just quit my job," she said.

"Oh. Well." I knew this couldn't be what had her all freaked. "Are congratulations in order?"

She flicked a glance to my right and I knew The Great Dick Tater had to be giving me the stink-eye because I said something to a customer that wasn't *What can I get for you today?* The GDT took his assistant manager responsibilities very seriously.

"I don't know what's in order. Everything's *out* of order." She glanced to my right again; the GDT must have been wearing a face that could sour milk. *Soy* milk.

"What can I get you today?" I said cheerfully.

Suzette's mouth opened but nothing came out.

"One medium American filter, mellow blend of the day, room for cow," I announced, repeating her order from yesterday. I rattled off the price while I double-cupped it to go, staring the GDT down with my back. Suzette paid and dropped a few coins in the tip jar. All the *baristas* split the tip jar, something you should keep in mind if you like your overpriced coffee without extras like employee saliva. Suzette was top of the no-spit list (posted conspicuously in the locker room, along with security camera photos to prevent episodes of mistaken identity), a policy that even the GDT respected.

Transaction done, Suzette went upstairs to sit. I gave it five minutes before announcing I was going on my break.

"Jeez, Pearl, what kept you?" Suzette said when I finally joined her.

That annoyed me; she knew damned well what the GDT was like. "Sorry," I said, taking off my apron and folding it up. "I couldn't just drop everything. Then I had to *walk* up the stairs because the teleporter's broken again."

Suzanne gave me a sharp look at that last.

"Kidding," I said; as she visibly unclenched, I added, "The teleporter's not *really* broken, I just needed the exercise."

Bam—she was white-knuckled all over her body again, which was a neat trick for someone with skin that dark. "Stop that," she growled. I felt a sudden seriously terrible pain in my upper arm; Suzette had me in a Death Grip of Doom.

"*Ow.*" I thought I could hear bone start to crack within the pulp formerly known as my bicep. "What kind of day are *you* having?"

"*Odd.*" Her grip loosened.

I pulled away fast before she changed her mind. "How odd?" I asked.

She took something out of her back pocket, unfolded it, put it on the table: a photograph. I winced; folding photographs goes against my personal code of fussy conduct. I'm no tight-ass—I'll tear the tags off pillows, jaywalk, even wear white after Labor Day. But fold a photograph? It's practically a physical pain.

"*Look* at that." Suzette tapped her finger on it hard. I winced again because touching the surface of a glossy-finish photograph is another of my fussy things.

"What is it?" I said.

"Rolling Stones, late 1960s."

"Really?" I almost forgot how fussy I was. It was an outdoor venue in sort of jungle-ish surroundings and the vantage point was onstage, far to the right. Only Keith Richards and Mick Jagger are in the photo. Keith Richards was still pretty rather than craggy, with the wide-eyed look of someone whose reality is exceeding his dreams, not the sneer of an old-timer who's seen it all. Mick Jagger was singing and pointing at a bunch of screaming girls. One had hoisted herself up on the others and seemed about to climb onto the stage in the hope of touching His Satanic Majesty.

"Where'd you get this?" I said. If it hadn't been for the folding and the fingerprints, the photo could have been taken the day before rather than forty-odd years ago. Heavy on the odd.

"My boss's desk," she said.

I was stunned. Suzette never stole from anyone, no matter how much they might have deserved it.

"He showed it around this morning. Said his uncle took the picture when he was a stringer for some music magazine back in the day."

I looked from the photo to her and back again, frowning. "And that made you, uh…kleptomaniacal?"

She tapped the photo hard again, her finger on the faces of the screaming girls. "See this woman? That's my Aunt Lillian. And the one trying to climb up on the stage?" She moved the photo so it was directly under one of the bright ceiling lights and pointed. "That's *my mother*."

"Are you sure?" I tried not to laugh and failed.

Suzette tossed her dreads, offended. "What, you think I don't know my own mother when I see her?"

"OK, so it's your mother. Why does that upset you?"

"Dammit, you're not *looking!*"

"Jeez, just tell me already." I drew back a little. "And then let me know if my head's still there or did you bite the whole thing off."

"Sorry," she said and managed to look it for all of a second. "But that's not my mother back in the day. That's her *now*."

"Oh?" I picked the photo up and angled it under the light. None of the people with her were very young. They were really cutting loose and that made them seem youthful but they hadn't been girls for some time.

"Or rather, it's how she *would* look now," she added.

I frowned, not understanding.

"She died when I was sixteen."

"Oh," I said. "Well, then, it can't be her."

"It *is*."

"OK, have it your way. It's her. Photoshopped. Do you know when your boss met your aunt? And did you know they were such tasteless practical jokers?"

Suzette grimaced impatiently. "I tried calling my Aunt Lillian. Some guy answered, said he's her house-sitter while she's on vacation. She's been gone two weeks and he's not sure exactly when she's coming back."

"Did he say where she went?"

Suzette's dark eyes seem to get even darker. "Where this picture was taken." Tap-tap-tap with her finger again. "Madagascar."

(I know what I said. Don't interrupt.)

Now, this next part is kind of a blur. It's not that I don't remember what happened, it's that I don't have a reasonable explanation for it.

It certainly seemed reasonable at the time—well, after listening to Suzette for a while—to go downstairs, toss my apron in The GDT's face, and walk out the front door with her.

First stop after I went home to pack a bag and grab my passport was Suzette's aunt's house in Chicago, to meet this alleged house-sitter and see, as Suzette put it, just what his shit was made of. That was an eight-hour drive in my ancient Geo, a subcompact car which a lot of my friends have described as being only just too large to hang on a charm bracelet. Taller people grumbled, then stopped when they found out what kind of gas mileage I could still get out of it. I'd have bought a hybrid a long time ago except that being virtuously green has always been the domain of the extremely wealthy, who probably weren't so virtuous while they were getting that way. Suzette and I discussed that on the road; by the time we hit the Loop, we had an airtight argument for why all the hideously rich had to help all the rest of us get virtuously green by buying us hybrids and solar panels and shit. If I ever remember it, there'll be one hell of a revolution.

Suzette's aunt's place was a condo halfway up a high-rise with a nice view of Lake Michigan. I was surprised but no more than Suzette was herself.

"You've never been here?" I asked as we got into the elevator.

"She moved here last year. Or maybe the year before, I can't remember."

"Haven't seen her for a while?"

"She's always busy," she said, sounding defensive. "You want to see her, you gotta make an appointment."

I started to tell her that I hadn't meant anything by that question but we were already at the right floor and heading down the hall, which smelled like a mix of potpourri and carpet shampoo. Suzette stopped at a door decorated with a wreath of artfully woven twigs and pussy willows, hesitated, then rapped on it hard, squarely in the middle of the wreath.

The guy who answered was better-looking than anyone calling himself a house-sitter had any right to be, tall, bearded and golden-skinned. We'd have stared even if he hadn't been wearing a turban.

"Ah, Suzette," he said. "I recognize you from your pictures." He stood back to let us in, giving me a polite little nod as if to say that I was welcome, too, even though there were no pictures to recognize me from.

His name was Jamail, he told us over coffee, and he was a student at Northwestern. One of his professors lived down the hall and when Suzette's aunt was looking for a house-sitter, he had introduced them. "I'm what you call a mature student," he said. "I believe learning is for life. Your aunt feels the same, obviously."

"How do you figure?" Suzette asked.

"I chose to go to university, she to Madagascar." He lowered his voice ever so slightly on the last word.

"Is that where *you're* from?" Suzette stared pointedly at his turban.

"No. I'm from Scottsdale."

"Scottsdale?" Suzette was openly skeptical.

He shrugged. "My grandparents were from India. I'm a Sikh." The only contact information he had for Suzette's aunt was an email address on Google Mail; there was no hotel or cell phone that he knew of, or so he claimed. Both Suzette and I found that hard to believe. Jamail took our suspicion graciously. He was really quite a sweet guy; I found myself wondering if Sikhs ever dated outside the church, so to speak.

Finally, he played the I-really-must-study-now card and started clearing away the coffee cups. As he turned toward the kitchen with his hands full, Suzette stopped him. "Thanks for letting me know my aunt's in Madagascar."

He smiled faintly. "Don't mention it."

"Did she take her wheelchair?"

Wheelchair? I looked around. Nothing suggested a wheelchair user had ever lived here.

"I'm sure she took everything she needed. Now, if you'll exc—"

Suzette shoved the photograph in his face. "And she never said anything about *this?*"

He dropped everything with a godawful crash. "Where did you get that?" He reached for the photo.

Suzette whipped it behind her back. "A friend."

"I see." Jamail hesitated, then went into the kitchen and came back with a small business card. "If anyone asks, you just found this somewhere," he told Suzette firmly, looking unhappy as he handed it over.

"OK. Thanks," Suzette replied.

I started to bend down. "Here, let me help y—"

"*Don't.*" He didn't snap or even raise his voice but the command was so forceful that we backed off immediately, and kept backing off, out the door and down the hall to the elevator.

"'Miles 2 Go,'" Suzette read from the card as the elevator descended. "'We'll Get You On Your Way. Jinx Gottmunsdottir, Senior Agent.'"

"Hey, does your aunt really use a wheelchair, or was that a trick question?" I asked.

She flicked a glance at me. "She's been in a wheelchair for ten years. I told you. What kind of a name is that?"

"No, you didn't and it's Icelandic, like Björk." I was only half listening. The elevator we'd gone up in had not had mirrored panels.

"I mean 'Jinx.'" Suzette was impatient again. "A travel agent named *Jinx?* Seriously? There's pushing your luck, there's tempting fate, and then there's teasing fate unmercifully till it bites you in the ass and gives you rabies."

"Is it rabies if this isn't the same elevator?" My reflections and I watched each other with wary solemnity on infinite repeat.

"What are you talking about?" Suzette glanced around quickly, then made a face. "So it's a different elevator. There're two. We went up in one and now we're coming down in the other." She studied the card again. "Address and phone number but no website. What kind of business doesn't have a website?"

I was busy trying not to feel spooked at my endless duplication. "This is *not* the same elevator. And when there are two, they're usually identical."

"So? I don't think there's a federal elevator law about it."

We went all the way to the ground floor without stopping and for a split second, I had the crazy idea that the doors would open onto a different lobby. If so, what should I do—go back up to Suzette's aunt's apartment and ask the Sikh's advice? Or just get off and take my chances with whatever was coming up next?

But it *was* the same lobby, of course, and there were, indeed, two elevators. The other one, however, was blocked off by a ladder with a sign taped to it that said OUT OF ORDER. I stared, sure that hadn't been there when we'd come in. Then something else occurred to me.

"Hey, Suzette, if your aunt's in a wheelchair—"

But she was already halfway across the lobby, muttering about bad names for travel agents.

Jinx Gottmunsdottir was a pink-cheeked strawberry blonde somewhere between fifty and sixty-five, with sapphire blue contact lenses and generous proportions made to look even more so by her cabbage rose print dress. She did business in an indoor market between a sports souvenirs stall and a place selling Russian nesting dolls custom-printed with your own face *(X-tra Faces = X-tra $—Ask 4 quote!)*. Her "office" was an ancient desk with an even older typist's chair, and two other chairs for clients: a molded white plastic thing and a vinyl beanbag that was a lot more bag than bean. Overlooking all of this was a poster stapled to a heavy dark blue drape, a generic landscape of rolling dark green hills with a glimpse of ocean in the background; flowery script at the bottom said, *Bulgaria…Let It HAPPEN…To YOU.*

She looked up without much interest from the motocross racing magazine on her desk. "If you want cut-rate fares to London or Paris, you're in the wrong place. I specialize in roads not taken." Suzette slapped the photograph down on her desk. Immediately, Jinx Gottmunsdottir swept the magazine into the center drawer. "Have a seat."

I let Suzette have the white plastic chair. The beanbag was hopeless so I just sat cross-legged on the floor.

"Normally, I have a spiel I go through," the woman said in an important, business-like tone. "However, you're obviously familiar with the caveats so I can save my breath."

Warning bells went off in my head. I got up on my knees to suggest she go through her spiel anyway and suddenly found myself rolling around on the floor; Suzette had pushed me over.

I pulled myself up on her chair. Suzette gave me a warning glare and mouthed *Shut up*.

"But I will remind you that you have to follow the itinerary *exactly*," Jinx Gottmunsdottir was saying as she took two ticket folders out of her right hand desk drawer. "Miss a connection and it's immediate cancellation. No refunds." She checked the contents of each folder, nodded, and smiled at Suzette expectantly. "We take all of the usual credit cards."

"Is there a discount for cash?" Suzette asked.

The woman blinked in mild surprise. "Do you have some?"

"No. I was just wondering."

"Ah. Well, no, it's the same price regardless. We don't do bulk, either. I'm sure you can see why."

Suzette, still bluffing, nodded; I decided to assert myself. "I don't."

Jinx Gottmunsdottir's professional smile disappeared, replaced by an expression of cold irritation with an undertone of revulsion.

"Don't mind her," Suzette said brightly. She produced a credit card and pushed it across the desk.

Jinx Gottmunsdottir produced a wireless electronic credit card machine and spent a lot more time tapping the keypad than seemed usual. When she offered it to Suzette, I saw that below the tiny screen there were two separate sets of keys, one with standard numbers and one with symbols that I mostly didn't recognize, although some of them seemed vaguely Greek or Cyrillic.

Suzette barely hesitated before entering a PIN. The woman pulled the machine back before we saw anything on the screen. Seconds crawled by while she stared at the device and we stared at her and I wondered if Suzette's bluff had failed. I actually hoped it had. Bluffing isn't anything I think you should do outside of poker and, truth be told, I'm not that wild about poker, either.

But then a slip of paper came out of a slot at the top of the machine and Jinx Gottmunsdottir beamed as she tore it off and handed it to

Suzette along with the folders. "Enjoy your trip."

"Will do," Suzette replied briskly and helped me to my feet. "Bye now."

Jinx Gottmunsdottir gave us a distracted wave. The racing magazine was already back on the desk in front of her.

Since our flight was at four-thirty the next morning, we found a hotel near the airport and didn't so much spend the night as take a nap. Normally, that alone would have been enough for me to bail—early morning is not my natural habitat. But Suzette and that damned picture seemed to have me under a spell.

Of course, the alternative was just another *barista* job, or temping in an office. Or cleaning it. Or trying to survive on unemployment until something else opened up in the great minimum-wage wasteland. Go to college, get a degree, they said. Yeah, because nothing impresses the civil servants at the unemployment office like someone reading Proust in the waiting room. Flying to Madagascar definitely seemed like the better option.

Suzette was also paying for everything at this point. She didn't even ask me for change. Any time I offered, she'd wave that credit card. Finally, over breakfast in the airport—coffee and limp croissants at one of those tall round tables where you have to stand up and eat (which I would like to go on record as saying is adding insult to the dual injury of the price and quality of the food, thank you so much), I said, "Haven't you maxed that thing out yet?"

She shook her head. "I couldn't find anything about a limit."

"What is it, platinum Amex?"

Suzette pulled it out of the back pocket of her jeans and studied it. "Actually, I don't know what it is."

"What?" I snatched it away from her. The bright colors seemed to be a mix of Visa, Master Card, and Sears; I had just enough time to see there was no name on the front and no signature strip on the reverse before she snatched it back. "Where'd you get it?"

"My aunt's place. I helped myself to some of her mail while What's-His-Name was making coffee."

"Really getting into this stealing thing, aren't you?" I said, mildly creeped out. "You sure it's hers? Maybe it's his—a special Sikh membership card."

Suzette frowned. "If there *is* such a thing, I doubt it would work like a credit card."

A new thought occurred to me. "How did you know the PIN number?"

"It was with the card."

"Credit card companies don't do that."

Suzette shrugged. "This one did."

"Did you take anything else?" I asked.

"A couple of bank statements. Nothing crucial."

"You think bank statements and a credit card with no limit are 'nothing crucial'?"

The sleepy-eyed man behind the counter perked up a bit. Suzette glared at me. "Keep it down, Ms Accessory-Before-and-After-the-Fact."

"*Unwitting*," I said emphatically.

"I was *kidding*, Pearl. This is *my aunt's*. She's *family*. My family wouldn't prosecute me. Would *yours?*"

I winced. "I've never told you about my family, have I?"

"Tell me later." Suzette finished her coffee in a gulp. "We'd better check in."

There was no line at the desk. Suzette handed over our tickets and then both she and the man behind the counter waited while I dug around for my passport.

When people take a long time checking in at the airport, I always wonder why. Everything's on the computer. Even if you don't have a seat assignment, how long can that take? If most of the flights I've been on are typical, the only ones left are middle seats in the last two rows.

Our check-in took a long time, apparently because there were a lot of connections. The man kept shuffling slips of paper and stamping them, reshuffling them, sorting them into two piles, which he recombined and shuffled through again. That was what it looked like to me, anyway. Finally, I said, "How many times do we change planes?"

He looked up at me sharply, as if this were an especially stupid question. "It's complicated." His gaze slid to Suzette and then back to me. "You know you *have* to make your connections, right?"

"Right," Suzette assured him.

"There's no taking a later flight, no re-booking, or anything like that."

"We know," Suzette said.

"I've got to match up all the arrivals and take-offs so you *can* make those connections. Some of these windows don't stay open very long and the ones that do aren't always at the right time in the right flight path. And then there's the fact that there's two of you." He sighed. "I'm sorry, I must sound like a crabby old man. This kind of thing gets more complicated every day."

I wanted to ask why we couldn't just fly direct but Suzette was standing on my foot with a glare that said *Shut up*. The man finished shuffling and stapling and tucked a sheaf of coupons and boarding passes into each of the ticket folders.

"I've stapled itineraries inside each wallet." He shoved mine at me and opened Suzette's on the counter to show it to both of us. "You'll have plenty of time to make each flight—"

"What if we're delayed?" I asked, a bit belligerently. "Can you guarantee we won't be delayed?"

His look said he thought I was insane as well as rude. "*Yes*. From Berlin, you go to Rome, then to Morocco, and then to Johannesburg. There'll be a lot of turbulence on the flight out of Jo'burg. Don't let it scare you. Just finish your drinks early and keep your seatbelts on. After that, you have the layover." He closed Suzette's folder and slid it under her hand. "Bon voyage."

I looked at the itinerary inside my folder. "Johannesburg to *Mombasa?* I thought we were going to Madagascar."

"*Don't mention Madagascar,*" the man snapped in a half-whisper.

"Thanks very much for all your help," Suzette said quickly, pulling me away. I wondered if the whole trip would be like this—me making people angry and her dragging me off before they took a swing at me.

Someone told me once that flying to London during the day rather than overnight made jetlag easier to handle. Or maybe I only dreamed that; I was a zombie. I gave up trying to tell what time of day it was as I marched through Heathrow behind Suzette. If I'd been even slightly more awake, I might have asked if we were going the right way. It seemed to be the long way; one hallway would let out onto a concourse which would take us to another hallway and then another. Occasionally someone in a uniform carrying a radio would wave us on. When I tried to stop and ask a woman in a maroon blazer a question, she told me to keep going, everything would be taken care of at The Desk. I could hear the capitals when she said it.

"I don't think there *is* a flight to Berlin," I said to Suzette as I shuffled down another hallway behind her. "We're actually walking there."

The hallway let out onto a concourse, smaller than any of the others and deserted except for a woman stationed at a counter in front of something that might have been one of those exclusive airline clubs, except there was no company name or logo. She reminded me a little of Jinx Gottmunsdottir, only a few decades younger and nowhere nearly as generously proportioned. I followed Suzette over and she greeted us with the restrained, professional smile people wear when they're not sure whether they'll have to let you in or throw you out.

"Is this The Desk?" Suzette asked.

The woman nodded. "Tickets, passports, and landing cards, please." She sorted, shuffled, and stamped, and sent us through a turnstile to a waiting room where the flight to Berlin was already boarding.

In Berlin, we debarked outdoors in the middle of what looked like a parking lot for airplanes and boarded a shuttle bus. Instead of getting off at the first stop with most of the other passengers, however, an attendant told us to stay on and we were ferried to another plane, much smaller than the one we had arrived in.

The flight attendant who checked our tickets as we boarded seemed more like a security guard. She pointed each passenger to a specific seat with an air that suggested she wouldn't look kindly on anyone wanting to switch places. I fell asleep before takeoff and didn't wake up till after we landed in Rome, which made me grouchy with disappointment—I'd hoped to get at least a glimpse of the city from the air.

Another shuttle bus took us to the next small aircraft. There were fewer passengers and no assigned seats. I had intended to stay awake but there was a long delay before takeoff. When I woke up, we were in a holding pattern over Morocco.

The shuttle bus waiting here was all but hermetically sealed against the heat and the windows had such a dark tint, it was practically impossible to see out of them. Tired, I leaned over to Suzette and whispered, "I'm exhausted. You go on, I'm gonna stay here and see when I can get a flight home."

"You are *not*." Suzette said, grabbing my arm in that Death Grip of Doom again. "You *can't*."

"I'll pay you back the airfare." I tried prying her fingers off me and couldn't.

"Pearl, you *can't* just bail. This is a trip for *two*. You're locked in." Suzette looked significantly at the uniformed man standing by the exit.

"Are you kidding me?" I started to get up and she pulled me down.

"*Don't*. He's *armed*." She leaned toward me and lowered her voice. "I'd have quit after Berlin. But we're committed."

"You can't *force* people to travel. It's illegal."

"It's not a matter of legal or illegal," said a firm voice. I looked up to see the guard standing over us. "You are *in transit*. You cannot leave a plane *in transit*. You stop when it stops." The bus came to a halt and he pointed at the exit door. It slid open to reveal the steps up to the next aircraft. "You haven't stopped yet."

The flight to Johannesburg was the longest and the one where sleep deserted me. The flight attendants looked as tired as I felt. I considered slipping one of them a note: *Help, I'm traveling against my will.* Seeing those morose faces, however, made me decide against it. They'd probably just tell me to be glad I was sitting down.

Someone had left a thick paperback book in the seat pocket in front of me. It seemed to be a thriller involving spies who had sex a lot but I couldn't be sure. It was in French, a language I'd had little acquaintance with since high school. Eventually, I got bored enough to try reading it and discovered that I could make out slightly more of the text than I'd expected but not, unfortunately, in any of the parts where the spies had sex a lot.

Suzette by contrast did sleep most of the time, and so heavily that I wondered if she had taken something. I hadn't seen her do anything like that but then I hadn't seen her steal her aunt's mail, either. I'd have to ask her when she woke up. Girlfriend, if you've got some Ambien on you, is it too much to ask you to share?

By the time the seatbelt sign came on for the descent into Johannesburg, I felt as if I'd spent a year in that stupid, lumpy seat. Again we exited the plane outside on the tarmac, far from any buildings. But this time, there was no shuttle bus. The plane for the final leg of the journey was waiting for us just a little ways away. A guard wearing the same uniform as the one who had spoken to me in Morocco led us over to it and checked our tickets at the foot of the steps before allowing us to board.

Just as I reached the open door, I heard a commotion at the bottom of the steps. A tall man with thinning brown hair was arguing with the guard, who was pushing him back. A jeep with three other uniformed people, two men and one woman, appeared out of nowhere and screeched to a stop beside the steps. All four of the guards were carrying the struggling man by his arms and legs toward the jeep when the relentlessly smiling flight attendant at the door pulled me inside and asked me to sit down in a way that made it sound like an offer I couldn't pass up instead of an order I didn't dare refuse.

I've since tried to figure out that technique for my own use but I always end up just straining my vocal cords.

All the attendants for this flight had relentless smiles; it was a special charter. They moved around the cabin distributing snacks, drinks and folders thick with information about the city of Mombasa as well as Mombasa District and the area of Kenya where it was located.

"Did you know this was a charter?" I asked Suzette, paging through a booklet on Kenya's flora and fauna.

"Does it matter?" She stuffed her folder in the seat pocket without looking at it.

"Hey, don't you want to keep that?"

"You *can't* keep it. It belongs to the charter company."

That was a non-answer if I'd ever heard one. "Then they'll have to catch me," I said, feeling contrary. "After seeing this, I kind of wish we really were going there instead of M—"

"Keep your voice down," Suzette snapped in a loud whisper.

I shrugged. "Fine. Sorry. But I don't know what all the big—" At that point, we hit the turbulence we'd been warned about and I lost my train of thought. Shortly after that, I also lost the drink I'd just finished along with the peanuts from the last flight and the pretzels from this one.

Nausea takes up all of my brain, leaving little room for anything other than wishing I were dead. But I did notice that the airsick bag was much larger and sturdier than average. It was made of untearable paper, printed with word games, riddles, and puzzles—*Fun Facts About Mombasa!*—and lined with heavy-duty plastic.

The turbulence lessened sometimes but never stopped. I kept the sick bag clamped to my face, wondering if anyone had ever died of nausea—not throwing up, just nausea. I couldn't remember ever feeling this bad. Was I just overtired or had those stupid snacks poisoned me? Suzette wasn't doing any better. Nor was anyone else on the plane, apparently. Even the flight attendants looked green.

Abruptly, there was a jolt so hard that if I hadn't been belted in, I'd have gone through the baggage compartment above me. Then the plane went into a nosedive.

Oxygen masks dropped out of flaps overhead. I couldn't hear myself scream over everyone else. I grabbed my oxygen mask, drew the bright yellow cup to my face and then hesitated. Passing out was probably preferable to feeling the impact—

Rough hands pushed the airsick bag away and forced the oxygen mask over my nose and mouth. Something fresh-smelling hit my nostrils and I inhaled deeply.

"*Don't hyperventilate! Breathe normally!*" scolded a flight attendant. There was no relentless smile behind the transparent oxygen mask she wore; it was attached to a small tank strapped to her back. She pulled herself up the aisle, checking on each passenger.

"Holy shit!" I shook Suzette, twisting around to stare after her. "That woman's a hero!"

"Just breathe already," Suzette said irritably. "And don't shake me or I'll—" She lifted her mask briefly so she could use the sick bag.

And all at once, the plane leveled out. Everyone screamed again, this time in a mix of surprise, relief and extreme joy. Well, that was why *I* screamed, anyway. The flight attendant reappeared complete with relentless smile, telling us to keep our masks on until after we landed. No problem; I didn't have the will or energy to take it off. I was feeling dizzy now as well as wrung out; dizzy, wrung out and sleepy.

"Sleeping through a landing after a nosedive isn't just being tired," I whispered to Suzette as we went up the walkway from the plane to the arrival area. "They must have sedated us."

Suzette shrugged. "Did you really want to be awake for the landing after that?"

"No," I admitted. "But don't you think that's sneaky?"

"It's a special charter. They have their own way of doing things."

That made no sense to me but I didn't argue. Instead of going through the arrival gate, we were led down a long ramp to an area I thought was customs, except it had no separate divisions for arrivals from different countries. We all waited together to be seen at one of two dozen numbered desks. Fewer than half of them were staffed but there weren't that many of us in line. Still, the wait seemed interminable anyway. To distract myself, I looked around at our fellow travelers, wondering if I'd recognize any of them. Not that I'd been paying much attention.

Only one person looked at all familiar, a tall man seven people behind me. It took a few seconds to place him and then I had to force myself not to stare. Either the man I had seen forcibly carried away by security guards in Johannesburg had an identical twin or the guards had brought him back and let him board the flight after all without my noticing.

The woman who saw us at desk 23 had very close-cropped hair, which showed the perfect shape of her head. She found Suzette's dreads fascinating.

"Have you worn those a long time, my sister?" she asked, looking from Suzette to her passport and back again. Her accent sounded musical to me; I was caught between wanting to hear more of it and trying to see where the tall man was now. To my surprise, he was already at a desk, having his passport stamped. A second later, he had been waved on. I watched as he disappeared down a corridor.

"Yeah, they're easy to take care of," Suzette was saying.

The woman looked from Suzette to her passport and then to the monitor on her desk. I couldn't see the screen. As tempted as I was to move so I could get a look at it, I had a feeling it would be a bad idea. Nearby, a tall guard in an immaculate khaki uniform held a weapon that looked both lethal and complicated. I stood very still.

"The information you need to book your new flights will be waiting for you at your accommodations," the woman said. "You will make your choices within twenty-four hours." She used the largest metal stamp I'd ever seen on our passports and gave them back to us. "Stay together, until you leave."

"We'll do everything we're told," I said solemnly. Suzette gave me a look; I was trying to speak loudly enough for the soldier to hear without actually shouting.

The woman beamed at us warmly. "Welcome to Madagascar! Enjoy your stay!"

We were directed to the baggage claim area where our baggage had already been claimed on our behalf and loaded onto a motorized cart.

"Welcome to Antananarivo, *mesdames.*" A dark-skinned man in light, loose-fitting shirt and trousers materialized beside us. He was holding a tablet notebook like a clipboard; a jute carrier bag dangled from one arm. "Your luggage will be taken to your accommodations for you—don't worry, we have never lost a single bag!" Chuckling, he reached into the bag and handed each of us a zippered 8 x 10 envelope; I could just make out a lot of printed documents inside the frosted plastic. "Everything you need for your layover is in there—food and drink vouchers, transport tickets, and of course the passes for your *famadihana.*"

"'Famadee-yan'?" I said, mystified.

"The bus is outside, you must go now." He shooed us toward the nearest exit.

There were a lot of buses lined up at the curb outside and they all seemed stuffed to capacity and beyond with people and luggage. "Maybe we're just supposed to get on anything with room for us," Suzette suggested doubtfully.

Abruptly, two women pushed us toward an ancient white school bus, already overcrowded with passengers. Suzette hesitated; as the people nearest the door pulled her up the steps, the tall man reappeared beside me. I was torn between wanting to ask him who he was and keeping track of Suzette. Smiling, he made an *after-you* gesture. Then I was being yanked up the metal steps while the two women gave me an unceremonious push from behind.

I had never been in such a crush. Every color and shape of humanity seemed to be represented—fair-haired Nordic types, Latins, Japanese, Chinese, Indians, Middle Easterns, North Africans, South Africans of all colors. People called to each other in Russian, Italian, French and other languages with clicks and glottal stops. It was so fascinating I almost forgot about the tall man.

I couldn't see him anywhere up front. Apparently I'd been the last sardine in. Maybe security guards had carried him off again. The bus started off with a jerk. There was nothing to hold onto, no hanging straps or poles within reach but it didn't matter. I couldn't possibly fall down. "How long do you think this'll take?" I asked Suzette, who was wedged under my left arm.

"I heard someone say it was ten miles to the city," she said.

The bus went over a large bump and I felt my feet leave the floor, along with everyone else around me. I'd barely caught my breath when we went over two more in quick succession, both larger than the first one so that the bus practically seesawed. As the front half dipped, the back end rose and I caught a glimpse of a familiar tall figure behind a young couple who were each holding a laughing toddler.

It couldn't be him, I thought. He'd have had to go past me and I knew he hadn't. No one had because no one could.

Another bump; the toddlers giggled as his hair flew up with the motion and fell down over his forehead. He laughed with them.

"See anything?" Suzette asked.

"Nothing I can explain," I said.

I looked for him when we finally all spilled out in front of the hotel but he had vanished again.

"The white umbrellas you see there, that's the Zoma." The man pointed out the open window of our hotel room. "Today is the biggest day for it, in fact. 'Zoma' means 'Friday.'"

I looked at Suzette. "Is today Friday?"

"Don't mind her," Suzette said. "We've been traveling for so long, she lost track."

"Oh. Yes. Of course you must be tired." The man looked apologetic. "But you will not be able to rest until after your *famadihana*. Now it's time to go."

"Can't we have five minutes to wash up and change?" I asked, looking longingly at my suitcase over in a far corner.

"I'm sorry, no," the man said briskly. "You must be exactly as you are for your *famadihana*."

"What *is* that?" I demanded.

"It's what you came here for," he said, herding us out of the room.

I tried not to budge and failed completely. "Actually, we came here to find *her* mother," I said, jerking my chin at Suzette. "Or have I been traveling for so long I've lost track of that, too?"

"Many come here to find mothers. Also fathers, siblings, friends, lovers, even themselves. The only way is the *famadihana*."

"But what is it?" Suzette asked.

"The Dance with the Dead."

I'd expected to see another bus or even the same one in front of the hotel. But the vehicle waiting for us was an old Geo that looked amazingly like the one I'd left sitting in O'Hare's long-term parking. The man thrust the plastic envelopes we'd been given at the airport into our hands and hustled us into the backseat, before getting into the front seat next to the driver. "You've come this far, you don't want to be late now!"

The driver looked over his shoulder at us. "Seatbelts on!"

We obeyed. As I clicked mine into place, I silently apologized to everyone who'd ever ridden in my Geo's backseat. It really was horrible.

Street-level Antananarivo went past in a blur and a cloud of dust; the many-windowed houses covering the hills stared into the distance. The man in the passenger seat was saying something about how the *famadihana* took place only during the dry season, from June to October.

"Practical reasons for that, of course," he said, peering around the back of his seat at us with a smile. "We restrict your *famadihana* to the same time. Out of season doesn't work as well for *vazaha*."

"What's a *vazaha*?" Suzette asked, leaning against me as we took a corner at 90.

"You are," said the driver cheerfully. "Means foreigner."

We took another corner on two wheels; the city vanished in a cloud of dust behind us. On the hills, the houses continued to stare impassively into the distance.

After a couple of miles, the sound of clarinets and drums came to us faintly under the chatter of the engine. Suzette and I looked at each other; she shrugged. As the music grew louder, I heard accordions and flutes as well.

"I don't think that's the Rolling Stones," I said more to myself than anyone else.

"Maybe it's their opening act," Suzette said.

The man in the front passenger seat turned to say something. Suzette shoved the photograph under his nose but before she could ask about her mother, the driver stood on the brakes.

My forehead hit the back of the seat in front of me—not so hard it hurt, just enough to be startling. The shoulder harness *did* hurt—I swore I could feel every fiber in the strap bruising my skin.

"What the hell, Suzette?" I yelled. "Couldn't you have waited till we stopped?"

"I didn't do anything!" she shouted over the chaotic mix of laughter, singing and music now surrounding the car. "I dropped it! Where is it? Give it back—"

"Is that *klezmer?*" I peered out the windows.

Children grinned back at me. "*Vazaha! Vazaha!*" They jumped around and mimed taking photos. Behind them, several adults went by, carrying a coffin. They were laughing and singing.

"What kind of a funeral is this?" I asked.

"Not a funeral—it's a *famadihana,*" the man told me. "The coffin has been removed from the family crypt. Now the family will dance with their dead, wrap the body in a new *lambamena,* and return it to the resting place, until next year."

Suzette and I looked at each other; she was as flabbergasted as I was.

"But my mother's not buried here. She's not buried at all. She was cremated and we scattered the ashes." Suddenly, she looked horrified. "My Aunt Lillian! Has something happened to *her?*"

The man reached down beside his seat and came up with the now dog-eared photo. "I do not know of any *vazaha* who has died here." His face creased with a mixture of amusement and pity as Suzette took it from him.

"Are you sure? Should we ask the police?" Suzette looked from him to me and back again.

"No, *no* police," said the driver. It was an order. He put the car in gear again and floored it. I looked out the window to see the people at the end of the procession waving goodbye.

Open country gave way to rainforest. Big green leaves slapped against the car windows. I sat forward, holding onto the back of the passenger seat and peered through the windshield. The "road" was a set of parallel wheel ruts. Very well-traveled wheel ruts—the Geo's off-road limit is an un-mowed lawn—so wherever they were taking us couldn't be too far from civilization.

Whose civilization, however, I wasn't sure of. After traveling to a place whose language and customs we didn't understand, Suzette and I had willingly gotten into a car with two strange men who were now driving us into a rainforest—jungle?—to a destination they hadn't even bothered to lie about because we hadn't bothered to ask them.

Was this the way your life began flashing before your eyes? Nothing remotely similar had happened when the plane had gone into a nosedive—

As if on cue, we were suddenly going down a steep hill into a tunnel. Suzette and I looked at each other; she had my arm in that Death Grip and I was returning the favor.

"Where—" Suzette started.

"Almost there," the man in the passenger seat said cheerfully. The driver put on the Geo's headlights but he didn't really have to: the tunnel lit the area immediately above us as well as a few yards ahead. The illuminated area traveled with us; I looked out the back window to see the lights going off behind us.

"What is this place?" I asked; I was thinking theme park.

The man in the passenger seat waved the question away. "Make sure you carry your documents and you can't get lost."

"I'm lost now," Suzette said. "Tell us where we're going right now or—" But of course, she didn't know how to finish that sentence and neither did I. This was Madagascar. Except right now it looked more like something out of a freaky movie.

The tunnel suddenly opened out into an enormous clear area paved with asphalt—outdoors. Waist-high barriers made of metal tubing held back the thick rainforest. I pressed my face against the window to look up at the sky, wondering if we really were outdoors again or if this were some sort of brilliant illusion.

Abruptly, we stopped in front of some ticket windows and turnstiles in front of what looked like an enormous sporting arena. The man got out of the car, then helped me and Suzette out of the backseat. He led us over to the counter, standing us in front of a specific window.

"Now I leave you." He made a little bow. "May each of you recognize what you seek in your *famadihana*." I was still trying to parse this when he got back in the car.

"What did *that* mean?" I asked Suzette as we stared after the car now disappearing into another tunnel entrance.

"Beats me," she said, "but I suspect it's not as good as he wants us to think it is."

"You must be able to recognize a good thing when you see it," said a voice behind us.

We turned to see a woman smiling at us with professional patience. She was in her late forties or early fifties, although her black hair had no strands of gray. She wore gorgeous blue and white printed material in intricate folds. I couldn't imagine where she had come from. Trapdoor? Transporter beam? At this point, either seemed likely.

"Documents, please."

Suzette slid her plastic envelope under the transparent divider. I started to do the same and she shook her head.

"One at a time, please." She opened the envelope and spread everything out on the counter. It was an odd assortment of things—cards of various sizes, some that looked an awful lot like old elementary school report cards, some that could have been I.D. cards or drivers' licenses or even library cards, a plastic thing that I knew was a hotel key-card but not one I recognized, and something that looked like a passbook for a savings account. All of them were marked with a barcode. I wondered what was in mine and decided to have a look.

"Don't do that," the woman said sharply, holding a barcode scanner in one hand and Suzette's high school photo in the other.

"I was just—"

"Don't. Do. That." She put down the photo and slid her hand under the barrier. "Here, we'll avoid temptation. Give it to me."

I hesitated. "Why can't I look?"

"It's not time." She frowned at Suzette, who took the envelope from me and passed it to her. She set it aside and went back to scanning barcodes. When she had finished, she did something under the counter and a flatscreen rose up from a slot that had been invisible thus far. I couldn't see what was on it from where I was standing; after checking for armed guards (none), I stood on tiptoe and tried to crane my neck. What little I could see didn't tell me anything—a few straight lines radiating from a point and a square the size of a postage stamp cycling through the color spectrum.

"There are many different routes from here but of course, not all of them are desirable—"

Suzette pressed the photo up against the barrier. "Is there one that goes here?"

The woman barely glanced at it. "No."

"Why not?"

"Because you're already here."

"Wait a minute." Suzette put the photo on the counter and pointed. "This is my mother. I'm trying to find her. And my Aunt Lillian—"

The woman motioned for her to pass it to her. "That narrows things down." She studied it for a moment and then concentrated on the screen, touching it occasionally, frowning at the result, touching it again, and frowning more deeply. After a few more touches, she stood back.

"I'm sorry, you can't get to her."

"What do you mean?" Suzette asked.

"There is no possible itinerary that will put you with her."

"You sound like you're booking flights," I said.

The woman nodded. "Yes, of course. What did you think you were doing here? However, I can give the both of you much better routes."

Suzette and I looked at each other. "What's that supposed to mean?" I asked.

She emptied my envelope and spread the contents out. It all looked like bus tickets, appointment cards, and the written portion of the driving test in Massachusetts. "I can give you both a route where you graduate from your respective universities *magna cum laude* and you meet for the first time during post-graduate study abroad." She touched the screen again. "It comes with single parenthood but you'll both be fairly well off."

"Magna cum laude in *what?*" I said. She was speaking English but nothing made sense.

The woman smiled. "That's up to you. Isn't that nice? You get the choice. Please pick something beneficial. You don't have to, of course, but if you did, it would make planning routes much easier in the future."

"My mother—"

"Your mother's itinerary does not intersect with yours. At least, not any more than it already has. Your flights in relation to her are unchanged."

Suzette shook her head, baffled.

"On *your* itinerary, she still dies when you're sixteen. But on *her* new itinerary, she never has children. I'm sorry, but there was no route *with* offspring that didn't include an early death. Once she understood this wouldn't affect your existence, she decided. I don't blame her."

"This," Suzette said, "*isn't* happening."

"Oh, it is. And it's not going to get any better, believe me." She put everything back into the envelopes and passed them back to us. "Through there," she said, pointing at the nearest turnstile.

We went through and down a passageway to a metal door. "This way to the egress," I said with a nervous laugh.

"On three," said Suzette. "One…two…"

We pushed through and the noise hit us like a physical blow.

We should have realized that it wasn't going to be a Rolling Stones concert, either in the late 1960s or from last week. I was actually hoping but when we pushed through that door, we found ourselves out on the tarmac at an airport. The wind was blowing and it sounded like a hundred jets were revving up for takeoff all at once. My inner ear suddenly turned against me and I felt myself falling. But before I could hit the ground, two strong hands caught me and set me on my feet again—an armed man in a uniform. He smiled at me and Suzette as he hustled us over to a shuttle bus and pushed us onto it.

The bus took us not to the airport building but to another plane. I was too boggled to do anything except get on board and sit where the flight attendant said to. "I guess this means we won't be enjoying the Zoma," I said to Suzette as we sat down. Another flight attendant standing nearby gave me a disapproving look.

"Keep your voice down," she said. "I don't think this is…you know."

"No," I said. "I don't know."

"Excuse me," Suzette called to the flight attendant. "What's the name of this airport?"

The woman raised one eyebrow, as if she thought Suzette was being rude in some way.

"The full official name, I mean."

"Moi," the attendant said. "Mombasa Moi International Airport."

"Thank you." Suzette turned to me with an I-told-you-so look.

"OK," I said. "Just tell me how we got here from Madagascar—"

"No, no, no," said the flight attendant, looming over us now. "You don't mention Madagascar."

"But—"

"*No.*" She raised a finger and I thought she was going to shake it in my face.

"This has got to be a trick," I said.

"It is," said the flight attendant. "And it's a very good one. So be quiet. Don't tell how the trick is done."

We'd been in the air an hour before Suzette realized she had left the photo behind.

We flew to New York and then to San Francisco, where we live. Suzette has a degree in economics and works on budget planning. I'm an architect, which I find amazing; I never thought I had it in me.

Neither of us is a parent yet. I don't think we're even close to it but the trajectory of this route allows for surprises. Other things, however, it doesn't allow for.

I'm more easygoing than ever, tearing the tags off pillows, jaywalking, wearing white after Labor Day. I got over my thing about folding photographs. People should live life just the way they want. So go ahead, dye *all* your hair purple, live in a tree, hitchhike your way around the world in a chicken suit. Whatever turns you on, yanks your crank or gets you through the night is OK with me.

Just don't mention Madagascar. At least, not where I can hear you.

ON THE ROAD

NNEDI OKORAFOR

A tiger does not proclaim its tigritude. It pounces.
—*Wole Soyinka*
Sub-Saharan Africa's first Nobel Laureate

I slammed the door in the child's face, a horrific scream trapped in my throat. I swallowed it back down.

I didn't want to wake my grandmother or auntie. They'd jump out of bed, come running down the stairs and in a string of Igbo and English demand to know what the fuck was wrong with me. Then I'd point at the door and they'd open it and see the swaying little boy with the evil grin and huge open dribbling red white gash running down the middle of his head. Split open like a dropped watermelon.

My stomach lurched and I shut my eyes and rubbed my temples, my hand still tightly grasping the doorknob. *Get it together*, I thought. But I knew what I'd seen—jagged fractured yellow white skull, flaps of hanging skin, startlingly red blood and some whitish gray jelly…brain? I shuddered. "Shit," I whispered to myself.

The boy had been standing in the rain. Soaked from head to toe, as everything outside was from the strange unseasonable three-day deluge. He'd been smiling up at me. He couldn't have been older than nine. I gagged. I couldn't just leave him out there.

Knock! Knock! Knock! In hard strong rapid succession. "Oh God," I whispered. "What the hell?" Every hair on my body stood on end. I took a deep breath. Before really thinking about what I was doing, my hand was turning the knob and pulling the door open. I kept my eyes down. His wet black shoes were clumped with red mud. Gradually I brought my eyes up, past his soaked navy blue school uniform pants, to his worn out and cracked black fake leather belt, his tucked in white dress shirt, the brown skin of his throat, his little boy face… cleaved open, all the way to his eyebrows. *Fuck!* I thought.

In all my five years as a cop on the south side of Chicago I'd *never* seen anything like this. Never. The boy laughed and spoke to me in Igbo, water dripping from his lips. "You, too," he said, his voice so much like that of the little boy that he was. "Me and you."

"You need…help," I whispered. I was about to reach out, despite my repulsion. I'd seen plenty of dead, mutilated, bleeding bodies. A year ago, I'd had a boy's life blood run over my hands as he stared sadly into my eyes. He'd been stabbed five times. His blood had been so warm on my hands and it remained under my nails for days. And that wasn't even my worst encounter with death. So I wasn't easily shaken. But this boy standing before me shook the hell out of me. He should have been dead or dying; not knocking hard on the door, smiling and saying ominous things.

Before I could reach for him, he reached for me. Lightning fast. He tapped my right hand. Just before it happened, I had a flashback of when I used to play tag in grade school. I loved playing tag.

"You're it," the boy said in Igbo. He laughed again.

The touch of his finger burned like a hot rough metal poker. I yelped. Then it was as if my very *being* was repulsed. I flew back about five feet before landing hard on my ass, the air knocked from my chest, my teeth rattling. Sharp pain shot all the way to my fingertips and toenails. I hit the coffee table and groaned as the clay vase on it fell to the floor and broke in two.

I heard footsteps upstairs. I looked at the door. The boy was gone.

"*O'u gini?*" Grandma shouted from the top of the stairs. She barely had her blue wrapper wrapped around her waist and she looked much older than her eighty years. Auntie Amaka was probably still sleeping, as she remained upstairs. Grandma looked at the door and then met my eyes. "Were you outside?" she asked.

I shook my head, trying to get up. Both my hands felt numb, though the boy had only touched one.

"But you opened the door," she said, still looking at the door like she expected armed robbers to burst in.

I didn't answer. So much adrenaline was flooding my system that I'd begun to feel faint.

"Who was at the door?" she demanded. When I didn't answer, she narrowed her eyes at me, sucked her teeth and said, "Stupid, stupid, girl."

Three days before, it had started raining cats and dogs. Out of nowhere. Thunder rolled in the skies, lightning crashed. The wind shook the trees and turned the red dirt to red mud. Three *days* of steady rain. It had stopped only minutes before the boy showed up at the door. This kind of weather *never* happened in this part of Nigeria during this time of the year. But who was I to question the doings of nature? Who was I?

I'd laughed to myself thinking, *Of course, it just has to happen right when I arrive.* I was only going to be in the village visiting my grandmother and grand aunt for two weeks and now the entire first week was going to be a guaranteed mud and mosquito fest. Little did I know that this was the least of my worries.

I told my grandmother everything. Without a word, she frowned and walked outside. I followed her. Squishing through the mud, we looked all over the yard for that creepy boy. Grandma even looked in the chicken coop and behind the noisy generator. We didn't find a trace of him. Even his footprints had disappeared in the mud. Above, the sky churned with exiting rain clouds. Already I could see peeks of sunlight but I was too bothered to be happy about it.

We went back inside. I took off my muddy shoes, picked up the two vase pieces and plopped down on a kitchen chair, rubbing my lower back and forehead. I was sore but I actually felt ok. I didn't mysteriously grow sick or break out in blue hives or start speaking in tongues. I was fine.

"Grandma, he should have been *dead*," I said yet again, pressing the pieces of vase together, as if that's all it would take to fix it. "I saw *brain*. Who would do that to a child? And where the heck would he *go*? This is so weird."

"Why were you stupid enough to open the door the second time?" she suddenly asked, crossing her arms over her chest, irritated. "If you see a monster at your doorstep, the wise thing to do is shut the door." She sucked her teeth and shook her head. "You Americanized Nigerians. No instinct."

"He was *hurt*," I insisted. "You can't just…"

"You knew better," she said, waving her hand dismissively at me. "Deep down, you knew not to open that door."

Ok, so she was right. I don't know why I opened the door again. It was like my hand had a mind of its own. Or maybe it was some sort of grim fascination? I put the vase pieces down.

"You feel alright?" Grandma asked.

I nodded, rubbing my hands together. They still felt a little numb.

She sighed. "We'll have to keep an eye on you."

"Have you ever…"

She held up a hand. "We speak of it no more," she said. "The mud is still wet."

Whatever that means, I thought. I got up, went to the bathroom and shut the door behind me. A large black wall spider occupied the ceiling corner above the toilet. A tiny pink wall gecko eyed it from the other corner. I chuckled despite myself. In the village, one is rarely ever truly alone. Not even in the bathroom.

I wiped my face with a towel and stared at myself in the mirror. I patted down my short 'fro and used some toilet paper to wipe the sweat from my brow. "Chioma, you're fine," I said with a laugh. *Just some weird shit, that's all*, I thought. *Maybe the boy's head wasn't as bad as it looked.*

I froze, the smile dropping from my lips. I smelled something. I sniffed at my clothes and my skin. No, it wasn't coming from those either. Not from me. But close to me. Like something unnatural breathing down my neck. Movement on the ceiling caught my eye. The wall gecko was slowly closing in on the spider. I quickly left the bathroom and sought out Grandma. She was sitting in the living room with my grand auntie Amaka.

They both wore the same blue wrappers but Grandma wore a t-shirt that I'd brought her from America and auntie Amaka wore a white blouse. Their rough wide feet dangled from the couch; their smallness always gives me pause as I'm over six feet tall. They looked at me with furrowed brows. Two old Igbo women with wrinkles so deep their eyes almost disappeared under the folds of skin whenever they made any facial expression.

"I'm fine." I assured them.

They knew I was lying. Yet they said nothing.

I laugh about it now. Of course they wouldn't have said anything.

That boy set something upon me. I was sure of it. Shit like that didn't just happen and that was it. Plus, I could still smell that weirdness in the air. Only I seemed to notice. It was like a bit of foulness. Something unpleasant definitely still lingered. Something unpleasant stayed.

The first few days, it was just that smell and odd shifts in the air. I'd be on my way to the bathroom and the leaves of the faux houseplant behind me would quiver softly. I'd turn around to see if someone was there. No one ever was. But that smell lingered a bit before fading away like an old fart. I started hearing whispers behind me, especially when I was the only one home. These were also accompanied by that smell and the sound of footsteps outside the house, loudly squelching in the drying mud. Not something you want to hear while in a rural village deep in southeast Nigeria. You're basically cut off from the rest of the world here. And then there were the lizards.

Normally, they ran about like squirrels, especially the large pine green and orange ones. They'd run up the cement block walls that surrounded the house, weaving between the protective shards of glass and razor wire at the top. They'd stop and do their lizardly push-ups. They were like little foul-tempered dragons. Corner one and you'd get to see just how wild and dragon-like they could get. I'd once seen one accidentally run into a plastic bag. The thing went temporarily insane when it couldn't figure out how to get out. Normally, the lizards of Nigeria were a source of hilarity for me.

When they started showing up everywhere accompanied by that unpleasant smell, they weren't so funny. I'd sit on the porch and three would show up and just look at me. If I stayed in one place for too long, those three lizards were joined by another seven. They'd scramble close. Watching me. As if they were waiting for something spectacular to happen. They only left me alone when I went in the house.

Being police, I know how to observe and listen. I'm *always* aware of my surroundings. I know when I'm being followed. Even when I'm on vacation in my mother's village visiting my grandmother and grandaunt. *Dammit, I wish I brought my gun,* I thought. How silly I was.

Days after the encounter with the boy, I had the shock of my life.

Upon my grandmother's request, we went with auntie Amaka to the village market. I was glad to get out of the house. Even if the "mud was still wet," whatever that meant. It was your usual affair. Piles of tomatoes here, piles of peppers there, boiled eggs, sacks of groundnut, stacks of hugely overpriced cell phone cards, bunches of plantains, pungent dried fish, flies, women in traditional or European-style clothes with their nosy eyes and ears and sharp-tongues, dodging the hot mufflers of overzealous shortcut-seeking *okada* drivers. I'd normally have enjoyed this, but I kept noticing lizards lurking too close to me, and the boy was still on my mind.

I closely followed my grandmother and auntie as they bought dried crayfish, plantain, oranges and so on. I guess we were going to have a feast tonight or something. As we walked, I felt like I was being watched again. When the feeling grew too intense, I whirled around, my hand going to my hip for the gun that wasn't there. I saw nothing but people going about their business. I sucked my teeth, my nerves sparking.

"Shit," I whispered. "This has got to stop, man. It's driving me nuts." Being this jumpy was so unlike me. We were standing at the booth of a fruit seller when I caught a whiff of sugariness, sweet and flammable. I turned my head toward the scent and met the eyes of a scruffy-looking palm wine seller.

"Good afternoon," he said, leaning on his ancient-looking dusty bicycle. His large brown gourds full of palm wine dangled from each handlebar. A basket of filled and empty green glass bottles hung from the front of the bars.

"Good afternoon," I responded, still preoccupied. I turned the other way and there *he* was, standing in the road. The boy who should have been dead. He wore a spotless pair of navy blue pants and a white pressed shirt. It was tucked in. And his head was shaven close. Nothing but a slightly gnarled gray brown scar ran down the middle of his head. He looked like a perfectly normal kid. Except for the knowing way he smiled at me. I stared back. He nodded, laughed and continued on his way, school books in the crook of his arm. No cars came down or from up the road. A lizard scrambled across the street feet from him.

"What the fuck," I whispered to myself.

The palm wine seller laughed and elbowed me. He leaned toward me and lowered his voice. "That boy's probably going to be the smartest kid in this village's history."

"W…why do you say that?" I asked, glancing at my auntie and grandmother. They were haggling hard with some old man over a large pineapple.

"You saw him, right?" he said. He pointed at me with a well-calloused finger. "It was you. Least that's what people are saying."

I wanted to ask, "What people?" Instead I just asked, "How can he be ok?"

The man nodded. "They took him into the forest."

"Not the hospital?" I asked, frowning.

"The hospital would have been no good for that boy."

"*Who* took him?"

"The women, of course." He kicked at a man inspecting his gourds of wine. "You buying or not?"

As the seller haggled with the customer, I watched the boy walk into the market crowd across the road. I watched until I couldn't see him anymore. I felt something cool against my hand and looked down. The tapper smiled, pressing it into my hand. A green bottle of palm wine. "On the house. You'll need it soon. One for the road."

I smiled uncomfortably, taking the bottle. "Uh…thanks." I had no intention of drinking it or anything else offered by a stranger that wasn't properly sealed. I mentally patted myself on the back again for thinking to bring all those packets of ramen noodles, my jar of peanut butter and canned salmon.

"What…what happened in the forest?" I asked him, lowering my voice and grasping the bottle.

He paused, then only shook his head as he laughed. "You ask too many questions. Go and drink that while you can."

That night, I tried to just go to bed and forget about the whole thing. Of course, I couldn't sleep. Outside, the warm wind blew hard. It should have been soothing but it wasn't. I could hear wet footsteps underneath the sound of the wind, squishing just below my window. Though my room was on the second floor of the house, I didn't dare look out.

I considered closing the window but that would have been like shutting myself inside a furnace. *Squish, squish, squish.* Someone was definitely just below my window. And was the ground that muddy? When I could take it no more, I grabbed a can of beef ravioli from my suitcase and went to the open window. Any weird shit I saw out there was going to get hit with that can.

I saw nothing but deep darkness. The power had been turned off an hour ago. Still, that piercing sensation of being watched increased tenfold. I stepped back and pulled the curtains closed. That didn't help. The wind made the curtains billow out like ghosts. I pulled them back open and spent the rest of the night huddled in my bed, staring at the window, the can in my lap, knowing whatever had smashed that boy's skull in was still out there. And now it was interested in me.

"What's wrong with you?" Grandma asked as I dragged myself into the kitchen. I felt sluggish but it was the kind of sluggish you feel after hours and hours of deep sleep. I was too rested. I'd finally fallen asleep near daybreak and now it was late evening. I'd slept the entire day away. It wasn't jetlag; I'd gotten over that by my second day there. Something else had made me sleep for over twelve hours.

My belly grumbled with hunger. My grand auntie Amaka was just walking in. She looked me up and down with way more scrutiny than I was willing to tolerate when I was so hungry. I resisted the urge to roll my eyes. She loudly sucked her few uneven white teeth.

"What?" I snapped, as I ladled some freshly made stew over the plate of steaming white rice my grandmother handed me. I loved my auntie Amaka. She talked a lot of shit about everyone. But once in a while her scrutinizing eye turned to me. Like now. The woman hadn't even finished walking in.

"She's looking thin," she told my Grandma in Igbo, ignoring me. As if I couldn't understand the language.

I scoffed. Maybe I'd lost a pound or two since getting here but I was still my usual thick-bodied Amazon build. My nicknames in the village were "giant" and "iroko tree."

Grandma nodded. "Like it's hollowing her out."

"So it can fill her up," Amaka finished.

"I don't think I've lost a pound," I said, sitting down with my huge mound of rice and stew. My mouth watered. *Gosh, I do feel empty, though*, I thought. *But I'm about to solve that problem.* I dug my spoon in, inhaling the smell of the spicy red stew and fragrant rice.

"Not physically," Grandma said.

I shook my head. "Whatever," I said, the spoon halfway to my mouth.

A loud *BUMP* came from the back of the house. Then a *CRASH*. I put the spoon of uneaten rice down. "What the…" Then a great roar that made me nearly jump out of my skin. About ten large brown, black and orange lizards skittered into the room, from the hallway, their tiny claws whispering on the wooden floor. Some climbed the walls, others scuttled across the floor. Neither grandma nor auntie moved. My eyes sought the nearest weapon. There. A large knife in the sink. My grandma had used it to chop meat. I jumped up and grabbed it.

A horrified look on her face, grandma grabbed auntie's shoulder and started speaking in rapid Efik, a language they only spoke when they didn't want me to understand. I frowned at them, but I was more concerned with whatever the hell was in the house.

The deep guttural roar came again, this time closer, from down the hall. The sound touched my very being. I held the knife more tightly, trying to think. I knew this was the thing that had been following me, biding its time. This was the thing that had smashed that boy's head open.

The movement of a black lizard on the wall caught my eye. I held the large knife more tightly, ignoring my grandmother and auntie's now angry and loud argument. I only vaguely wondered what the hell they were shouting about. Slowly, knife held before me, I moved toward the hallway. I could see a large shadow creeping forth. Whatever it was was breathing deep and hard. The air grew warm and took on the smell of tar. I realized that this was what that weird smell reminded me of. Tar and maybe soil or crushed leaves?

I glanced at the front door. Still open. I ran for it. This thing meant to take me. On instinct, I knew this. I ran out of the house. It was after me, not my grandmother and auntie. At least I could save them. I surprised myself. I really *was* one of those people who would happily die to save the ones they loved.

I ran onto the dirt road. At some point, I must have dropped the knife. It was pitch dark out there. People were awake most likely. Deep in their homes. But tonight, no one played cards on the porch. No one stood in the doorway, smoking a cigarette. I think people sensed it was a bad time to be out. So I ran and I ran alone. I wasn't even wearing flip flops.

I could hear it coming. Slobbering. Wheezing. Blowing a strange wind. The smell of broken leaves and tar in the air. The half-moon in the sky gave a little light. I could have sworn there were hundreds of lizards running with me, some crisscrossing my path. It felt like I stepped on some as I ran. I only managed to stay on my feet because I knew the shape of the dirt road.

I passed the last home and entered the stretch of palm trees.

My eyes had adjusted to the darkness. *I'm going to die out here,* I knew. *Just as the boy should have.* A burning heat descended on me from behind. I fell to the dirt road, coughing as I inhaled its dust. Lizards scampered over me like ants on a mound of sugar. I felt their rough feet and claws nipping at my skin. Something grabbed my hands as a great shadow fell on me. Yes, a shadow in the darkness. It was blacker than black.

The air was sucked from my lungs.

My eyes stung with dust.

The road beneath me grew hard as stone, as concrete.

My arms were pulled over my head and ground into the concrete beneath me.

First the left hand and then the right. At the wrist. Something bit right through. I felt painful pressure, then tendons, bone, blood vessels snapping and cracking and then separating. I heard it; the sound was brittle and sharp. Then the wet spattering and squirting of my blood. I only smelled warm paved road. A pause. Then bright white pain flashed through me, blinding the rest of my senses. *Like Che Guevara,* I thought feebly. *Now no one will know who I am.*

Time passed. I remember none of it clearly.

The sound of grass and twigs bending and snapping roused me. The feeling of hands roughly grasping me. I dared to open my eyes. They carried me. One woman carried my hands, like two dead doves. I almost blacked out again from the sight but I held on.

"Hurry," one of the women said quietly. "She's going to die."

"It takes what it will," another woman said.

"She'll be fine." This was my grandmother's voice. My own grandmother was one of these women!

"It's still best to move faster." Auntie Amaka!

Suddenly we came upon a road. It was paved, black, shiny, new. Something you didn't normally see in Nigeria.

"Listen," one of the women hissed, looking around.

All of them froze. I was too weak to do anything. The edges of my vision were starting to fade. I heard the sound of my own blood hitting the concrete as it spurted to the beat of my heart from the stumps of my wrists. It soaked quickly into the concrete.

"It's coming," one of the women said.

There was a mad scramble. They dumped me on the hard concrete. Two items dropped beside me. *SLAP! SLAP!* My hands. Then other items. Some cocoa yams that rolled to rest against my leg. Tomatoes that rolled in all directions. A bowl of still steaming rice that shattered, some of the porcelain and hot rice hitting my face. A bunch of cell phones that clattered to the ground; the ones I could see were still on. And some other things I couldn't see from where I lay.

"What are you…" my voice was weak and I had no energy to finish my question.

After a glance up the road, the women started running off. I couldn't get up, I couldn't speak. Soon, I wouldn't be breathing. Their feet made soft sounds in the grass as they ran into the forest.

I was alone in the middle of a road in Nigeria. I couldn't get up. My hands were cut off. I was going to be run over, bleed to death or both. All I could think of was how hungry I was. That I'd give anything for sweet fried plantain, egusi soup heavy with goat meat and stock fish, garri, spicy jallof rice, chin chin, red stew with chicken, ogba…

I stared at my severed hands. My long fingers were curved slightly. My thumbs were both bent inward. My nails still had their French manicure. The bronze ring my boyfriend gave me two years ago was still on my left middle finger. I could see the palm of my right hand with its small calluses from my regular days at the gym lifting free-weights.

The middle finger of my right hand twitched. I blinked. Then all five fingers wiggled and the hand flipped over, reminding me of a spider flipping back onto its feet. My left hand was rising up, too. Barely a sound escaped my lips as my eyes started to water from sheer terror. I was too afraid to move. If one of them came near me, I knew I'd pass out. Instead they both just "stood" there; again that strange waiting that I'd also witnessed with the lizards.

Suddenly, the concrete grew hot. I tried to get up but fell back. The road shook. And as I stared down the road, I wondered, *What the god-damn fucking hell is that?* I tried to get up again; anything to get away from my hands and the chaos happening up the road.

About a fourth of a mile away, the concrete road undulated as if it were made of warm taffy. It broke apart and crumbled in some places and piled up in others. It rippled and folded and fell back into a road as the chaos progressed toward me. I looked at the sky. It was black but starting to burn. I didn't know if this was morning's approach or my own death. I did care. I didn't want to die. But I knew I was dying. Still, not a car came up or down this mystery road. No one would save me. My grandmother and grand auntie had left me.

The noise was deafening. Like a thousand dump trucks dumping hot gravel all at the same time. The air reeked of bitter tar. The closer it got, the clearer its shape. Slabs of road the size of houses arranged themselves into a giant body, tail, legs, short arms, and finally a horrible reptilian head. Vines whipped out of the forests flanking the strange road creature and attached themselves to the slabs. They started snaking up to the items the women had dropped. Snatching up the yam tubers, cell phones, tomatoes. They took every scoop of rice, right down to the grains on my face. Every piece of broken porcelain. They left nothing but me.

It stood several stories high, the vague shape of a monstrous lizard of hot gravel. It snapped and tore connected vines as it moved, only for more vines to reconnect. It slithered toward me, its hot black gravel sizzling.

Vines snatched up my hands, which wriggled about like captured crabs. Then the vines snatched my wrists. They dragged me close to the creature. By this time, I was done. I had nothing left. I don't even know why I was conscious.

The vines connected to my open wrists and I could feel them… pumping something into me. It was warm and that warmth ran up my arms, to my shoulders, to my chest, all the way to my toes. I felt like I was going to be sick. How can one who is dying feel sick?

The moment the sensation made it to my toes, I experienced a terrible stab of pain that radiated from all over my body. Like a light switch had been turned on, my mind cleared. Just like that.

I screamed.

My eye landed on the horrific creature again. I screamed again. The vines were doing something to my severed hands and wrists. I could hear a soft wet smacking sound. When I finally chanced a look, I saw that the vines were knitting. They were knitting my veins and arteries.

Lying on my back, I turned my head to the side and vomited. That road monster was hovering over me like an over-attentive doctor. Hot pebbles and stones rained on me. The sky was brightening as the day broke. From where I lay, I could now see that it had several lizards running about its body, mainly those large orange and green ones.

Then the worst happened. Its attention focused on me. Every muscle in my body tightened, every one of my physical senses sharpening. I felt that which is "me" fear for her very existence.

The creature brought its huge stone face up to mine. Within inches. Heat dripped from it like sweat. Its bitter tar odor stung my nostrils. Beneath the stench there was another scent, something distinctively native. That woody, rich perfume that I always noticed as soon as I got off the airplane. There was life and death in that scent. But I was only thinking about death, as the smell filled my nasal passage.

It moved closer, within a half-inch. Its appearance began to shift. Stone became wood, elongating into a giant long-faced mask of black ebony with prominent West African features. I nearly started laughing, despite is all. You saw this face in many markets; it was that generic face of most West African ebony masks. I had many masks with this very face on my wall back home.

But this was the *real* one, the *living* one, the *first* one. This was the face that people were selling. My ears rung and my eyes watched; no species of terror could have been more profound. Its thick lips puckered, the deep deep eyes piercing. Over its shoulders, I could see the hard faces of others. They floated like puffs of powder and undulated like oil. They had large eyes, wide-nostrilled noses, cheekbones like granite. Many of them were familiar to me, also. Even more were not.

Some had what looked like ants skittering about their faces. Others had red eye lids and deep tribal scars on their cheeks and foreheads. Blue horns. The face of a great red bird. A tree frog sitting on its forehead. Eyes like mud. Skin like leaves. Some radiated beautiful liquid light. Others sprouted pink flowers. Spirits, masquerades, ghosts, and ancestors, these were deep deep *mmuo!* I was actually seeing *mmuo!* Me, Chioma, born in the USA. Why *me?*

These ethereal faces crowded far far back, tens, thousands, millions, billions, an infinite number of them peering from infinity. Looking over the creature's shoulders. Watching. Seeing *me*. Like those lizards, they were waiting for something to happen to me. Can you imagine?

My chest felt like a block of ice and my eyes burned. My scalp itched. Then I felt it. It was pleasure and pain, black and white, cacophony and stillness, perfumed and pungent. Something inside me both died and was birthed. I moaned, looking into its eyes. At once, there was clarity. I saw a young woman with a chain of thick red-orange beads woven into her tightly braided hair. She danced slowly, lizards following the movement of her feet. And there was a vertical line scarring each of her ankles. Her feet had been cut off and reattached. Yet look at her dance. *Was she the first?* I wondered. *First what?*

Then, just like that, the vines retreated. The lizards scattered. And the road dragon monster ancestor creature grunted and quickly began to shamble back down the road. It was like they all feared the sunlight. I dunno. What do I know?

When I sat up, I was in the middle of a lumpy dirt road and there was a car coming right at me. I jumped up and ran out of the way. The driver didn't even see me! *Am I invisible?* I wondered. I realized I knew where I was, less than a mile from the house. There was no dense forest near the house, never had been. It was all impossible.

Images of *mmuo* rose and fell in my mind and I swayed. I steadied myself by looking at my hands. Slowly, I brought them up. There were dark bruises on my wrists, as if someone had tied them too tightly with heavy ropes. There was dried blood, too. But my hands looked…normal. They weren't turning purple or black as they should have been nor were they behaving like independent creatures. And most importantly, they were connected to my wrists. I dared to move a finger. It worked just fine. Except for a weird tingle I felt in the fingertips.

I made a fist and wiggled and flexed all my fingers. Still that weird tingle. But that was it. My hands were still alive and they were my own. I wiped my lips with the back of my hand, the taste of vomit still in my mouth. Even my vomit was gone from the ground.

I walked home.

I killed a man once. With my bare hands. This was before I was a cop. It's probably the reason I *became* a cop. It was during my second year in college. I was twenty. He followed me home one night and dragged me between the dorms onto a narrow road that ran between the buildings. He was bigger than me. Stronger, too. I'm tall and a rather strong woman, but just a woman nonetheless. So there we were on the concrete, his hands squeezing the air from my neck. I was seeing stars, galaxies, black outer space. There was a ringing in my ears. My head was full of pressure. Tears were in my eyes. I was fading.

Then something swept over me. I raised my hands and grabbed his neck, too. He looked surprised at first but didn't seem too bothered. Until my hands locked on his neck like a vice. Suddenly I knew I could crush stones with my hands. I crushed his neck like it was one of the stones I was imagining.

My parents are lawyers and somehow they kept it all away from the press. And somehow they kept me out of jail, thank God, though that was the easy part. The guy had apparently done to several women within the state what he tried to do to me. Since then, I've always been suspicious of my hands.

Typically when you think of one's identity, you think face, right? The eyes are the windows to the soul. You cut off one's head and the person dies. You see a picture where a woman's face is not shown but her body is and you think misogyny, no? She becomes objectified, nothing but a body. But what of the hands? Fingerprints are as distinctive as one's face, as unique.

When we want to really identify a suspect, we go to his or her prints. Again, I think of Che Guevara and the depth of the insult in cutting off his hands. The depth of attempted annihilation. So what happens when your hands kill a man? What happens when those hands are cut off and then start behaving like freed spiders? What happens when those hands are reattached by some fucking dragon monster Nigerian ancestor being made of rolling hot gravel and vines and wood? What just happened to me?

As I slowly walked back to my grandmother's house, my stomach groaned and my temples throbbed. *Grandma and auntie*, I thought. *They just…left me there.* I heard the crunch of my bones, the snap of my arteries and veins, the splatter of my blood. I saw my own hands moving about on their own. I saw billions of *mmuo*, all staring at me. I stopped, put my hands on my knees and bent forward. My stomach heaved but thankfully I had nothing in it. Tears dribbled from my eyes. More cars passed me by. I wiped the tears away but more tears came. It took me a half-hour to make the ten-minute walk to the house. By the time I arrived, I was deeply pissed off.

I threw the front door open. "Grandma! Auntie! Where are you?" I screamed in Igbo. I stood there, breathing heavily, wiping the tears from my eyes, so I could clearly see the looks on their faces. I watched them descend the stairs looking guilty as hell. I shouted and cursed and accused them of everything from black magic and Satanism to witchcraft and juju; anything that would make them feel ashamed, as I knew they both claimed to be good Catholics. Spit flew from my mouth, snot from my nose. My voice quivered as my entire body began to shudder. I started sobbing, images and sounds and scents racing through my mind again. And my grandma and auntie leaving me.

Then I blurted the story of the murderer who tried to murder me and instead got murdered. I laughed wildly through my sobs, feeling lightheaded, frightened, desperate and confused.

"Oh we knew about you killing that man," grandma calmly responded.

My mouth hung open. I sat on the couch, my heart slamming in my chest.

Auntie Amaka sat beside me and took my hand in hers. I yanked it away from her. I had a brief thought of leaving my severed hand in her hands. I had to work hard not to screech. "Don't touch me!" I snapped.

"My dear, we could have told you, yes," Auntie Amaka said, delicately. "But once…once you opened that door…"

"No," Grandma said. "Once it started to rain, I think. And you being here."

"Regardless," Auntie Amaka said. "It was going to happen."

I ran my hand over my face. Who knew what the fuck they were talking about? "What was… that thing?" I asked.

"It has many names. We speak none of them," Grandma said.

"Why the boy, then?"

"All we can guess is that it was because he outsmarted a great snake that was meant to kill him," Grandma said. "It was last year. The snake was about to strike as he passed through a field. The boy somehow knew. Before the snake could do the job the boy smashed its head with his school book."

"Again, not his fault," Grandma said. "It never is."

"So you're saying we were both supposed to die but something…"

Grandmother laughed. I felt like slapping her. "You think this is about you?" she asked, ignoring the irate look on my face. "You think it had anything to do with any of us specifically?" She shook her head. "In this village, when it rains for three days during Harmattan, certain people start… getting maimed. Us women know where to take them and what to bring. It's been like that since anyone can remember."

"But we don't know the why or the how of it," Auntie added. "It doesn't happen often. Maybe once every ten years." She shrugged and both women looked at me apologetically.

It was like being the victim of an unsolved hit and run. No one knew the motive. No real answers. No revelation. No "aha" moment. So all I knew was pain, mystification, terror and the eerie feeling of having my face seductively licked by death. I looked at my hands. The thin green lines on my wrists had faded some. I was heading home in a few days.

I sit looking out the airplane window now. We land soon. I never return home from Nigeria the same person I was before. But this time takes the cake.

Minutes after takeoff, I felt a rush of relief like no other. I was glad to be leaving the motherland. After what happened, I needed some serious space. I scratched at a mosquito bite on my arm. It was red and inflamed and I knew I should leave it alone. But damn, the thing was itchy. Nigerian mosquito bites were always the worst. You never feel them land on you and then you can't stop feeling the itch of their bites.

I was glad to be sitting near the window. The plane was pretty packed, so turning to the window gave me at least a little privacy. I looked closely at my mosquito bite, rubbing it with my thumb as opposed to digging at it with my nail, the way I wanted to. The more I rubbed, the better it felt. The less itchy. The less red.

"Oh shit," I whispered. The guy beside me looked at me with raised eyebrows. I smiled at him and shook my head.

It was as if I'd rubbed off the mosquito bite. My skin was healed back to its usual brown. I quickly got up.

"Excuse me," I whispered as I made my way into the aisle. I went straight to the bathroom. Once inside, I unbuttoned my blouse. I had all types of scratches from the incident. I touched the painful bruise on my side and ran my finger across it. Erased like chalk on a chalkboard. I undid my jeans and rubbed the scratches on my legs. I rubbed my hands all over. Then, naked, I stood up and looked at myself in the mirror. Not a scratch, bruise, pimple or blemish on my body.

I was thirty-nine years old. Happy with my life. "Why?" I whispered. "Shit, shit shit! No, no, no." I was a cop. And I loved being a cop. Now what will I become? I wondered. I considered asking my hands. *But what if they answer?* I thought.

I sit here looking out the window at the ocean below. What will become of me?

I hear a sharp scream behind me. Then a gasp. "I… I didn't… he tried to…" The sound of commotion. A woman yells, "Get his hands!"

"Oh my God!"

Grunting, screeching, shouting. I jump up along with everyone around me. We're all probably thinking of the same thing. Terrorists, 9/11. I whirl around to see what's happening. It's a sight to behold.

There are five men piled in the aisle. Two of them are dark-skinned Africans; one wears a white caftan and there is bright red blood smeared on it. One of them is Asian, he wears a black suit with a golden dragon pin on the left breast pocket. Two of them are white men; one in jeans and a t-shirt, another in a navy blue suit. They sit on, hold down, and punch a young white man, mashing his head to the floor. The young man's wide eyes water and he sweats profusely. His face is beet red. He's breathing heavily and babbling, "Get me off this goddamn plane! I want to get off! GET ME OFF!"

In the seat before them, a woman lies in a man's arm. She coughs, her hands to her throat. A yellow number two pencil protrudes from the side of her neck. Blood spurts and dribbles down. The man holding her, an old Igbo-looking man in Western attire, looks absolutely lost.

I look at my hands. I don't even hesitate.

SWELL

ELIZABETH BEAR

Of course you notice the blind girl.

After you've packed up the merchandise table and started clearing the stage, she lingers, beached with small white hands wrapping the edges of her little café table like bits of seaweed dried there. She clings to scarred black wood as if something might sweep her adrift and drown her.

The crowd breaks and washes around her, flowing toward the door. The wrist loop of her white cane pokes over the back of her chair like a maritime signal flag, in case you somehow missed the opacity of her face-wrapping black shades in the near-dark of the club. And still she remains, a Calypso on her tiny island, while you coil patch cables and slide your warm mahogany fiddle into its case, while the café staff lift chairs onto tables and bring the house lights up glaringly bright, until you start to wonder if whoever she's waiting for is coming to assist her.

The tall redheaded bartender polishes glasses, her apron tossed over the Sam Adams Boston Lager draft handle. Up in the crude timber-built mezzanine, institutional stoneware makes flat clicking sounds and sticky food smells as someone piles it into a washtub. Your sweat's turned cold with the stage lights off, and your flat shoes reek of spilled beer. You're just packing the fiddle pickup into its hand-cut foam when you see Little Eddie the house manager (*little* to keep him straight from *Big* Eddie the redheaded bartender) come through the kitchen doors and notice the blind girl.

He starts forward, turning sideways to miss skinny dreadlocked Clara as she pauses with the washtub full of plates, but you set the pickup on the closed fiddle case and hop off the riser so you can get to the girl first. Nobody needs Little Eddie at the end of a bad night. You've had enough bad nights here to know.

He sees you coming and lets his steps go purposeless, turning to stack the glasses on the worst table in the joint—behind the pillar, next to the kitchen—so he can keep a hairy eyeball on you. You come over to the blind girl's table, careful to make some noise, and stop four feet from her.

"Miss, do you need some help?"

She doesn't lift her chin to seek your voice, which makes you think she's been blind since birth. She does tilt her head, however, a vertical crease appearing on her brow.

"You're the singer," she says. She sounds like the cold outside has gotten into her sinuses, her voice rough as if its nap caught on a sandpaper throat. "Has everyone gone home, then? I like to wait for the crowds to clear."

When she lets go of the table-edge, you can imagine you hear her flesh peel free of the wood. It wobbles as she releases it, rocking back and forth on crooked coaster feet for a moment before settling down with a little list to the left. House left. Her left. Your right.

"Everybody's gone," you say. "We're closing up. Do you have somebody to help you get home?"

"Oh," she says, "I can manage."

She's plain, with bland colorless hair to go with the transparent skin, but even stuffy and hoarse, her voice lifts the fine hairs on your nape like a breath.

Dubiously, you glance at the light jacket draping her chair, the summerweight, girl-cut t-shirt stretched over her bony shoulders. Even more dubiously, you glance at the door. Each time it opens, the cold washes into the café. Each time, it takes two seconds for the cold to cross the open floor and curdle on your skin.

Of course, she can't read your body language. So you clear your throat and say, "You know it's January out there."

"I know my way home." As if to prove her point, she stands and gathers her red-tipped cane and jacket. She starts working her way into the latter one sleeve at a time, but the cane gets in her way. You'd offer to take it, but there's no way to catch her eye.

"Sure," you say. "But I can drop you. I'm parked out back."

"You want me to get into a car with a stranger?"

You laugh. "What's going to happen?"

"Sometimes serial killers have women who find victims for them," she says, and you'd think she was totally sincere if the corner of her mouth wasn't turning upward just a little.

"You can call home before we leave and tell them I'm bringing you. And everybody here will see us leave together."

She's on the hook, but it's not set yet. She chews the inside of her cheek.

"I'll even warm the car up before I bring it around," you promise, and just like that she says, "Okay."

She moves toward you, cane swinging, and you stand aside. She taps expertly towards the door. You follow her from the music hall, thinking that it's weird that after all that she didn't give you a chance to go and fetch the car. She's still going to have to wait while you load your gear.

One nice thing about a blind girl: you don't have to be embarrassed by the un-vacuumed state of your ride. Or the fact that it's a Corolla with a quarter million touring miles on it. It used to be red about six years ago.

You know you shouldn't ask her, but who can resist? After she gives you directions you ask, "So how did you like the show?"

Her silence is enough warning to brace yourself for honesty. But then what she says is thoughtful, and not as bad as you were expecting. "You still sound like everybody else," she says. "But that won't be forever. You'll find your voice."

You nod, and realize again that she can't see you. You know you're generic. Everybody starts off generic. All garage bands sound the same, as a girl you used to know liked to say. So you're generic. But you're still growing. It's a slow, painful process, though, and there's always the fear you'll die before you finish.

Evolution is the most awful god of all.

"That stuff you sing about," she said. "You really believe it?"

"I believe it's important to say it out loud," you say, because you have to say something. She makes a little noise of consideration or disapproval, like a thumped violin, and you're afraid to ask which.

You can't really talk, so you just reach across the center console and touch the back of her hand, lightly, with two fingers. The side road whirs by under the Toyota's wheels, the verges studded with bare trees burnt-bone stark against dirty snow. The blind girl's not wearing any gloves. You don't think she had any. Her hand is cold.

Cold flesh, not the surface cold of human chill with the sense of warmth under it, but cold to the bone.

"You must be freezing!"

"I'm always cold," she says, and pulls her hand away. "Bad circulation. I was born that way."

"What's your name?" you ask, because it seems like a good way to apologize.

She says "Ashley," you think, but when you repeat it she corrects you. She has to say it twice more before it dawns that what she's saying is *Aisling*, only she's pronounced it the Irish way, correctly.

By the time you've repeated it to her satisfaction, you're wondering how she meant to walk all the way out here with no sidewalks and no sight. And who on earth would let her try it. She can't be more than seventeen. Even if you weren't sure from her skin, she doesn't have on the purple wristband the café uses for over twenty-one.

"What does your house look like?" you ask.

"It has a big porch," she says. "The front lawn is overgrown but there's a slate walk. The trees kind of clear out around it. When the echoes get sharp you're nearly there."

Of course, you think, but then you deserve it for asking what the place looks like, don't you? And up ahead you can see a break in the trees, a place where the headlights stop catching on crossed black trunks.

"The driveway's not plowed," you say, pulling up to the curb. There's a tromp line through the snow which must mark out the route of that slate path, and—as promised—a big deep three-season porch that wraps the front of the ramshackle, light-colored farmhouse like a grin.

"We don't have a car," she says.

There's no porch light, and the light pole in the stand of birches by the street looks like it hasn't worked in years. White paint shags from the cast iron like the bark of the young trees that surround it, all clearly delineated in moonlight amplified by snow.

She opens the car door while you're still wondering if you should get out and help her, but the stiffness in her neck says she wants to do this for herself, and she doesn't seem to have any problem finding the path through the snow. Her cane seems to waver before her like a snake's tongue tasting the air.

"Thank you," she says. She shuts the door and moves forward confidently. Caught on the horns of your dilemma, you opt to drape your hands over the steering wheel and watch, just watch. To make sure she gets into the house, that's all.

She climbs the snowy steps without mishap. The lights in the house don't come on when she rattles the porch door open and steps inside.

The door is shut behind her before you realize you never told her your name, and she never asked it.

You keep a musician's schedule, but when you wake up early the next afternoon you haven't overslept. You've still got a couple hours of daylight and it's Tuesday, so no gig tonight, though you're supposed to be driving to Boston on Thursday and Albany Friday night. The memory of the girl and the steps haunts you all through cold spaghetti breakfast, too much coffee, a shower that washes the stiff stage sweat from your hair. At least you don't reek of cigarettes, the way you used to after a gig back when you started.

It's not until you're wrapping the robe around your shoulders that you realize the steps Aisling climbed last night had not been shoveled, and that while there were footsteps leading towards the house, there hadn't been any leading in the door.

You're skinning into jeans, wool socks, a thermal top and flannel shirt before you realize you've made a decision. More coffee tumbles, black, into a travel mug, and with a jingle of metal you lock the door behind you.

It's crisp clear winter as you descend the wooden steps, ice melt crunching under lace-up boots, but the air breathed through the alpaca scarf your sister knitted is warm and smells of lanolin. You scrape the windows of the Toyota, saving gas and the environment by choosing not to warm it up before you climb in and drive away. It starts on the second attempt, grinding and complaining, but bumps out of the driveway easily enough, as if it were just following its nose.

You remember the way, and twenty minutes later you're pulled up in front of Aisling's house.

In daylight, it looks even more disreputable. The gutters along the edge of the porch roof sag. One has frozen saplings sprouting. You pull the Toyota over into the snow bank until the tires crunch on ice and get out. Even though this is the country, city habits die hard. You lock the doors behind.

It's cold enough that the snow squeaks under your boots, and the sun hasn't yet made a brittle crust on top. You stride through it, noticing two sets of footprints—one big and one small, one boots and one sneakers—and stop by the front porch door. Footprints lead around the side of the house, off towards the oak wood, but on the steps only two trails break: one up and one down.

The ones leading down cross over the ones leading up.

You fish a miniature Maglite out of your pocket and shine it through a grimed louvered window, though you already suspect what you're going to see inside. Boxes, torn and waterstained. Mouse droppings. Blown leaves curled like brown dead spiders. There are footprints in the dirt on the boards, but they stop right inside the door and turn around.

A ghost-story chill chases around your shoulders, or maybe that's just the wind sneaking between your scarf and your hat. Deep in the woods, the metallic call of a cardinal blurs through naked branches: *wheet, wheet, chipchipchipchipchipchip*. Nobody lives here, and hasn't in years.

You catch yourself looking over your shoulder and shake your head. No one is sneaking up behind you and you'd be sure to hear them crunching if they were. Still, when you step back from the window, you hunch your shoulders at more than the cold.

The trail leads around the left side of the house. You stuff your gloved hands into your coat pockets and rub the sleek case of your cellphone with leathered fingertips. You'd call 911, but what would you tell them? *I dropped a girl off here late last night and I'm not sure she was really blind?* You're not even sure if she was really *here*.

If you call, you won't have to find what you might find in a snowdrift. But then if you call and there's nothing, what will that look like? Better to go check for yourself, just to make sure.

Maybe somebody was waiting here for her. There's the other set of footprints. Maybe there's a carriage house around back, an in-law apartment or something, and that's where people live.

Sniffing deeply, you can imagine you smell woodsmoke. But when you come around the corner into the back yard, there's nothing but those two sets of tracks, still laid over one another, one big and one little. They cross the yard diagonally, past a trio of blueberry bushes in torn wire cages, and vanish among the trees. The snow is well-trampled, too: you don't think these are the marks of only one passage, or even just a couple.

You glance over your shoulder again. Then, shoulder squared, eyes front, you start forward, whistling the jaunty cardinal's song back at him.

You hope to see him flicker through the trees—red wings would be a welcome distraction from a world of white and black—but the only movement is the pall of your breath hung on the air, the way it curls to either side when you move through it. A hundred yards into the trees, just the other side of a snowy scramble over a humped stone wall that must once have marked a field boundary, the paths diverge—larger booted footsteps back towards the road, smaller sneakers deeper into the wood.

"Two roads diverged in a snowy wood," you mutter, conflating two poems, but Frost isn't here to correct your misquotation and, furthermore, it amuses you. The problem is, neither of them looks particularly less-traveled. But you're guessing that the smaller feet must be Aisling's, which means you should go that way. Deeper into the woods, in the fading afternoon.

Well, if it gets dark, you have a flashlight.

The wool socks and your insulated boots keep your toes warm, so when they start to hurt it's just from walking downhill and getting jammed up against the front of the boots. The slope turns into a hill, and at the bottom of the hill you spot a broad swift brook, running narrow now between ice-gnarled stony banks. The chatter of the water against stone reaches you along with the smell.

Somebody told you once that ice and water don't smell. When the scent of this fills you up, you wonder if their nose was broken. It's clean and sharp and somehow, counterintuitively, *earthy*. Rich. Satisfying.

Aisling's trail—if it is Aisling's trail—ends at the ice.

"Shit!" You slalom down the slope, though there's no point in hurrying. Whatever happened here happened hours ago, and there's no sign of Aisling. Her footprints vanish when they reach the stream.

There's an obvious course of action. Wool socks will keep your feet warm even wet, your boots are reasonably waterproof, and it'll be safer to splash through the water than try to walk on the icy rocks. As you teeter into the brook, arms outstretched, an icy gout leaps up inside the leg of your jeans. You'd shriek, but the cold is so intense it's silencing.

You're committed now. You turn upstream, at a guess, because a guess is all you have. Some other bird is singing now, something more flutelike and complicated than the cardinal, and it seems to come from this direction. Under the circumstances, music seems as good a guide as any.

You're still trying to decide if you've chosen the right direction when the brook vanishes among jumbled boulders into the side of the hill.

"Well, fuck," you say. Water can go where you can't. Downstream, then, you think, and turn.

The music is coming from out of the ground. An acoustic illusion, some trick of how sound conducts around the stones. But you turn back nonetheless, unable to resist the lure of a mystery, and inch closer to the stones. Wool socks or not, your toes numb in their boots. Despite that, when you kick a rock by accident the pain spikes to your knee.

When you put a hand on the rocks and lean into the gap, the echoes tell you it goes on. The entrance is tight, but you could squeeze through without stripping. The rock under your hand tells you something else, too: it's a known cave, one with regular visitors. The stone is polished as if in a tumbler, rubbed smooth by many years of passages, the wear of cloth against stone.

You grope in your pocket for the light, twist it on. The floor's all mud within, frozen and sticky, but you can see a trail down the corridor where someone's crunched through surface ice into the muck beneath.

Inside, the singing reverberates. There's no mistaking it now: it's a human voice, distorted by resonances, rippling with overtones and echoes. And it's singing one of your songs.

Your heart squeezes so hard it chokes you, a triphammer beat of relief and excitement and fear. You have to clear your throat twice to speak, but when you get your voice unstuck you shape a breath and call out "Aisling?"

The singing stops, but the echoes trail, complexifying before they die. Away in the cave you hear a splash, and that echoes too.

"Aisling? I have a light. Talk to me, so I can find you?"

There's a pause, when you expected hysterical calls for help. And then she says, "I'm back where the water is. Come and find me."

You follow the stream again, this time through the muddy deposits and then over clean stones. Your light skitters over gray and black and pale, streaks and circles, and some of that must be fossils because you don't think stones grow in those shapes. You've always heard that the dark in a cave is supposed to be oppressive, that the weight of stone over your head should press you down. But it's peaceful here, quiet and sweet, calm as a cathedral. The water rings on stone like a Zen fountain, and Aisling sings harmonies around it to guide you.

The deeper into the cave you get, the warmer the air becomes. Not *warm*, actually, but no longer freezing either. The mud underfoot stops crunching, and when the stream drops off sharply you step out of the flow and onto the well-worn trail beside it.

When you step on the bra, you almost drop your light.

It's a black bra, the stiff seamless under-a-t-shirt kind, and piled beside it, soaked on the cave floor, are white panties and a thin blue t-shirt. No jeans and no shoes. Sometimes, don't people get crazy with hypothermia and take off their clothes because they think they're dying of heat when they're already freezing?

"Aisling?"

"Down here," she says. "In the water."

You shine the light down, to where the cave opens away from a winding braided channel and becomes something like a room. Its rays reflect from a rippled surface, the limpid waters of an underground lake, so transparent that even with the flashlight glare you can see the weird white limestone structures that hump and glide across its bottom. And you can see Aisling in the water, *through* the water, her colorless hair all around her like seaweed, teacup breasts white as the rock she floats over, the featureless flesh where her eyes should be, the wide slash of her lipless mouth, and the ragged plumy sweep of her long, light-scattering tail.

"You're a mermaid," you say, as if it were the most natural thing in the world. Listening to your own level voice shocks you more, right now, than Aisling does. "You're a mermaid in a cave."

"Very good," she tells you, her voice a reedy, layered thing. "Most people are much worse about denying the evidence of their eyes. Come on in, my darling. The water's fine."

The water, in point of fact, is freezing, or very nearly so. Ice crystals brush your naked arms and legs, the water sucking heat from your liver and ovaries. You start to shiver before you're even fully immersed, a bone-rattling chill that makes you fear for your tongue should you attempt to speak. And yet still you walk to her, until the cave water laps your collarbones like desperate tongues, until the finny spikes of her webbed outreached fingertips scratch the calluses on your own.

The flashlight, left propped on a stone, spreads sallow light around the cave, inadequate to touch its corners. The blind mermaid still seems clearly delineated, as if she collected light or as if some inner light illuminated her. Maybe mermaids are bioluminescent. Maybe nobody's ever done the research.

Don't be an idiot. The research?

Her knobbled-slick hands close on your wrists and she draws you into water so cold you can't feel it, can't really feel the moment when your feet lose contact with the knobbled-slick limestone floor. Her brawny tail pries between your legs, fish-slippery, hard muscle rasping-rough with the scales that sparkle. Fins hook your ankles, glass-sharp on knobby bone, and her hands glide wide on your scapulae, so you can feel the prickle of their roughness and also the way your bony edges press into her palms. She has breasts, and why on earth would a mermaid have milk and mammal breasts when she is so obviously not a mammal? But there they are, floating against your own, nipples as hard and white as the rest of her.

When she kisses you on the mouth you feel the prick of all her sharp sharp teeth. You kiss her back, eyes drifting closed, shivering so hard you barely find her mouth, and her best of voices whispers, "Open your eyes."

You do, and see the dim light glitter on the cave roof as she floats you. The cold is sinking deep, deep into your meat and organs, so you shake already like a woman in orgasm.

The blind mermaid doesn't care. You put your hands in the dilute cloud of her hair, so she pulls against your grip as she kisses down your throat—leaving rings of pinpricks on your collarbone—down the slopes of your breasts until you grind against her strong uncooperative body, arching back, crying out.

She scrapes your belly like rough stone, her hands pressing the small of your back up to hold your face in air. She hums to you as she kisses until you could drown here, drown in her voice, drown in this desperate cold and die happy. Water falls from the cave roof, strikes your mouth and eyes. You imagine the stalactites it's forming, each single droplet a force for legacy.

"Sing for me," she says, half-underwater. Her lips scrape the skin over your hip ridge until you whine. She likes to kiss where the bones come up under the surface of your body like gliding fish. "Sing for me, or I kiss no more."

"Cold," you manage, though it falls from you like a whisper. Your teeth aren't knocking themselves to pieces in your head anymore. You think that means you're dying: that your body won't shiver anymore.

"Sing," she says, with a flicker of her tongue that—cold or not—makes you cry.

So you sing in the mermaid's arms, in whispers and tiny sharp gasps of breath that blue your lips with cold, expecting her touch will be your death and not caring, for the beauty of the frozen song.

You awaken stiff and alone with your scrapes and bruises, when you expected not to awaken at all. Someone has heaped stained cloth and a torn old sleeping bag under and over you. In sleep you've curled tight as a grub, your abdominal muscles aching with contraction. There's light: it must be the next morning.

You hope it's only the next morning. When you lift your head, you realize that you're not in the cave any longer.

You lie on a plywood floor before the soot-stained brick pad that supports a cast-iron woodstove. The walls are peeling metal and seem very close to either side and from about waist-height they're mostly made of rows of windows, as if you were in an airplane fuselage. The windows are covered in a layer of transparent plastic, condensation misting the enclosed side and turning to frost on the metal-framed windows.

That woodstove ripples with heat. Radiant energy flattens against your face, picking moisture from your cheeks and eyelids. You turn from it and try to find the strength to roll away, but your arms won't move you, so you pull the edge of the sleeping bag up as a shield, instead and assess the damage.

Your skin burns everywhere she kissed you, swollen in chilblains red as lipstick prints. They smart when you press them, though your fingertips are cold enough that all you can feel is how much they hurt when you touch anything.

The plywood shudders with footsteps, and this time the adrenaline gives you enough energy to sit. Half-sit, anyway, slumped forward on locked elbows with your hair draggled in your eyes like a shipwrecked survivor pushing herself up from the surf. You feel castaway, cast-off. Seawracked and adrift, or maybe fetched up hard against the rocks and dashed there.

"Oh, good," a voice says, too loud. "You lived. Don't bother talking until you can look at me. Save your strength, 'cause I can't hear you."

You get your head up as he squats down, scarred boots laced only partway and the ragged cuffs of his dungarees spattered with salt and mud and (mostly) sawdust. He's a white guy, hair gray and thinning on top and not long. His cheeks were clean-shaven about three days ago: now silver hairs sparkle against dull skin. He's not a big guy and he's not a young guy, and even though he's dirty and ragged and you're naked on the floor under a pile of rags he doesn't make you scared. You wonder if you'll ever feel scared again, after the cave, after the mermaid inside it.

He tugs the sleeping bag up over your shoulders with a rough-skinned hand and steps back. "I'll get you some coffee," he says. "And some clothes."

By the time he comes back with a flannel shirt, t-shirt, cardigan, and too-big men's jeans washed soft, you've managed to edge away from the crisping heat of the woodstove and get yourself wedged into a lad-derback chair. An enamel pan sits atop the stove, steam rising from the water that must be simmering inside, but you can't tell that it's making any difference to the humidity. A few steps away from the stove, you can feel the baffling cold seeping through the metal walls of what you now realize is an ancient schoolbus, probably up on blocks and defi-nitely not in any condition to ever go anywhere again, because from here you can see the holes in the firewall where the steering column and gearshift used to go.

He leaves the clothes and turns his back, except you're not sure you can get the pants on by yourself. You'd call him, but you don't know his name, and after you say "Hey!" a couple of times you remember what he said about not being able to hear, and how loud he spoke.

Well, you made it into the chair. You can probably make it into the trousers.

With a little help from the chair you do. You're pulling the flannel shirt over the t-shirt when he comes back with a big blue plastic travel mug with a gas station logo on the side. It steams when he gives it over. Some of the warmth within seeps through the empty spaces between its inner and outer walls and stings your hands, but you cup it close anyway. It's white, which makes it cool enough to drink, and you don't stop until you've drained it to the bottom. It tastes like oily vanilla creamer and boiled coffee grounds and enough sugar to make your teeth ache and leave grit on your tongue and at the bottom of the cup, which right this second makes it the best thing you've ever tasted.

When you hand the cup back to the man, he fills it up from a ther-mos that sits on a knocked-together wood table along one side of the schoolbus. He must sleep underneath it, because a cot mattress is just visible behind the curtains tacked up to its underside. The second mug of coffee you cradle between your palms and savor, and when he's look-ing at your mouth you say, "Thank you."

Your voice startles you a little. Maybe it's the cold stopping up your ears, but it sounds plummier and more resonant than it should.

"T'ain't nothing," he says, and grins. "You're not the first one to meet the girl in the cave and come off worse—and better—for it." He touches his ear. "I can't hear her singing anymore, but I keep an eye out for anybody else who does."

"Are there a lot of us?"

He shrugs. "Every five, ten years or so. It's been a while since the last one. You'll probably more or less recover, given time."

"More or less?" You swallow more coffee, scrub the sweet sand of sugar across your palate with your tongue.

"Don't expect you won't be changed. By the way, I'm Marty."

"I'm Missy," you say, which is what your mom called you when she wasn't mad. You nerve yourself, as if bracing against some cold that's inside you, and say, "She's under my skin."

"She gets there," he says. "What are you going to do about it?"

You shrug. He hands you a pair of wool socks—your own socks, washed out and damp still.

"I've got some work," he says. "You're welcome to stay in here until you feel well enough to go. There's soup in the cupboard. You can heat it on the stove if you want."

He points, tins in a series of stacked Guida crates. You see Progresso lentil, Campbell's clam chowder. Boxes of crackers stuffed inside plastic freezer bags so the mice don't smell them.

"Thanks," you say. "I'm good. What kind of work?"

"Excuse me?"

"Your work," you say. "What kind of work do you do?"

"Oh." He stares down at his hands. "I make dulcimers and stuff."

"You're a musician?" He's not looking at you when you say it, though, and you have to repeat.

He shakes his head. "Luthier," he says. His eyes slide shyly aside. "I make instruments for other people. Do you want to see my shop?"

You put on your boots, which he must have rescued from the cave also. When you get outside in the cold, you realize that the schoolbus is parked in a clearing in the midst of a winter-bare multiflora rose and blackberry bramble, the canes bent and the sprays of withered crimson hips, no bigger than the head of a big sewing pin, bowed under tiny hats of snow. Beyond them, reached by tunnel-like paths that Marty must clear with a machete during the growing season, lies a ring of trees—the border of the woods, with its cave and its mermaid.

Other than the cold and the thorns, the first thing you notice when you step outside is the hum of a diesel generator, isolated off to the side in a little tin shack, its feet propped off the ground on cinder blocks. Marty's "shop" proves to be a wooden shed, also on blocks from what you can see through the snow, up against the side of the schoolbus so the bus serves as a windbreak. On the far side is the rusted out corpse of a DeSoto, the hood tatted to lacework by years.

The shed's other three walls have hay bales stacked against them, which might make you worry about fire, but the hay looks so wet it wouldn't burn if you soaked it in gasoline.

When he opens the door, heat comes out like a sticky wall. You hear the crackle of a woodstove in here too, and smell sharp sweet frankincense. A handful of resin smokes on the iron stove lid, giving the sixteen-by-sixteen room funereal or cathedral airs. Sawdust covers the floor inside, worktables lining every wall, lathes and sanders greased and dirty. Shaker pegboards circle eighteen inches below the topwall, unfinished instruments dangling by their necks. Dulcimers, yes. Mandolins, basses, guitars. A single white unsanded fiddle hanging from a neck like the wrung neck of a swan, like the curled tendril of a fern.

You draw a breath full of sawdust and incense and think, *Too perfect.* You might even say it, but Marty wouldn't hear you, and sometimes talking to yourself is really talking to be overheard. So you wait until he turns to check your reaction, moving into the warm shop with the snow dripping off your cuffs, and you say, "You made all these?"

"Every one." He reaches out and taps the hull of a double bass, the face striped purpleheart and rosewood and something gold. It thumps like a melon, sweet and ripe, so you wonder if he can feel the resonance through lingering fingertips.

"Do you sell them?" You want to touch the jazz guitar hanging over the lathe. Its faceplate is honey-colored, riddled with holes from worms that must have worked in the tree after it was fallen. The neck is mahogany, and it too has small scars, the imperfections of salvaged wood.

"I give them away," he says, and lifts down the guitar you were eyeing. It's finished and strung; he sets an electric tuner on the bench and bends over the strings. You probably couldn't tune as fast by ear as he does in his deafness.

When he's done, he scoops up the beast and holds it out to you like a toddler, archtop gleaming under the worklights. It's strung left-handed, and you wonder how he knew.

He says, "Care to try her?"

Your cold-stung fingers itch for it. "Give them away?" you ask. "How can you afford that?"

He gestures around and grins. "It doesn't take a lot of money to live like this, and I made some when I was young. When I still played myself, a little. Go on, take the guitar."

He has a point there. So you lift the guitar off his palms and stroke it for a second, finding where your hands should fall. You glance up, about to ask him what he wants to hear, and find him staring at your fingers. Oh, of course.

So you pick out a Simon and Garfunkel tune, because it's easy and fun and suits the instrument. And then you play a little Pete Seeger something, until your cracked fingertips start to more-than-sting. You don't bother singing: Marty's not listening, and you want to hear the *guitar*. You'd give it back, but it feels good in your arms, close and friendly, so you let it sit there and puppy-snuggle for a minute while you chat. You play a couple of bars of "Peggy Sue" and a couple of bars of "I Wanna Be Sedated," and it all sounds good. You expect a little buzz at the bottom of the neck, but it's clean all the way down.

"Who do you give them away to?"

"Deserving folks," he says. "Folks with music people listen to. Folks whose music makes a better world. That one's yours."

Your right hand locks on the neck. "I can't take this."

"I made it for you," he says. "The siren called you, Missy. There's no two ways about it. That there's your guitar."

You'd have expected to be too ill and exhausted to continue your vest-pocket tour, but you wake up rested and strong on Thursday, and in fine voice as if in spite of having been half-drowned in ice water and left on the stones. You hum to yourself in the mirror while you fix your hair, and you pick out a white button shirt and patchwork vest with swingy glass bead fringe across the chest to pull on over threadbare jeans. Spiked up hair and too much makeup gives you cheekbones that will read from stage. You're getting too old for the scapegrace gamine schtick.

At the last minute, as you're packing up the Toyota, you decide to bring the new guitar.

Boston and Albany are great, better than good, CDs flying out of the booth, and in Albany you pick up a gig in Portsmouth for May and a business card from a booking agent who sounds six kinds of excited and impressed.

"You're a lot better live," she says, tossing bottle-red hair behind her shoulder. "We need to get you into bigger venues, get some quality production on those CDs."

You think you like her.

Two weeks later, when you make it back to play for the Eddies again, you've figured out something is up. The crowd treats you differently since the mermaid. It's not about the guitar, nice as the guitar is, because you experiment with using other instruments and it doesn't seem to change anything.

You have to stop yourself from scanning the crowd for the mermaid. *She won't be here*, you tell yourself, wondering why it's so hard to believe.

It's no surprise when Little Eddie sidles up after the second set and asks you for a return booking in another four weeks, at the same fee. You tell him you have to check your calendar and your booking agent will call him. You make a note to negotiate him up, and sharply.

But when he walks away, you catch Big Eddie looking over the bar at you and you can see the shine in her eyes. That rattles you. Big Eddie doesn't get like that. She never lets anything get under her skin.

You walk over on the excuse of a beer—the second set ends and the café closes before last call, so it's still legal to serve—and drape yourself over a stool.

Big Eddie slides it in front of you and says, "What did you do to your voice?"

"Does it sound bad?" You clear your throat, sip beer, and try again. "I kind of fell in some water and wound up with hypothermia on a hike, and it's sounded funny since."

You didn't miss the way your voice has changed, and not just the timbre: it's your phrasing and your range as well. It took a little while and some messing around with a digital recorder to understand what you were hearing. The tentativeness, the derivative garage-band sound the mermaid commented on, have been washed from your music, leaving something etched and rough-edged and labyrinthine as sea caves.

You love it. You haven't been able to stop singing—to the cat, to yourself, in the shower, walking down the street—since she kissed you. Your new voice fills you up, clothes you in bright glory. You know how everyone else who hears it feels, because you feel it too.

Eddie says, "No, no. It sounds great. But it doesn't sound like you."

You have to bang on the door of Marty's shop to get his attention. When the door creaks open on sawdust-clogged hinges, he blinks at the brightness of sun off snow and covers it by pushing up his safety glasses. "Problem with the guitar, Missy?"

"Actually, just the opposite," you say, shaping the words so he can read them on your lips and tongue. "The guitar is wonderful. It's something else I need to give back, and I was hoping you'd come with me. Because I don't know what I'll do if I hear her singing. I'd really—" You look down in embarrassment, force yourself to look up again. If he can't see your face, he can't understand what you're saying. "—I'd really owe you one."

You already owe him one. More than one. Closer to a dozen. Your impression that he's a good guy is reinforced by the fact that he hangs the goggles on a nail inside the shop threshold, pulls his coat and gloves on without a word, and only pauses long enough to padlock the door.

You go down into the earth like pilgrims, making obeisance to the gods of deep places, sometimes scraping on your bellies over rough stones. Marty takes you deeper and by different passages than you went before, and all you can do is follow. You can't talk to him in the dark, not unless you make him turn and shine his light into your face, and so you listen to what he has to say instead.

"I had a daughter your age," he says, and you notice the verb tense and don't ask, just let your fingers brush the back of his wrist. In the cave, echoing from stone, shimmering from the moving surface of the underground river, his voice takes on the resonances and harmonics that have come to invest your own.

But then he adds, "She was a guitar player too." And, after another moment, "Kids are stupid. And maybe God protects fools, drunks and musicians, but all three at once is a bit much to ask of anybody."

You touch his shoulder in the dark, and realize it wasn't the deafness that made him give up playing. He leans into it for a second before walking forward, placing feet carefully on the rippled stones, ducking sideways to bend under a low roof. Water's worn scallops on the floor of the cave; they look like ripples in sand where a river's flowed over it. Wave patterns, sine patterns, like sound.

Water and music are the same thing, at the core.

You stop at the edge of a pool deeper and wider and even more pellucid than the one in which you met the mermaid before. The water moves only where slow drips scatter into it from the ceiling, the beams of your flashlight and Marty's scattering where they're reflected.

You half-expected the mermaid to be waiting, maybe even for her to sing you in, but the only sound is the arrhythmic plink of droplets. She's taken what she wanted and given what she chose to give. She's done and the rest is yours now.

Except you want it all to be yours, earned, not borrowed glory. You wonder if Marty—if anyone—can get her to let you go this time, let you come up out of the darkness again. You wonder if she'll be angry that you're rejecting her gift. You wonder what she'll say, and if she'll curse you.

You breathe deep of wet air to fill yourself up, and nerve yourself to call her up with your song. Because even if it's quick and easy, even if you've already paid for it, even if it's the most beautiful sound you'll ever make, you don't want to echo her voice forever.

You want to grow your own.

USELESS THINGS

MAUREEN F. MCHUGH

"Señora?" The man standing at my screen door is travel-stained. Migrant, up from Mexico. The dogs haven't heard him come up but now they erupt in a frenzy of barking to make up for their oversight. I am sitting at the kitchen table, painting a doll, waiting for the timer to tell me to get doll parts curing in the oven in the workshed.

"Hudson, Abby!" I shout, but they don't pay any attention.

The man steps back. "Do you have work? I can, the weeds," he gestures. He is short-legged, long from waist to shoulder. He's probably headed for the Great Lakes area, the place in the U.S. with the best supply of fresh water and the most need of farm labor.

Behind him is my back plot, with the garden running up to the privacy fence. The sky is just starting to pink up with dawn. At this time of year I do a lot of my work before dawn and late in the evening, when it's not hot. That's probably when he has been traveling, too.

I show him the cistern, and set him to weeding. I show him where he can plug in his phone to recharge it. I have internet radio on, Elvis Presley died forty-five years ago today and they're playing "(You're So Square) Baby I Don't Care." I go inside and get him some bean soup.

Hobos used to mark code to tell other hobos where to stop and where to keep going. Teeth to signify a mean dog. A triangle with hands meant that the homeowner had a gun and might use it. A cat meant a nice lady. Today the men use websites and bulletin boards that they follow, when they can, with cheap smartphones. Somewhere I'm on a site as a "nice lady" or whatever they say today. The railroad runs east of here and it's sometimes a last spot where trains slow down before they get to the big yard in Belen. Men come up the Rio Grande hoping to hop the train.

I don't like it. I was happy to give someone a meal when I felt anonymous. Handing a bowl of soup to someone who may not have eaten for a few days was an easy way to feel good about myself. That didn't mean I wanted to open a migrant restaurant. I live by myself. Being an economic refugee doesn't make people kind and good and I feel as if having my place on some website makes me vulnerable. The dogs may bark like fools, but Hudson is some cross between Border collie and golden retriever, and Abby is mostly black Lab. They are sweet mutts, not good protection dogs, and it doesn't take a genius to figure that out.

I wake at night sometimes now, thinking someone is in my house. Abby sleeps on the other side of the bed, and Hudson sleeps on the floor. Where I live it is brutally dark at night, unless there's a moon—no one wastes power on lights at night. My house is small, two bedrooms, a kitchen and a family room. I lean over and shake Hudson on the floor, wake him up. "Who's here?" I whisper. Abby sits up, but neither of them hear anything. They pad down the hall with me into the dark front room and I peer through the window into the shadowy back lot. I wait for them to bark.

Many a night, I don't go back to sleep.

But the man at my door this morning weeds my garden, and accepts my bowl of soup and some flour tortillas. He thanks me gravely. He picks up his phone, charging off my system, and shows me a photo of a woman and a child. "My wife and baby," he says. I nod. I don't particularly want to know about his wife and baby but I can't be rude.

I finish assembling the doll I am working on. I've painted her, assembled all the parts and hand rooted all her hair. She is rather cuter than I like. Customers can mix and match parts off of my website—this face with the eye color of their choice, hands curled one way or another. A mix and match doll costs about what the migrant will make in two weeks. A few customers want custom dolls and send images to match. Add a zero to the cost.

I am dressing the doll when Abby leaps up, happily roo-rooing. I start, standing, and drop the doll dangling in my hand by one unshod foot.

It hits the floor head first with a thump and the man gasps in horror.

"It's a doll," I say.

I don't know if he understands, but he realizes. He covers his mouth with his hand and laughs, nervous.

I scoop the doll off the floor. I make reborns. Dolls that look like newborn infants. The point is to make them look almost, but not quite real. People prefer them a little cuter, a little more perfect than the real thing. I like them best when there is something a little strange, a little off about them. I like them as ugly as most actual newborns, with some aspect that suggests ontology recapitulating phylogeny; that a developing fetus starts as a single celled organism, and then develops to look like a tiny fish, before passing in stages into its final animal shape. The old theory of ontology recapitulating phylogeny, that the development of the human embryo follows the evolutionary path, is false, of course. But I prefer that my babies remind us that we are really animals. That they be ancient and a little grotesque. Tiny changelings in our house.

I am equally pleased to think of Thanksgiving turkeys as a kind of dinosaur gracing a holiday table. It is probably why I live alone.

"Que bonita," he says. How beautiful.

"Gracias," I say. He has brought me the empty bowl. I take it, and send him on his way.

I check my email and I have an order for a special. A reborn made to order. It's from a couple in Chicago, Rachel and Ellam Mazar—I have always assumed that it is Rachel who emails me but the emails never actually identify who is typing. There is a photo attached of an infant. This wouldn't be strange except this is the third request in three years I have had for exactly the same doll.

The dolls are expensive, especially the specials. I went to art school, and then worked as a sculptor for a toy company for a few years. I didn't make dolls, I made action figures, especially alien figures and spaceships from the *Kinetics* movies. A whole generation of boys grew up imprinting on toys I had sculpted. When the craze for *Kinetics* passed, the company laid off lots of people, including me. The whole economy was coming apart at the seams. I had been lucky to have a job for as long as I did. I moved to New Mexico because I loved it and it was cheap, and I tried to do sculpting freelance. I worked at a big box store. Like so many people, my life went into freefall. I bought this place—a little ranch house that had gone into foreclosure in a place where no one was buying anything and boarded up houses fall in on themselves like mouths without teeth. It was the last of my savings. I started making dolls as a stopgap.

I get by. Between the little bit of money from the dolls and the garden, I can eat. Which is more than some people.

A special will give me money for property tax. My cistern is getting low and there is no rain coming until the monsoon in June, which is a long way from now. If it's like last year, we won't get enough rain to fill the cistern anyway. I could pay for the water truck to make a delivery. But I don't like this. When I put the specials on my website, I thought about it as a way to make money. I had seen it on another doll site. I am a trained sculptor. I didn't think about why people would ask for specials.

Some people ask me to make infant dolls of their own children. If my mother had bought an infant version of me I'd have found it pretty disturbing.

One woman bought a special modeled on herself. She wrote me long emails about how her mother had been a narcissist, a monster, and how she was going to symbolically mother herself. Her husband was mayor of a city in California, which was how she could afford to have a replica of her infant self. Her emails made me uncomfortable, which I resented. So eventually I passed her on to another doll maker who made toddlers. I figured she could nurture herself up through all the stages of childhood.

Her reborn was very cute. More attractive than she was in the image she sent. She never commented. I don't know that she ever realized.

I suspect the Mazars fall into another category. I have gotten three requests from people who have lost an infant. I tell myself that there is possibly something healing in re-creating your dead child as a doll. Each time I have gotten one of these requests I have very seriously considered taking the specials off my website.

Property tax payments. Water in the cistern.

If the Mazars lost a child—and I don't know that they did but I have a feeling that I can't shake—it was bad enough that they want a replica. Then a year ago, I got a request for the second.

I thought that maybe Rachel—if it is Rachel who emails me, not El-lam—had meant to send a different image. I sent back an email asking were they sure that she had sent the right image?

The response was terse. They were sure.

I sent them an email saying if something had happened, I could do repairs.

The response was equally terse. They wanted me to make one.

I searched online, but could find out nothing about the Mazars of Chicago. They didn't have a presence online. Who had money but no presence online? Were they organized crime? Just very very private? Now a third doll.

I don't answer the email. Not yet.

Instead I take my laptop out to the shed. Inside the shed is my oven for baking the doll parts between coats of paint. I plug in the computer to recharge and park it on a shelf above eye level. I have my parts cast by Tony in Ohio, an old connection from my days in the toy industry. He makes my copper molds and rotocasts the parts. Usually, though, the specials are a one-off and he sends me the copper supermaster of the head so he doesn't have to store it. I rummage through my molds and find the head from the last time I made this doll. I set it on the shelf and look at it.

I rough sculpt the doll parts in clay, then do a plaster cast of the clay mold. Then from that I make a wax model, looking like some Victorian memorial of an infant that died of jaundice. I have my own recipe for the wax—commercial wax and paraffin and talc. I could tint it pink, most people do. I just like the way they look.

I do the fine sculpting and polishing on the wax model. I carefully pack and ship the model to Tony and he casts the copper mold. The process is nasty and toxic, not something I can do myself. For the regular dolls, he does a short run of a hundred or so parts in PVC, vinyl, and ships them to me. He keeps those molds in case I need more. For the head of a special he sends me back a single cast head and the mold.

All of the detail is on the inside of the mold, outside is only the rough outline of the shape. Infants' heads are long from forehead to back of the skull. Their faces are tiny and low, their jaws like porkchop bones. They are marvelous and strange mechanisms.

At about seven, I hear Sherie's truck. The dogs erupt.

Sherie and Ed live about a mile and a half up the road. They have a little dairy goat operation. Sherie is six months pregnant and goes into Albuquerque to see an obstetrician. Her dad works at Sandia Labs and makes decent money so her parents are paying for her medical care. It's a long drive in and back, the truck is old and Ed doesn't like her to go alone. I ride along and we pick up supplies. Her mom makes us lunch.

"Goddamn it's hot," Sherie says as I climb into the little yellow Toyota truck. "How's your water?"

"Getting low," I say. Sherie and Ed have a well.

"I'm worried we might go dry this year," Sherie says. "They keep whining about the aquifer. If we have to buy water I don't know what we'll do."

Sherie is physically Chinese, one of the thousands of girls adopted out of China in the nineties and at the turn of the century. She said she went through a phase of trying to learn all things Chinese, but she complains that, as far as she can tell, the only thing Chinese about her is that she's lactose intolerant.

"I had a migrant at my door this morning," I say.

"Did you feed him?" she asks. She leans into the shift, trying to find the gear, urging the truck into first.

"He weeded my garden," I say.

"They're not going to stop as long as you feed them."

"Like stray cats," I say.

Albuquerque has never been a pretty town. When I came it was mostly strip malls and big box stores and suburbs. Ten years of averages of four inches of rain or less have hurt it badly, especially with the loss of the San Juan/Chama water rights. Water is expensive in Albuquerque. Too expensive for Intel, which pulled out. Intel was just a larger blow in a series of blows.

The suburbs are full of walkaway houses—places where homeowners couldn't meet the mortgage payments and just left, the lots now full of trash and windows gone. People who could went north for water. People who couldn't did what people always do when an economy goes soft and rotten, they slid, to rented houses, rented apartments, living in their cars, living with their family, living on the street.

But inside Sherie's parents' home it's still twenty years ago. The countertops are granite. The big screen plasma TV gets hundreds of channels. The freezer is full of meat and frozen Lean Cuisine. The air conditioner keeps the temperature at a heavenly 75 degrees. Sherie's mother, Brenda, is slim, with beautifully styled graying hair. She's a psychologist with a small practice.

Brenda has one of my dolls, which she bought because she likes me. It's always out when I come, but it doesn't fit Brenda's tailored, airily comfortable style. I have never heard Brenda say a thing against Ed. But I can only assume that she and Kyle wish Sherie had married someone who worked at Los Alamos or at Sandia or the university, someone with government benefits like health insurance. On the other hand, Sherie was a wild child, who, as Brenda said, "Did a stint as a lesbian," as if being a lesbian were like signing up for the Peace Corps. You can't make your child fall in love with the right kind of person. I wish I could have fallen in love with someone from Los Alamos. More than that, I wish I had been able to get a job at Los Alamos or the university. Me, and half of Albuquerque.

Sherie comes home, her hair rough-cut in her kitchen with a mirror. She is loud and comfortable. Her belly is just a gentle insistent curve under her blue Rumatel goat dewormer t-shirt. Brenda hangs on her every word, knows about the trials and tribulations of raising goats, asks about Ed, the truck. She feeds us lunch.

I thought this life of thoughtful liberalism was my birthright, too. Before I understood that my generation was to be born in interesting times.

At the obstetrician's office, I sit in the waiting room and try not to fall asleep. I'm stuffed on Brenda's chicken and cheese sandwich and corn chowder. *People Magazine* has an article about Tom Cruise getting telemerase regeneration therapy which will extend his lifespan an additional forty years. There's an article on some music guy's house, talking about the new opulence: cutting edge technology that darkens the windows at the touch of a hand and walls that change color, rooms that sense whether you're warm or cold and change their temperature, and his love of ancient Turkish and Russian antiques. There's an article on a woman who has dedicated her life to helping people in Siberia who have AIDs.

Sherie comes out of the doctor's office on her cell phone. The doctor tells her that, if she had insurance, they'd do a routine ultrasound. I can hear half the conversation as she discusses it with her mother. "This little guy," Sherie says, hand on her belly, "is half good Chinese peasant stock. He's doing fine." They decide to wait for another month.

Sherie is convinced that it's a boy. Ed is convinced it's a girl. He sings David Bowie's "China Girl" to Sherie's stomach which for some reason irritates the hell out of her.

We stop on our way out of town and stock up on rice and beans, flour, sugar, coffee. We can get all this in Belen, but it's cheaper at Sam's Club. Sherie has a membership. I pay half the membership and she uses the card to buy all our groceries then I pay her back when we get to the car. The cashiers surely know that we're sharing a membership, but they don't care.

It's a long hot drive back home. The air conditioning doesn't work in the truck. I am so grateful to see the trees that mark the valley.

My front door is standing open.

"Who's here?" Sherie says.

Abby is standing in the front yard and she has clearly recognized Sherie's truck. She's barking her fool head off and wagging her tail, desperate. She runs to the truck. I get out and head for the front door and she runs towards the door and then back towards me and then towards the door, unwilling to go in until I get there, then lunging through the door ahead of me.

"Hudson?" I call the other dog, but I know if the door is open, he's out roaming. Lost. My things are strewn everywhere, couch cushions on the floor, my kitchen drawers emptied on the floor, the back door open. I go through to the back, calling the missing dog, hoping against hope he is in the back yard. The back gate is open, too.

Behind me I hear Sherie calling, "Don't go in there by yourself!"

"My dog is gone," I say.

"Hudson?" she says.

I go out the back and call for him. There's no sign of him. He's a great boy, but some dogs, like Abby, tend to stay close to home. Hudson isn't one of those dogs.

Sherie and I walk through the house. No one is there. I go out to my workshop. My toolbox is gone, but evidently whoever did this didn't see the computer closed and sitting on the shelf just above eye level.

It had to be the guy I gave soup to. He probably went nearby to wait out the heat of the day and saw me leave.

I close and lock the gate, and the workshop. Close and lock my back door. Abby clings to me. Dogs don't like things to be different.

"We'll look for him," Sherie says. Abby and I climb into the truck and for an hour we drive back roads, looking and calling, but there's no sign of him. Her husband Ed calls us. He's called the county and there's a deputy at my place waiting to take a statement. We walk through the house and I identify what's gone. As best I can tell, it isn't much. Just the tools, mainly. The sheriff says they are usually looking for money, guns, jewelry. I had all my cards and my cell phone with me, and all my jewelry is inexpensive stuff. I don't have a gun.

I tell the deputy about the migrant this morning. He says it could have been him, or someone else. I get the feeling we'll never know. He promises to put out the word about the dog.

It is getting dark when they all leave and I put the couch cushions on the couch. I pick up silverware off the floor and run hot water in the sink to wash it all. Abby stands at the backdoor, whining, but doesn't want to go out alone.

It occurs to me suddenly that the doll I was working on is missing. He stole the doll. Why? He's not going to be able to sell it. To send it home, I guess, to the baby in the photo. Or maybe to his wife, who has a real baby and is undoubtedly feeling a lot less sentimental about infants than most of my customers do. It's a couple of weeks of work, not full time, but painting, waiting for the paint to cure, painting again.

Abby whines again. Hudson is out there in the dark. Lost dogs don't do well in the desert. There are rattlesnakes. I didn't protect him. I sit down on the floor and wrap my arms around Abby's neck and cry. I'm a stupid woman who is stupid about my dogs, I know. But they are what I have.

I don't really sleep. I hear noises all night long. I worry about what I am going to do about money.

Replacing the tools is going to be a problem. The next morning I put the first layer of paint on a new doll to replace the stolen one. Then I do something I have resisted doing. Plastic doll parts aren't the only thing I can mold and sell on the internet. I start a clay model for a dildo. Over the last couple of years I've gotten queries from companies who have seen the dolls online and asked if I would consider doing dildos for them. Realistic penises aren't really any more difficult to carve than realistic baby hands. Easier, actually. I can't send it to Tony, he wouldn't do dildos. But a few years ago they came out with room temperature, medical grade silicon. I can make my own molds, do small runs, hand finish them. Make them as perfectly lifelike as the dolls. I can hope people will pay for novelty when it comes to sex.

I don't particularly like making doll parts, but I don't dislike it either. Dildos, on the other hand, just make me sad. I don't think there is anything wrong with using them, it's not that. It's just…I don't know. I'm not going to stop making dolls, I tell myself.

I also email the Chicago couple back and accept the commission for the special, to make the same doll for the third time. Then I take a break and clean my kitchen some more. Sherie calls me to check how I'm doing and I tell her about the dildos. She laughs. "You should have done it years ago," she says. "You'll be rich."

I laugh, too. And I feel a little better when I finish the call.

I try not to think about Hudson. It's well over 100 today. I don't want to think about him in trouble, without water. I try to concentrate on penile veins. On the stretch of skin underneath the head (I'm making a circumcised penis.) When my cell rings I jump.

The guy on the phone says, "I've got a dog here, has got this number on his collar. You missing a dog?"

"A golden retriever?" I say.

"Yep."

"His name is Hudson," I say. "Oh thank you. Thank you. I'll be right there."

I grab my purse. I've got fifty-five dollars in cash. Not much of a reward, but all I can do. "Abby!" I yell. "Come on girl! Let's go get Hudson!"

She bounces up from the floor, clueless, but excited by my voice.

"Go for a ride?" I ask.

We get in my ancient red Impreza. It's not too reliable, but we aren't going far. We bump across miles of bad road, most of it unpaved, following the GPS directions on my phone, and end up at a trailer in the middle of nowhere. It's bleached and surrounded by trash—an old easy chair, a kitchen chair lying on its side with one leg broken and the white unstained inside like a scar, an old picnic table. There's a dirty green cooler and a bunch of empty 40-ounce bottles. Frankly, if I saw the place my assumption would be that the owner made meth. But the old man who opens the door is just an old guy in a baseball cap. Probably living on social security.

"I'm Nick," he says. He's wearing a long-sleeved plaid shirt despite the heat. He's deeply tanned and has a turkey wattle neck.

I introduce myself. Point to the car and say, "That's Abby, the smart one that stays home."

The trailer is dark and smells of old man inside. The couch cushions are covered in cheap throws, one of them decorated with a blue and white Christmas snowman. Outside, the scrub shimmers, flattened in the heat. Hudson is laying in front of the sink and scrabbles up when he sees us.

"He was just ambling up the road," Nick says. "He saw me and came right up."

"I live over by the river, off 109, between Belen and Jarales," I say. "Someone broke into my place and left the doors open and he wandered off."

"You're lucky they didn't kill the dogs," Nick says.

I fumble with my purse. "There's a reward," I say.

He waves that away. "No, don't you go starting that." He says he didn't do anything but read the tag and give him a drink. "I had dogs all my life," he says. "I'd want someone to call me."

I tell him it would mean a lot to me and press the money on him. Hudson leans against my legs to be petted, tongue lolling. He looks fine. No worse for wear.

"Sit a minute. You came all the way out here. Pardon the mess. My sister's grandson and his friends have been coming out here and they leave stuff like that," he says, waving at the junk and the bottles.

"I can't leave the other dog in the heat," I say, wanting to leave.

"Bring her inside."

I don't want to stay, but I'm grateful, so I bring Abby in out of the heat and he thumps her and tells me about how he's lived here since he was in his twenties. He's a Libertarian and he doesn't trust government and he really doesn't trust the New Mexico state government which is, in his estimation, a banana republic lacking only the fancy uniforms that third-world dictators seem to love. Then he tells me about how lucky it was that Hudson didn't get picked up to be a bait dog for the people who raise dogs for dog fights. Then he tells me about how the American economy was destroyed by operatives from Russia as revenge for the fall of the Soviet Union.

Half of what he says is bullshit and the other half is wrong, but he's just a lonely guy in the middle of the desert and he brought me back my dog. The least I can do is listen.

I hear a spitting little engine off in the distance. Then a couple of them. It's the little motorbikes the kids ride. Nick's eyes narrow as he looks out.

"It's my sister's grandson," he says. "Goddamn."

He gets up and Abby whines. He stands, looking out the slatted blinds.

"Goddamn. He's got a couple of friends," Nick says. "Look you just get your dogs and don't say nothing to them, okay? You just go on."

"Hudson," I say and clip a lead on him.

Outside, four boys pull into the yard, kicking up dust. They have seen my car and are obviously curious. They wear jumpsuits like prison jumpsuits, only with the sleeves ripped off and the legs cut off just above the knees. Khaki and orange and olive green. One of them has tattoos swirling up his arms.

"Hey Nick," the tattooed one says, "new girlfriend?"

"None of your business, Ethan."

The boy is dark but his eyes are light blue. Like a Siberian Husky. "You a social worker?" the boy says.

"I told you it was none of your business," Nick says. "The lady is just going."

"If you're a social worker, you should know that old Nick is crazy and you can't believe nothing he says."

One of the other boys says, "She isn't a social worker. Social workers don't have dogs."

I step down the steps and walk to my car. The boys sit on their bikes and I have to walk around them to get to the Impreza. Hudson wants to see them, pulling against his leash, but I hold him in tight.

"You look nervous, lady," the tattooed boy says.

"Leave her alone, Ethan," Nick says.

"You shut up, Uncle Nick, or I'll kick your ass," the boy says absently, never taking his eyes off me.

Nick says nothing.

I say nothing. I just get my dogs in my car and drive away.

Our life settles into a new normal. I get a response from my dildo email. Nick in Montana is willing to let me sell on his sex site on commission. I make a couple of different models, including one that I paint just as realistically as I would one of the reborn dolls. This means a base coat, then I paint the veins in. Then I bake it. Then I paint an almost translucent layer of color and bake it again. Six layers. And then a clear over layer of silicon because I don't think the paint is approved for use this way. I put a pretty hefty price on it and call it a special. At the same time I am making my other special. The doll for the Chicago couple. I send the mold to Tony and have him do a third head from it. It, too, requires layers of paint, and sometimes the parts bake side by side.

Because my business is rather slow, I take more time than usual. I am always careful, especially with specials. I think if someone is going to spend the kind of money one of these costs, the doll should be made to the best of my ability. And maybe it is because I have done this doll before, it comes easily and well. I think of the doll that the man who broke into my house stole. I don't know if he sent it to his wife and daughter in Mexico, or if he even has a wife and daughter in Mexico. I rather suspect he sold it on eBay or some equivalent—although I have watched doll sales and never seen it come up.

This doll is my orphan doll. She is full of sadness. She is inhabited by the loss of so much. I remember my fear when Hudson was wandering the roads of the desert. I imagine Rachel Mazar, so haunted by the loss of her own child. The curves of the doll's tiny fists are porcelain pale. The blue veins at her temples are traceries of the palest of bruises.

When I am finished with her, I package her as carefully as I have ever packaged a doll and send her off.

My dildos go up on the website.

The realistic dildo sits in my workshop, upright, tumescent, a beautiful rosy plum color. It sits on a shelf like a prize, glistening in its topcoat as if it were wet. It was surprisingly fun to make, after years and years of doll parts. It sits there both as an object to admire and as an affront. But to be frank, I don't think it is any more immoral than the dolls. There is something straightforward about a dildo. Something much more clear than a doll made to look like a dead child. Something significantly less entangled.

There are no orders for dildos. I lie awake at night thinking about real estate taxes. My father is dead. My mother lives in subsidized housing for the elderly in Columbus. I haven't been to see her in years and years, not with the cost of a trip like that. My car wouldn't make it, and nobody I know can afford to fly anymore. I certainly couldn't live with her. She would lose her housing if I moved in.

If I lose my house to unpaid taxes, do I live in my car? It seems like the beginning of the long slide. Maybe Sherie and Ed would take the dogs.

I do get a reprieve when the money comes in for the special. Thank God for the Mazars in Chicago. However crazy their motives, they pay promptly and by internet, which allows me to put money against the equity line for the new tools.

I still can't sleep at night and instead of putting all of the money against my debt, I put the minimum and I buy a 9 millimeter handgun. Actually, Ed buys it for me. I don't even know where to get a gun.

Sherie picks me up in the truck and brings me over to the goat farm. Ed has several guns. He has an old gun safe that belonged to his father. When we get to their place, he is in back, putting creosote on new fence posts, but he is happy to come up to the house.

"So you've given in," he says, grinning. "You've joined the dark side."

"I have," I agree.

"Well, this is a decent defensive weapon," Ed says. Ed does not fit my pre-conceived notions of a gun owner. Ed fits my pre-conceived notions of the guy who sells you a cell phone at the local strip mall. His hair is short and graying. He doesn't look at all like the kind of guy who would either marry Sherie or raise goats. He told me one time that his degree is in anthropology. Which, he said, was a difficult field to get a job in.

"Offer her a cold drink!" Sherie yells from the bathroom. In her pregnant state, Sherie can't ride twenty minutes in the sprung-shocked truck without having to pee.

He offers me iced tea and then gets the gun, checks to see that it isn't loaded, and hands it to me. He explains to me that the first thing I should do is check to see if the gun is loaded.

"You just did," I say.

"Yeah," he says, "but I might be an idiot. It's a good thing to do."

He shows me how to check the gun.

It is not nearly so heavy in my hand as I thought it would be. But, truthfully, I have found that the thing you thought would be life changing so rarely is.

Later he takes me around to the side yard and shows me how to load and shoot it. I am not even remotely surprised that it is kind of fun. That is exactly what I expected.

Out of the blue, an email from Rachel Mazar of Chicago.

I am writing you to ask you if you have had any personal or business dealings with my husband, Ellam Mazar. If I do not get a response from you, your next correspondence will be from my attorney.

I don't quite know what to do. I dither. I make vegetarian chili. Oddly enough, I check my gun which I keep in the bedside drawer. I am not sure what I am going to do about the gun when Sherie has her baby. I have offered to baby-sit, and I'll have to lock it up, I think. But that seems to defeat the purpose of having it.

While I am dithering, my cell rings. It is, of course, Rachel Mazar.

"I need you to explain your relationship with my husband, Ellam Mazar," she says. She sounds educated, with that eradication of regional accent that signifies a decent college.

"My relationship?" I say.

"Your email was on his phone," she says, frostily.

I wonder if he is dead. The way she says it sounds so final. "I didn't know your husband," I say. "He just bought the dolls."

"Bought what?" she says.

"The dolls," I say.

"Dolls?" she says.

"Yes," I say.

"Like…sex dolls?"

"No," I say. "Dolls. Reborns. Handmade dolls."

She obviously has no idea what I am talking about, which opens a world of strange possibilities in my mind. The dolls don't have orifices. Fetish objects? I tell her my website and she looks it up.

"He ordered specials," I say.

"But these cost a couple of thousand dollars," she says.

A week's salary for someone like Ellam Mazar, I suspect. I envision him as a professional, although, frankly, for all I know he works in a dry cleaning shop or something.

"I thought they were for you," I say. "I assumed you had lost a child. Sometimes people who have lost a child order one."

"We don't have children," she says. "We never wanted them." I can hear how stunned she is in the silence. Then she says, "Oh my God."

Satanic rituals? Some weird abuse thing?

"That woman said he told her he had lost a child," she says.

I don't know what to say so I just wait.

"My husband…my soon to be ex-husband," she says. "He has apparently been having affairs. One of the women contacted me. She told me that he told her we had a child that died and that now we were married in name only."

I hesitate. I don't know legally if I am allowed to tell her about transactions I had with her husband. On the other hand, the emails came with both their names on them. "He has bought three," I say.

"Three?"

"Not all at once. About once a year. But people who want a special send me a picture. He always sends the same picture."

"Oh," she says. "That's Ellam. He's orderly. He's used the same shampoo for fifteen years."

"I thought it was strange," I say. I can't bear not to ask. "What do you think he did with them?"

"I think the twisted bastard used them to make women feel sorry for him," she says through gritted teeth. "I think he got all sentimental about them. He probably has himself half-convinced that he really did have a daughter. Or that it's my fault that we didn't have children. He never wanted children. Never."

"I think a lot of my customers like the *idea* of having a child better than having one," I say.

"I'm sure," she says. "Thank you for your time and I'm sorry to have bothered you."

So banal. So strange and yet so banal. I try to imagine him giving the doll to a woman, telling her that it was the image of his dead child. How did that work?

Orders for dildos begin to trickle in. I get a couple of doll orders and make a payment on the credit line and put away some towards real estate taxes. I may not have to live in my car.

One evening, I am working in the garden when Abby and Hudson start barking at the back gate.

I get off my knees, aching, but lurch into the house and into the bedroom where I grab the 9 mm out of the bedside table. It isn't loaded, which now seems stupid. I try to think if I should stop and load it. My hands are shaking. It is undoubtedly just someone looking for a meal and a place to recharge. I decide I can't trust myself to load and, besides, the dogs are out there. I go to the back door, gun held stiffly at my side, pointed to the ground.

There are in fact two of them, alike as brothers, indian looking with a fringe of black hair cut in a straight line above their eyebrows.

"Lady," one says, "we can work for food?" First one, then the other sees the gun at my side and their faces go empty.

The dogs cavort.

"I will give you something to eat, and then you go," I say.

"We go," the one who spoke says.

"Someone robbed me," I say.

"We no rob you," he says. His eyes are on the gun. His companion takes a step back, glancing at the gate and then at me as if to gauge if I will shoot him if he bolts.

"I know," I say. "But someone came here, I gave him food, and he robbed me. You tell people not to come here, okay?"

"Okay," he says. "We go."

"Tell people not to come here," I say. I would give them something to eat, something to take with them. I hate this. They are two young men in a foreign country, hungry, looking for work. I could easily be sleeping in my car. I could be homeless. I could be wishing for someone to be nice to me.

But I am not. I'm just afraid.

"Hudson! Abby!" I yell, harsh, and the two men flinch. "Get in the house."

The dogs slink in behind me, not sure what they've done wrong.

"If you want some food, I will give you something," I say. "Tell people not to come here."

I don't think they understand me. Instead they back slowly away a handful of steps and then turn and walk quickly out the gate, closing it behind them.

I sit down where I am standing, knees shaking.

The moon is up in the blue early evening sky. Over my fence I can see scrub and desert, a fierce land where mountains breach like the petrified spines of apocalyptic animals. The kind of landscape that seems right for crazed gangs of mutants charging around in cobbled-together vehicles. Tribal remnants of America, their faces painted, their hair braided, wearing jewelry made from shiny CDs and cigarette lighters scrounged from the ruins of civilization. The desert is Byronic in its extremes.

I don't see the two men. There's no one out there in furs, their faces painted blue, driving a dune buggy built out of motorcycle parts and hung with the skulls of their enemies. There's just a couple of guys from Nicaragua or Guatemala, wearing t-shirts and jeans.

And me, sitting, watching the desert go dark, the moon rising, an empty handgun in my hand.

THE CORAL HEART

JEFFREY FORD

His sword's grip was polished blood coral, its branches perfect doubles for the aorta. They fed into a guard that was a thin silver crown, beyond which lay the blade (the heart); slightly curved with the inscription of a spell in a language no one could read. He was a devotee of the art of the cut, and when he wielded this weapon, the blade exactly parallel to the direction of motion, the blood groove caught the breeze and whistled like a bird of night. He'd learned his art from a hermit in the mountains where he'd practiced on human cadavers.

That sword had a history before it fell to Ismet Toler. How it came to him, he swore he would never tell. Legend had it that the blade belonged first to the ancient hero who'd beheaded the Gorgon: a creature whose gaze turned men to smooth marble. After he'd slain her, he punctured her eyeballs with the tip of his blade and then bathed the cutting edge in their ichor. The character of the weapon seized the magic of the Gorgon's stare and, ever after, if a victim's flesh was sliced or punctured to any extent where blood was drawn, that unlucky soul would be turned instantly to coral.

The statuary of Toler's skill could be found throughout the realm. Three hardened headless bodies lay atop the Lowbry Hill, and on the slopes three hardened heads. A woman crouching at the entrance to the Funeral Gardens. A score of soldiers at the center of the market at Camiar. A child missing an arm, twisting away with fear forever, resting perfectly on one heel, in the southeastern corner of the Summer Square. All deepest red and gleaming with reflection. There were those who believed that only insanity could account for the vast battlefields of coral warriors frozen in the kill, but none was brave enough to speak it.

The Valator of Camiar once said of The Coral Heart, "He serves the good because it is a minority, leaving the majority to slay in the name of Truth." The Valator is now, himself, red coral, his head cleaved like a roasted sausage. Ismet dispatched evil with dedication and stunning haste. It was said that the fate of the sword was tied to that of the world. When enough of its victims had been turned to coral, their accumulated weight would affect the spin of the planet and it would fly out of orbit into darkness.

There are countless stories about The Coral Heart, and nearly all of them are the same story. Tales about a man who shares a name and a spirit with his weapon. They're always filled with fallen ranks of coral men. Some he kicks and shatters in the mêlée. There is always betrayal and treachery. A few of these stories involve the hermit master with whom he'd studied. Most all of them mention his servant, Garone, a tulpa or thought-form creation physically coalesced from his focused imagination. The descriptions of killing in these classical tales are painstaking and brutal, encrusted with predictable glory.

There are a handful of stories about The Coral Heart, though, that do not end on a battlefield. You don't hear them often. Most find the exploits of the weapon more enchanting than those of the man. Your average citizen enjoys a tale of slaughter. You, though, if I'm not mistaken, understand as well the deadly nature of the human heart and would rather decipher the swordsman's dreams than the magic spell engraved upon his blade.

And so… in the last days of summer, in The Year of the Thistle, after transforming the army of the Igridots, upon the dunes of Weilawan, into a petrified forest, Ismet Toler wandered north in search of nothing more than a cold day. He rode upon Nod, his red steed of a rare archaic stock—toes instead of hooves and short, spiral horns, jutting out from either side of its forelock. Walking beside Toler, appearing and disappearing like the moon behind wind-driven clouds, was Garone, his tulpa. The servant, when visible, drifted along, hands clasped at his waist, slightly hunched, the hood of his brown robe always obscuring any definitive view of his face. You might catch a glimpse of one of his yellow eyes, but never both at once.

As they followed a trail that wound beneath giant trees, leaves falling everywhere, Toler pulled the reins on Nod and was still. "Was that a breeze, Garone?"

The tulpa disappeared but was as quickly back. "I believe so," he said in a whisper only his master could hear.

Another, more perceptible gust came down the trail and washed over them. Toler sighed as it passed. "I'm weary of turning men to coral," he said.

"I hadn't noticed," said Garone.

The Coral Heart smiled and nodded slightly.

"Up ahead in these yellow woods, we will find a palace and you will fall in love," said the servant.

"There are times I wish you wouldn't tell me what you know."

"There are times I wish I didn't know it. If you command me to reveal my face to you, I will disappear forever."

"No," said Toler, "not yet. That day will come, though. I promise you."

"Perhaps sooner rather than later, master."

"Perhaps not," said Toler and nudged his mount in the ribs. Again moving along the trail, the swordsman recalled the frozen expressions of his victims at Weilawan, each countenance set with the same look of terrible surprise.

In late afternoon, the travelers came to a fork in the trail, and Garone said, "We must take the right-hand path to reach that palace."

"What lies to the left?" asked Toler.

"Tribulation and certain death," said the servant.

"To the right," said the swordsman. "You may rest now, Garone."

Garone became a rippling flame, clear as water, and then disappeared.

As twilight set in, Toler caught sight of two towers silhouetted against the orange sky. He coaxed Nod into a gallop, hoping to arrive at the palace gates before nightfall. As he flew from the forest and across barren fields, the cool of the coming night refreshing him, he thought, "I have never been in love." Every time he tried to picture the face of one of his amorous conquests, what came before him instead were the faces of his victims.

He arrived just as the palace guards were about to lift the moat bridge. The four men saw him approaching and drew their weapons.

"An appeal for lodging for the night," called Toler from a safe distance.

"Who are you?" one of the men shouted.

"A traveler," said the swordsman.

"Your name, fool," said the same man.

"Ismet Toler."

There was a moment of silence, and then a different one of the guards said, in a far less demanding tone, "The Coral Heart?"

"Yes."

The guard who had spoken harshly fell to his knees and begged forgiveness. Two others sheathed their swords and came forward to help the gentleman from his horse. The fourth ran ahead into the palace, announcing to all he passed that The Coral Heart was at the gate.

Toler dismounted and one of the men took Nod's reigns. The swordsman approached the guard who knelt on the ground, and said, "I'll not be killing anyone tonight. I'm too weary. We'll see what tomorrow brings." The man rose up, and then the three guards, with Toler's help, turned the huge wooden wheel that lifted the moat bridge.

Inside, the guards dispersed and left Toler standing at the head of a hall with vaulted ceiling, all fashioned from blue limestone. People came and went quietly, keeping their distance but stealing glances. Eventually, he was approached by a very old man, diminutive of stature, with the snout and mottled skin of a toad. When the little fellow spoke, he croaked, "A pleasure, sir," and offered his wet hand as a sign of welcome.

Toler took it with a shiver. "And you are?" he asked.

"Councilor Greppen. Follow me." The stranger led on down the vast hall, padding along at a weary pace on bare, flat feet. The slap of his soles echoed into the distance.

"May I ask what manner of creature you are?" said Toler.

"A man, of course," said the Councilor. "And you?"

"A man."

"No, no, from what I hear you are Death's own Angel and will one day turn the world to coral."

"What kind of Councilor can you be if you believe everything you hear?" said Toler.

Greppen puffed out his cheeks and laughed; a shrewd, wet sound. He shuffled toward the left and turned at another long hall, a line of magnificent fountains running down its center. "The Hall of Tears," he croaked and they passed through glistening mist.

As Toler followed from hall to hall, he gradually adopted the old man's pace. The journey was long, but Time suddenly had no bearing. The swordsman studied the people who passed, noticed the placement of the guard, marveled at the colors of the fish in the fountains, the birds that flew overhead, the distant glass ceiling through which the full moon stared in. As if suddenly awakened, he came to at the touch of the Councilor's damp hand on his arm.

"We have arrived," said Greppen.

Toler looked around. He was on a balcony that jutted off the side of the palace. The stars were bright and there was a cold breeze, just the kind he'd wished for when heading north from Weilawan. He took a seat on a simple divan near the edge of the balcony, and listened as Greppen's footfalls grew faint. He closed his eyes and wondered if this was his lodging for the night. The seat was wonderfully comfortable and he leaned back into it.

A moment passed, perhaps an hour, he wasn't sure, before he opened his eyes. When he did, he was surprised to see something floating toward the balcony. It was no bird. He blinked and it became clear in the resplendent starlight. It was a woman, dressed in fine golden robes, seated in a wooden chair, like a throne, floating toward him out of the night. When she reached the balcony and hovered above him, he stood to greet her.

"The Coral Heart," she said as her chair settled down across from the divan.

"You may be seated."

Toler bowed slightly before sitting.

"I am Lady Maltomass," she said.

The swordsman was intoxicated by the sudden scent of lemon blossoms, and then by the Lady's eyes—large and luminous. No matter how he scrutinized her gaze, he could not discern their color. At the corners of her lips there was the very slightest smile. Her light brown hair was braided and strung with beads of jade. There was a thin jade collar around her neck, and from there it was a quick descent to the path between her breasts and the intricately brocaded golden gown.

"Ismet Toler," he finally said.

"I grant you permission to stay this night in the palace," she said.

"Thank you," he said. There was an awkward pause and then he asked, "Who makes your furniture?"

She laughed. "The chair, yes. My father was a great scholar. By way of his research, he discovered it beneath the ruins of an Abbey at Cardeira-davu."

"I didn't think the religious dabbled in magic," said Toler.

"Who's to say it's not the work of God?"

The swordsman nodded. "And your Councilor, Greppen? Another miracle?"

"Noble Greppen," said the Lady.

"Pardon my saying, Lady Maltomass, but he appears green about the gills."

"There's no magic in it," she said. "His is a race of people who grew out of the swamp. They have a different history than we do, but the same humanity."

"And what is your story?" said Toler. " Are you magic or miracle?"

She smiled and looked away from him. "I'll ask the questions," she said. "Is that The Coral Heart at your side?"

"Yes," he said, and moved to draw the sword from its sheath.

"That won't be necessary," she said. "I see the coral from here."

"Most people prefer not to see the blade," he said.

"And pardon my asking, Ismet Toler, but how many have you slain with it?"

"Enough," he said.

"Is that a declaration of remorse?"

"Remorse was something I felt for the first thousand."

"You're a droll swordsman."

"Is that a compliment?" he asked.

"No," said Lady Maltomass. "I hear you have a tulpa."

"Yes, my man Garone."

To Toler's left, there was a disturbance in the air, which became a pillar of smoke that swirled and coalesced into the hooded servant.

"Garone, I present to you the Lady Maltomass," said Toler, and swept his arm in her direction. The tulpa bowed and then disappeared.

"Very interesting," she said.

"Not a flying chair, but I try," he said.

"Well, I also have a tulpa," said the Lady.

"No," said Toler.

"Mamresh," she said, and in an instant, there appeared, just to the right of the flying chair the presence of a woman. She was naked and power-fully built. A warrior, thought the swordsman. His only other impression, before she disappeared—the deep red color of her voluminous hair.

"You surprise me," he said to the Lady.

"If you'll stay tomorrow," she said, "I'll show you something I think you'll be interested in. Meet me among the willows in the garden after noon."

"I'm already there," he said.

She smiled as the chair rose slowly above the balcony. It turned in midair and then floated out past the railing. "Good night, Ismet Toler," she called over her shoulder.

As the chair disappeared into the dark, Greppen approached. He led the swordsman to a spacious room near the balcony. The Councilor said nothing but lit a number of candles and then called goodnight as he pushed the door closed behind him.

Toler undressed, weary from travel and the aftereffects of the drug that was Lady Maltomass. He lay down with a sigh, and then summoned his servant. The tulpa appeared at the foot of the bed.

"Garone, while the palace is sleeping I want you to search around and see what you can discover about the Lady. A mysterious woman. I want to know everything about her. Take caution, though, she also has a tulpa." Then he wrapped his right hand around the sheath of The Coral Heart, clasped the grip with his left and fell asleep to a dream of kissing Lady Maltomass beneath the willows.

Toler arrived early to the gardens the following day. The entrance led through a long grape arbor thick with vine and dangling fruit. This opened into an enormous area sectioned into symmetrical plots of ground, and, in each, stretching off into the distance, beds of colorful flowers and pungent herbs. Their aromas mixed in the atmosphere and the scent confused him for a brief time. Everywhere around him were bees and butterflies and members of Greppen's strange race, weeding, watering, fertilizing. The swordsman asked one where the willows were, and the toad man pointed down a narrow path into the far distance.

It was past noon when he arrived amid the stand of willows next to a pond with a fountain at its center. He discovered an ancient stone bench, partially green with mold, and sat upon it, peering through the mesh of whiplike branches at sunlight glistening on the water. There was a cool breeze and orange birds darted about, quietly chirping.

"Garone," said Toler, and his servant appeared before him. "What have you to report about the Lady?"

"I paced through every inch of the palace, down all its ostentatious halls, and found not a scrap of a secret about her. In the middle of the night I found her personal chambers, but could not enter. I couldn't pass through the walls nor even get close to them."

"Is there a spell around her?" asked the swordsman.

"Not a spell; it's her tulpa, Mamresh. She's too powerful for me. She's blocking me with her will from approaching the Lady's rooms. I summoned all my strength and exerted myself and she merely laughed at me."

Toler was about to speak, but just then heard his name being called from deeper in amidst the willows. Garone disappeared and the swordsman rose and set off in the direction of the voice. Brushing the tentacles of the trees aside, he pushed his way forward until coming upon a small clearing. At its center sat Lady Maltomass in her flying chair. Facing her was another of the ancient stone benches.

"I heard someone speaking off in the distance, and knew it must be you," she said. He walked over and sat down across from her.

"I hope you slept well," said the Lady.

"Indeed," said Toler. "I dreamt of you."

"In your dream, did I tell you I don't like foolishness?"

"Perhaps," he said, "but the only part of it I witnessed was when we kissed."

She shook her head. "Here's what I wanted to show you," she said, lifting a small book that appeared to be covered with a square of Greppen's flesh.

"Is the cover made of toad?" he asked, leaning forward to get a better look at it.

"Not precisely," she said, "but it's not the cover I wanted to show you. She opened the book to a page inside, and then turned the volume around and handed it to him. "What do you see there?" She pointed at the left-hand page.

There was a design that was immediately familiar to him. He sat back away from her and drew his sword. Bringing the blade level with his eyes, he studied the design of the inscribed spell. He then looked back to the book. Three times he went from blade to book and back before she finally said, "I'll wager they are identical."

"How did you come upon this?" asked Toler, returning his sword to its sheath. "The blade has never left my side since it came to me."

"No, but the weapon is old, and it has passed through many men's hands. In fact, there was a people who had possession of it, two centuries past, who deemed it too dangerous to be at large in the world. They didn't destroy it but studied it. One of the things they were interested in was the spell. For all of their effort, though, they were only able to decipher two words of it. There might be as many as ten words in that madly looping script. My father, digging in the peat bogs north of the Gentious quarry, hauled two clay tablets out of a quivering hole in the ground. Those heavy ancient pages contained reference to the sword, to its legend, and the design of the blade's script. Also included was the translation of the two words."

"What were they?" he asked, wrapping his fingers again around the grip of the weapon.

"My father worked with what was given on the tablet and deciphered three more of the spell's words."

"What were they?"

"The words he was certain of were—Thanry, Meltmoss, Stilthery, Quasum, and Pik."

"All common herbs," said Toler.

She nodded. "He believed that all the words constituted a kind of medicine, that if prepared and inserted into one of your victim's coral mouths, it would reverse the sword's power and return them to flesh. The blade's damage could, of course, have been a death blow, in which case there would be no chance of returning them to life, but those who succumbed to only a nick, a scratch, a cut would again be flesh and bone and draw breath."

"I've often wondered about the inscription," he said. "Your father was a wise man."

"I'm giving you the book," she said. "When I heard you'd turned up at the gate, I remembered my father telling me about his discoveries. The book should belong to the man who carries the weapon. I have no use for it."

"Why would the blade hold an antidote to the sword's effects, and yet be written in a language no one can understand?" asked Toler.

"That fact suggests a dozen possible motives, but I suppose the real one will remain a mystery." She held the book out toward him. As he leaned forward to take it from her, she also leaned forward, and as his fingers closed on the book, her lips met his. She kissed him eagerly, her mouth open. They parted and he moved closer to the edge of the stone bench. He put his hands on her shoulders and gently drew her toward him.

"Wait, is that Greppen, spying?" she said, bringing her arms up between them. Toler drew his sword as he stood and spun around, brandishing it in a defensive maneuver. He saw no sign of Greppen, heard no movement among the willow branches. What he heard instead was the laughter of Lady Maltomass. When he turned back to her, she was gone. He looked up to see the chair rising into the blue sky. As she floated away toward the tree line, he yelled, "When will I see you next?"

"Soon," she called back.

Two days passed without word from her, and in that time, all Toler could think of was their last meeting. He tried to stay busy within the walls of the palace, and the beauty of the place kept his attention for half a day, but, ultimately, in its ease and refinement, palace life seemed hollow to one who'd spent most of his life in combat.

On the evening of the second day, after dinner, he summoned Councilor Greppen, who was to see to his every need. They met in Toler's room, and the toad man had brought a bottle of brandy and two glasses. As he poured for himself and The Coral Heart, he said, "I can smell your frustration, Ismet Toler."

"You can, can you, Prince of Toads? Tell her I want to see her."

"She'll summon you when she's ready."

"She is in every way a perfect woman," said Toler, sipping his brandy.

"Perfection is in the eye of the beholder," said Greppen. "If you were to see my wife, considered quite a beauty among our people, you might not agree."

"I'm sure she's lovely," said the swordsman, "but I feel if I don't soon have a tryst with Lady Maltomass, I'm going to go mad and turn the world to coral."

Greppen laughed. "The beast with two backs? Your people are comical in their lust."

"I suppose," said Toler. "How do you do it? With a thought?" He sipped at the brandy.

"Very nearly," said Greppen, lifting the bottle to refill his companion's glass.

"Here's a question for you, Councilor," said Toler. "Does she ever leave the chair?"

"Only to go to bed," he said. "I would think of all people, you might understand best. She shares her spirit with it as you do The Coral Heart. She knows what the world looks like from above the clouds. She can fly."

Toler finished his second drink, and told Greppen he was turning in. On the way out the door the Councilor called back, "Patience." Once in bed, again he summoned Garone and sent him forth to discover any secrets he might. The swordsman then grasped the sheath and the grip and fell into a troubled sleep.

He tossed and turned, his desire for the Lady working its way into his dreams. Deep in the night, her face rose above the horizon bigger than the moon. He looked into her eyes to see if he could tell their color, but in them he saw instead the figures of Garone and Mamresh on the stone bench, beneath the willows, in the moonlight. His tulpa's robe was pulled up to his waist, and Mamresh sat upon his lap, facing away, her legs on either side of his. She was panting and moving quickly to and fro, and he was grunting. Then Garone tilted his head back and the hood began to slip off.

Toler woke suddenly to avoid seeing his servant's face. He was drenched in sweat and breathing heavily. I've got to get away from here," he said. Still, he stayed three more days. On the evening of the third day, he gave orders for the grooms to ready Nod for travel early in the morning. Before turning in, he went to the balcony and sat, staring out at the stars. "Garone, you were right," he said aloud. "I've fallen in love, but tribulation and certain death might have been preferable." He dozed off.

A few minutes later, he awoke to the sound of Greppen's footfalls receding into the distance. He sat up, and as he did he discovered a pale yellow envelope in his lap. *For The Coral Heart* was inscribed across the front. The back was affixed with wax, bearing, what he assumed, was the official seal of the House of Maltomass, ornate lettering surrounding the image of an owl with a snake writhing in its beak. He tore it open and read, "*Come now to my chambers. Your Lady.*"

He sprang off the divan and summoned Garone to lead him. They moved quickly through the halls, the tulpa skimming along above the blue limestone floors like a ghost. In the Hall of Tears, they came upon a staircase and climbed up four flights. At the top of those steps was a sitting room, at the back of which was a large wooden door, opened only a sliver. Toler instructed Garone to stand guard and to alert him if anyone approached. He carefully opened the door and entered into a dark room that led into a hall at the end of which he saw a light. He put his left hand around the grip of the sword and proceeded.

Before reaching the lighted chamber he smelled the vague scent of orange oil and cinnamon. As he stepped out of the darkness of the hall, the first thing that caught his attention was Lady Maltomass, sitting up, supported by large silk pillows, in her canopied bed. The coverlet was drawn up to her stomach and she was naked. The sight of her breasts halted his advance.

"Come to practice your swordsmanship?" she said.

He swallowed hard and tried to say, "At your service."

She laughed at his consternation. "Come closer," she said, her voice softer now, "and dispense with those clothes."

He undressed before her, quickly removing every article of clothing. When he stood naked before her, though, he still had on his belt and the sheathed sword.

"One sword is useful here, the other not," she said.

"I never take it off," he said.

"Hurry now. Put it right here on my night table."

He reluctantly removed the sword. Then he sat on the edge of the bed and put his arms around her. They kissed more passionately than they had in the clearing. He ran his fingers through her hair as she clasped her hands behind his back and kissed his chest. He moved his hands down to her breasts and she reached for his prick. When their ardor was well inflamed, she pulled away from him, and then slowly leaning forward, whispered in his ear, "Do you want me?"

"Yes," he said.

"Then, come in," she said and, grabbing the corner of the blanket, threw it back for him.

For a moment, Ismet Toler wore the same look of terrible surprise fixed forever on the faces of his victims, for Lady Maltomass, was, from the waist down, blood coral. He glimpsed the frozen crease between her legs and cried out.

Garone appeared suddenly at his side, shouting, "Treachery." Toler turned toward his servant just as Mamresh, bearing a smile, appeared and pulled back the hood of his tulpa's robe. The swordsman glimpsed his own face with yellow eyes in the instant before the thought form went out like a candle. He buckled inside from the sudden loss of Garone. Then, from out of the dark, he was punched in the face.

Toler came to on the floor, gasping as if he'd been under water. Greppen was there, helping him off the floor. Once Toler had regained his footing and clarity, he turned back to the bed.

"Imagine," said Lady Maltomass, "your organ of desire transformed into a fossil."

Toler was speechless.

"Some years ago, my father took me to the market at Camiar. He'd been working on the translation of the spell upon your sword, and he'd heard that you frequented a seller there who dispensed drams of liquor. He wanted to present you with what he'd discovered from the ancients about the sword's script. Just as we arrived at the market, a fight broke out between five swordsmen and yourself. You defeated them, but in the melee you struck a young woman with an errant thrust and she was turned to coral."

"Impossible!" he shouted.

"You're an arrogant fool, Ismet Toler. The young woman was me. My father brought me back here a statue, and prepared the five herbs from his research into an elixir. He poured it down my hard throat, and because it was made of only half the ingredients of the cure, only half of me returned."

Greppen tapped Toler upon the hip and, when the swordsman looked down, handed him The Coral Heart.

"Now you face my tulpa," said the Lady.

Toler heard Mamresh approaching and drew the sword, dropping the sheath upon the bed. He ducked and sidled across the floor, the weapon constantly moving. He turned suddenly and was struck twice in the face and once in the chest. He stumbled, but didn't go down. She moved on him again, but this time he saw her vague outline and sliced at her torso. The blade passed right through her and she kicked him in the balls. He doubled over and went down again.

"Get up, snake," called Lady Maltomass from the bed.

"Please, rise, Ismet Toler," said Greppen, now standing before him.

He lifted himself off the floor and resumed a defensive crouch. He kept the blade in motion, but his hands were shaking. Mamresh attacked. Her hard knuckles seemed to be everywhere at once. No matter how many times Toler swung The Coral Heart, it made no difference.

After another pass, Mamresh had him staggered and reeling from side to side. Blood was running from his nose and mouth.

"I've just given her leave to beat you to death," said Lady Maltomass.

The vague outline of a muscled arm swept out of the air, and Toler slid beneath it, turned and made the most exquisite cut to the ghostly figure's spine. The blade didn't even slow in its arc.

She closed his left eye and splintered his shin with a kick. Toler was on the verge of panic when he saw Greppen standing in the corner, tiny fists raised in the air, urging Mamresh to the kill. The tulpa came from the left this time. The swordsman had learned the sound of her breathing. Before she could strike, he tucked his head in and rolled into the corner where Greppen stood. He could hear her right behind him.

He reached out with his free hand and grabbed the toad man by the ankle. Then, as Toler rose, he lifted the blade, and with unerring precision, gave a deft slice to the Councilor's neck. He turned quickly, and Greppen's blood sprayed forth in a great geyser. It washed over Mamresh, and she became visible to him as she threw a punch at his left eye. He moved gracefully to the side, tossing Greppen's now coral body at her. It passed through her face, briefly blocking her view of him. Toler calmly sought a spot where the blood revealed his assassin and then lunged, sending the blade there.

Mamresh gasped, and her visible face contorted in terror as she crackled into blood coral. He turned back to the bed, and the Lady was still. He now could ascertain the color of her eyes and they were a deep red. He'd made her mind coral in the act of defeating her tulpa. He dropped the sword and lay down beside her. Pulling her to him, he tried to kiss her, but her teeth were shut and a slow stream of drool issued from the corner of her mouth.

Toler discovered Nod gutted and decapitated in a heap upon the stable floor. After that, he spared no one, but worked his way down every hall and through the gardens, killing everything that moved. It was after midnight when he left the palace in the flying chair and disappeared into the western mountains.

People wondered what had happened to The Coral Heart. Some said he'd died of frostbite, some, of fever. Others believed he'd finally been careless and turned himself into a statue. Seven long years passed and the violence of the world had been diminished by half. Then, in the winter of The Year of Ice, a post rider galloped into Camiar and told the people that he'd seen a half-dozen bandits turned to coral on the road from Totenhas.

IT TAKES TWO

NICOLA GRIFFITH

It began, as these things often do, at a bar—a long dark piece of mahogany along one wall of Seattle's Queen City Grill polished by age and more than a few chins. The music was winding down. Richard and Cody (whose real name was Candice, though no one she had met since high school knew it) lived on different coasts, but tonight was the third time this year they had been drinking together. Cody was staring at the shadows gathering in the corners of the bar and trying not to think about her impersonal hotel room. She thought instead about the fact that in the last six months she had seen Richard more often than some of her friends in San Francisco, and that she would probably see him yet again in a few weeks when their respective companies bid on the Atlanta contract.

She said, "You ever wonder what it would be like to have, you know, a normal job where you get up on Monday and drive to work, and do the same thing Tuesday and Wednesday and Thursday, every week, except when you take a vacation?"

"You forgot Friday."

"What?" They had started on mojitos, escalated through James Bonds, and were now on a tequila-shooter-with-draft-chaser glide path.

"I said, you forgot Friday. Monday, Tuesday—"

"Right," Cody said. "Right. Too many fucking details. But did you ever wonder? About a normal life?" An actual life, in one city, with actual friends.

Richard was silent long enough for Cody to lever herself around on the bar stool and look at him. He was playing with his empty glass. "I just took a job," he said. "A no-travel job."

"Ah, shit." She remembered how they met, just after the first dotcom crash, at a graduate conference on synergies of bio-mechanics and expert decision-making software architecture or some such crap, which didn't really make sense if you stopped to consider that he started out in cognitive psychology and she in applied mathematics. But computers were the alien glue that made all kinds of odd limbs stick together and work in ways never intended by nature. *Like Frankenstein's monster*, he had said when she mentioned it, and she had bought him a drink, because he got it. They ran into each other at a similar conference two months later, then again at some industry junket not long after they'd both joined social media startups. The pattern repeated itself, until, by the time they were both pitching venture capitalists at trade shows, they managed to get past the required cool, the distancing irony, and began to email each other beforehand to arrange dinners, drinks, tickets to the game. They were young, good-looking, and very, very smart. Even better, they had absolutely no romantic interest in each other.

Now when they met it was while traveling as representatives of their credit-starved companies to make increasingly desperate pitches to industry-leading Goliaths on why they needed the nimble expertise of hungry Davids.

Cody hadn't told Richard that lately her pitches had been more about why the Goliaths might find it cost-effective to absorb the getting-desperate David she worked for, along with all its innovative, motivated, bootstrapping employees whose stock options and 401(k)s were now worthless. But going back to the groves of academe was really admitting failure.

She sighed. "Where?"

"Chapel Hill. And it's not... Well, okay, it is sort of an academic job, but not really."

"Uh huh."

"No, really. It's with a new company, a joint venture between Wishtle. net and the University of North—"

"See."

"Just let me finish." Richard could get very didactic when he'd been drinking. "Think Google Labs, or Xerox PARC, but wackier. Lots of money to play with, lots of smart grad students to do what I tell them, lots of blue sky research, not just irritating Vice Presidents saying I've got six months to get the software on the market even if it is garbage."

"I hear you on that." Except that Vince, Cody's COO, had told her that if she landed the Atlanta contract she would be made a VP herself.

"It's cool stuff, Cody. All those things we've talked about in the last six, seven years? The cognitive patterning and behavior mod, the modulated resonance imaging software, the intuitive learning algorithms—"

"Yeah, yeah."

"—they *want* me to work on that. They want me to define new areas of interest. Very cool stuff."

Cody just shook her head. Cool. Cool didn't remember to feed the fish when you were out of town, again.

"Starts next month," he said.

Cody felt very tired. "You won't be in Atlanta."

"Nope."

"Atlanta in August. On my own. Jesus."

"On your own? Think of all those pretty girls in skimpy summer clothes."

The muscles in Cody's eyebrows felt tight. She rubbed them. "It's Boone I'm not looking forward to. And his sleazy strip club games."

"He's the customer."

"Your sympathy's killing me."

He shrugged. "I thought that lap-dancing hooker thing was your wet dream."

Her head ached. Now he was going to bring up Dallas.

"That's what you told us in—now where the hell was that?"

"Dallas." Might as well get it over with.

"You were really into it. Are you blushing?"

"No." Three years ago she had been twenty-eight with four million dollars in stock options and the belief that coding cowboy colleagues were her friends. Ha. And now probably half the geeks in the South had heard about her most intimate fantasy. Including Boone.

She swallowed the last of her tequila. Oily, ugly stuff once it got tepid. She picked up her jacket.

"I'm out of here. Unless you have any handy hints about landing that contract without playing Boone's slimeball games? Didn't think so." She pushed her shot glass away and stood.

"That Atlanta meeting's when? Eight, nine weeks?"

"About that." She dropped two twenties on the bar.

"I maybe could help."

"With Boone? Right." But Richard's usually cherubic face was quite stern.

He fished his phone from his pocket and put it on the bar. He said, "Just trust me for a minute," and tapped the screen. The memo icon winked red. "Whatever happens, I promise no one will ever hear what goes on this recording except you."

Cody slung on her jacket. "Cue ominous music."

"It's more an, um, an ethics thing."

"Jesus, Richard. You're such a drama queen." But she caught the bartender's eye, pointed to their glasses, and sat.

"I did my Atlanta research too," he said. "Like you, I'm pretty sure what will happen after you've made your presentations to Boone."

"The Golden Key," she said, nodding. Everyone said so. The sun rises, the government taxes, Boone listens to bids and takes everyone to the Golden Key.

"—but what I need to know from you is whether or not, to win this contract, you can authorize out-of-pocket expenses in the high five figures."

She snorted. "Five figures against a possible eight? What do you think?"

He pointed at the phone.

"Fine. Yes. I can approve that kind of expense."

He smiled, a very un-Richard-like sliding of muscle and bone, like a python disarticulating its jaw to swallow a pig. Cody nearly stood up, but the moment passed.

"You'll also have to authorize me to access your medical records," he said.

So here they were in Marietta, home of the kind of Georgians who wouldn't fuck a stranger in the woods only because they didn't know who his people were: seven men and one woman stepping from Boone's white concrete and green glass tower into an August sun hot enough to make the blacktop bubble. Boone's shades flashed as he turned to face the group.

"All work and no play makes Jack a dull boy. And Jill," with a nod at Cody, who nodded back and tried not to squint. Squinting made her look like a moron: not good when all around you were wearing sleek East Coast summer business clothes and gilded with Southern tans. At least the guy from Portland had forgotten his shades too.

They moved in a small herd across the soft, sticky parking lot: the guy from Boston would have to throw away his fawn loafers.

Boone said to the guy from Austin, "Dave, you take these three. I know you know where we're going."

"Sure do," Dave said, and the seven boys shared that we're-all-men-of-the-world-yes-indeedy laugh. Cody missed Richard. And she was still pissed at the way he'd dropped the news on her only last week. Why hadn't he told her earlier about not coming to Atlanta? Why hadn't he told her in Seattle? The whole thing was weird. And a university job: What was up with that? Asshole. But she wished he was here.

Boone's car was a flashy Mercedes hybrid in silver. He opened the passenger door with a Yeah-I-know-men-and-women-are-equal-but-I-was-born-in-the-South-so-what-can-you-do? smile to which Cody responded with a perfect, ironic lift of both eyebrows. Hey, couldn't have managed that in shades. The New York guy and Boston loafers got in the back. The others were climbing into Dave's dark green rental SUV. A full-sized SUV. Very uncool. He'd lose points for that. She jammed her seatbelt home with a satisfying click.

As they drove to the club, she let the two in the back jostle for conversational space with Boone. She stared out of the window. The meeting had gone very well. It was clear that she and Dave and the guy from Denver were the only ones representing companies with the chops for this contract, and she was pretty sure she had the edge over the Denver people when it came to program rollout. Between her and Dave, then. If only they weren't going to the Golden Key. God. The thought of all those men watching her watch those women made her scalp prickle with sweat. In the flow of conditioned air, her face turned cold.

Two days before she left for Atlanta she'd emailed Vince to explain that it wasn't she who would be uncomfortable at the strip club, but the men, and that he should at least consider giving Boone a call and setting her presentation up for either the day before or the day after the others. She'd got a reply half an hour later, short and to the point: *You're going, kid, end of story.* She'd taken a deep breath and walked over to his office.

He was on the phone, pacing up and down, but waved her in before she could knock. He covered the receiver with one hand, "Gotta take this, won't be long," and went back to pacing, shouting, "Damn it, Rick, I want it done. When we had that meeting last week you assured me—Yeah. No problem, you said. No fucking problem. So just do it, just find a way." He slammed the phone down, shook his head, turned his attention to her. "Cody, what can I do for you? If it's about this Atlanta thing I don't want to hear it."

"Vince—"

"Boone's not stupid. He takes people to that titty club because he likes to watch how they behave under pressure. You're the best we've got, you know that. Just be yourself and you won't fuck up. Give him good presentation and don't act like a girl scout when the nipples start to show. Can you handle that?"

"I just resent—"

"Jesus Christ, Cody. It's not like you've never seen bare naked ladies before. You want to be a VP? Tell me now: yes or no."

Cody took a breath. "Yes."

"Glad to hear it. Now get out of here."

The Golden Key was another world: cool, and scented with the fruity overtones of beer; loud, with enough bass to make the walls of her abdomen vibrate; dark at the edges, though lushly lit at the central stage with its three chrome poles and laser strobes. Only one woman was dancing. It was just after six, but the place was already half-full. Somewhere, someone was smoking expensive cigars. Cody wondered who the club paid off to make that possible.

Boone ordered staff to put two tables together right by the stage, near the center pole. The guy from New York sat on Boone's left, Dave on his right. Cody took a place at the end, out of Boone's peripheral vision. She wouldn't say or do anything that wasn't detached and ironic. She would be seamless.

A new dancer: shoulder-length red hair that fell over her face as she writhed around the right-hand pole. She wore a skirt the size of a belt, and six-inch heels of translucent plastic embedded with suggestive pink flowers. Without the pole she probably couldn't even stand. Did interesting things to her butt, though, Cody thought, then patted surreptitiously at her upper lip. Dry, thank god. Score one for air conditioning.

New York poked her arm. He jerked his thumb at Boone, who leaned forward and shouted, "What do you want to drink?"

"Does it matter?"

He grinned. "No grape juice playing at champagne here. Place takes its liquor seriously."

Peachy. "Margarita. With salt." If it was sour enough she wouldn't want to gulp it.

The dancer hung upside down on the pole and undid her bra. Her breasts were a marvel of modern art, almost architectural.

"My God," Cody said, "it's the Hagia Sophia."

"What?" New York shouted. "She's called Sophia?"

"No," Cody shouted back, "her breasts… Never mind."

"Fakes," New York said, nodding.

The drinks came, delivered by a blonde woman wearing nothing but a purple velvet g-string and a smile. She called Boone *Darlin'*—clearly he was a regular—and Cody *Sugar*.

Cody managed to lift her eyes from the weirdness of unpierced nipples long enough to find a dollar bill and drop it on the drinks tray. Two of the guys were threading their tips under the g-string: a five and a ten. The blonde dropped Cody a wink as she walked away. New York caught it and leered. Cody tried her margarita: very sour. She gulped anyway.

The music changed to a throbbing remix of mom music: the Pointer Sisters' "Slowhand." The bass line was insistent, pushing on her belly like a warm hand. She licked her lips and applied herself to her drink. Another dancer with soft black curls took the left-hand pole, and the redhead moved to center stage on her hands and knees in front of their table, rotating her ass in slow motion, looking at them over her shoulder, slitting her eyes at them like a cat. Boone, Dave, all the guys had bills in their hands: "Ooh mama, I've got what you need." The redhead backed towards them in slow motion, arching her spine now in apparent ecstasy—but not so far gone as to ignore the largest bill at the table: Boone's twenty. She let him tease her with it, stroking up the inside of her thigh and circling a nipple before she held out the waistband of the pseudo-skirt for the twenty. They probably didn't notice that she plucked them of their bills in order—Boone's twenty, Dave's ten, the two fives. Then she was moving to her right, to a crowd of hipster suits who had obviously been there longer than was good for them: two of them were holding out fifties. The dancer pretended to fuck the fifty being held out at pelvis level. She had incredible muscle control. Next to Cody, New York swallowed hard, and fumbled for his wallet. But it was too late. The hipster was grinning hard as the redhead touched his cheek, tilted her head, said something. He stood and his friends hooted encouragement as he and the redhead disappeared through a heavily frosted glass door in the back.

"Oh, man…" Dave's face was more red than tan now. He pulled a fifty from his wallet, snapped it, folded it lengthways, and held it out over the stage to the remaining dancer. "Yo, curlyhead, come and get some!"

"Yeah!" said New York in a high voice. Portland and Boston seemed to be engaged in a drinking game.

Boone caught Cody's eye and smiled slightly. She shrugged and spread her hand as if to say, Hey, it's their money to waste, and he smiled again, this time with a touch of skepticism. Ah, shit.

"Sugar?" The waitress with the velvet g-string, standing close and bending down so that her nipples brushed Cody's hair, then dabbed her cheek.

Cody looked at her faded blue eyes and found a ten dollar bill. She smiled and slipped it into the g-string at the woman's hip and crooked a finger to make her bend close again.

"I'd take it as a personal favor if you brought me another of these wonderful margaritas," she said in the woman's ear, "without the tequila."

"Whatever you say. But I'll still have to charge for the liquor."

"Of course you do. Just make sure it looks good." Cody jerked her head back at the rest of the table.

"You let me take care of everything, Sugar. I'm going to make you the meanest looking margarita in Dixie. They'll be amazed, purely amazed, at your stamina. It'll be our little secret." She fondled Cody's arm and shoulder, let the back of her hand brush the side of Cody's breast. "My name is Mimi. If you need anything, later." She gave Cody a molten look and headed for the bar. The skin on her rotating cheeks looked unnaturally smooth, like porcelain. Cosmetics, Cody decided.

Curlyhead had spotted Dave's fifty and was now on her back in front of their table. Cody imagined her as a glitched wigglebot responding to insane commands: clench, release, arch, whip back and forth. Whoever had designed her had done a great job on those muscles: each distinct, plump with strength, soft to the touch. Shame they hadn't had much imagination with the facial expressions or managed to put any spark in the eyes.

Breasts swaying near her face announced the arrival of her kickless drink. She slipped a five from her wallet and reached for Mimi's g-string.

Mimi stepped back half a pace, put her tray down, and squeezed her breasts together with her hands. "Would you like to put it here instead, Sugar?"

Cody blinked.

"You could slide it in real slow. Then maybe we could get better acquainted." But like the wigglebot, her eyes stayed blank.

"You're too hot for me, Mimi." Cody snapped the bill into her g-string and tried not to feel Mimi's flash of hatred. She sipped her drink and took a discreet peek in her wallet. This was costing the company a fortune.

Boone watched Dave and New York with a detached expression. Then he turned her way with a speculative look. An invitation to talk?

She stood. And turned to look at the stage just as a long-haired woman in cowboy boots strode to the center pole.

For Cookie it was all routine so far, ankle holding up better than she thought it might. The boots helped. She couldn't remember when she'd written that note to herself, *Cowboys and Indians!* but it was going to be inspired. She flexed and bent and pouted and pointed her breasts on automatic pilot. Should she get the ankle x-rayed? Nah. It was only a sprain. Two ibuprofen and some ice would fix it.

Decent crowd for a Tuesday night. Some high spenders behind the pillar there, but Ginger had taken them for four lapdances already. Well, hey, there were always more men with more money than sense. She glanced into the wings. Danny had her hat. He nodded. She moved automatically, counted under her breath, and just as the first haunting whistle of Morricone's *The Good, the Bad, and the Ugly* soundtrack echoed from the speakers she held out her hand, caught the hat, and swept it onto her head. Ooh, baby, perfect today, perfect. She smiled and strutted downstage. A woman at the front table was standing. Cookie saw the flash of a very expensive watch, and for no particular reason was flooded with conviction that tonight was going to go very well indeed. Cookie, baby, she told herself, tonight you're gonna get rich.

And with that catch of the hat, that strut, just like that, Cody forgot about Boone and his contract, forgot about being seamless, forgot everything. The dancer was fine, lean and soft, strong as a deer. The name *Cookie* was picked out in rhinestones on her hat, and she wore a tiny fringed buckskin halter and something that looked like a breech-clout—flaps of suede that hung from the waist to cover front and back, but not the sides—and wicked spurs on the boots. She looked right at Cody and smiled, and her eyes were not blank.

Part of Cody knew that Boone had seen her stand, and was now watching her watch this dancer, and that she should stop, or sit, or keep walking to Boone's end of the table, but the other part—the part that liked to drink shots in biker bars, to code all night with Acid Girls pounding from the speakers and the company's fortunes riding on her deadline, the part that had loaded up her pickup and left Florida to drive all the way to the West Coast on her own when she was just nineteen, that had once hung by her knees from a ninth floor balcony just because she could—that part cared about nothing but this woman with the long brown hair.

The hair was Indian straight and ended just once inch above the hem of the breechclout, and the way she moved made Cody understand that the hat and spurs were trophies, taken from a dead man. When the dancer trailed her hands across her body, Cody knew they held knives. When the male voices began their rhythmic chanting, she could see this woman riding hard over the plain, vaulting from her pony, stripping naked as she walked.

The music shifted but again it was drums, and now Cookie swayed like a maiden by a pool, pulling the straps of her halter off her shoulders, enough to expose half her breasts but not all, and she felt them thoughtfully, and began to smear them with warpaint. When she had painted all she could see, she pushed the buckskin down further, so that each breast rested like a satsuma on its soft shelf, then she turned her back on the audience, twisted her hair over one shoulder and examined the reflection of her ass in the water. She turned a little, this way and that, lifting the back flap, one corner then another, dropping it, thinking, stroking each cheek experimentally, trying to decide how to decorate it. Then she smoothed the buckskin with both hands so it pulled tight, and studied that effect. She frowned. She traced the outline of her g-string with her index finger. She smiled. She stuck her butt out, twitched it a couple of times, hooked both thumbs in the waistband of her g-string, and whipped it off. The breechclout stayed in place. She was still wearing the halter under her breasts.

And the little dyke liked that, Cookie could tell. She smiled smooth as cream, danced closer, saw the stain creeping up the woman's cheeks, the way her lips parted and her hands opened. Professionally manicured hands; clothes of beautifully cut linen, shoes handmade. The men in the room faded to irritation. This was the prize.

One of the men at the table reached out and slipped a twenty between the rawhide tie of her breechclout and her hip, but Cookie barely took her eyes from the woman. Twenty here or fifty there was small change compared to this. *For you*, she mouthed and turned slightly, and tightened down into a mushroom of skin-sheathed muscle, took off her hat, and reached back and pulled the flap of her breechclout out of the way.

She was aware of some shouting, the tall guy with the red face and the fifty, but she kept her eyes fixed on the woman.

And then the music changed, and Ginger was back from her lapdance, and she saw Donna was hand in hand with a glazed-looking mark, about to leave for the backroom, and it was time for Cookie to put some of her clothes back on and work the floor.

Five minutes, she mouthed to the woman.

Cookie, Cody thought, as the dancer flicked the suede flap back in place, stood gracefully, and put her hat back on. Cookie. She watched as Cookie left the stage and took all the heat and light with her. She would come back, wouldn't she? Five minutes, she had said.

"Cunt!" Dave shouted again, "my money not good enough for you? Goddamned—No, you get off of me." He pushed Boone's hand from his arm, then realized what he'd done. "Shit. That's—It's just—You know how it is, man. But fifty bucks…."

"Hell, Dave, maybe she knew it was counterfeit," Boone said jovially.

Dave forced a laugh, thrust the bill in his pocket. "Yeah, or maybe she just doesn't understand size matters." Boone laughed, but everyone at the table heard the dismissive note.

"Maybe it's time to call it a night, folks."

But Cody wasn't listening because Cookie was standing before her: no hat, buckskins and g-string back in place.

"Okay guys, looks like we lost Cody." Boone laughed, nothing like the laugh he'd given Dave. "Hey, girl, you make sure you get a cab home, hear? Mention my name to the doorman. Come on guys, we're outta here."

"Cody. Is that your name?" said Cookie, and took her hand. Cody nodded dumbly. "I'm Cookie. It's so good to find another woman here."

Another nod. *How are you?* Cody wanted to say, but that made no sense.

"Would you like to dance with me? Just you and me in private?"

"Yes."

"We'd have to pay for the room."

"Yes."

"But it wouldn't be like work, not with you. I love dancing for women. It gets me going, turns me on. I understand what women want, Cody. Would you like me to show you?"

"Yes," said Cody, and was mildly amazed when her legs worked well enough to follow Cookie to the frosted-glass door.

Midnight in her hotel room. Cody sat on the bed, naked, too wired to lie down. Streetlight slanted through the unclosed drapes, turning the room sodium yellow. The air conditioning roared, but her skin burned. Cookie. Cookie's lips, Cookie's hips, Cookie's cheek and chin and belly.

Her thighs and ass and breasts. Oh, her breasts, their soft weight on Cody's palms.

She lifted her hands, turned her palms up, examined them. They didn't look any different. She unsnapped her watch and rubbed her wrist absently. Cookie.

Stop it. What the fuck was the matter with her? She'd gone to a strip club and paid for sex. It was a first, okay, so some confusion was to be expected, but it was sordid, not romantic. She had been played by an expert and taken for hundreds of dollars. Oh, God, and Boone... She had made a fucking fool of herself.

So why did she feel so happy?

Cody, you're so beautiful, she'd said. *Oh, yes, yes, don't stop, Cody. Give it to me, give me all of it.* And Cody had. And Cookie had...Cookie had been perfect. She had understood everything, anticipated everything. What to say, what to do, when to cajole and goad, when to smile and be submissive, when to encourage, when to resist. Like a mind reader. And she had felt something, Cody knew it. She had. You couldn't fake pupil dilation, you couldn't fake that flush, you couldn't fake that sheen of sweat and luxuriant slipperiness. Could you?

Christ. She going mad. She rubbed her eyebrows. Cookie was a pro, and none of it was real.

She got up. The woolen carpet made her bare feet itch. That was real. Her clothes were flung across the back of the chair by the desk; they reeked of cigar smoke. No great loss. She'd no idea why she'd chosen to wear those loose pants, anyway. Hadn't worn them for about a year. Hadn't worn that stupid watch for about as long, come to think of it. Cookie hated the smell of cigars, she'd said so, when she was unbuttoning—

Stop it. Stop it now.

She carried her pants to the bed and pulled the receipts from the pockets. Eight of them. She'd paid for eight lapdances, and the size of the tips... Jesus. That was two month's rent. What had she been thinking?

We have to pay for the room, Cookie said, *but I'll pay you half back. It's just that I can't wait. Oh, please, Cody. I want you again.*

"God *damn* it!" Her ferocity scared her momentarily and she stilled, listening. No stirrings or mutterings from either room next door.

Give me your hotel phone number, Cookie had said. *I'll call you tomorrow. This has never happened before. This is real.*

And if it was... She could reschedule her flight. She'd explain it to Vince somehow.

Christ. That huge contract gone, in a flash of lust. Vince would kill her.

But, oh, she'd had nearly three hours of the best sex she'd ever had. It had gone exactly the way she'd imagined it in her fantasies. I know just what you want, she'd said, and proved it.

But Cody had known too, that was the thing. She had *known* when the hoarse breath and clutching hands meant it was Cookie's turn, meant that Cookie now wanted to be touched, wanted to break every single personal and club rule and be fucked over the back of the chair, just for pleasure.

Cody stirred the receipts. She couldn't make it make sense. She had paid for sex. That was not romance. But she had felt Cookie's vaginal muscles tighten, felt that quiver in her perineum, the clutch and spasm of orgasm. It wasn't faked. It hadn't been faked the second time, either.

Cody shivered. The air conditioning was finally beginning to bite. She rubbed her cold feet. Cookie's feet were long and shapely, each toe painted with clear nail polish. She'd twisted her ankle, she'd said. Cody had held the ankle, kissed it, stroked it. Cookie's smile was beautiful. *How did you sprain it?* Cody had asked, and Cookie had told her about falling five feet from the indoor climbing wall, and they had talked about climbing and rafting, and Cody had told her of the time when she was seven and had seen Cirque de Soleil and wanted to be one of the trapeze artists, and that led to talk of abdominal muscles, which led to more sex.

She padded into the bathroom, still without bothering with the light. When she lifted her toothbrush to her mouth, the scent on her fingers tightened her muscles involuntarily. She dropped the toothbrush, leaned over the sink, and wept.

A blue, blue Atlanta morning. Cody hadn't slept. She didn't want breakfast. Her plane wasn't until four that afternoon.

She'd lost the contract, lost a night's sleep, lost her mind and her self-respect, and flushed two months' rent down the toilet. She would never see Cookie again—and she couldn't understand why she cared.

The phone rang. *Cookie!* she thought, and hated herself for it.

"Hello?"

"Your cell phone's off, but I called Vince back in Frisco and he told me you were at the Westin."

Boone. She shut her eyes.

"Plane's not till four, am I right? Cody, you there?"

"Yes. I'm here."

"If you're not too tuckered out, maybe you wouldn't mind dropping by my office. We'll give you lunch."

"Lunch?"

"Yep. You know, food. Don't they do lunch on the West Coast?"

"Yes. I mean, why?"

He chuckled. "Because we've got a few details to hammer out on this contract. So should we say, oh, eleven-thirty?"

"That's, yes, fine. Good," she said at random, and put the phone down.

She stared at her bag. Clothes. She'd need to change her clothes. Was he really giving her the contract?

The phone rang again. "Hello?" she said doubtfully, expecting anyone from god to the devil to reply.

"Hey, Cody. It's me."

"Richard?"

"Yeah. Listen, how did it go?"

"I don't… Things are…" She took a deep breath. "I got the contract."

"Hey, that's great. But how did last night go?"

"Christ Richard, I can't gossip now. I don't have the time. I'm on my way to Boone's, iron out a few details." She had to pull it together. "I'll call you in a week or two, okay?"

"No, wait, Cody. Just don't do anything you—"

"Later, okay." She dropped the phone in its cradle. How did he know to call the Westin? What did he care about her night? She rubbed her forehead again. Food might help with the contract. The headache, she meant. And she grinned: the contract. She'd goddamned well won the contract. She was gonna get a huge bonus. She was gonna be a Vice President. She was gonna be late.

In the bathroom, she picked up the toothbrush, rinsed off the smeared paste, and resolutely refused to think about last night.

Cookie dialed the hotel.

"This is Cody. Leave a message, or reach me on my cell phone," followed by a string of numbers beginning with 216. San Francisco. That's right. She'd told Cookie that last night: San Francisco with its fog and hills and great espresso on Sunday mornings.

That might be okay. Anything would beat this Atlanta heat.

Boone didn't want to talk details so much as to laugh and drink coffee and teach Cody how to eat a po' boy sandwich. After all, if they were gonna be working together, they should get to know each other, was he right? And there was no mention of strip clubs or lapdances until the end when he signed the letter of intent, handed it to her, and said, "I like the way you handle yourself. Now take that Austin fella, Dave. No breeding. Can't hold his liquor, can't keep his temper, and calls a woman names in public. But you: no boasting, no big words, you just sit quiet then seize the opportunity." He gave her a sly smile. "You do that in business and we'll make ourselves some money."

And somehow, with his clap on the back, the letter in her laptop case and the sun on her face while she waited for the car for her trip to the airport, she started to forget her confusion. She'd had great sex, she'd built the foundations of a profitable working relationship, she was thirty-one and about to be a Vice President, and she didn't even have a hangover.

The car came and she climbed into the cool, green-tinted interior.

She let the outside world glide by for ten minutes before she got out the letter of intent. She read it twice. Beautifully phrased. Strong signature. Wonderful row of zeroes before the decimal point. If everything stayed on track, this one contract would keep their heads above water until they could develop a few more income streams. And she had done it. No one else. Damn she was good! Someone should buy her a great dinner to celebrate.

She got out her phone, turned it on. The signal meter wavered as the car crossed from cell to cell. Who should she call? No one in their right mind would want to have dinner with Vince. Richard would only want all the details, and she didn't want to talk about those details yet; he was in the Carolinas, anyway. Asshole.

The signal suddenly cleared, and her phone bleeped: one message.

"Hey. This is Cookie. I know you don't go until the afternoon. If you... I know this is weird but last night was... Shit. Look, maybe you won't believe me but I can't stop thinking about you. I want to see you, okay? I'll be in the park, the one I told you about. Piedmont. On one of the benches by the lake. I'm going there now, and I'll wait. I hope you come. I'll bring doughnuts. Do you like doughnuts? I'll be waiting. Please."

Oooh, you're different, ooh, you're so special, ooh, give it to me baby, just pay another thousand dollars and I'll love you forever. Sure. But Cookie's voice sounded so soft, so uncertain, as though she really meant it. But of course it would. That was her living: playing pretend. Using people.

Cody's face prickled. Be honest, she told herself: Who really used who, here? Who got the big contract, who got to have exactly what she wanted: great sex with no complications, and on the expense account no less?

It was too confusing. She was too tired. She was leaving. It was all too late anyhow, she thought, as the car moved smoothly onto the interstate.

A woman sitting on her own on a bench, maybe getting hot, maybe getting thirsty, wanting to use the bathroom. Afraid to get up and go pee because she might miss the one she was waiting for. Maybe the hot sweet scent of the doughnuts reminded her she was hungry, but she wouldn't eat them because she wanted to present them in their round-dozen perfection to her sweetie, see her smile of delight. She would pick at the paint peeling on the wooden bench and look up every time someone like Cody walked past; every time, she'd be disappointed. This one magical thing had happened in her life, something very like a miracle, but as the hot fat sun sinks lower she understands that this miracle, this dream is going to die because the person she's resting all her hopes on is worried she might look like a fool.

Cody blinked, looked at her watch. She leaned forward, cleared her throat.

The driver looked at her in his mirror. "Ma'am?"

"Where is Piedmont Park?"

"Northeast of downtown."

"Do we pass it on the way to the airport?"

"No, ma'am."

She was crazy. But all that waited for her at home was a tankful of fish. "Take me there."

Without the hat and boots, wearing jeans and sandals and the kind of tank top Cody herself might have picked, Cookie looked young. So did her body language. Her hair was in a braid. She was flipping it from shoulder to shoulder, twisting on the bench to look to one side, behind her, the other side. When she saw Cody, her face opened in a big smile that was naked and utterly vulnerable.

"How old are you?" Cody blurted.

The face closed. "Twenty-six. How old are you?"

"Thirty-one." Cody didn't sit down.

They stared at each other. "Dirt on my face?"

"No. Sorry. It looks…you look different."

"You expect me to dress like that on my day off?"

"No! No." But part of her had. "So. You get a lot of days off?"

A short laugh. "Can't afford it. No expense accounts for me. No insurance, no 401(k), no paid vacation."

Cody flushed. "Earning two thousand bucks a night isn't exactly a hard luck story."

"Was I worth it?"

Her smell filled Cody's mouth. *Yes!* she wanted to shout. *Yes, a hundred times over.* But that made no sense, so she just stood there.

"You paid twenty-two hundred. The house takes sixty percent off the top. Out of my eight-eighty, Danny takes another twenty percent and, no, he's a bouncer, not a pimp, and I've never done that before last night. And no, I don't expect you to believe me. Then there's costumes, hair, waxing, makeup…" She leaned back, draped both arms along the back of the bench. "You tell me. Would fucking a complete stranger for three hours be worth five hundred dollars?"

Her mouth stretched in a hard smile but her eyes glistened. She put one ankle up on the other knee.

"Does your ankle still hurt?" It just popped out.

Cookie turned away, blinked a couple of time. Cody found herself kneeling before the bench.

"Cookie? Cookie, don't cry."

"Susanna," she said, still turned away.

"What?"

"Susanna. It's my real name. Susanna Herrera." She turned to Cody, and her face was fierce. "I am Susanna Herrera. I'm a dancer, I'm not a whore, and I want to know what you've done to me."

"What I've…?"

"I dance. I tease, I hint. It makes you feel good, you give me money, which makes me feel good. Sometimes I give a lapdance, but always by the rules: hands on the armrest, clothes on, a little bump and grind, because I need the extra tips. I dance, you pay. It's my job. But this, this isn't a job! I don't know what it is. It's crazy. I let you—" Her cheeks darkened. "And I would do it again, for no money. For nothing. It's crazy. I feel… It's like… I don't even know how to say it! I want to talk to you, listen to you talk about your business. I want to see your house. I didn't sleep last night. I thought about you: your smile, your hands, how strong it made me feel to give you pleasure, how warm I felt when you wrapped your arms around me. And I'm scared."

"Me too," Cody said, and she was, very, because she was beginning to get an idea what was wrong with them and it felt like a very bad joke.

"You're not scared." Susanna folded her arms, turned her face again.

"I am. Cook—Susanna, do you suppose... Shit. I feel ridiculous even saying this. Look at me. Please. Thank you. Do you suppose this is what I—"

She couldn't say it. She didn't believe it.

After a very long pause, Susanna said, "Dancers don't fall in love with the marks."

That cut. "Marks don't fall in love with whores."

"I'm not a—"

"Neither am I."

They stared at each other. Cody's phone rang. She thumbed it off without looking. "My full name is Candice Marcinko. I have to fly back to San Francisco this afternoon, but I could come back to Atlanta at the end of the week. We could, you know, talk, go to the movies, walk in the park." Jesus, had she left any stereotype unturned? She tried again. "I want to meet your, your cat."

"I don't have a cat."

"Or your dog," she said. *Stop babbling.* But she couldn't. "I want to learn how long you've lived in Atlanta and what kind of food you like and whether you think the Braves will win tonight and how you feel when you sleep in my arms." She felt like an idiot.

Susanna looked at her for a while, then picked up the box at her side. "Do you like Krispy Kreme?"

When Cody turned her phone on again at the airport, there was a message from Richard: *Call me, it's important.* But she had to run for her plane.

In the air she leaned her head against the window and listened to the drone of the engines.

Susanna, sitting on the bench while the sun went down, thinking, *Love, love is for rich people.*

A cream labrador runs by, head turned to watch its owner running alongside. Its tongue lolls, happy and pink. *Dogs love. Dogs are owned.*

She tears the last three doughnuts to pieces and throws them to the ducks.

On Thursday, Vince and the executive team toasted her with champagne. She took the opportunity to ask for Friday and two days next week off. Vince couldn't say no without looking chintzy, so he told her VPs didn't have to ask permission.

VP. She grinned hard and for a minute she felt almost normal. VP. Top dog.

Friday morning she had just got out of the shower when the doorbell rang. She was so surprised she barely remembered to pull on a robe before she opened the door.

"Well, that's a sight for sore eyes."

"Richard!"

"Not that I don't appreciate the gesture but could you please tighten that belt, at least until we've had coffee? Here you go, quad grande, two percent."

She went to get dressed. When she emerged, drying her hair with a towel, he was sitting comfortably on the couch, ankle crossed at the knee, just like Susanna in the park.

"I envy you that dyke rub-and-go convenience."

She draped the towel round her neck, sat, and sipped the latte. "To paraphrase you, it's not that I don't appreciate the coffee, but…why the fuck are you here?"

He put his phone on the table next to her latte. "Remember this?"

"It's your phone?"

He took a thumbdrive from his laptop case and gave it, then her, a significant look.

"Richard, I've had a real weird few days and I'm on a plane in four hours. Maybe." Maybe she was crazy, maybe she should cancel… "Anyhow, could you please just get to the point?"

"Drink your coffee. You're going to need it. And tell me what happened on Tuesday night." He held up his hand. "Just tell me. Because my guess is you had a hell of a night with a lovely young thing called Cookie."

She didn't say anything for a long, long time. "Susanna," she said finally.

"Ah. You got that far? Susanna Herrera, aged twenty-four—"

"Twenty-six."

"Twenty-four. Trust me. Mother Antonia Herrera, father unknown. Dunwoody community college, degree in business administration—oh, the look on your face—and one previous arrest for possession of a controlled substance. Healthy as an ox. Not currently taking any medication except contraceptive pills."

"The pill?"

"What's the matter?"

"Nothing. Go on."

"No known allergies to pharmaceuticals, though a surprising tolerance to certain compounds, for example sodium thiopental and terpazine hydrochloride."

Cody seized on something that made sense. "Wait. I know that drug. It's—"

"RU486 for the mind. That's the one."

"Oh, Jesus, Richard, you didn't *give* her that! You didn't make her forget what happened!"

"Not what happened Tuesday."

Cody, confused, said nothing.

He plugged the thumbdrive into his laptop and turned the screen so she could see the sound file icons. "It will all make sense when you've listened to these."

"But I don't have time. I have a plane—"

"You'll want to cancel that, if it's to Atlanta. Just listen. Then I'll answer questions."

He tapped play.

"*…ever happens, I promise no one will ever hear what goes on this recording except you.*"

"*Cue ominous music.*"

She jumped at the sound of her own voice. "What—"

"Shh."

"*—more an, um, an ethics thing.*"

"*Jesus, Richard. You're such a drama queen.*" Pause. Clink.

"*I've done my research, too. Like you, I'm pretty sure what will happen after you've made your presentations to Boone.*"

"*The Golden Key.*"

"*—but what I need to know from you is whether or not you can authorize out-of-pocket expenses in the high five figures to win this contract.*"

He touched pause. "Ring any bells?"

"No." Cody's esophagus had clamped shut. She could hardly swallow her own spit, never mind the latte. But the cardboard was warm and smooth in her hand, comforting, and behind Richard her fish swam serenely back and forth.

"Terpazine is a good drug. We managed to calculate your dosage beautifully. Susanna's was a bit more of a challenge. Incredible metabolism."

"You said you didn't give her—"

"Not in the last couple of weeks. But you've had it six times, and she seven. Now keep listening."

Six times?

"—*the exploration of memory and its retrieval. So exciting. A perfect dovetail with the work I've been doing on how people form attachments. It's all about familiarity. You let someone in deep enough, or enough times, then your brain actually rewires to recognize that person as friend, or family.*"

Pause.

"*There are ways to make it easier for someone to let you in.*"

Clink of bottle on glass.

"*I've told you about those studies that show it's as simple as having Person A anticipate Person B's needs and fulfill them.*"

"*So don't tell me again.*"

She sounded so sure of herself, bored even. A woman who had never thought to use the world *love*.

"—*jumpstart the familiarization process. For example, Person A works in a bookshop and is lonely, and when she's lonely chocolate makes her feel better. And one day Person B arrives mid-afternoon with some chocolate, says, Hey, you look sorta miserable, when I'm miserable chocolate makes me feel better, would you like one? and A eats a chocolate and thinks, Wow, this B person is very thoughtful and empathic and must be just like me, and therefore gets slotted immediately into the almost-friend category. It's easy to set something like that up. You just have to know enough about Person A.*"

Know enough.

Cody pushed the laptop from her. "I don't believe this."

"No?"

Cody didn't say anything.

"You sat in that bar, and you listened, and then you signed a temporary waiver." He placed a piece of paper on the table by her hand. It was her signature at the bottom—a little sloppy, but hers. "Then you took some terpazine and forgot all about it."

"I wouldn't forget something like this."

He held up his hand. Reached with his other and nudged the sound file slider to the right.

"*Take the pill.*"

"*All right, all right.*" *Pause. Tinkle of ice cubes.* "*Jesus. That tastes vile.*"

"*Next time we'll put it in a capsule. Just be grateful it's not the vasopressin. It would make you gag. I speak from experience.*"

He tapped the file to silence. "It really does. Anyhow, a week after Seattle I came here and you signed a more robust set of papers." He handed her a thick, bound document. "Believe me, they're bombproof."

"Wait." She dropped the document on her lap without looking. "You came here? To my apartment?"

"I did. I played the recording you've just heard, showed you the initial waiver. Gave you that." He nodded at her lap. "You signed. I gave you the sodium thiopental, we had our first session. You took another terpazine."

"I don't remember."

He shrugged. "It happened." He tapped the paper in her lap. "There's a signed waiver for every session."

"How many did you say?"

"Six. Four here, twice in North Carolina."

"But I don't remember!"

The fish in her tank swam back and forth, back and forth. She closed her eyes. Opened them. The fish were still there. Richard was still there. She could still remember the weight of Susanna's breasts in her hands.

"You'd better listen to the rest. And read everything over."

He tapped *play*.

"*Okay. Think about what it would be like if you knew enough about someone and* then *you met: you'd know things about her and she'd know things about you, but all you'd be aware of is that you recognize and trust this person and you feel connected. Now imagine what might happen if you add sex to the equation.*"

"*Good sex, I hope.*"

"*The best. There are hundreds of studies that show how powerful sex bonding can be, especially for women. If a woman has an orgasm in the presence of another person, her hormonal output for the next few days is sensitized to her lover: every time they walk in the room, her system floods with chemical messengers like oxytocin saying Friend! Friend! This is even with people you know consciously aren't good for you. You put that together with someone compatible, who fits—whether they really fit or just seem to fit—and it's a chemical bond with the potential to be human superglue. That's what love is: a bond that's renewed every few days until the brain is utterly rewired. So I wanted to know what would happen if you put together two sexually compatible people who magically knew exactly—exactly!—what the other wanted in bed but had no memory of how they'd acquired that knowledge…*"

It took Cody a moment to pause the sound. "Love," she said. "*Love?* What the fuck have you done to me?"

"You did it to yourself. Keep listening."

And she did. After she had listened for an hour, she accepted the sheaf of transcripts Richard handed her from his case.

She looked at the clock.

"Still thinking about that plane?"

Cody didn't know what she was thinking.

"Is it refundable?" he said. "The flight?"

Cody nodded.

"Give me the ticket. I'll cancel for you. You can always rebook for tomorrow. But you need to read."

She watched, paralyzed, as Richard picked up the phone and dialed. He turned to her while he was on hold, mouthed *Read*, and turned away again.

So she began to read, only vaguely aware of Richard arguing his way up the airline hierarchy.

After the first hundred pages of *Subject C* and *Subject S*, he brought her fresh coffee. She paused at one section, appalled.

"What?"

"I can't believe I told you that."

He peered over her shoulder. "Oh, that's a juicy one. Stop blushing. I've heard it all before. Several times now. Sodium thiopental will make you say anything. Besides, you don't remember telling me, so why bother being embarrassed?"

She watched her fish. It didn't matter. Didn't matter. She picked up the paper again and plowed on. May as well get it over with.

Somewhere around page three hundred, he went into the kitchen to make lunch. She didn't remember eating it, but when she set aside the final page at seven o'clock that evening, she saw that the plate by her elbow was empty, and heard the end of Richard's order to the Chinese takeout place on the corner. It was clearly something he'd done before. From her phone, in her apartment. And she didn't remember.

She wished there was a way to feed him terpazine so he would forget all those things she'd never said to another soul before.

She tried to organize her thoughts.

He had asked for her permission to use her in an experiment. It would mean she would feel comfortable at the club in Atlanta, that she might even have a good couple of hours, and it would further his work while being paid for to some extent by her expense account. He had traveled to the Golden Key and picked Susanna as the most likely dancer to fit her fantasies—and he knew a little about her preferences from that stupid, stupid night in Dallas—and made the same pitch to her. Only Susanna got paid.

Twice, Cody thought. *I paid her too.*

And so Richard had flown to Cody's apartment in San Francisco and given her sodium thiopental, and she had talked a blue streak about her sexual fantasies, every nuance and variation and degree of pleasure. In North Carolina, she had talked about her fantasies again, even more explicitly, encouraged to imagine in great detail, pretend it was happening, while they had her hooked up to both a functional MRI and several blood-gas sensors.

Richard put down the phone. "Food in thirty minutes."

Cody forced herself to stay focused, to think past her embarrassment. "What were the fMRIs for, the fMRIs and—" she glanced at the paper, "—TMS during the, the fantasy interludes?"

"We built a kind of mind and hormone map of how you'd feel if someone was actually doing those things to you. A sort of super-empathy direction finder. And one from Susanna, of course. We played your words to each other, along with transcranial magnetic stimulation to encourage brain plasticity—the rewiring."

"And," she hunted through the pages for the section labeled *Theoretical Underpinnings*. "You gave me, us, oxytocin?"

"No. We wanted to separate out the varying factors. You supplied the oxytocin on your own, later." He beamed. "That's the beautiful part. It was all your own doing. Your hopes, your hormones, your needs. Yours. We made a couple of suggestions to each of you that you might not have come up with on your own: that expensive watch and the loose clothes, Cookie's hat and spurs. The rest was just you and Cookie, I mean Susanna. But you two were primed for each other, so if that wasn't the best sex of your life, I'll eat this table." He rapped the table top in satisfaction.

All her own doing.

"You can't publish," she said.

"Not this, no." He picked up one of the fMRIs and admired it. "It's enough for now to know that it works."

She waited for anger to well up, but nothing happened. "Is this real?"

"The project? Quite real."

Project. She watched him gather all the documents, tap them into a neat pile.

"Not the project," she said. "Not the TMS, the fMRIs, the terpazine. This." She tapped her chest. "Is it real?"

He tilted his head. "Is love real? A lot of people seem to think so. But if you mean, is that what you're feeling, the answer is, I don't know. I don't think a scan could give you that answer. But it could tell us if you've changed: your data have been remarkably clear. Not like Cookie's. Susanna's." He held the fMRI image up again, admired it some more, then put it back in the pile.

"What do you mean?"

"The data. Yours were perfectly consistent. Hers were… erratic."

"Erratic." Her mind seemed to be working in another dimension. It took an age for the thought to form. "Like lying?"

"She's lied about a lot of things."

"But she could have been lying to me? About how she feels?"

He shrugged. "How can we ever know?"

She stared at him. "The literature," she said, trying to force her slippery brain to remember what she'd just read. "It says love's a feedback loop, right?"

"In terms of individual brain plasticity, yes."

"So it's mutual. I can't love someone if she doesn't love me." If it was love.

He gave her a look she couldn't interpret. "The data don't support interdependence." He paused, said more gently, "We don't know."

Pity, she realized. He pities me. She felt the first flex and coil of something so far down she couldn't identify it. "What have you done to me? What *else* have you done to me?"

"To you? For you."

"You made me feel something for a woman who fucked for money. Who had her mind fucked for money."

"So did you, if you think about. Just at one remove."

"I didn't."

"So, what, you did it for science?"

Cody changed direction. "Does Susanna know?"

"I'm flying to Atlanta tomorrow."

"Do you have her sound files with you?"

"Of course."

"Let me hear them."

"That would be unethical."

Unethical. "I think you might be a monster," she said, but without heat.

"I have a strange way of showing it, then, wouldn't you say? For the price of a few embarrassing experimental sessions you won't ever remember, I won you a contract, a girlfriend and a night on the town."

She stared at him. "You expect me to be grateful…"

"Well, look at this place. Look at it. Bare walls. Fish, for god's sake."

"Get out."

"Oh, come on—"

"Out."

"By tomorrow it will all fall into perspective."

"I swear to god, if you don't leave now I'll break your face." She sounded so weirdly calm. Was this shock, or was it just how people in love, or whatever, behaved? She had no idea. "And you can put those papers down. They're mine, my private thoughts. Leave them right there on the table. The thumbdrive, too."

He pulled the drive, laid it on the papers, stowed his laptop and stood. She held the door open for him.

He was halfway through the door when she said, "Richard. You can't tell Susanna like this."

"No?"

"It's too much of a shock."

"You seem to be coping admirably."

"At least I already knew you. Or thought I did. You'll be a complete stranger to her. You can't. You just can't. It's…inhumane. And she's so young."

"Young? Don't make me laugh. She makes you look like an infant." He walked away.

Cookie danced. She didn't want to think about the phone call. Didn't want to think about any of it. Creep.

But there was the money.

The lights were hot, but the air conditioning cold. Her skin pebbled.

"Yo, darlin', let's you and me go to the back room," the suit with the moustache and bad tie said. He was drunk. She knew the type. He'd slip his hands from the chair, try cop a feel, get pissed off when she called in Danny, refuse to pay.

"Well, now," she said, in her special honey voice. "Let's see if you've got the green," and pushed her breasts together invitingly. He flicked a bill across her breasts. "A five won't buy you much, baby."

"Five'll buy you, babydoll," he said, hamming for his table buddies. One of them giggled. Ugly sound in a man, Cookie thought. "Five'll buy you five times!"

"And how long did it take you to come up with that, honey?"

"The fuck?" He looked confused.

"I said, your brain must be smaller than your dick, which I'd guess is even smaller than your wallet, only I doubt that's possible," and she plucked the bill from his fingers, snapped it under her g-string and walked away.

In the dressing room she looked at herself in the mirror. Twenty-four was too old for this. Definitely. She had no idea what time it was.

She stuck her head out of the door. "Danny!"

"Yes, doll."

"Time is it?" She'd have to get herself a watch someday. A nice expensive watch.

"Ten after," Danny said.

"After what?"

"Ten."

Three hours earlier on the West Coast. She stacked her night's take, counted it, thought for a minute, peeled off two hundred in fives and ones. She stuck her head out of the door again. "Danny!"

"Here, doll."

"I'm gone."

"You sick?" He ambled up the corridor, stood breathing heavily by the door.

"Sick of this."

"Mister Pergoletti says—"

"You tell Pergoletti to stick it. I'm gone. Seriously." She handed him the wad of bills. "You take care of these girls, now. And have a good life."

"Got something else lined up?"

"Guess we'll find out."

There was one bottle of beer in Cody's fridge. She opened it, poured it carefully into a glass, stared at the beige foam. A glass: she never drank beer from a glass. She poured it down the sink. She had no idea what was real anymore but she was pretty sure alcohol would only make things worse.

She made green tea instead and settled down in the window seat. The sun hung low over the bay. What did Susanna see from her apartment? Was her ankle better? Contraceptive pills, Jesus. And, oh, the smell of her skin.

She was losing her mind.

She didn't know who she hated more: Richard for making the proposal, or herself for accepting it. Or Susanna. Susanna had done it for money.

Or maybe... But what about those contraceptive pills?

And what if Susanna did feel...whatever it was? Did that make it real? It was all an experiment, all engineered. Fake.

But it didn't feel fake. She wanted to cradle Susanna, kiss her ankle better, protect her from the world. The Richards of the world.

She picked up the phone, remembered for the tenth time she had neither address nor phone number. She called information, who told her there was no listing under Susanna Herrera in the Atlanta Metro area. She found herself unsurprised, though surprised at how little it mattered.

She got the number for the Golden Key instead.

A man called Pergoletti answered. "Cookie? She's gone. They always go." The music thumped. Cody's insides vibrated in sympathy, remembering.

"—don't have a number. Hey, you interested in a job?"

Cody put the phone down carefully. Sipped her tea. Picked up the phone again, and called Richard.

It was open mic night at Coffee to the People. Richard was in the back room on a sofa, as far from the music as possible. Two cups on the table. One still full.

"You knew I'd call."

"I did."

"Did you program that, too?"

"I didn't program anything. I primed you—and only about the sex." He patted the sofa. "Sit down before you fall down."

She sat. Blinked. "Give me her phone number."

"I can't. She gave me a fake. I called her at the club, but she hung up on me." He seemed put out.

"What does she know?"

"I talked fast. I don't know how much she heard. But I told her she wouldn't get the rest of the money until we'd done follow up."

The singer in the other room sang of love and broken hearts. It was terrible, but it made Cody want to cry anyway.

"How long does it last?"

"Love? I don't know. I avoid it where possible."

"What am I going to do?"

Richard lifted his laptop bag. "I planned for this eventuality." He took out a small white cardboard box. He opened it, shook something onto his hand. A grey plastic inhaler.

"What is it?"

"A vasopressin analogue, formulated to block oxytocin receptors in the nucleus accumbens. That is, the antidote."

They both looked at it.

"It works in voles," he said. "Female voles."

Voles. "You said it tasted bad."

"I've used it. Just in case. I prefer my sex without complications. And I've had a lot of sex and never once fallen in love." He arched his eyebrows. "So, hey, it must work."

The elephant whistle hypothesis. *Hey, Bob, what's that whistle? Well, Fred, it keeps elephants away. Don't be an asshole, Bob, there aren't any elephants around here. Well, Fred, that's because of my whistle.*

"Cody." He did his best to look sincere. "I'm so very sorry. I never thought it would work. Not like this. But I do think the antidote might work." His face went back to normal. He hefted the inhaler. "Though before I give it to you, I have a favor to ask."

She stared at him. "On what planet do I owe you anything?"

"For science, then. A follow-up scan, and then another after you take the antidote."

"Maybe I won't take it. Give me the number."

"Love is a form of insanity, you know."

"The number."

In the other room, the bad singing went on and on.

"Oh, all right. For old time's sake." He extracted a folder from his bag, and a piece of paper from the folder. He slid it across the table towards her, put the inhaler on top of it.

She nudged the inhaler aside, picked up the paper. Handwritten. Susanna's writing.

"Love's just biochemical craziness," he said, "designed to make us take a leap in the dark, to trust complete strangers. It's not rational."

Cody said nothing.

"She screwed us."

"She screwed you," Cody said. "Maybe she fell in love with me." But she took the inhaler.

Cody sat in the window seat with the phone and the form Susanna had filled in. Every now and again she punched in a different combination of the numbers Susanna had written and got the *Cannot be completed as dialed* voice. Every now and again she touched the form with the tip of her middle finger; she could feel the indentation made by Susanna's strong strokes. Strong strokes, strong hands, strong mouth.

She didn't think about the grey inhaler in its white box, which she had put in the fridge—to stay viable a long time, just in case.

After a while she stopped dialing and simply waited.

When her phone lit up at 11:46 she knew who it was—even before she saw the 404 area code on the screen.

"Do you feel it?" Susanna said.

"Yes," and Cody did. Whatever it was, wherever it came from, it was there, as indelible as ink. She wanted to say, I don't know if this is real, I don't know if it's good. She wanted to ask, Had you ever had sex with anyone for money before me? and, Does it matter? She wanted to know, Have you ever loved anyone before? and, How can you know?

She wanted to say, Will it hurt?

Walking through the crowds at the airport, Cody searched for the familiar face, felt her heart thump every time she thought she saw her. Panic, or love? She didn't know. She didn't know anything except that her throat ached.

Someone jostled her with his bag, and when she looked up, there was the back of that head, that smooth brown hair, so familiar, after just one night, and all her blood vessels seemed to expand at once, every cell leapt forward.

She didn't move. This was it, the last moment. This was where she could just let the crowd carry her past, carry her away, out into the night. Walk away. Go home. Use the inhaler in the fridge.

That was the sensible thing. But the Cody who had hung from the ninth-story balcony, the Cody who had risked the Atlanta contract without a second thought, that Cody thought, *Fuck it*, and stepped forward. *Will it hurt?* You could never know.

SLEIGHT OF HAND

PETER S. BEAGLE

She had no idea where she was going. When she needed to sleep she stopped at the first motel; when the Buick's gas gauge dropped into the red zone she filled the tank, and sometimes bought a sandwich or orange juice at the attached convenience store. Now and then during one of these stops she spoke with someone who was neither a desk clerk nor a gas-station attendant, but she forgot all such conversations within minutes, as she forgot everything but the words of the young policeman who had come to her door on a pleasant Wednesday afternoon, weeks and worlds ago. Nothing had moved in her since that point except the memory of his shakily sympathetic voice, telling her that her husband and daughter were dead: ashes in a smoking, twisted, unrecognizable ruin, because, six blocks from their home, a drowsy adolescent had mistaken his accelerator for his brake pedal.

There had been a funeral—she was present, but not there—and more police, and some lawyer; and Alan's sister managing it all, as always, and for once she was truly grateful to the interfering bitch. But that was all far away too, both the gratitude and the old detestation, made nothing by the momentary droop of a boy's eyelids. The nothing got her snugly through the days after the funeral, dealing with each of the endless phone calls, sitting down to answer every condolence card and e-mail, informing Social Security and CREF of Alan's death, going with three of his graduate students to clean out his office, and attending the memorial on campus, which was very tasteful and genuinely moving, or so the nothing was told. She was glad to hear it.

The nothing served her well until the day Alan's daughter by his first marriage came to collect a few of his possessions as keepsakes. She was a perfectly nice girl, who had always been properly courteous in an interloper's presence, and her sympathy was undoubtedly as real as good manners could make it; but when she had gone, bearing a single brown paper grocery bag of photographs and books, the nothing stepped aside for the meltdown.

Her brother-in-law calmed her, spoke rationally, soothed her out of genuine kindness and concern. But that same night, speaking to no one, empty and methodical, she had watched herself pack a small suitcase and carry it out to Alan's big old Buick in the garage, then go back into the house to leave her cell phone and charger on Alan's desk, along with a four-word note for her sister-in-law that read *Out for a drive*. After that she had backed the Buick into the street and headed away without another look at the house where she used to live, once upon a time.

The only reason she went north was that the first freeway on-ramp she came to pointed her in that direction. After that she did not drive straight through, because there was no *through* to aim for. With no destination but away, without any conscious plan except to keep moving, she left and returned to the flat ribbon of the interstate at random intervals, sometimes wandering side roads and backroads for hours, detouring to nowhere. Aimless, mindless, not even much aware of pain—that too having become part of the nothing—she slogged onward. She fell asleep quickly when she stopped, but never for long, and was usually on her way in darkness, often with the moon still high. Now and then she whistled thinly between her teeth.

The weather was warm, though there was still snow in some of the higher passes she traversed. Although she had started near the coast, that was several states ago: now only the mountains were constant. The Buick fled lightly over them, gulping fuel with abandon but cornering like a deer, very nearly operating and guiding itself. This was necessary, since only a part of her was behind the wheel; the rest was away with Alan, watching their daughter building a sandcastle, prowling a bookshop with him, reaching for his hand on a strange street, knowing without turning her head that it would be there. At times she was so busy talking to him that she was slow to switch on the headlights, even long after sunset. But the car took care of her, as she knew it would. It was Alan's car, after all.

From time to time the Buick would show a disposition to wander toward the right shoulder of the road, or drift left into the oncoming lane, and she would observe the tendency with vague, detached interest. Once she asked aloud, "Is this what you want? I'm leaving it to you—are you taking me to Alan?" But somehow, whether under her guidance or its own, the old car always righted itself, and they went on together.

The latest road began to descend, and then to flatten out into farm and orchard country, passing the occasional township, most of them overgrown crossroads. She had driven for much of the previous night, and all of today, and knew with one distant part of herself that it would soon be necessary to stop. In early twilight, less than an hour later, she came to the next town. There was a river winding through it, gray and silver in the dusk, with bridges.

Parking and registering at the first motel with a *Vacancy* sign, she walked three blocks to the closest restaurant, which, from the street, looked like a bar with a 1950s-style diner attached. Inside, however, it proved larger than she had expected, with slightly less than half of the booths and tables occupied. Directly to the left of the *Please Wait To Be Served* sign hung a poster showing a photograph of a lean, hawk-nosed man in late middle age, with white hair and thick eyebrows, wearing evening dress: tailcoat, black bowtie, top hat. He was smiling slightly and fanning a deck of playing cards between long, neat fingers. There was no name under the picture; the caption read only *DINNER MAGIC*. She looked at it until the young waitress came to show her to her booth.

After ordering her meal—the first she had actually sat down to since leaving home—she asked the waitress about Dinner Magic. Her own voice sounded strange in her ears, and language itself came hard and hesitantly. The girl shrugged. "He's not fulltime—just comes in now and then, does a couple of nights and gone again. Started a couple of weeks ago. Haven't exchanged two words with him. Other than my boss, I don't know anybody who has."

Turning away toward the kitchen, she added over her shoulder, "He's good, though. Stay for the show, if you can."

In fact, the Dinner Magic performance began before most of the current customers had finished eating. There was no stage, no musical flourish or formal introduction: the man in evening dress simply walked out from the kitchen onto the floor, bowed briefly to the diners, then tossed a gauzy multicolored scarf into the air. He seized it again as it fluttered down, then held it up in front of himself, hiding him from silk hat to patent-leather shoes…

…and vanished, leaving his audience too stunned to respond. The applause began a moment later, when he strolled in through the restaurant's front door.

Facing the audience once more, the magician spoke for the first time.

His voice was deep and clear, with a certain engaging roughness in the lower range. "Ladies, gentlemen, Dinner Magic means exactly what it sounds like. You are not required to pay attention to me for a moment, you are free to concentrate on your coffee and pie—which is excellent, by the way, especially the lemon meringue—or on your companion, which I recommend even more than the meringue. Think of me, if you will, as the old man next door who stays up all night practicing his silly magic tricks. Because that, under this low-rent monkey suit, is exactly what I am. Now then."

He was tall, and older than the photograph had suggested—how old, she could not tell, but there were lines on his cheeks and under his angled eyes that must have been removed from the picture; the sort of thing she had seen Alan do on the computer. From her booth, she watched, chin on her fist, never taking her eyes from the man as he ran through a succession of tricks that bordered on the miraculous even as his associated patter never transcended a lounge act. Without elephants or tigers, without a spangled, long-legged assistant, he worked the room. Using his slim black wand like a fishing rod he reeled laughing diners out of their seats. Holding it lightly between his fingertips, like a conductor's baton or a single knitting needle, he caused the napkins at every table to lift off in a whispering storm of thin cotton, whirl wildly around the room, and then settle docilely back where they belonged. He identified several members of his audience by name, address, profession, marital status, and, as an afterthought, by driver's license state and number. She was never one of these; indeed, the magician seemed to be consciously avoiding eye contact with her altogether. Nevertheless, she was more intrigued—more *awakened*—than she had meant to let herself be, and she ordered a second cup of coffee and sat quite still where she was.

Finishing at last with an offhanded gesture, a bit like an old-fashioned jump shot, which set all the silverware on all the tables chiming applause, the magician walked off without bowing, as abruptly as he had entered. The waitress brought her check, but she remained in her booth even after the busboy cleared away her dishes. Many of the other diners lingered as she did, chattering and marveling and calling for encores. But the man did not return.

The street was dark, and the restaurant no more than a quarter full, when she finally recollected both herself and her journey, and stepped out into the warm, humid night. For a moment she could not call to mind where she had parked her car; then she remembered the motel and started in that direction. She felt strangely refreshed, and was seriously considering the prospect of giving up her room and beginning to drive again. But after walking several blocks she decided that she must have somehow gone in the wrong direction, for there was no motel sign in sight, nor any landmark casually noted on her way to the restaurant. She turned and turned again, making tentative casts this way and that, even starting back the way she had come, but nothing looked at all familiar.

Puzzlement had given way to unease when she saw the magician ahead of her, under a corner streetlamp. There was no mistaking him, despite his having changed from evening clothes into ordinary dress. His leanness gave him the air of a shadow, rather than a man: a shadow with lined cheeks and long bright eyes. As she approached, he spoke her name. He said, "I have been waiting for you." He spoke more slowly than he had when performing, with a tinge of an accent that she had not noticed.

Anxiety fled on the instant, replaced by a curious stillness, as when Alan's car began to drift peacefully toward the guardrail or the shoulder and the trees. She said, "How do you know me? How did you know all about those other people?"

"I know nearly everything about nearly everyone. That's the curse of my position. But you I know better than most."

She stared at him. "I don't know you."

"Nevertheless, we have met before," the magician said. "Twice, actually, which I confess is somewhat unusual. The second time was long ago. You were quite small."

"That's ridiculous." She was surprised by the faint touch of scorn in her voice, barely there yet still sharp. "That doesn't make any sense."

"I suppose not. Since I know how the trick's done, and you don't, I'm afraid I have you at a disadvantage." He put one long finger to his lips and pursed them, considering, before he started again. "Let's try it as a riddle. I am not entirely what I appear, being old as time, vast as space, and endless as the future. My nature is known to all, but typically misunderstood. And I meet everyone and everything alive at least once. Indeed, the encounter is entirely unavoidable. Who am I?"

She felt a sudden twist in the nothing, and knew it for anger. "Show's over. I'm not eating dinner anymore."

The magician smiled and shook his head very slightly. "You are lost, yes?"

"My motel's lost, I'm not. I must have taken a wrong turn."

"I know the way," the magician said. "I will guide you."

Gracefully and courteously, he offered his arm, but she took a step backward. His smile widened as he let the arm fall to his side. "Come," he said, and turned without looking to see whether she followed. She caught up quickly, not touching the hand he left open, within easy reach.

"You say we've met before. Where?" she asked.

"The second time was in New York City. Central Park," the magician said. "There was a birthday party for your cousin Matthew."

She stopped walking. "Okay. I don't know who you are, or how you knew I grew up in New York City and have a cousin named Matthew. But you just blew it, Sherlock. When we were kids I *hated* stupid, nasty Matthew, and I absolutely never went to any of his birthday parties. My parents tried to make me, once, but I put up such a fuss they backed down. So you're wrong."

The magician reached down abruptly, and she felt a swift, cool whisper in her hair. He held up a small silver figure of a horse and asked with mock severity, "What are you doing, keeping a horse up in there? You shouldn't have a horse if you don't have a stable for it."

She froze for an instant, wide-eyed and open-mouthed, and then clutched at the silver horse as greedily as any child. "That's *mine!* Where did you get it?"

"I gave it to you." The magician's voice sounded as impossibly distant as her childhood, long gone on another coast.

And then came his command: "*Remember.*"

At first she had enjoyed herself. Matthew was fat and awful as usual, but his birthday had been an excuse to bring together branches of the family that rarely saw one another, traveling in to Central Park from places as whispered and exotic as Rockaway and Philadelphia. She was excited to see her *whole* family, not just her parents and her very small baby brother, and Matthew's mother and father, but also uncles and aunts and cousins, and some very old relatives she had never met before in her life. They all gathered together in one corner of the Sheep Meadow, where they spread out picnic blankets, coverlets, beach towels, anything you could sit down on, and they brought out all kinds of old-country dishes: *piroshki, pelmeni, flanken, kasha, rugelach, kugel mit mandlen,* milk bottles full of *borscht* and *schav*—and hot dogs and hamburgers too, and baked beans and deviled eggs, and birthday cake and candy and cream soda. It was a hot blue day, full of food.

But a four-year-old girl can only eat and drink so much...and besides, after a while the uncles all began to fall asleep on the grass, one by one, much too full to pay attention to her…and all the aunts were sitting together telling stories that didn't make any sense…and Matthew was fussing about having a "stummyache," which she felt he certainly deserved. And her parents weren't worth talking to, since whenever she tried they were busy with her infant brother or the other adults, and not really listening. So after a time she grew bored. Stuffed, but bored.

She decided that she would go and see the zoo.

She knew that Central Park had a zoo because she had been taken there once before. It was a long way from the picnic, but even so, every now and then she could hear the lions roaring, along with the distant sounds of busses and taxis and city traffic that drifted to her ears. She was sure that it would be easy to find her way if she listened for the lions.

But they eluded her, the lions and the zoo alike. Not that she was lost, no, not for a minute. She walked along enjoying herself, smiling in the sunlight, and petting all the dogs that came bouncing up to her. If their owners asked where her parents were, she pointed firmly in the direction she was going and said, "right up there," then moved on, laughing, before they had time to think about it. At every branching of the path she would stop and listen, taking whatever turn sounded like it led toward the lions. She didn't seem to be getting any closer, though, which eventually grew frustrating. It was still an adventure, still more exciting than the birthday picnic, but now it was beginning to annoy her as well.

Then she came around a bend in the path, and saw a man sitting by himself on a little bench. To her eyes he was a *very* old man, almost as old as her great-uncle Wilhelm—you could tell that by his white hair, and the deep lines around his closed eyes, and the long red blanket that his legs stretched out in front of him. She had seen other old men sitting like that. His hands were shoved deep into his coat pockets, and his face lifted to the angle of the afternoon sun.

She thought he was asleep, so she started on past him, walking quietly, so as not to wake him. But without opening his eyes or changing his position, he said in a soft, deep voice, "An exceptional afternoon to you, young miss."

Exceptional was a new word to her, and she loved new words. She turned around and replied, trying to sound as grown up as she could, "I'm very exceptional, thank you."

"And glad I am to hear it," the old man said. "Where are you off to, if I may ask?"

"I'm going to see the lions," she told him. "And the draffs. Draffs are excellent animals."

"So they are," the old man agreed. His eyes, when he opened them, were the bluest she had ever seen, so young and bright that they made the rest of him look even older. He said, "I used to ride a draff, you know, in Africa. Whenever I went shopping."

She stared at him. "You can't ride a draff. There's no place to *sit*."

"I rode way up on the neck, on a little sort of platform." The old man hadn't beckoned to her, or shifted to make room for her on the bench, but she found herself moving closer all the same. He said, "It was like being in the crow's-nest on the mast of a ship, where the lookout sits. The draff would be swaying and flowing under me like the sea, and the sky would be swaying too, and I'd hang onto the draff's neck with one hand, and wave to all the people down below with the other. It was really quite nice."

He sighed, and smiled and shook his head. "But I had to give it up, because there's no place to put your groceries on a draff. All your bags and boxes just slide right down the neck, and then the draff steps on them. Draffs have very big feet, you know."

By that time she was standing right in front of him, staring into his lined old face. He had a big, proud nose, and his eyebrows over it were all tangly. To her they looked mad at each other. He said, "After that, I did all my shopping on a rhinoceros. One thing about a rhinoceros"—and for the first time he smiled at her—"when you come into a store, people are always remarkably nice. And you can sling all your packages around the rhino's horn and carry them home that way. *Much* handier than a draff, let me tell you."

He reached up while he was talking and took an egg out of her right ear. She didn't feel it happen—just the quick brush of his long fingers, and there was the egg in his hand. She grabbed for her other ear, to see if there might be an egg in there too, but he was already taking a quarter out of that one. He seemed just as surprised as she was, saying, "My goodness, now you'll be able to buy some toast to have with your egg. Extraordinary ears you have—my word, yes." And all the time he was carrying on about the egg, he was finding all kinds of other things in her ears: seashells and more coins, a couple of marbles (which upset him—"You should *never* put marbles in your ears, young lady!"), a tangerine, and even a flower, although it looked pretty mooshed-up, which he said was from being in her ear all that time.

She sat down beside him without knowing she was sitting down. "How do you *do* that?" she asked him. "Can *I* do that? Show me!"

"With ears like those, everything is possible," the old man answered.

"Try it for yourself," and he guided her hand to a beautiful cowrie shell tucked just behind her left ear. Then he said, "I wonder...I just wonder..." And he ruffled her hair quickly and showed her a palm full of tiny silver stars. Not like the shining foil ones her preschool teacher gave out for good behavior, but glittering, sharp-pointed metal stars, as bright as anything in the sky.

"It seems your hair is talented, too. *That's* exceptional."

"More, please!" she begged him.

The old man looked at her curiously. He was still smiling, but his eyes seemed sad now, which confused her.

"I haven't given you anything that wasn't already yours," he said. "Much as I would otherwise. But *this* is a gift. From me to you. Here." He waved one hand over his open palm, and when it passed she saw a small silver figure of a horse.

She looked at it. It was more beautiful, she thought, than anything she had ever seen.

"I can keep it? Really?"

"Oh yes," he said. "I hope you will keep it always."

He put the exquisite figure in her cupped hands, and closed her fingers gently over it. She felt the curlicues of the mane, blowing in a frozen wind, against her fingertips.

"Put it in your pocket, for safekeeping, and look at it tonight before you go to bed." As she did what he told her, he said, "Now I must ask where your parents are."

She said nothing, suddenly aware how much time had passed since she had left the picnic.

"They will be looking everywhere for you," the old man said. "In fact, I think I can hear them calling you now." He cupped his hands to his mouth and called in a silly, quavering voice, "Elfrieda! *Elfrieda!* Where are you, Elfrieda?"

This made her giggle so much that it took her a while to tell him, "*That's* not my name." He laughed too, but he went on calling, "*Elfrieda! Elfrieda!*" until the silly voice became so sad and worried that she stood up and said, "Maybe I ought to go back and tell them I'm all right." The air was starting to grow a little chilly, and she was starting to be not quite sure that she knew the way back.

"Oh, I wouldn't do that," the old man advised her. "If I were you, I'd stay right here, and when they come along you could say to them, 'Why don't you sit down and rest your weary bones?' That's what *I'd* do."

The idea of saying something like that to grownups set her off giggling again, and she could hardly wait for her family to come find her. She sat down by the old man and talked with him, in the ordinary way, about school and friends and uncles, and all the ways her cousin Matthew made her mad, and about going shopping on rhinoceroses. He told her that it was always hard to find parking space for a rhino, and that they really didn't like shopping, but they would do it if they liked you. So after that they talked about how you get a rhinoceros to like you, until her father came for her on the motorcycle.

"I lost it back in college." She caressed the little object, holding it against her cheek. "I looked and looked, but I couldn't find it anywhere." She looked at him with a mix of wonder and suspicion. She fell silent then, frowning, touching her mouth. "Central Park…there was a zoo in Central Park."

The magician nodded. "There still is."

"Lions. Did they have lions?" She gave him no time to answer the question. "I do remember the lions. I heard them roaring." She spoke slowly, seeming to be addressing the silver horse more than him. "I wanted to see the lions."

"Yes," the magician said. "You were on your way there when we met."

"I remember now," she said. "How could I have forgotten?" She was speaking more rapidly as the memory took shape. "You were sitting with me on the bench, and then Daddy…Daddy came on a motorcycle. I mean, no, the *policeman* was on the motorcycle, and Daddy was in the…the sidecar thing. I remember. He was so furious with me that I was glad the policeman was there."

The magician chuckled softly. "He was angry until he saw that you were safe and unharmed. Then he was so thankful that he offered me money."

"Did he? I didn't notice." Her face felt suddenly hot with embarrassment. "I'm sorry, I didn't know he wanted to give you money. You must have felt so insulted."

"Nonsense," the magician said briskly. "He loved you, and he offered what he had. Both of us dealt in the same currency, after all."

She paused, looking around them. "This isn't the right street either. I don't see the motel."

He patted her shoulder lightly. "You will, I assure you."

"I'm not certain I want to."

"Really?" His voice seemed to surround her in the night. "And why would that be? You have a journey to continue."

The bitterness rose so fast in her throat that it almost made her throw up. "If you know my name, if you know about my family, if you know things *I'd* forgotten about, then you already know why. Alan's dead, and Talley—my Mouse, oh God, *my little Mouse*—and so am I, do you understand? I'm dead too, and I'm just driving around and around until I rot." She started to double over, coughing and gagging on the rage. "I wish I were dead with them, that's what I wish!" She would have been desperately happy to vomit, but all she could make come out were words.

Strong old hands were steadying her shoulders, and she was able, in a little time, to raise her head and look into the magician's face, where she saw neither anger nor pity. She said very quietly, "No, I'll tell you what I really wish. I wish *I* had died in that crash, and that Alan and Talley were still alive. I'd make that deal like a shot, you think I wouldn't?"

The magician said gently, "It was not your fault."

"Yes it was. It's my fault that they were in my car. I asked Alan to take it in for an oil change, and Mouse…Talley wanted to go with him. She loved it, being just herself and Daddy—oh, she used to order him around so, pretending she was me." For a moment she came near losing control again, but the magician held on, and so did she. "If I hadn't asked him to do that for me, if I hadn't been so selfish and lazy and sure I had more important things to do, then it would have been me that died in that crash, and they'd have lived. They *would* have lived." She reached up and gripped the magician's wrists, as hard as she could, holding his eyes even more intently. "You see?"

The magician nodded without answering, and they stood linked together in shadow for that moment. Then he took his hands from her shoulders and said, "So, then, you have offered to trade your life for the lives of your husband and daughter. Do you still hold to that bargain?"

She stared at him. She said, "That stupid riddle. You really *meant* that. What *are* you? Are you Death?"

"Not at all. But there are things I can do, with your consent."

"My consent." She stood back, straightening to her full height. "Alan and Talley…nobody needed *their* consent—or mine, either. I meant every word."

"Think," the magician said urgently. "I need you to know what you have asked, and the extent of what you think you mean." He raised his left hand, palm up, tapping on it with his right forefinger. "Be very careful, little girl in the park. There *are* lions."

"I know what I wished." She could feel the sidewalk coiling under her feet.

"Then know this. I can neither take life nor can I restore it, but I *can* grant your wish, exactly as it was made. You have only to say—and to be utterly certain in your soul that it *is* your true desire." He chuckled suddenly, startlingly; to her ear it sounded almost like a growl. "My, I cannot recall the last time I used that word, *soul*."

She bit her lip and wrapped her arms around herself, though the night continued warm. "What can you promise me?"

"A different reality—the exact one you prayed for just now. Do you understand me?"

"No," she said; and then, very slowly, "You mean, like running a movie backward? Back to…back to *before*?"

The old man shook his head. "No. Reality never runs backward; each thing is, and will be, as it always was. Choice is an uncommon commodity, and treasured by those few who actually have it. But there *is* magic, and magic can shuffle some possibilities like playing cards, done right. Such craft as I control will grant your wish, precisely as you spoke it. Take the horse I have returned to you back to the place where the accident happened. The *exact* place. Hold it in your hand, or carry it on your person, and take a single step. One single step. If your commitment is firm, if your choice is truly and finally made, then things as they always were will *still* be as they always were—only now, the way they always were will be forever different. Your husband and your daughter will live, because they never drove that day, and they never died. *You* did. Do you understand now?"

"Yes," she whispered. "Oh, yes, *yes*, I do understand. Please, do it, I accept, it's the only wish I have. Please, *yes*."

The magician took her hands between his own. "You are certain? You know what it will mean?"

"I can't live without them," she answered simply. "I told you. But… how—"

"Death, for all His other sterling qualities, is not terribly bright. Efficient and punctual, but not bright." The magician gave her the slightest of bows. "And I am very good with tricks. You might even say exceptional."

"Can't you just send me there, right this minute—transport me, or e-mail me or something, never mind the stupid driving. Couldn't you do that? I mean, if you can do—you know—*this*?"

He shook his head. "Even the simplest of tricks must be prepared…and this one is not simple. Drive, and I will meet you at the appointed time and place."

"Well, then." She put her hands on his arms, looking up at him as though at the sun through green leaves. "Since there are no words in the world for me to thank you with, I'm just going to go on back home. My family's waiting."

Yet she delayed, and so did he, as though both of them were foreigners fumbling through a language never truly comprehended: a language of memory and intimacy. The magician said, "You don't know why I am doing this." It was not a question.

"No. I don't." Her hesitant smile was a storm of anxious doubt. "Old times' sake?"

The magician shook his head. "It doesn't really matter. Go now."

The motel sign was as bright as the moon across the street, and she could see her car in the half-empty parking lot. She turned and walked away, without looking back, started the Buick and drove out of the lot. There was nothing else to collect. Let them wonder in the morning at her unruffled bed, and the dry towels never taken down from the bathroom rack.

The magician was plain in her rear-view mirror, looking after her, but she did not wave, or turn her head.

Free of detours, the road back seemed notably shorter than the way she had come, though she took it distinctly more slowly. The reason, to her mind, was that before she had been so completely without plans, without thought, without any destination, without any baggage but grief. Now, feeling almost pregnant with joy, swollen with eager visions—*they will live, they will, my Mouse will be a living person, not anyone's memory*—she felt a self that she had never considered or acknowledged conducting the old car, as surely as her foot on the accelerator and her hands on the wheel. A full day passed, more, and somehow she did not grow tired, which she decided must be something the magician had done, so she did not question it. Instead she sang nursery songs as she drove, and the sea chanteys and Gilbert and Sullivan that Alan had always loved. *No, not loved. Loves! Loves now, loves now and will go on loving, because I'm on my way. Alan, Talley, I'm on my way.*

For the last few hundred miles she abandoned the interstate and drove the coast road home, retracing the path she and Alan had taken at the beginning of their honeymoon. The ocean was constant on her right, the massed redwoods and hemlocks on her left, and the night air smelled both of salt and pinesap. There were deer in the brush, and scurrying foxes, and even a porcupine, shuffling and clicking across the road. Once she saw a mountain lion, or thought she had: a long-tailed shadow in a shadow, watching her shadow race past. *Darlings, on my way!*

It was near dawn when she reached the first suburbs of the city where she had gone to college, married, and settled without any control—or the desire for control—over very much of it. The city lay still as jewels before her, except when the infrequent police siren or fire-engine clamor set dogs barking in every quarter. She parked the Buick in her driveway, startled for a moment at her house's air of abandonment and desolation. *What did you expect, disappearing the way you did, and no way to contact you?* She did not try the door, but stood there for a little, listening absurdly for any sound of Alan or Talley moving in the house. Then she walked away as calmly as she had from the magician.

Six blocks, six blocks. She found the intersection where the crash had occurred. Standing on the corner angle of the sidewalk, she could see the exact smudge on the asphalt where her life had ended, and this shadowy leftover had begun. Across the way the light grew beyond the little community park, a glow as transparent as seawater. She drank it in, savoring the slow-rising smells of warming stone and suburban commuter breakfasts. *Never again…never again*, she thought. Up and down the street, cars were backing out of garages, and she found herself watching them with a strange new greed, thinking, *Alan and Mouse will see them come home again, see the geese settle in on the fake lake for the night. Not me, never again.*

The street was thickening with traffic, early as it was. She watched a bus go by, and then the same school van that always went first to the furthest developments, before circling back to pick up Talley and others who lived closer to school. *He's not here yet*, she thought, fingering the silver horse in her pocket. *I could take today. One day—one day only, just to taste it all, to go to all the places we were together, to carry that with me when I step across that pitiful splotch—tomorrow? My darlings will have all the other days, all their lives…couldn't I have just the one? I'd be right back here at dawn, all packed to leave—surely they wouldn't mind, if they knew? Just the one.*

Behind her, the magician said, "As much as you have grieved for them, so they will mourn you. You say your life ended here; they will say the same, for a time."

Without turning, she said, "You can't talk me out of this."

A dry chuckle. "Oh, I've suspected that from the beginning."

She did turn then, and saw him standing next to her: unchanged, but for a curious dusk, bordering on tenderness, in the old, old eyes. His face was neither pitying nor unkind, nor triumphant in its foreknowledge, but urgently attentive in the way of a blind person. "There she was, that child in Central Park, stumping along, so fierce, so determined, going off all alone to find the lions. There was I, half-asleep in the sun on my park bench…"

"I don't understand," she said. "Please. Before I go, tell me who you are."

"You know who I am."

"I don't!"

"You did. You will."

She did not answer him. In silence, they both turned their heads to follow a young black man walking on the other side of the street. He was carrying an infant—a boy, she thought—high in his arms, his round dark face brilliant with pride, as though no one had ever had a baby before. The man and child were laughing together: the baby's laughter a shrill gurgle, the father's almost a song. Another bus hid them for a moment, and when it passed they had turned a corner and disappeared.

The magician said, "Yet despite your certainty you were thinking, unless I am mistaken, of delaying your bargain's fulfillment."

"One day," she said softly. "Only to say goodbye. To remind myself of them and everything we had, before giving it all up. Would that…would it be possible? Or would it break the…the spell? The charm?"

The magician regarded her without replying immediately, and she found that she was holding her breath.

"It's neither of those. It's just a trick, and not one that can wait long on your convenience." His expression was inflexible.

"Oh," she said. "Well. It would have been nice, but there—can't have everything. Thank you, and goodbye again."

She waited until the sparse morning traffic was completely clear. Then deliberately, and without hesitation, she stepped forward into the street. She was about to move further when she heard the magician's voice behind her. "Sunset. That is the best I can do."

She wheeled, her face a child's face, alight with holiday. "*Thank* you! I'll be back in time, I promise! Oh, *thank* you!"

Before she could turn again the magician continued, in a different voice, "I have one request." His face was unchanged, but the voice was that of a much younger man, almost a boy. "I have no right to ask, no claim on you—but I would feel privileged to spend these hours in your company." He might have been a shy Victorian, awkwardly inviting a girl to tea.

She stared back at him, her face for once as unreadable as his. It was a long moment before she finally nodded and beckoned to him, saying, "Come on, then—there's so little time. Come on!"

In fact, whether or not it was due to his presence, there was time enough. She reclaimed the Buick and drove them first up into the hills, to watch the rest of dawn play itself out over the city as she told him stories of her life there. Then they joined an early morning crowd of parents and preschoolers in the local community playground. She introduced the magician to her too-solicitous friends as a visiting uncle from Alan's side of the family, and tried to maintain some illusion of the muted grief she knew they expected of her; an illusion which very nearly shattered with laughter when the magician took a ride with some children on a miniature train, his knees almost up to his ears. After that she brought them back down to the bald flatlands near the freeway, to the food bank where she had worked twice a week, and where she was greeted with cranky affection by old black Baptist women who hugged her and warned her that she needn't be coming round so soon, but if she was up to it, well, tomorrow was likely to be a particularly heavy day, and Lord knows they could use the extra hand. The magician saw the flash of guilt and sorrow in her eyes, but no one else did. She promised not to be late.

Time enough. They parked the car and took a ferry across the bay to the island where she had met Alan when they were both dragged along on a camping trip, and where she and Alan and Talley had picnicked often after Talley was born. Here she found herself chattering to the magician compulsively, telling him how Alan had cured their daughter of her terror of water by coaxing her to swim sitting up on his back, pretending she was riding a dolphin. "She's become a wonderful swimmer now, Mouse has, you should see her. I mean, I guess you *will* see her—anyway you *could* see her. I won't, but if you wanted to…" Her voice drifted away, and the magician touched her hand without replying.

"We have to watch the clock," she said. "I wouldn't want to miss my death." It was meant as a joke, but the magician did not laugh.

Time enough. Her vigilance had them back at the house well before sunset, after a stop at her family's favorite ice-cream shop for cones: coffee for herself—"Double scoop, what the hell?"—and strawberry, after much deliberation, for the magician. They were still nibbling them when they reached the front door.

"God, I'll miss coffee," she said, almost dreamily; then laughed. "Well, I guess I won't, will I? I mean, I won't know if I miss it or not, after all." She glanced critically up at the magician beside her. "You've never eaten an ice-cream cone before, have you?"

The magician shook his head solemnly. She took his cone from him and licked carefully around the edges, until the remaining ice-cream was more or less even; then handed it back to him, along with her own napkin. "We should finish before we go in. Come on." She devoted herself to devouring the entire cone, crunching it up with a voracity matching the sun's descent.

When she was done she used her key to open the door, and stepped inside. She was halfway down the front hall, almost to the living room, when she realized the magician had not followed.

"Hey," she called to him. "Aren't you coming?"

"I thank you for the day, but this moment should be yours alone. I will wait outside. You needn't hurry," he said, glancing at the sky. "But don't dawdle, either."

With that he closed the door, leaving her to the house and her memories.

Half an hour later, six blocks away, she stood slightly behind him on the sidewalk and studied the middle of the intersection. He did not offer his hand, but she lifted it in both of hers anyway. "You are very kind."

He shook his head ruefully. "Less than you imagine. Far less than I wish."

"Don't give me that." Her tone was dismissive, but moderated with a chuckle. "You were waiting for me. You said so. I would have bumped into you wherever I drove, wouldn't I? If I'd gone south to Mexico, or gotten on a plane to Honolulu or Europe, sooner or later, when I was ready to listen to what you had to say, when I was ready to make this deal, I'd have walked into a restaurant with a sign for Dinner Magic. Right?"

"Not quite. You could only have gone the way you went, and I could only have met you there. Each thing is, and will be, as it always was. I told you that."

"I don't care. I'm still grateful. I'm still saying thanks."

The magician said softly, "Stay."

She shook her head. "You know I can't."

"This trick...this misdirection...I can't promise you what it will buy. Your husband and daughter will live, but for how long cannot be known by anyone. They might be killed tomorrow by another stupid, sleepy driver—a virus, a plane crash, a madman with a gun. What you are giving up for them could be utterly useless, utterly pointless, by next sunrise. Stay—do not waste this moment of your own choice, your own power. *Stay.*"

He reached out for her, but she stepped away, backing into the street so suddenly that a driver honked angrily at her as he sped by. She said, "Everything you say is absolutely true, and none of it matters. If all I could give them was one single extra second, I would."

The old man's face grew gentle. "Ah. You are indeed as I remembered. Very well, then. I had to offer you a choice. You have chosen love, and I have no complaint, nor would it matter if I did. In this moment you are the magician, not I."

"All right, then. Let's do this."

The huge red sun was dancing on tiptoe on a green horizon, but she waited until the magician nodded before she started toward the intersection. Traffic had grown so heavy that there was no way for her to reach the stain that was Alan and Talley's fading memorial. The magician raised his free hand, as though waving to her, and the entire lane opened up, cars and drivers frozen in place, leaving her free passage to where she needed to be. Over her shoulder she said, "Thank you," and stepped forward.

The little girl shook her head and looked around herself. She was confused by what she saw, and if anyone in the park other than the old man had been watching, they would have wondered at the oddly adult way that she stood still and regarded her surroundings.

"Hello," the magician said to her.

"This…isn't what I expected."

"No. The audience sees a woman cut in half, while the two women folded carefully within separate sections of the magic box experience it quite differently. You're in the trick now, so of course things are different than you expected. It's hardly magic if you can guess in advance how it's done."

She looked at her small hands in amazement, then down the short length of her arms and legs. "I *really* don't understand. You said I would die."

"And so you will, on the given day and at the given time, when you think about asking your husband to take care of your oil change for you and then decide—in a flickering instant, quite without knowing why—that you should do this simple errand yourself, instead." He looked enormously sad as he spoke. "And you will die now, in a different way, because that one deeply buried flicker is the only hint of memory you may keep. You won't remember this day, or the gifts I will give you, or me. The trick won't work, otherwise. Death may not be bright, but he's not stupid, either—all the cards have to go back in the deck, or he *will* notice. But if you and I, between us, subtly mark one of the cards…that should slip by. Just."

He stopped speaking; and for a little it seemed to the woman in the girl, staring into the finality of his face as though into a dark wood, that he might never again utter a word. Then he sighed deeply. "I told you I wasn't kind."

She reached up to touch his cheek, her eyes shining. "No one could possibly be kinder. You've not only granted my wish, you're telling me I'll get to see them again. That I'll meet Alan again, and fall in love again, and hold my little Mouse in my arms, exactly as before. That *is* what you are saying, isn't it?"

He held both his hands wide, elegant fingers cupped to catch the sun. "You are that child in Central Park, off to see the lions. And I am an old man, half-asleep on a bench…from this point on the world proceeds just as it ever was, and only one thing, quite a bit ahead of today and really not worth talking about, will be any different. Please look in your pocket, child."

She reached into the front of her denim coverall, then, and smiled when she felt her four-year-old hand close around the silver horse. She took it out, and held it up to him as if she were offering a piece of candy.

"I don't know who you are, but I know what you are. You're something good."

"Nonsense," he said, but she could see he looked pleased. "And now…" The magician placed his vast, lined hands around hers, squeezed once, gently, and said "*Forget.*" When he took his hands away the silver horse was gone.

The little girl stood on the green grass, looking up at the old man with the closed eyes. He spoke to her. "Where are you off to, if I may ask?"

"I'm going to see the lions," she told him. "And the draffs. Draffs are excellent animals."

"So they are," the old man agreed, tilting his head down to look at her. His eyes, when he opened them, were the bluest she had ever seen.

THE PRETENDERS' TOURNEY

DANIEL ABRAHAM

The serfs and peasants of Castrwick said a star had fallen from Heaven. Or an angel. The night had gone bright as an instant of noon. The thunder of it left the church bells chiming as if they'd been struck. A plague-blinded baby regained her sight by being bathed in that divine light, so they said.

Now, only a light rain fell, dotting the heather with silver. A dozen local men, their caps in their hands, stood around the three nobles who had come from Westford Keep: Dafyd's mother, the newly widowed Dowager Duchess; his childhood friend Rosmund Colp, fourth son of Lord Andigent and now family priest of Westford; and Dafyd himself, once the youngest son of Westford, and now by grace of God its Duke.

"It *might* be miraculous," Rosmund said.

The wound in the land gaped wider than a man's height and three times as long. The stone itself rested on a rough pallet of cut saplings.

"Of course it is," Dafyd's mother said. "It fell from Heaven as a sign from God."

Rosmund looked at his knees, his wide brow taking on the furrows they always did when the Duchess started declaiming upon the Divine.

Dafyd dropped to the ground and walked closer. The village men, once his father's property and now his own, stepped aside to let him pass. Their gazes never rose above his knee and none of them spoke, but something in the way they held themselves crackled with excitement. Dafyd had seen boys no more than ten stand the same way just before a children's melee, but these were men. Gray-haired, some of them. It struck him again that he was the youngest person present.

Black as soot, the stone was shapeless as a blighted apple. The word of God made stone: twisted, diseased, ambiguous.

"It's good iron, that," one of the men behind him said.

Dafyd turned to him. A broad-shouldered man, missing his lower teeth, his hands were knobbed with muscle and his arms were both wider than the young man's thigh. He could have broken Dafyd over his knee like a twig, but instead he blushed under his gaze and looked ashamed for having spoken. Dafyd tried to recall the man's name. Herdlick, he thought. Or that might have been the smith at the next village on. His father would have known.

"If you please, sir," he said toward Dafyd's feet.

"We shall have a new blade forged," the Duchess said. Her eyes were bright as candles. "A new blade for a new age."

The subtle sound came, barely audible over the tapping of raindrops, of a dozen men taking in a breath at once. Nothing, Dafyd thought, suited his mother as well as theater, and the weight of her drama settled across his shoulders like a yoke. Anger crawled up his throat, and he spoke more sharply than he intended to.

"There isn't time. We leave for court in a fortnight."

"It will be done, my lord," the smith who might have been Herdlick said. His face was round as the moon and as bright. "I ain't a sword-smith by trade. That was Ableson, and him plague-took. But I know as much as anyone in the Duchy and, by my honor, my lord, if I have to kill myself and both my 'prentices doing it, it'll be in your hand when that day comes."

That day. The words nipped Dafyd's belly like bad meat.

"It is the will of God," his mother said. Dafyd stepped back to his horse, heaved himself up into the saddle, and pulled her head back toward the path more roughly than she deserved. He felt an instant stab of regret.

Rosmund and his slow nag caught up with Dafyd before the first turning. They rode for half a mile in silence. The rain grew harder, the low gray sky more nearly the color of steel.

"I'm not sure running off helps," Rosmund said.

"I'm not running," Dafyd said. "And a fat lot of good you were."

"What did you want me to say? That stones fall from the sky all the time?"

"You could have said that being odd doesn't make something holy. Or that it was an omen that I *shouldn't* be king," Dafyd said. "The best you could offer was it *might* be miraculous?"

"Well, it might."

"Or?"

Rosmund shrugged. The rain had plastered his hair to his skull. He looked like a drowned cat.

"Or it might not," he said. "But that's not the question. Is it?"

The plague had come in late summer, seven weeks before the harvest. It began as a cough, and then a fever. Those who fell before it took to their beds. Two days after the first cough, the fever began to rise and fall, and the ill lost their minds. Many were tormented by dreams of demons lurking in the shadows. Some were possessed by lust.

At five days, their joints swelled and ached. At six, some respite came; lucidity returned, joints moved more freely, fever cooled. On the seventh day, just as the power of the illness seemed broken, they died. A glimmer of hope before the grave, a small added cruelty that made mere tragedy into something worse. Dafyd's infant sister had even taken milk once—the first in days—before her tiny lips stilled.

Some villages lost only one or two people. Others were killed to the last man. Plague-death struck where it struck and passed over the houses it passed with a will of its own.

It took the Duke of Westford, silencing his cool wit and ending forever his warm embraces and drunken midwinter songs. It took Dafyd's sister, Ydel, before she could walk or speak; her toothless grin gone still. It took his eldest brother, fair-eyed Racian, who Dafyd had grown up believing to be invincible. It took his older brother, Caersin, from his library at seminary. It took the family tutor, the dancing master, and twenty servants.

It spared the Duchess, though the grief released a religious fervor that had survived through twenty-five years of marriage to the Duke. Dafyd suffered no cough, no fever, no delirium or swollen hands.

How much of him had survived was an open question.

Riding back now, Rosmund at his side, the lethal season they had left behind showed in small ways. Here a field lay fallow, all the hands that worked it the year before now lying beneath it. There, a dyer's yard with windows stopped up with wooden planks and jute to keep out snow long since melted. The smiles and bows offered by the men and women they passed showed ghosts behind the eyes. No one was untouched.

Both of the princes had also died, and the king's brother, Lord Saratyn. They said the king died at midnight on the longest night of the year, but that seemed too poetic to be true. Even as the plague went on its deadly way, the Council Regent studied the genealogies and precedents, argued points of law and cited examples of succession. At the first thaw, they agreed that the impasse could not be settled by mortal means.

The debate hinged on whether the ascendance of King Abdemar of Essen three hundred years before had been legitimate or not, and reasonable men could have different opinions on the subject. If it had been, then, by its precedent, Sir Ursin Palliot, Duke of Lakefell and Warden of the South, was the royal cousin set to inherit the throne.

If it had not, then Westford ascended, and by the grace of the God who had slaughtered his family, Dafyd Laician would become king.

And God, so the Council Regent said, was to answer the question in His traditional manner: trial by combat. Whose arm He lent strength would be king.

"It isn't as simplistic as you make it sound," Rosmund said.

"No?" Dafyd asked.

"Of course not."

In the privacy of the Ducal stead, a dry cassock and his hair only damp and both Duchess and laity safely distant, Rosmund looked more like a priest. The fire burning in the grate pushed back the spring chill and filled the room with the smell of pine sap and smoke, driving out the scent of rain. Rosmund poured himself another cup of wine as he spoke.

"There are also political considerations. Lord Palliot is willing to set aside the cane field grants that Earl Haver wants, and so Haver is against you. Our former King, God keep him, had fallen three years behind in paying tithes. The bishop knows you and I are on good terms, and suddenly he's moved to write an opinion that the Essen ascension was based on scriptural misreading."

"Money and ambition, then. I don't find that comforting."

Rosmund drank the wine, his throat working with each swallow. The cup clicked against the table.

"I think you're underestimating the comfort money and ambition can bring," he said contemplatively, and the door behind him burst open.

"You are never," the Duchess said, storming into the room, "*never* to disgrace this family that way again."

The words struck her son like a slap.

"Disgrace?" Dafyd said, rising to his feet. "You spout the will of God like a zealot! Fine. But don't pretend that I have to carry it."

Her cheeks were red and thick, her lips almost blue, and her hands balled in fists. Rosmund poured himself a fresh cup of wine as they shouted.

"You run off like a little boy whenever you're…"

"Like it or not, Mother, I am Duke of Westford now, and if you…"

"…faced with the reality of God's presence. Well it…"

"…feel that you've become a prophet of God…"

"…might have been charming when you were a *child*, but…"

"…you can tell Him that I have no use for…"

Rosmund made a slurping sound. They both wheeled on him, chests working like bellows. He looked up at them, wide-eyed.

"Sorry," he said.

"Dafyd," the Duchess said, her voice quieter now, but sharp. "Every man in that field was looking to you, and you disappointed them. And me. And your father. Never do it again."

She wheeled before he could answer and swept from the room, slamming the door behind her. Dafyd said something obscene. Rosmund shrugged, refusing even in her absence, to cross the woman.

"*Hypocrite*," Dafyd said, accusing the closed door she'd passed through. "Says I'm acting like a child the same breath that I'm to do exactly what my mother tells me? She will never listen."

"Well. When you're king, maybe," Rosmund said.

Dafyd threw a cup at his head.

The journey to Cyninghalm could have been no more than a dozen days, but the weight of ceremony and allegiance slowed them to a crawl. The wide road, centuries old and still as solid as the day the stones were set, filled around their carts and carriages. Knights on huge warhorses waited at every crossroads, ready to join their banners to Westford's own. High lords and low fell in behind them wearing enameled armor so light and gaudy Dafyd couldn't help but think of beetles. As they passed, the trees themselves seemed to bow to them.

To him.

And with every league he traveled, his own robes and the black-and-silver of his court armor seemed more ridiculous. With every night's camp spent presiding over the grand pavilion, with every beery, weeping man laced into his best tournament silk, Dafyd felt more a pretender.

"He was a great man, your da," the Earl of Anmuth said. "A *great* man."

"Thank you," Dafyd said.

The old man bent back his head, gold beard shot with gray pointing toward the moon. Tears ran from his rheumy eyes, and his voice was thick with phlegm and sorrow.

"I was there the day he bested Easin's three top fighters. You wouldn't have been born then, but God, it was a day. Your da, he was brilliant. And after, when he took us all aside and swore that we… that we…"

He sobbed. The others—there must have been a dozen men in the pavilion, even that late—watched as if Dafyd were the entertainment. He set his jaw and prayed the old idiot would pass out. Anmuth wiped his eyes with the back of one wide, meaty hand, then leaned close. His breath smelled like the wind from a brewery.

"Lord Bessin came to me," he said softly. "Ass-licker offered to make me Warden of Rivers if I threw in with Palliot. Told him I'd rather muck stables. And I would, too. I would."

Dafyd nodded solemnly. The old man's bleary gaze locked on his, waiting for Dafyd to speak. He didn't know what he was expected to say. *Thank you* or *I will be avenged.*

"My father would appreciate that," he said. "He always counted you among his most trusted friends."

It might have been true, for all Dafyd could say. It sounded kind enough. New tears welled up in Anmuth's eyes and spilled down his cheeks. His beard squeezed together, completely obscuring his lips. He nodded once, clapped Dafyd on the shoulder, and walked unsteadily away.

Dafyd waited, troubled by something he couldn't quite express. The moon made its slow arc across the dark sky. Musicians played on flute and tambour. A minstrel declaimed the story of King Almad and the Dragon, which Dafyd had sat through unmoved a thousand times before. But when King Almad ascended to Heaven *this* time, he felt his throat thickening and his eyes tearing up. His brothers would have laughed.

And through it all, something Anmuth said bothered him like a stone in his boot. It wasn't until he lay down to sleep that he knew what it was.

Rosmund's tent wasn't quite as overbuilt as his own, but it still had its own framed door and walls too thick for sound to pass through easily. Dafyd shook the priest's door servant—a thin-framed boy in a cheap, greasy cassock—awake, and waited no more than a minute before Rosmund opened the door and waved him in. Rosmund wore a thick cotton night dress unlaced down the front, and his hair stood at a hundred different angles.

"Long time since we kept a midnight meeting," he said, and yawned. "We would have been twelve, I think."

"Are we alone?"

His bleary eyes sharpened.

"No," he said, "but she's well asleep, and I'd rather not wake her."

"Be sure," Dafyd said.

Rosmund went through the thick leather flap of the tent's interior wall and door. The Duke sat on a tapestried cushion until the priest came back.

"Snoring deeply," Rosmund said. "What's the matter?"

"Why is Lord Bessin trying to get men to side with Palliot?" Dafyd asked. "Trial by arms isn't about who's cheering or where they sit."

Rosmund shrugged and waited for Dafyd to tell him. They had known one another too long.

"Allies don't help in single combat," Dafyd said. "They're very useful in a war. I don't think my lord the Duke is going to accept a loss."

Rosmund's eyebrows rose toward his hairline. He whistled low, soft and appreciative.

"Insurrection. That would be a very, very stupid thing to do."

"You think I'm wrong then?"

"No," he said. "I think grief drives people mad, and anything, no matter how ill-advised, becomes possible."

"Grief?"

"Look around. The kingdom's caught a fever, and it's touched everyone. Not just you."

A soft wind shook the thick leather walls. The candle flickered and the woman in the next room murmured something inchoate.

"I'm not at issue here. We're talking about civil war," Dafyd said, his voice cool.

"We're talking about mastering a world that's just shown everyone that it will take everything from them anytime it wishes," Rosmund said, his voice growing deep and passionate in a way it rarely did when speaking at the pulpit.

"I don't…" Dafyd began, but Rosmund talked over him.

"Your mother's turned to piety and prayer. Bessin and Palliot have turned to intrigue. I've turned to sex. Back to sex. These are different dressings on the same wound. The plague reminded us that we're powerless, and now we're trying to forget."

"This isn't about the plague," Dafyd said.

"Of course it is."

"It's *not!*"

Rosmund looked down, lips pressed tight.

"I didn't come here to talk about the plague or God or the wounds of the kingdom," Dafyd said, venom in his voice. "I came because I thought of all the men I know, I could tell my suspicions to you. That you would *listen*."

They were silent for a moment.

"And didn't I?" Rosmund asked.

A woman's voice came, slushy and warm and dazed.

"Love? Did something happen?"

"Nothing, sweet thing," Rosmund said. "It's nothing. A bad dream."

Dafyd gathered himself to leave, but Rosmund put a hand on his arm. His touch was gentle and familiar, and Dafyd had to force himself not to push it away.

"You weren't like this before the plague," Rosmund said.

"Like what?"

"Angry. Afraid," he said. And then, "You didn't whine as much."

Sleep didn't come easily. In the privacy of his imagination, Dafyd told Rosmund exactly why the priest was an idiot. He dressed down his mother and her overbearing piety. He confronted Lord Bessin and Duke Palliot. His words unanswerable and his logic profound, his opponents abased themselves before him. The rage that kept the Duke from rest didn't cool.

He lay in the darkness of his bed until the quiet murmurs of the guards changed and the first, tentative songs that the birds sang before first light began. He would have said sleep had never come had a rough voice not wakened him.

"The Duchess sent for you. It's here, my lord," the servant said.

The Duke sat up, field bed creaking under him. His eyes felt too large for their sockets, and more than his weight pulled him back toward the bed.

"What's come?"

The pause lasted less than a heartbeat. The answer came with barely hidden awe.

"The *blade*," the servant said.

A chill mist clung to the ground. The Duchess, wearing a high-collared black dress with a thin silver chain around her neck, stood waiting in the camp's main yard. Beside her, the blacksmith knelt. He looked sick with fatigue; pale skin, bloodshot eyes, and a looseness in his spine that left Dafyd afraid the man would collapse on the spot. Westford's men and allies stood arrayed behind them in an eerie silence. He didn't see Rosmund anywhere. As he walked toward the assembly, it occurred to him exactly how he would look; mist at his ankles, the risen sun shining off his face. It couldn't have been better staged if it had been a theater piece.

With a visible effort, the blacksmith pulled himself straight and held out a sheathed blade.

"Damn near killed us, my lord," he said. "But we got it done."

Dafyd felt a moment's sympathy for the man and his apprentices. The smith had truly done himself damage, and he at least believed it was for the Duke. The Duchess might have smiled, or Dafyd might only have imagined it. He couldn't answer the smith's loyalty to Dafyd's father with rudeness again. The Duchess had known he couldn't.

Dafyd nodded gravely and took the scabbard. There were tears in the smith's eyes. His huge hands shook. Dafyd drew the sword. The best blades sing when they pull free. This one didn't. Dafyd tapped the fresh metal against its scabbard, and it clanked like a metal stick. There was no groove down the center. When he pressed against the flat, it barely flexed at all. The edge was sharp enough, but the blade was ill-balanced and brittle. He had seen boys at play with better.

In deep, stark letters, the smith had engraved *God's Will* into the blade.

"Westford!" someone cried. "Westford and Honor! Westford and *God!*"

The men took up the call, pumping their fists and shouting at the morning sun. Dafyd looked at his mystical and blessed blade, hardly better than pot metal. With this he was supposed to win the crown. With this, they wanted him to best Palliot and then most likely lead them into civil war. With this, they wanted him to heal the kingdom. To avenge his father against God. To make all wrong things right.

They might as well have asked him to put his heels against the sky and lift the world.

The first time Dafyd had gone to court, he was just past his seventh birthday. Cyninghalm had been a name to conjure with: the high court, foundation of the kingdom, center of the world. For weeks before, he had dreamed of silvered spires and vast, exotic gardens. The truth was grayer and squat. The great men and women of the court turned out to be much like the people in Westford, but less impressed by his father's status. While grand, and some truly beautiful, no buildings matched the stories he'd conjured about them. Likely nothing could.

This time, he saw graves.

They began five miles from the city walls, the freshest first. Wide fields with headstones like rough, demonic teeth. Turned earth as long as a man or a woman or, more often, a child. With each mile, the graves themselves showed their age by the height of the grass upon them. By the time he saw the rising hill and the city upon it glowing in the afternoon sun, he had left the evidence of the winter's plague behind.

Still, he didn't know how deeply the honor guard of the dead had shaken him until his company passed through the city gates to the flowers and gaudy cloth of the tourney festival. The local folk thronged the streets; they shouted and smiled and sang the praises of God and Westford. He knew they had done the same for Palliot three days before. The new and rightful king had come to Cyninghalm, and only a few people seemed uneasy not to know when precisely it had happened.

Dafyd watched their faces as they passed. Ruddy, laughing, sometimes grinning through tears. The crowds followed him from the city gates, up three hills, to the inner wall, and then to the palace itself. Men and women he didn't know, had never seen, shouting and waving and begging that he should bless them. Dafyd washed through the city on a flood of something that another man at another time might have mistaken for love. Rosmund had known its real name. It might have worn its particolored clothes, but grief was still grief.

The tourney itself had begun a week before; jousts and melees, archery and axe throwing, song and strife and games of honor. A minor knight with third-hand armor stunned the court by beating Sir Laren Esterbrand. Corriot Mander of Evenhall had worn a token from another man's wife into the melee. Sir Ander Anson's lance had shattered in his first tilt on the jousting grounds, and a splinter of it had pierced his leg; the funeral would come tomorrow. Between the ceremonies of welcome and the press of court followers anxious to ingratiate themselves to the Duke of Westford and claimant to the throne, it was after nightfall before Dafyd went hunting Lord Bessin.

Trials by combat were held at the court within the court, a great hall with tiered benches six deep around a tile-marked square in the central floor and a ceiling so dark and high that, in the torchlight, it might have been the sky. Two men in light chain with blunt swords grunted and shoved in the square. Perhaps a hundred men watched and called out encouragement or derision. Bessin sat alone at the lowest tier, near to the combatants.

A smaller man than Dafyd remembered, Bessin was gray at the temples with a sharp beard and bright, foxlike eyes. A tip of pink tongue wetted his lips and he sat forward, leaning in toward the spectacle.

"A word, my lord?" Dafyd said.

Bessin's smile didn't falter. No hint of unease touched his eyes. It was enough to make Dafyd wonder if he had been wrong. On the court, the smaller knight disengaged, backing perilously close to the border mark.

"Westford," Bessin said. "I heard you'd come. I trust the journey wasn't too arduous."

"Weather was good," Dafyd said, sitting beside him. "Too much company, though. I travel better light."

Lord Bessin made a companionable sound in his throat. The larger knight swung a few low, testing blows. The smaller opponent tried to dodge around to the relative safety of the center. His face, toward Dafyd, was flushed and sweat-soaked and chagrined.

"I need to talk to him," Dafyd said. "Now. Before the trial."

Bessin forgot the battle on the floor and turned his attention to Dafyd. The polite veneer gone, suspicion took its place.

"I don't know who you mean," Bessin said.

"Yes, you do. Everyone knows you're running his errands. You can stop it now. Just tell him that a private word with me will make his life easier."

The larger knight made his move. Roaring like a bear, he charged. The smaller man raised his shield, only to have it batted away. The two armored bodies came together with a crash. The crowd rose to its feet around Dafyd and Bessin as the smaller knight bent slowly backward, heels just inside of the border mark and struggling not to take a single step back. Even as close as they sat, the howl of voices almost drowned out Bessin's words. The two of them might have been alone.

"Without an assurance of his safety," Bessin said carefully, "my lord Palliot would be a fool to be in private with his rival for the throne."

"If I wanted to assassinate him, I wouldn't come to his known ally and ask for an audience."

"No?" Bessin said. "And how *would* you assassinate Lord Palliot?"

The smaller knight grunted, screamed, and dropped twisting to his knees. Suddenly off-balance, the larger opponent windmilled his arms and stumbled forward. His foot passed the border mark, and the smaller man leaped up, mailed fists raised in victory. The crowd erupted in cheers and derision.

"I'll provide a hostage," Dafyd said. "Tell Palliot to come to the winter garden at moonset. He can bring as many men as he likes, but tell him to bring only the ones he trusts."

Dafyd walked away before Bessin could respond. His heart raced and his hands shook.

He found Rosmund in a fire circle, clapping and singing along as women in too little clothing danced through the flames. Dafyd put his hand on the priest's shoulder.

"I need a favor," he whispered. Rosmund lost the beat, then stopped clapping.

"What's the matter?"

"I need a favor," Dafyd said again.

Rosmund broke away from the circle and followed him into darkness without word or question, and Dafyd loved him for it.

The winter garden spread out at the southern edge of the palace, wide paths of stone and gravel winding through low hedge and dwarf trees all within webwork walls of glass and iron. Dafyd's father had said the king could grow iris and rose in it all year round, but there were no blooms now. The still air smelled of rotting plants and soil. The two sat on a low stone bench lit by a single candle as the crescent moon slipped below the distant, dark horizon. The pale flicker of lamp light came from a darkened arch, growing steadily brighter. Bessin and five men in the colors of his house approached.

The Duke stood.

"This is the hostage?" Bessin asked.

"Apparently so," Rosmund said.

"If you will join us, father," Bessin said.

Rosmund stood, took a long, deep breath, and met Dafyd's gaze with an expression both skeptical and determined.

"It'll be fine," Dafyd said.

"I'm reassured."

Bessin, Rosmund, and the men at arms walked away together, vanishing under the archway. Dafyd didn't sit. A moment later, Palliot appeared with three swordsmen behind him. The guards stopped short; Palliot came on, his steps slow and wary. He was a tall man, broad across the shoulder. His jaw ran toward jowls though he wasn't more than three years older than Dafyd. His fair hair was pulled back and his dark eyes shifted through the darkness.

"Duke Palliot."

"Westford," he replied with a small but formal bow. "You wanted words."

"Yes," Dafyd said, then took a deep breath. "The kingdom's in pain. It needs a king strong enough to hold it together while the wounds knit."

"It does," Palliot said, as if answering an accusation.

"You should do it."

Palliot crossed his arms, head cocked as if he'd heard an unfamiliar sound.

"You're forfeiting the trial?"

"Not that. I can't. There are too many people who back me for my father's sake," Dafyd said. "If we don't go through with it, there'll be talk that your rule isn't legitimate. I can't forfeit. But I can lose."

"Lose," Palliot repeated.

"A few good blows for each of us for the sake of form. I'll come too near the border mark, and you'll knock me over it. I'll swear my fealty to you, and no one need ever doubt it was a fair fight."

"And in return you want… what?"

Dafyd laughed, surprised by the bitterness in the sound.

"The last year undone," he said. "I want the dead alive. I want the graves undug. I want God to say it was a mistake and that He takes it back. But failing that, I want it to be *your* problem and not mine."

Somewhere in the speech, tears had stolen into his eyes, and he wiped them away with a sleeve. Palliot was quiet for a long moment.

"You'd give up your honor? This trial isn't to the death."

"Yes, it is," he said. "If not on the court, then in the field. Let's not pretend otherwise."

The larger man laughed. Dafyd thought there was relief in it.

"You're wiser than I expected," Palliot said, his eyes still narrow and his voice cautious.

"We understand one another, then?" Dafyd said.

Palliot was silent for longer than Dafyd liked, the dark eyes searching the empty air before the man grunted.

"Will you swear to it before God?" Palliot asked.

It was all Dafyd could do not to laugh.

"If you'd like," he said. "I swear before God."

"Then I do as well," Palliot said, and held out his hand. Dafyd took it. Palliot had an impressive grip.

They stood together for a moment, and then Dafyd watched Palliot walk back to his men, head held high. Silently, they vanished into the shadows, leaving him to sit on the bench. Someone approached, gravel complaining at each footstep. And then a wet sound, and Rosmund said something obscene.

"You're well?" Dafyd asked as his friend sat beside him. Rosmund's right leg was caked to the ankle with a greenish muck.

"Ruined my hose," he said ruefully. "And you?"

"I said what I came to say."

"Well, I'm pleased they didn't kill me over it."

The single candle flickered, then stood straight again. The air wasn't particularly cold, but Dafyd was shivering.

"Rosmund, can I ask you something?"

"As a friend or a priest?"

"Priest."

"Anything you like, my child," he said, only half-mocking. Dafyd took a long, slow breath.

"Does God have a plan for us?"

"I assume so. Everyone seems to think He does."

"I believe God is evil," Dafyd said. It was the first time he had said the words aloud, and he felt the air itself clear when he said them.

"Is that why you're conspiring to lose the trial?" Rosmund asked, his voice as comfortable as if they'd been discussing nothing more than food or which girls were prettiest. "To take the decision away from Him?"

"I suppose so."

"It won't work. It can't. Whatever happens tomorrow will have been God's will," Rosmund said. "You win? God did it. Palliot? God will have done that too. You both fall down when you step on the court and stub your toes too badly to walk? Still God."

"I'll know," Dafyd said. "That's enough."

"What if ceding to Palliot was God's plan all along? How would you know?"

Dafyd growled, a small noise in the back of his throat. Rosmund didn't seem to hear it.

"It doesn't matter whether God is good or God is evil," the priest went on. "It doesn't even matter if God is God. As long as He's a tale told after the fact, He's inevitable. You *can't* beat Him."

"Watch me," Dafyd said.

"Listen to me. As a priest, I'm telling you the dice are shaved. The cards are marked. Good or evil or a fairy story grown fat on too many tellings, it doesn't matter. Even if there is no God, He *will* win."

Dafyd Laician, Duke of Westford, spent the following day in one of two equally placed couches overlooking the melee field. Grass still clung to the margins, but days of battles and games had reduced the center to mud. There were four combats planned: a children's melee at dawn, a battle of ten against ten with maces and flails, a great battle of twenty to a side in the early afternoon, and the generally comic infirm melee at evening where the wounded and spent of the previous days' games took the field in splints and bandages.

His mother had arranged to have the sword *God's Will* hung behind his chair and draped with cloth-of-gold. If she hadn't sat beside him the whole day through, he would have taken the thing down. Across the field, Palliot sat in a seat that mirrored his. For all the battles and entertainments, more eyes were on the pair of them than the field. Only when Sir Emund Loak, having survived the blow that caved in his armor, died when his breastplate's straps were cut did the drama of the day turn from the succession. And then only briefly.

Night came with a great feast. Some master of entertainments with an overactive sense of humor placed the high table crosswise from its usual orientation, with Palliot on one end and Dafyd at the other, the court etiquette fashion of asking *which is the king?*

Dafyd retired to his rooms early, claiming the need to rest and prepare for the next day's trial. Palliot did the same. There would be time enough for wine and song when the succession was decided.

A fire burned low in the grate, red coals casting dim shadows on the walls. The air stifled, and rather than call for a servant, Dafyd opened the window shutters himself and stood in the cool air, watching the stars in the sky and the lights of the palace wink at each other.

The door opened behind him, then shut.

"Will you pray with me?" the Duchess asked, her voice small. Almost fearful. She glowed red in the dim light. The thin line of her mouth and the severe knot of her hair made her an ascetic. He wondered what had happened to the woman with long, soft hair who had sung to him when he was a boy. He wondered what had happened to the boy.

"No," Dafyd said. And then, "I'm sorry. But no. I can't."

"I can pray for you," she said. She meant *I will make it all right*, and the sorrow in her eyes meant she knew she couldn't. They stood for a moment in silence, a gulf between them more painful than the one separating them from the dead. He was the first to look away.

"You have to kill him," she said. "If he gives you an opportunity dur-ing the trial, you must kill him. It will stop any chance of his leading an insurrection later."

"Is that what God tells you?" Dafyd said more harshly than he'd meant. He braced himself against her anger. She sighed faintly.

"It is what my experience says, and it is what I fear he is thinking of you. I wish that your father…" she began, then shook her head. "I love you, perfect child. Sleep well."

He wanted to turn to her, to call her back, but he loved her too well to do it. The door closed again, leaving him to himself.

When Dafyd had found Bessin, a hundred men or less had lounged on the tiered benches around the court within the court. Now there were thousands. The noise of voices could have drowned out a heavy surf. The air hung low and thick, stale as children hiding too long under a blanket.

Dafyd wore his best armor, black and silver scale and fit for a body slightly changed by the months since its making. His shield dragged at his left arm, and the new sword hung at his side in a scabbard of gems and silver like a milkmaid wearing silk. As he passed the benches, he saw a hundred faces that he knew. His father's men and allies. He saw the anxiety in their eyes, the hope and the fear. He was about to disappoint them all. It was the choice he'd made and he told himself the shame would be worth the relief.

The Duchess sat on the front bench in a dress whose cut owed as much to a nun's habit as to the glamour of court. Rosmund, behind her, wore his cassock and a grave expression.

What if ceding to Palliot was God's plan all along?

Across the court, Dafyd's opponent wore armor of enameled scales the blue of the sky; his shield bore a bronze sun. When their eyes met, Dafyd nodded. Palliot didn't return the gesture.

The high priest entered the court and raised his hands. His voice rang clear and pure and totally at odds with the pandemonium around him. As he chanted out a benediction, all heads bowed except Dafyd's. Even Palliot cast his gaze down. Dafyd felt singled out, even embarrassed, but his neck would not bend. The prayer echoed off the distant ceiling, giving the words a sense of depth and grandeur. He wondered whether the architects had designed the room just for moments like this.

When the high priest was done, the two combatants strapped on their helmets and stepped over the border mark together. There was no court official to remind them of the rules of combat, no priest to declare that God would strengthen the arm of the righteous. Everyone knew.

Dafyd drew his sword. Palliot did the same. They stepped to the center of the court to determine the fate of the kingdom and, Dafyd thought bitterly, through their violence, heal the world.

Palliot shifted to his right, swinging his blade low and slow, no more than the testing blow that any fight might begin with. Dafyd moved away rather than block with his shield, and countered with a half-hearted swing at Palliot's exposed arm. Palliot pulled back, moving carefully, his weight forward.

Dafyd's eyes were narrow, and he found his body reacting as if the fight were genuine. With a sudden roar, Palliot charged, his shield slamming against Dafyd and shoving him off balance. Dafyd bent low, and his enemy's blade skittered off the face of his shield.

Dafyd swung at Palliot's leg, turning the blade at the last moment to slap him with the flat of it. To the crowd, it would look like a missed chance; a cut tendon would have ended the issue, only not the way Dafyd had chosen.

Palliot danced back, his face flushed. He held his blade high behind him, as his father had taught. In a true battle, it would leave his opponent uncertain of which angle his attack might come from. Dafyd met the man's eyes, nodded, and swung a high overhand toward Palliot's skull. Palliot blocked with his shield. Dafyd's sword clanked, and the power of the blow made his fingers smart. The poor balance left his arm aching already.

Palliot pushed back, and Dafyd gave way, moving plausibly and unmistakably toward the border mark. Palliot shifted forward, bringing a heel down hard on Dafyd's foot. The sudden pain confused and surprised him, and he hesitated as Palliot got around his guard, pushing him back toward the center court like a sheep dog holding its flock.

Fear bloomed in Dafyd's breast, and he looked a question at his opponent. He might as well have asked it of stone. Palliot swung hard and fast; the edge of Dafyd's shield only pushed the blade aside from its target. He felt its point catch at his hip, and then a deeper pain. Leaping back, Dafyd saw a glimpse of red at the tip of Palliot's blade.

It is what my experience says, and it is what I fear he is thinking of you.

Dafyd felt a brief, shrill panic washing away grief and despair both. And then, a heartbeat later, his teeth ground against each other, his heart glowed with rage. He screamed wordlessly as he attacked.

Bent low, his shield forward, Dafyd pushed close, swinging hard, a blow more outrage than technique. Palliot blocked easily with his shield and struck back. He was hellishly strong. At the third blow, Dafyd's shield began to buckle, the metal cutting into the flesh of his arm. When he staggered back, Palliot loped around, cutting off the court's edge again.

There was glee in Palliot's face now. His dark eyes glittered, and the thin lips were pulled back into something between a smile and a threat. Dafyd's arm ached. His sword hand was nearly numb. He shouted again, pushed forward, and slammed Palliot with his breaking shield. Palliot fell back a step more from surprise than the attack itself, then roared and shifted again, keeping Dafyd from the border mark. Fight or die, Dafyd would not even be permitted surrender.

Palliot leaped forward with a high side swing. It felt like nothing more than a hard tap with a stick, and then it hurt much worse. Dafyd tried to fall back, but Palliot was on him. Fury or ecstasy fueled the man's arm, and he rained blows on Dafyd's shield and helmet, hammering him down. Dafyd cried out, his fear coming in sobs. His cut hip had been bleeding down his leg unnoticed until he slipped on the blood and fell to one knee.

Like a man swearing fealty, Dafyd knelt, a parody of the ending he hoped for. God's last joke. Palliot's eyes widened, enchanted by the image of his own victory. He lifted his blade, hewing down like an axeman splitting wood. Dafyd raised sword and shield together in a desperate block. Their blades met.

Dafyd felt his break.

Palliot staggered back, blood pouring down his face. A flap of pale skin open in his forehead showed where the flying sword point had slipped past the helmet's brim. Dafyd rose.

All through the court, men were on their feet, screaming and cheering like a storm wind.

Dafyd felt blood cooling on his leg. The pain in his side might have been burning or cold, but whichever it grew worse with each breath. The knuckles of his sword hand ached.

With a sinking, sick rage, Dafyd knew what he had to do if he was to live.

"You swore before God," Dafyd said, softly enough that only the pair of them could hear him. "Now, oathbreaker, you will surrender or you will die."

Palliot glanced around him, uncertain. Afraid.

And, his mother's son after all, Dafyd gathered his breath and spoke louder, his head high, declaiming with every ounce of theater that he could muster.

"Ursin Palliot, you have been tested by God! As His agent upon this earth, I bear witness to your failure. Kneel before me. Kneel before God and confess your sins, or else die here and die *forever!*"

Dafyd lifted his sad, shattered sword, and it might have been a blade of fire. Palliot took a step back.

"Look in my eyes," Dafyd said, softly again. He used the same tone

Rosmund had in speaking of shaved dice and marked cards: sorrowful, sympathetic, and made terrible by its truth. "You cannot win."

For a moment, Dafyd thought Palliot would kneel, and then that the man would strike him down.

Ursin Palliot, Duke of Lakefell and Warden of the South, turned and fled. When he passed the border mark, every man and woman in the court drew in a breath, and then their voices rose as one—like breaking waves, thunder, a landslide of rock and stone—to bear witness to the trial's end.

Dafyd dropped his sword, turned, and spat. At the exultant Duchess's side, Rosmund smiled, and then shrugged, and then looked away. Only the two of them understood that in his victory, Dafyd had lost. Dafyd Laician, once Duke of Westford, and now—by the grace of God—King.

YES WE HAVE NO BANANAS

PAUL DI FILIPPO

1.
INVASION OF THE SHOREBIRDS

Thirty years' worth of living, dumped out on the sidewalk, raw pickings for the nocturnal Street Gleaners tribe. Not literally yet, but it might just as well be—would be soon, given the damn rotten luck of Tug Gingerella. He was practically as dead as bananas. Extinct!

How was he going to manage this unwarranted, unexpected, inexorable eviction?

Goddamn greedy Godbout!

The space was nothing much. One small, well-used, five-room apartment in a building named The Wyandot. Bachelor's digs, save for those three tumultuous years with Olive. Crates of books, his parents' old Heywood-Wakefield furniture that he had inherited, cheaply framed but valuable vintage lobby poster featuring the happy image of Deanna Durbin warbling as *Mary Poppins*. Shabby clothes, mostly flannel and denim and Duofold, cargo shorts and Sandwich Island shirts; cast-iron cornbread skillets; favorite music on outmoded media: scratch slates, holo transects, grail packs, and their various stacked players, natch. Goodfaith Industries metal-topped kitchen table, Solace Army shelves, a painting by Karsh Swinehart (a storm-tossed sailboat just offshore from local Pleistocene Point, Turneresque by way of Thomas Cole).

All the beloved encumbering detritus of a life.

But a life lived to what purpose, fulfilling what early promise, juvenile dreams? All those years gone past so swiftly...

No. Maundering wouldn't cut it. No remedies to his problems in fruitless recriminations and regrets. Best to hit the streets of Carrollboro in search of some aid and comfort.

Tug shuffled into a plaid lumberjacket, red-and-black Kewbie castoff that had wandered south across the nearby border like some migrating avian apparel and onto the Solace Army Store racks, took the two poutine-redolent flights down to ground level at a mild trot, energized by his spontaneous and uncharacteristic determination to act, and emerged onto Patrician Street, an incongruously named grand-dame-gone-shabby avenue cutting south and north through the Squirrel Hills district, and full of gloriously decaying sister buildings to The Wyandot, all built post-War, circa 1939: The Lewis and Jonathan, The Onondowaga, The Canandaigua, The Lord Fitzhugh, and half a dozen others.

Mid-October in Carrollboro: sunlight sharp as honed ice-skate blades, big irregularly gusting winds off Lake Ondiara, one of the five Grands. Sidewalks host to generally maintaining citizens, everyday contentment or focus evident, yet both attitudes tempered with the global stresses of the Big Retreat, ultimate source of Tug's own malaise. (And yet, despite his unease, Tug invariably spared enough attention to appraise all the beautiful women—and they were *all* beautiful—fashionably bundled up just enough to tease at what was beneath.)

Normally Tug enjoyed the autumn season for its crisp air and sense of annual climax, prelude to all the big holidays. Samhain, Thanksgiving, the long festive stretch that began with Roger Williams' birthday on December 21 and extended through Christmas and *La Fête des Rois*...

But this year those nostalgia-inducing attractions paled, against the harsh background of his struggle to survive.

Patrician merged with Tinsley, a more commercial district. Here, shoppers mixed with browsers admiring the big gaudy windows at Zellers and the Bay department stores, even if they couldn't make a purchase at the moment.

Carrollboro's economy was convulsing and churning in weird ways, under the Big Retreat. Adding ten percent more people to the city's population of two-hundred-thousand had both boosted and dragged down the economy, in oddly emergent ways. The newcomers were a representatively apportioned assortment of rich, poor and middle-class refugees from all around the world, sent fleeing inland by the rising seas. "Shorebirds" all, yet differently grouped.

The poor, with their varied housing and medical and educational needs, were a drain on the federal and state government finances. They had settled mostly in the impoverished Swillburg and South Wedge districts of Carrollboro.

The skilled middle-class were undercutting wages and driving up unemployment rates, as they competed with the natives for jobs in their newly adopted region, and bought up single-family homes in Maplewood and Parkway.

And the rich—

The rich were driving longtime residents out of their unsecured rentals, as avaricious owners, seeking big returns on their investments, went luxury condo with their properties.

Properties like The Wyandot, owned by Narcisse Godbout.

Thoughts of his heinous landlord fired up Tug and made him quicken his pace.

Maybe Pavel would have some ideas that could help.

2.
OCARINA CITY

Just a few blocks away from the intersection of Tinsley with Grousebeck, site of the Little Theatre and Tug's destination, Tug paused before Dr. Zelda's Ocarina Warehouse, the city's biggest retailer of fipple flutes.

Carrollboro had been known as Ocarina City ever since the late 1800s.

The connection between metropolis and instrument began by chance in the winter of 1860, when an itinerant pedlar named Leander Watts passed through what was then a small town of some five-thousand inhabitants, bearing an unwanted crate full of Donati "Little Goose" fipple flutes, which Watts had grudgingly accepted in Manhattan in lieu of cash owed for some other goods. But thanks to his superb salesmanship, Watts was able to unload on the citizens of Carrollboro the whole consignment of what he regarded as useless geegaws.

In their heimal isolation and recreational desperation, the citizens of Carrollboro had latched on to the little ceramic flutes, and by spring thaw the city numbered many self-taught journeymen and master players among the populace.

From Carrollboro the fascination with ocarinas had spread nationally, spiking and dying away and spiking again over the subsequent decades, although never with such fervor as at the epicenter. There, factories and academies and music-publishing firms and cafés and concert halls and retail establishments had sprung up in abundance, lending the city its nickname and music-besotted culture.

Today the window of Dr. Zelda's held atop russet velvet cushions the fall 2010 models from Abimbola, von Storch, Tater Innovator, Xun Fun, Charalambos and many other makers. There were small pendant models, big two-handed transverse models and the mammoth three-chambered types. Materials ranged from traditional ceramics to modern polycarbonates, and the surface decorations represented an eye-popping decorative range from name designers as varied as Fairey, Schorr and Mars.

Piped from outdoor speakers above the doorway came the latest ocarina hit, debuting on the Billboard charts at Number Ten, a duet from Devandra Banhart and Jack Johnson, "World Next Door."

Tug himself was a ham-fingered player at best. But his lack of skill did not deter his covetous admiration of the display of instruments. But after some few minutes of daydreaming fascination, he turned away like a bum from a banquet.

Simply another thing he couldn't afford just now.

3.
UNPLANNED OBSOLESCENCE

The Art Vrille movement that had swept the globe in the 1920s and 1930s had left behind several structures in Carrollboro, not the least of which was the Little Theatre. An ornate music-box of a structure, it had plainly seen better days, with crumbling stucco ornaments, plywood replacement of lapidary enamelled tin panels, and a marquee with half its rim's lightbulbs currently missing.

Today, according to that marquee, the Little Theatre was running a matinee in one of its four rooms, subdivided from the original palace-like interior: a double feature consisting of Diana Dors in *The Girl Can't Help It* and Doris Day in *Gun Crazy*. Tug had seen both films many times before, and was glad he wasn't the projectionist for them. Tonight, though, he anticipated his duty: screening the first-run release of *Will Eisner's The Spirit*. Early reviews had Brendan Fraser nailing the role.

Tug tracked down Pavel Bilodeau in the manager's office.

The short, mid-thirtyish fellow—casually dressed, blond hair perpetually hayricked, plump face wearing its default expression of an elementary-school student subjected to a pop quiz on material unmastered—was busy behind his desktop ordinateur, fingers waltzing across the numerical keypad to the right of the alpha keys. Spotting his unexpected visitor, Pavel said, "Right with you, Tug." He triggered output from the noisy o-telex (its carriage chain needed oiling), got up, burst and shuffled together the fanfold printout, and approached Tug.

"This is a spreadsheet of the Little Theatre's finances, Tug."

Tug got a bad feeling from Pavel's tone. Or rather, Tug's recently omnipresent bad feeling deepened. "Yeah?"

"Receipts are down—way down. I've got to cut costs if I want to keep this place open."

"I read about this cheap butter substitute for the popcorn concession—"

"I need bigger savings, Tug. Like your salary."

"I'm being fired?"

Pavel had the grace to look genuinely miserable. "Laid off. Starting today. You can collect."

Tug sank into a chair like a used-car-lot Air Dancer deprived of its fan. "But I was coming here to ask for more hours—and if you had found any leads on a place for me to stay."

Pavel clapped a hand on Tug's shoulder. "You know the worst now, Tug."

Regarding his newly-ex-employer, Tug suddenly realized the gap of years between them, over two decades' worth. Pavel looked incredibly young and callow—like the growing majority of people Tug encountered lately. Kids! They were all kids these days! He tried not to let his resentment of Pavel's relative youth and prospects surface in his voice.

"But how will you run the place without me? Dave and Jeff can't work round-the-clock on four machines."

"I'm installing automated digital projectors. The new Cinemeccanica o-500s. No more film. It's a bit of a capital investment, but it'll pay off quickly. Jeff will handle days, and Dave nights. They'll have to take a pay cut too. Together, after the cut, they'll still make less than you do now. They're young and inexperienced, so they won't mind so much. Oh, and shipping charges on the rentals come down dramatically too. The files get transmitted over CERN-space."

"I'll take the pay cut!"

"No, Tug, I think this is best. You wouldn't be happy just pressing virtual buttons on a monitor screen. You're too old-school. You're filaments and sprockets and triacetate, not bits and bytes and command language strings."

Tug wanted to voice more objections, to protest that he could change—but a sudden realization stilled his tongue.

What Pavel said was true. His age and attitudes had caught up with him. If he couldn't manually load the reels of film and enjoy guiding their smooth progress through the old machines for the enjoyment of the audience, he would feel useless and unfulfilled. The new technology was too sterile for him.

Tug got wearily to his feet. "All right, if that's how it's gotta be. Do I dare ask if you stumbled on any housing leads?"

"No, I haven't. It's incredible. The shorebirds have totally deranged the rental landscape. But listen, here's what I can offer. You can store all your stuff in the basement here for as long as you want."

The basement of the Little Theatre was a huge labyrinth of unused storage space, save for some ancient props from the days of the live-performer Salmagundi Circuit.

"Okay, that's better than nothing. Thanks for all the years of employment, Pavel. The Little Theatre always felt like my second home."

"Just think of it as leaving the nest at last, Tug. It's gonna work out fine. Bigger and better things ahead."

Tug wished he could be as optimistic as Pavel, but right this minute he felt lower than Carole Lombard's morals in *Baby Face*.

4.
TRASH PLATTER CHATTER

Hangdogging his way through the lobby, Tug ran into the Little Theatre's lone janitor and custodian.

Pieter van Tuyll van Serooskerken was a Dikelander. Like a surprisingly uniform number of his countrymen and countrywomen, Pieter was astonishingly tall and fair-skinned. In the average crowd of native brunette and ruddy-faced Carrollborovians, he resembled a stalk of white asparagus set amid a handful of radishes. Today, alone in the lobby and leaning daydreamily on his broom, he seemed like a lone droopy stalk tethered to a supportive stake.

Pieter's native country had been one of the first to collapse under the rising oceans. Dikeland now existed mostly underwater, its government in exile, its citizens dispersed across the planet. The Dikelanders were among the longest-settled Big Retreat immigrants in Carrollboro and elsewhere in the USA, hardly considered an exotic novelty any longer.

Back home, Pieter had been a doctor. Informed, upon relocation to America, of the long tedious bureaucratic process necessary to requalify, he had opted out of the prestigious field, although still young, hale and optimally productive. Tug suspected that Pieter's discovery of Sal-D, or Ska Pastora, had contributed to his career change. Blissfully high throughout much of each day and night on quantities of Shepherdess that would turn a novice user's brain to guava jelly, Pieter found janitorial work more his speed.

With a paradoxically languid and unfocused acuity, Pieter now unfolded himself and hailed Tug.

"Hey, Ginger Ale."

Pieter, in his perfect, nearly accentless yet still oddly alien English, was the only person who ever called Tug Gingerella by that nickname. The Dikelander seemed to derive immense absurdist humor from it.

"Hey, Pete. What's new?"

"I have almost gotten 'Radar Love' down. Apex of Dikelander hillbilly-skiffle music. Wanna hear?"

Pieter drew a pendant ocarina from beneath his work vest and began to raise it to his lips.

"Naw, Pete, I'm just not in the mood right now."

"How is that?"

Tug explained all his troubles, starting with his eviction and culminating in his dismissal from the Little Theatre.

Pieter seemed truly moved. "Aw, man, that sucks so bad. Listen, we approach lunchtime. Let me treat you to a trash platter, and we can talk things through."

Tug began perforce to salivate at the mention of the Carrollboro gastronomic speciality. "Okay, that's swell of you, Pete."

"So long as *I* still possess a paycheck, why not?"

Pieter stood his broom up in a corner with loving precision, found a coat in the cloakroom—not necessarily his own, judging by the misfit, Tug guessed—and led the way five blocks south to the Hatch Suit Nook.

The clean and simple proletarian ambiance of the big diner instantly soothed Tug's nerves. Established nearly a century ago, the place ranked high in Carrollboro traditions. Tug had been dining here since childhood. (Thoughts of his departed folks engendered a momentary sweet yet faded sorrow, but then the enzymatic call of his stomach overpowered the old emotions.) Amidst the jolly noise of the customers, Tug and Pieter found seats at the counter.

Composing one's trash platter was an art. The dish consisted of the eater's choice of cheeseburger, hamburger, red hots, white hots, Italian sausage, chicken tender, haddock, fried ham, grilled cheese, or eggs; and two sides of either home fries, French fries, baked beans, or macaroni salad. Atop the whole toothsome farrago could be deposited mustard, onions, ketchup, and a proprietary greasy hot sauce of heavily spiced ground beef. The finishing touch: Italian toast.

Pieter and Tug ordered. While they were waiting, Pieter took out his pipe. Tug was appalled.

"You're not going to smoke that here, are you?"

"Why not? The practice is perfectly legal."

"But you'll give everyone around us a contact high."

"Nobody cares but you, Ginger Ale. And if they do, they can move off. This helps me think. And your fix demands a lot of thinking."

Pieter fired up and, as he predicted, no neighbors objected. But they were all younger than Tug. Another sign of his antiquity, he supposed.

After a few puffs of Shepherdess, Pieter said, "You could come live with me."

Pieter lived with two women, Georgia and Carolina, commonly referred to as "The Dixie Twins," although they were unrelated, looked nothing alike and hailed from Massachusetts. Tug had never precisely parsed the exact relations among the trio, and suspected that Pieter and the Dixie Twins themselves would have been hard-pressed to define their menage.

"Again, that's real generous of you, Pete. But I don't think I'd be comfortable freeloading in your apartment."

Pieter shrugged. "Your call."

The trash platters arrived then, and further discussion awaited wholehearted ingestion of the jumbled mock-garbage ambrosia....

Pieter wiped his grease-smeared face with a paper napkin and took up his smoldering pipe from the built-in countertop ashtray. Sated, Tub performed his own ablutions. A good meal was a temporary buttress against all misfortunes....

"Maybe you could live with Olive."

Tug's ease instantly evaporated, to be replaced by a crimson mélange of guilt, frustration, anger and shame: the standard emotional recipe for his post-breakup dealings with Olive Ridley.

"That—that is not a viable idea, Pete. I'm sorry, it's just not."

"You and Olive had a lot going for you. Everybody said so."

"Yeah, we had almost as much going for us as we had against. There's no way I'm going to ask her for any charity."

Pete issued hallucinogenic smoke rings toward the diner's ceiling. His eyes assumed a glazed opacity lucid with reflections of a sourceless starlight.

"Tom Pudding."

Tug scanned the menu board posted above the grill. "Is that a dessert? I don't see—"

Pieter jabbed Tug in the chest with the stem of his pipe. "Wake up! The *Tom Pudding*. It's a boat. An old canal barge, anchored on the

Attawandaron. People are using it as a squat. Some guy named Vasterling runs it. He fixed it all up. Supposed to be real nice."

Tug pondered the possibilities. A radical recasting of his existence, new people, new circumstances… Life on a houseboat, rent-free. The romantic, history-soaked vista of the Attawandaron Canal. Currier & Ives engravings of grassy towpath, overhanging willow trees, merry bargemen singing as they hefted bales and crates—

"I'll do it! Thanks, Pete!"

But Pieter had already lost interest in Tug and his plight, the Dikelander's Shepherdess-transmogrified proleptic attention directed elsewhere. "Yeah, cool, great."

Tug helped his hazey-dazey friend stand and don his coat. They headed toward the exit.

Pieter stopped suddenly short and goggled in amazement at nothing visible to Tug. Other customers strained to see whatever had so potently transfixed the Dikelander.

"A Nubian! I see a Nubian princess! She's here, here in Carrollboro!"

"A Nubian princess? You mean, like a black woman? From Africa?"
"Yes!"

Tug scratched his head. "What would a black woman be doing in Carrollboro? I've never seen one here in my whole life, have you?"

5.
MOVING DAY MORN

After his impulsive decision at the Hatch Suit Nook—a decision to abandon all his old ways for a footloose lifestyle—Tug had nervous second thoughts. So in the two weeks left until his scheduled eviction on November first, he searched for a new job. But the surge of competing talented shorebirds made slots sparse.

Tug's best chance, he thought, had come at the Aristo Nodak Company. That large, long-established national firm, purveyor of all things photographic, ran a film archive and theater, mounting retrospective festivals of classic features, everything from Hollywood spectacles such as *Elizabeth Taylor's Salammbô* to indie productions like Carolee Schneemann's avant-garde home movies of the 1960s, featuring her hillbilly-skiffle-playing husband John Lennon. With their emphasis on old-school materials, there'd be no nonsense about Cinemeccanica o-500s. But, despite a sympathetic and well-carried interview, Tug had come in second for the lone projectionist job to a Brit shorebird who had worked for the drowned Elstree Studios.

Despondent at the first rejection, Tug had immediately quit looking. That was how he always reacted, he ruefully acknowledged. One blow, and he was down for the count. Take his only serious adult romantic relationship, with Olive. The disintegration of that affair a few years ago had left him entirely hors de combat on the fields of Venus.

But what could he do now about this fatal trait? He was too damn old to change....

Tug didn't own a fancy o-phone or even a cheap laptop ordinateur. The hard drive on his old desktop model had cratered a year ago, and he had been too broke to replace the machine. Consequently, he used a local o-café, The Happy Applet, to manage his sparse o-mail and to surf CERN-space. A week before his scheduled eviction, he went to Craig's List and posted a plea for help with getting his possessions over to the Little Theatre. Too proud and ashamed to approach his friends directly, Tug hoped that at least one or two people would show up.

Far from that meager attendance, he got a massive turnout.

The morning of October 31 dawned bright, crisp and white as Jack Frost's bedsheets, thanks to an early dusting of snow. (The altered climate had pushed the typical wintry autumn weather of Tug's youth back into December, and he regarded this rare October snow, however transitory, as a good omen.) After abandoning his futile job search, Tug had furiously boxed all his treasured possessions, donating quite a bit to Goodfaith Industries. Handling all the accumulated wrack of thirty years left him simultaneously depressed and nostalgic. He had set aside a smattering of essential clothes, toiletries and touchstones, stuffing them all into a beat-up North Face backpack resurrected from deep within a closet, token of his quondam affiliation with a hiking club out near Palmyra.

At six a.m. he sat on a box at a window looking down at Patrician Street, backpack nestled between his feet, sipping a takeout coffee. An hour later, just when he had prematurely convinced himself no one was coming, the caravan arrived: miscellaneous trucks and cars to the number of a dozen. Out of them tumbled sleepy-eyed friends, acquaintances and strangers.

Jeff, Dave, Pavel and Pieter from the Little Theatre. Tug's second cousin, Nick, all the way from Bisonville. Brenda and Irene, baristas from The Happy Applet. Those nerdy guys with whom for a few years he had traded holo transects of rare Salmagundi Circuit novelty tunes. The kid who sold him his deli lunch each day and who had had an obsession with Helen Gahagan ever since Tug had introduced the kid to her performance in *The Girl in the Golden Atom*. And others, of deeper or shallower intimacy.

Including—yes, that fireplug of a figure was indeed Olive Ridley.

6.
OLD HABITS DIE HARD

Tug hastened down the stairs, and was greeted with loud acclamations. Smiling broadly yet a bit nervously at this unexpected testament to his social connectivity, he nodded to Olive but made no big deal of her presence. Someone pressed a jelly doughnut and a fresh coffee into his hands, and he scarfed them down. Then the exodus began in earnest.

The first sweaty shuttling delivered nearly half his stuff to the basement of the old movie palace. Then came a refreshment break, with everyone gently ribbing Tug about this sea-change in his staid life, and subtly expressing their concern for his future, expressions he made light of, despite his own doubts. The second transfer netted everything out of the melancholy, gone-ghostly apartment except about a dozen small boxes. These were loaded into a single car. Sandwiches and pizza and drinks made the rounds, and a final salvo of noontide farewells.

Then Tug was left alone with Olive, whose car, he finally realized, bore the last of his freight.

But before he could expostulate, Narcisse Godbout arrived on the scene in his battered Burroughs Econoline van.

Born some seventy years ago in Montreal, the fat, grizzled, foul-mouthed Kewbie wore his usual crappy cardigan over flannel shirt, stained gray wool pants and scuffed brogans. Although resident in Carrollboro for longer than his Montreal upbringing, he had never lost his accent. For thirty years he had been Tug's landlord, a semi-distant albeit intermittently thorny source of irritation. Godbout's reasonable rents had been counterbalanced by his sloth, derision and ham-handed repairs. To preserve his below-market rent, Tug had always been forced to placate and curry the man's curmudgeonly opinions. And now, of course, with his decision to evict Tug, Godbout had shifted the balance of his reputation to that of extremely inutile slime.

"You got dose fucking keys, eh, Gingerella?"

Tug experienced a wave of violent humiliation, the culmination of three decades of kowtowing and forelock-tugging. He dug the apartment keys from his pocket and threw them at Godbout's feet into the slush. Then Tug summoned up the worst insult he could imagine.

"You—you *latifundian!*"

Yes, it fit. Like some peon laboring without rights or privileges for the high-hatted owner of some Brazilian plantation, Tug had been subservient to the economic might of this property-owner for too long. But now he was free!

Tug's brilliant insult, however, failed to register with Godbout or faze the ignorant fellow. Grunting, he stooped for the keys, and for a moment Tug expected him to have a heart attack. But such perfect justice was not in the cards. An unrepentant Godbout merely said, "Now I get a better class of tenant, me. Good goddamn riddance to all you boho dogshits."

The landlord drove off before Tug could formulate a comeback.

Leaving Tug once again alone with Olive.

Short and stout and a few years younger than Tug, Olive Ridley favored unadorned smock dresses in various dull colors of a burlap-type fabric Tug had never seen elsewhere, at least outside of barnyard settings, complemented by woolly tights of paradoxically vivid hues and ballet-slipper flats. She wore her long grey-flecked black hair in a single braid thick as a hawser. Her large plastic-framed glasses lent her face an owlish aspect.

Tug and Olive had met and bonded over their love of vintage postcards, bumping into each other at an ephemera convention, chatting tentatively, then adjourning for a coffee at a nearby branch of Seattle's ubiquitous Il Giornale chain. Subsequent outings found them exploring a host of other mutual interests: from movies, of course, through the vocal stylings of the elderly Hank Williams. Their middle-aged, cool-blooded romance, such as it was, progressed through retrospectively definable stages of intimacy until moving in together seemed inevitable.

But cohabitation disclosed a plethora of intractable quirks, crotchets, demands and minor vices held by both partners, fossilized abrasive behavior patterns that rendered each lover unfit for longterm proximity—at least with each other.

Three years after putting her collection of Felix the Cat figurines—including the ultra-rare one depicting Felix with Fowlton Means' Waldo—on Tug's shelves, Olive was tearfully shrouding them in bubblewrap.

Despite this heavy history, Tug vowed now to deal with Olive with neutral respect. She had worked hard all morning to help him move, and now obviously sought some kind of rapprochement.

Olive's words bore out Tug's intuition.

"I wanted to have some time for just us, Tug. I thought we could grab some ice cream at Don's Original, and talk a little."

Don's Original had been their favorite place as a couple. Tug was touched.

"That—that's very kind of you, Olive. Let's go." Tug tossed his pack in the car, and climbed in.

The drive to Culver Road took only a few minutes. (With no car of his own, Tug felt weird to be transiting the city in this unaccustomed fashion.) They mostly spoke of the inarguable: what a Grade-A jerk Narcisse Godbout had unsurprisingly proved himself to be.

Inside Don's, Tug and Olive both paused for a sentimental moment in front of the Banana Split Memorial. Fashioned of realistic-looking molded and colored silicone, like faux sushi, the dusty monument never failed to bring a sniffle to any viewer of a certain age.

Forty years ago, the beloved and familiar Cavendish banana—big creamy delicious golden-skinned monocultured artifact of mankind's breeding genius—had gone irrevocably extinct, victim of the triple-threat of Tropical Race 4, Black Sigatoka and Banana Bunchy Top Virus. In the intervening decades, alternative cultivars had been brought to market. Feeble, tiny, ugly, drab and starchy as their plantain cousin, these banana substitutes had met with universal disdain from consumers, who recalled the unduplicatable delights of the Cavendish.

Tug's own childhood memories of banana-eating were as vivid as any of his peers'. How thoughtlessly and gluttonously they had gorged on the fruit, little anticipating its demise! Sometimes after all these years of abstinence he believed he could not recall the exact taste of a banana. Yet at other unpredictable moments, his mouth flooded with the familiar taste.

But this particular moment, despite the proximity of the banana simulacrum, did not provide any such Proustian occasion.

Tug and Olive found a booth, ordered sundaes, and sat silent for a moment, before Olive asked, "Tug, precisely what are you doing with yourself?"

"I—I don't know exactly. I'm just trying to go with the flow."

"Squatting with a bunch of strangers—yes, Pete told me about it—is not exactly a longterm plan."

"I'm thinking...maybe I can write now. Now that I've shed everything that kept me down. You know I've always wanted to write. About movies, music, my everyday life—"

Olive's look of disgust recalled too many similar, rankling moments of harsh condemnation, and Tug had to suppress an immediate tart rejoinder.

"Oh, Tug, you could have written at any time in the past twenty years. But you let those early rejections get to you, and you just caved in and gave up."

Unspeaking, Tug poked pensively and peevishly at his melting ice cream. Then he said, "Can you drop me off in Henrietta? I've got to find the *Tom Pudding.*"

7.
IN PURSUIT OF THE *TOM PUDDING*

At its inception the Attawandaron Canal had stretched unbroken for nearly four hundred miles, from Beverwyck on the Hudson River, the state's capital, all the way to Bisonville on the shores of Lake Attawandaron, another of the Grands. Constructed in the mid-1800s during the two terms of President Daniel Webster, the Canal had been an engineering wonder, and came to occupy a massive place in American history books, having opened up the Midwest to commerce with the established East, and also generated an immense folklore, still fondly recalled. The Canal Monster, Michel Phinckx, Sam Patch and other archetypes. Bypassed now by other modes of transport, chopped by development into long and short segments, the old Canal had become a recreational resource and prominent talismanic presence in Carrollboro and environs.

Tug had chosen the Henrietta district as a likely starting point for his search for the *Tom Pudding.* Beginning at Carrollboro's city lines where the Canal entered town, he would follow its riverine length until he encountered the utopic loafer's haven limned by Pete.

Tug waved goodbye to Olive's dwindling rear-view mirror, shouldered his pack, and looked at the westering sun. Their trip to the Little Theatre to drop off Tug's last load of stuff had chewed up more time. Now he had barely a few hours before frosty autumnal dusk descended. No plans for how to spend the night. Better get moving.

Tug's earlier whimsy of inhabiting a vanished Currier & Ives era intermittently materialized as he began to hike the Canal. Stretches of the original towpath, paved or not, served as a bike and pedestrian trail, alongside the somnolent unworking waters channeled between meticulously joined stone walls, labor of a thousand anonymous Irish and Krakówvian workers. The mechanisms of the old locks hulked like rusted automatons. The whole scene radiated a melancholy desuetude most pleasing to Tug. Something older even than him, yet still useful in its decrepit fashion.

Of course, at other points the Canal fought with modernity—and lost. It vanished under grafitti'd bridges or potholed pavement, was pinched between ominous warehouses, paralleled by gritty train tracks: a Blakean straitened undine.

Tug was brought up short at one point as the Canal slipped liquidly beneath a razor-wire-topped fence surrounding an extensive auto junk-yard. Furious big dogs hurled themselves at the chainlink, bowing it outward and causing Tug to stumble backwards. He worked his way around the junkyard by gritty alleys and continued on.

By ten p.m. exhaustion had set in. The neighborhood around him held no familiar landmarks, a part of Carrollboro unvisited by Tug be-fore, despite his long tenure in the city. He found a Tim Horton's open all night, bought a coffee and donut as requisite for occupying a booth unmolested by the help. But the desultory kids behind the counter cared little about his tenancy anyhow. He drowsed on and off, dreaming of a Narcisse Godbout big as a mountain, up whose damp woolen flank Tug had to scrabble.

In the morning, he performed some rudimentary ablutions in the donut shop rest room, his mouth tasting like post-digested but pre-processed civet-cat coffee beans. Then he went on hunting the elusive barge full of slackers.

He made it all the way out past Greece Canal Park to Spencerport, before deciding that it was unlikely for the *Tom Pudding* to be berthed further away. Then he turned around and began wearily to retrace his steps, following the fragments of the Attawandaron Canal as if he were Hansel lacking a Gretel, seeking a way home.

Luckily that day featured pleasant weather. Tug had a pocket full of cash, his first unemployment money, so he was able to eat well. He even took a shower at Carrollboro's downtown branch of the Medicine Lodge, changed his underwear and dozed in the kiva chapel with some winos, despite the shaman's chants and the rattle of his gourds.

Tug extended his search beyond Henrietta. No luck. He spent the night in another Tim Horton's, emerging smelling like a stale cruller.

Eliminating the unlikely distal regions, the third day saw him repeat the whole central portion of his fruitless quest, traversing every acces-sible inch of the Canal without seeing so much as the *Tom Pudding*'s oil slick.

When dusk arrived, Tug found himself at the edge of the sprawl-ing park adjacent to the University of Carrollboro in the city's center, one hundred acres of path-laced greenery, wild as Nature intended in spots.

Slumped against a foliage-rich oak tree atop a dry carpet of last year's leaves (trees stayed seasonally green longer these days), Tug polished off a can of Coke. Dispirited and enervated, he mused on this latest failure.

Why hadn't he gotten Pete to nail down the location of the *Tom Pudding*? If the place was unknown, he should have discarded the option, despite its romantic allure. But having chosen to search, why couldn't he accomplish this simple task? It was as if the world always turned a cold shoulder to him. Why couldn't he ingratiate himself with anyone? Was he too prickly, too proud? Would he die a bitter, lonely, unrequited fellow?

Tug's thoughts turned to a wordless pall along with the descent of darkness. He stewed for several hours.

Then lilting ocarina music infiltrated his blue funk.

Tug had heard ocarina music intermittently for the past three days: from street musicians, lunchtime amateurs, kids in playgrounds, commercial loudspeakers. Fipple flute music provided the background buzz of Ocarina City, and he mostly paid little attention to it.

But he had never heard an ocarina sound like this. The music conjured up vivid pictures of foreign locales, an almost sensory buzz.

From out the bushes of the park emerged a dim figure, source of the strangely gorgeous sounds. Tug strained his eyes—

He saw Pete's Nubian Princess.

The black woman was bundled up against the cold in a crazyquilt assortment of shawls and scarves. Tug suspected the patterned garments would be gaudy and colorful by day. Lithe, tall, thin, she moved like a swaying giraffe. Her indistinctly perceived facial features seemed more Arabic or Semitic than Negroid. Her hair was a dandelion explosion.

She stopped a few yards away from Tug and continued to play, a haunting melody unfamiliar to the man.

Tug got to his feet. What were the odds he'd encounter such an exotic creature, given that the whole of North America hosted perhaps only ten thousand Africans at any given moment, and those mostly diplomats and businessmen? Could she be a foreign student attending Carrollboro's University? Unlikely, given the prestige of schools in Songhai, Kanen-Bornu and the Oyo Empire. Nor was it likely she'd be a shorebird, given that Africa's displaced coastal citizens had all been taken care of at home.

Tug took a step toward the outré apparition. The woman ceased playing, smiled (teeth very white against dark skin), turned, then resumed playing and began to walk into the undergrowth.

Tug could do nothing but follow. Had not an ounce of will left otherwise.

Deeper into the park she led him. Tug could smell water. But not the semi-stagnant Canal water. Fresh, running water. He realized that they must be approaching the Cunhestiyuh River as it cut through the park and city.

Sure enough, they were soon at its banks, and could not cross. The woman led the way leftward along the shore until they reached a line of thick growth perpendicular to the river. Employing a non-obvious gap amidst the trees and bushes, she stepped through, Tug just steps behind.

No more ocarina music, and the woman had vanished.

Tug became more aware of his surroundings, as if awaking from a dream.

He stood on the edge of an artificial embankment. He suddenly realized the nature of the spot.

The Attawandaron Canal had been connected to the Cunhestiyuh River at intervals by short feeder canals, to refresh its flow. This was one such. A leaky yet still mostly functioning feedgate on the riverside was still in place, barring ingress of the river and making for a low water level in the feeder chute. Entering the Canal on the opposite side from the towpath, this feeder inlet, perhaps overgrown on its far end too, had been totally overlooked by Tug in his quest.

Tug looked down.

Nearly filling the narrow channel, the *Tom Pudding* floated below, lit up like an Oktoberfest beer garden with colored fairy lights, its deck busy with people. A ladder ran from the top of the feeder canal on down to the barge's broad roof.

A fair-haired man looked up then and spotted Tug. The man said, "Pellenera's brought us another one. Hey, pal, c'mon down!"

8.
VASTERLING'S MAD AND MARVELOUS MENAGERIE

The planning and rehearsing for the quantum physics chautauqua were complete. A vote among the barge's citizens had affixed the title of "Mystery Mother and Her Magic Membranes" onto the production, passing over such contenders as "The Heterotic Revue"; "Branes! Branes!

Escape from the Zombie Universe"; "I've Got the Worlds on a String"; and "Witten It Be Nice? Some Good Sub-Planckian Vibrations."

The one and only performance of the educational saturnalia was scheduled for this very night, at the Carrollboro venue that generally hosted visiting chautauquas, the Keith Vawter Memorial Auditorium. Franchot Galliard had paid for the rental of the space, reluctantly tapping into his deep family fortunes, despite an inherent miserliness that had caused him, about four years previously, to purchase the *Tom Pudding* at scrapyard prices and take up residence aboard, whilst leasing out his Ellwanger Barry-district mansion at exorbitant rates to rich shorebirds.

Oswaldo Vasterling was just that persuasive.

The young visionary self-appointed captain of the permanently moored barge full of oddballs could have herded cats into a swimming pool, Tug believed. Short and roly-poly, his complexion a diluted Mediterranean olive hue, the stone-faced twenty-one-year-old struck most first-time interlocutors as unprepossessing in the extreme. (Tug suspected a bit of Asperger's, affected or otherwise, in Vasterling's character.)

Gorm Vasterling, Oswaldo's dad, had been an unmarried Dikelander resident in Fourierist Russia, an agriculture specialist. When the Omniarch of the Kiev Phalanx ordered Gorm to transplant his talents to Cuba, to aid the Fourierist brethren there, Gorm instantly obeyed.

Upon relocation to Cuba, Gorm's Dikelander genes almost immediately combined with the Latina genes of Ximena Alcaron, a Fourier Passionologist specializing in Animic Rehabilitation. The result was a stubby, incipiently mustachio'd child who had received the least appealing somatic traits of each parent.

But in brainpower, little Oswaldo was not scanted.

Some three years ago, in 2007, at age eighteen, educationally accelerated Oswaldo was already doing post-doc work in M-theory with Lee Smolin at the Perimeter Institute for Theoretical Physics, a semi-independent think-tank headquartered on the campus of Carrollboro U. But Smolin and his star student had clashed violently over some abstruse quantum heresy, and Oswaldo Vasterling had been cast out from the sanctum

He hadn't gone far, though, ending up just a mile or so away from the campus, serendipitously stumbling upon Franchot Galliard's welcoming barge. There, he commandeered several rooms as his lab-cum-sleeping quarters and set up a rococo experimental apparatus resembling the mutant offspring of a Portajohn and a digital harmonium, attached to a small-scale radio-telescope, a gravity-wave interferometer and a bank of networked ordinateurs, the whole intended to replicate what he had left behind at the PITP.

Forever short of money for his unperfected equipment, he perpetually harassed the stingy Galliard for dough, generally with little success, and inveigled everyone else onboard to participate in money-raising schemes, of which the chautauqua was the latest. (The city had been plastered with advertisements, both wheat-pasted and CERN-spaced, and if Oswaldo's show filled half of Vawter's seats with paying customers, he'd net a hefty sum—especially since all the performers were volunteers.)

But the mixed-media performance also stood as Oswaldo's intended refutation of his ex-comrades at the PITP. He had invited them all to witness his theories rendered in music and dance, light and sound, hoping they would repent and acknowledge the Vasterling genius. And his quondam colleagues had accepted en masse, in the spirit of those anticipating a good intellectual brawl.

Tug's part in this affair? He had been placed in charge of stage lighting, on the crack-brained logic that he had worked before with machines that projected light. Luckily, the boards at the Vawter were old-fashioned, non-o consoles, and Tug had mastered them easily in a few rehearsals, leaving him confident he could do his part to bring off "Mystery Mother and Her Magic Membranes" successfully.

So in the hours remaining before showtime, Tug had little to do save hang out with Sukey Damariscotta. He looked for her now.

The vast open cargo interior of the old decommissioned barge had been transformed over the past four years into a jerry-built, multi-level warren of sleeping, dining, working and recreational spaces by the resident amateur carpenters (and by one former professional, the surly alcoholic Don Rippey, who managed just barely to ensure that every load-bearing structure met minimal standards for non-collapse, that the stolen electricity was not fed directly into, say, the entire hull, and that the equally purloined plumbing did not mix inflow with outflow). Consequently, there were no straight paths among the quarters, and finding anyone involved something just short of solving the Traveling Voyageur problem.

If the layout of the *Tom Pudding* remained still obscure to Tug even after a month's habitation, he felt he finally had a pretty good fix on most of the recomplicated interpersonal topography of the barge. But initially, that feature too had presented an opaque façade.

Hailed from the barge that night of discovery, Tug had descended the ladder into a clamorous reception from a few dozen curious strangers. Supplied, sans questioning, with a meal, several stiff drinks and a bunk, he had fallen straight asleep.

In the morning, Tug stumbled upon the same fellow who had first spotted him. Brewing coffee, the ruggedly handsome guy introduced himself as Harmon Frawley. Younger than Tug by a decade or more, boyish beyond his years, Frawley had been an ad copywriter in Toronto until a painful divorce, after which he had gone footloose and impoverishedly free. He still favored his old wardrobe of Brooks Brothers shirts and trousers, but they were getting mighty beat.

Sipping coffee and running a big hand through his blond bangs, Harmon explained the origin, ethos and crew of the *Tom Pudding* to Tug.

"So Galliard owns this floating commune, but Vasterling is the boss?"

"Right. Insofar as anyone is. Call Ozzie the 'Prime Mover' if you need a more accurate title. Frankie just wants to be left alone with his collection."

When Tug eventually met Franchot Galliard, he was instantly reminded of Adolphe Menjou in his starring role in *Where the Blue Begins*, lugubrious canine makeup and all. Galliard's penchant for antique eight-millimeter stag films, especially those starring the young Nancy Davis, struck Tug as somewhat unhealthy, and he was glad the rich collector knew how to operate his own projector. Still, who was he to criticize any man's passion?

"And he doesn't care who crashes here?"

"Not at all! So long as it doesn't cost him anything. But you know, not many people find us here. And even the ones who do don't always stay. The hardcores are special. Particularly since Pellenera showed up."

Mention of the enigmatic Nubian Pied Piper sent mystical frissons down Tug's spine. The story of her origin lacked no complementary mystery or romance.

"It was a dark and stormy night. Really. About six months ago, sometime in May. Ozzie announced that he was gonna power up his brane-buster for the first time. Bunch of us gathered down in his lab around midnight. Boat was rocking like JFK trying to solve the Cuban Seafloor Colony Crisis. So Ozzie straps himself in and starts playing the keys of that electronic harmonium thingy that's at the core of the device. Weirdest music you've ever heard. Flashing lights, burning smells, the sound of about a dozen popping components self-destructing simultaneously—Then the inside of the booth part of the gizmo goes all smoky-hazy-like, and out pops this naked African chick! She looks around for a few seconds, not scared, just amazed, says a few words no one understands, then runs off into the night!"

Tug's erotic imagination supplied all too vividly the image of the naked ebony charms of Pellenera—conjured up a picture so distracting that he missed the next few words from Harmon Frawley.

"—Janey Vogelsang. She was the first one Pellenera led back here, a week later. Marcello named her that, by the way. Just means 'black hide.' And you're, oh, about the tenth."

"And she never speaks?"

"Not since that first night. She just plays that demon ocarina. You ever heard the like?"

"Never."

Harmon scratched his manly chin. "Why she's leading people here, how she chooses 'em—that's anybody's guess."

"Does she live onboard?"

"Nope. Roams the city, so far as anyone can tell."

And so Tug entered the society of the *Tom Pudding* as one cryptically anointed.

He came now to a darkened TV room, whose walls, floor and ceiling had been carpeted with heterogenous scavenged remnants. An old console set dominated a couch on which were crowded Iona Draggerman, Jura Burris and Turk Vanson.

"Hey, Tug, join us! We're watching *Vajayjay and Badonkadonk!*"

"It's that episode where Vajayjay's relatives visit from India and have to go on a possum hunt!"

The antics of Kaz's animated Hindi cat and Appalachian mule, while generally amusing, held no immediate allure for Tug.

"Aren't you guys playing the part of quarks tonight? Shouldn't you be getting your costumes ready?"

"We've got hours yet!"

"We don't dance every time Ozzie pulls our strings!"

Tug moved on, past various uncanny or domestic tableaux, including the always spooky incense-fueled devotional practice of Tatang, the mono-named shorebird from the sunken Kiribati Islands.

At last he found Sukey Damariscotta, sitting all bundled up and cross-legged in a director's chair on deck, sketching trees upon the shoreline.

Only twenty-four, Sukey possessed a preternatural confidence derived from her autodidactic artistic prowess. Tug had never met anyone so capable of both meticulous fine art and fluent cartooning.

Sukey's heritage included more Amerind blood than most other Americans possessed. In her, the old diffuse and diluted aboriginal strains absorbed by generations of colonists had recombined to birth a classic pre-Columbian beauty, all cheekbones, bronze skin and coal-black hair, styled somewhat incongruously in a Dead Rabbits tough-girl cut repopularized recently by pennywhistlers the Pogues.

Tug was more than a little in love with the talented and personable young woman, but had dared say nothing to her of his feelings so far.

Dropping down to the December-cold deck, Tug admired the drawing. "Sweet. I like the lines of that beech tree."

Sukey accepted the praise without false humility or ego. "Thanks. Hey, remember those caricatures I was working on?"

Sukey's cartoon captures of the cast of the ongoing *Tom Pudding* farcical drama managed to nail their personalities in a minimum of brisk, economical lines. Tug had been a little taken aback when she showed him his own depiction. Did he really look like such a craggy, aged misanthrope? But in the end, he had to confess the likeness.

"Sure. You added any new ones?"

Sukey tucked her charcoal stick behind one ear and flipped the pages of her sketchbook.

Tug confronted an image of Pellenera in the guise of the enormous demi-barebreasted Statue of Marianne on her island home in New York Harbor. The statue's fixed pose of torch held aloft had been modified to feature Pellenera cradling all the infantilized *Tom Pudding* crew to her bosom.

When Tug had finished laughing, he said, "Hey, you ever gotten interested in bande dessinée? With an image like that, you're halfway there."

"Oh, I can't tell a story to save my life."

"Well, what if we collaborate? Here, give me that pad and a pencil, and I'll rough something out."

"What's the story going to be about?"

"It'll be about—about life in Carrollboro."

Tug scrawled a three-by-three matrix of panels and, suddenly inspired, began populating them with stick figures and word balloons.

Sukey leaned in close, and Tug could smell intoxicating scents of raw woodsmoke and wild weather tangled in her hair.

9.
"MORE OCARINA!"

Tug had never been subjected to a one-on-one confrontation with Oswaldo Vasterling before. The circumstances of their first dialogue added a certain surreal quality to what would, in the best of conditions, have been a bit of an unnerving trial.

The two men stood in a semi-secluded corner backstage at the Keith Vawter Memorial Auditorium, illuminated only by the dimmest of caged worklights that seemed to throw more shadows than photons. All around them was a chaos one could only hope would exhibit emergent properties soon.

Don Rippey was bellowing at people assembling a set: "Have any of you guys ever even *seen* a hammer before?!?"

Janey Vogelsang was trying to make adjustments to two costumes at once: "No, no, your arrow sash has to go *counter*clockwise if you're a gluon!"

Turk Vanson was coaching a chorus of ocarina players. "Why the hell did I bother writing out the tablatures if you never even studied them!?!"

Crowds of other actors and dancers and musicians and crew-bosses and directors and makeup artists and stagehands and techies surged around these knots of haranguers and haranguees in the usual pre-chautauqua madness.

But Ozzie remained focused and indifferent to the tumult, in a most unnatural fashion. His lack of affect disturbed Tug. Despite Ozzie's youth and a certain immaturity, he could appear ageless and deep as a well. Now, with Sphinxlike expression undermined only slightly by the juvenile wispy mustache, he had Tug pinned down with machine-gun questions.

"You're sure you know all your cues? Did you replace those torn gels? What about that multiple spotlight effect I specified during the Boson Ballet?"

"It's all under control, Ozzie. The last run-through was perfect."

Oswaldo appeared slightly mollified, though still dubious. "You'd better be right. A lot is depending on this. And I won't be here to supervise every minute of the production."

"You won't be? I thought this spectacle was going to be your shining moment. Where are you going?"

The pudgy genius realized he had revealed something secret, and showed a second's rare disconcertment. "None of your business."

Oswaldo Vasterling turned away from Tug, then suddenly swung back, exhibiting the most emotion Tug had yet witnessed in the enigmatic fellow.

"Gingerella, do you like this world?"

Tug's turn to feel nonplussed. "Do I like this world? Well, yeah, I guess so… It's a pretty decent place. Things don't always fall out in my favor, or the way I'd wish. I lost my job and my home just a month ago. But everyone has ups and downs, right? And besides, what choice do I have?"

Oswaldo stared intently at Tug. "I don't think you really *do* care for this universe. I think you're like *me*. You see, I know this world for what it is—a fallen place, a botch, an imperfect reflection of a higher reality and a better place. And as for choices—well, time will tell."

On that note, Oswaldo Vasterling scuttled off like Professor T. E. Wogglebug in Baum's *The Vizier of Cockaigne*.

Tug shook his head in puzzlement at this Gnostic Gnonsense, then checked his watch. He had time for one last curtain-parting peek out front.

The well-lighted auditorium was about a third full, with lots more people flowing in. Ozzie might make his nut after all, allowing him to continue with his crazy experiments….

Hey, a bunch of Tug's old crowd! Pete, Pavel, Olive—essentially, everyone who had helped him move out of The Wyandot. Accidental manifestation, or solidarity with their old pal?

Wow, that move seemed ages ago. Tug experienced a momentary twinge of guilt. He really needed to reconnect with them all. That mass o-mail telling them he was okay and not to worry had been pretty bush league. But the *Tom Pudding* experience had utterly superseded his old life, as if he had moved to another country, leaving the patterns of decades to evanesce like phantoms upon the dawn….

Tug recognized Lee Smolin in another section of seats, surrounded by a claque of bearded nerds. The physicist's phiz was familiar, the man having attained a certain public profile with his CBC documentaries such as *The Universal Elegance*….

The voice of Harmon Frawley, director-in-chief, rang out, "Places, everyone!"

Tug hastened back to his boards.

He found Sukey Damariscotta waiting there. She wore purple tights and leotard over bountiful curves. Tug's knees weakened.

"Doing that bee-dee together this afternoon was lots of fun, Tug.

Let's keep at it! Now wish me luck! I've never portrayed a membrane before!"

Sukey planted a kiss on Tug's cheek, then bounced off.

Glowing brighter than any floodlight, Tug turned to his controls. He tilted the monitor that showed him the stage to a better viewing angle.

And then "Mystery Mother and Her Magic Membranes" was underway.

Under blood-red spotlights *Pudding* person Pristina Immaculata appeared, raised from below through a trap, an immense waterfall of artificial hair concealing her otherwise abundant naked charms, Eve-style. Pristina's magnificent voice, Tug had come to learn, made Yma Sumac's seem a primitive instrument.

Warbling up and down the scale, Pristina intoned with hieratic fervor, "In the beginning was the Steinhardt-Turok model, and the dimensions were eleven…"

A rear-projection screen at the back of the stage lit up with one of Franchot Galliard's B&W stag films, the infamous orgy scene from *Les Vacances de Monsieur Hulot*, involving Irish McCalla, Julie Newmar, Judy Holliday and Carole Landis.

Low-hanging clouds of dry-ice fog filled the stage. Tug's hands played over his controls, evoking an empyrean purple realm. A dozen women cartwheeled across the boards. The imperturbable South-Pacifican Tatang wheeled out on a unicycle, barechested and juggling three machetes.

"I shift among loop gravity, vacuum fluctuations and supergravity forever!"

After that, things got weird.

Tug was so busy at his boards that he paid little heed to the audience reaction, insofar as it even penetrated his remove. Retrospectively, he recalled hearing clapping, some catcalls, whistles and shouts of approval. All good reactions.

But then, at the start of the second hour, the riot began.

What triggered it seemed inconsequential to Tug: some bit of abstruse physics jargon, recited and then pantomimed by a bevy of dancers wearing fractal-patterned tights. But the combined assertion of their words and actions outraged Lee Smolin and his clan. No doubt Oswaldo Vasterling had penned the speech with just this result in mind.

On his monitor, Tug saw the performance come to a confused halt. He abandoned his station and raced out front.

The staff of the Perimeter Institute for Theoretical Physics had jumped to their feet and were shaking their fists at the stage, hollering insults.

Others in the audience told the dissenters to shut up and sit down. This enraged the unruly scientists further. Some bumrushed the stage, while others engaged in fisticuffs with the shushers. Gee, those guys could sure punch surprisingly hard for a bunch of electron-pushers.

The brawl spiralled outward from the principled nucleus, but without rhyme or reason. Soon the whole auditorium was churning with fighters and flighters.

Turk Vanson rushed onstage followed by his stalwart ocarina players. "We've got a fever, and my prescription is—more ocarina! Blow, guys, blow!"

The musicians launched into "Simple Gifts," practically the nation's second anthem ever since the tenure of Shaker Vice-President Thomas McCarthy during President Webster's second term. But the revered music had no effect.

Someone uncorked a fire extinguisher or three, and Tug caught a blast of foam in the face.

Tug cleared his vision just in time to dodge a flying bottle that clipped Vanson's head and sent him reeling, the projectile then tearing through the movie screen and passing right through the image of Bunny Yeager's split beaver.

A woman collided with Tug and they both went smashing down. Sukey? No? Where was she? Was she okay…?

Tatang rode over Tug's legs with his unicycle, causing him to grunt in pain and to forget anything else.

Sirens obtruded over the screams….

At the adamant urging of Ozzie, Franchot Galliard reluctantly posted bail for all the *Tom Pudding* arrestees the next morning.

Tug met Sukey outside the police station. She had sheltered on a catwalk during the worst of the fracas, dropping sandbags on rogue quantum theoreticians.

Back on the barge, Tug took a shower, then went to one of the galleys to rustle up some breakfast.

A copy of that morning's *Whig-Chronicle* lay on the table. The main headline, natch, concerned the debacle at the Vawter.

But buried inside the paper lurked an even more intriguing lede:

"Authorities report a break-in last night at the Perimeter Institute for Theoretical Physics…."

10.
AMERICAN SPLENDOR

Tug and Sukey worked on their bee-dee throughout December. Projected as an anthology of several tales, some just a page, some many pages, the nascent book chronicled a bare handful of anecdotes from Tug's colorful years in Carrollboro. Events and characters came welling up from memory in a prodigious rush, producing laughter and incredulous head-shaking from his collaborator. He knew he had enough material for years of such books. And things always went on happening to him, too.

"You've led quite a life, Tug."

"Yeah. Yeah, I guess I have."

Tug had never been happier, or felt more creative. He blessed the day miserable bastard Narcisse Godbout had kicked him out of his comfortable rut, the day Pete had pointed him toward the *Tom Pudding*, the night alluring Pellenera had approached him, and the day he had impulsively snatched Sukey's sketchpad.

The cartooning team paused in their intense work only long enough to celebrate the birthday of Roger Williams on December 21, along with the rest of the nation. Watching the traditional televised parades with Sukey, with their cheesy floats celebrating what had come to be known and worshipped as the Williams Creed, in all its archaically glorious phrasing—"No red man to be kept from our hearths and bedchambers; no black man to be imported to these shores against his will; no gods above the minds and hearts of mankind"—Tug experienced a simple national pride he had not felt in many years.

During these weeks, Tug and the rest of the barge's crazyquilt crew braced themselves for some new manifestation of Oswaldo Vasterling's brane-buster. The day after the catastrophic chautauqua, Ozzie had radiated a certain smug self-satisfaction at odds with his usual semblance of lordly indifference. Whatever he had purloined from the PITP must have promised immediate success. He immured himself in his lab, and the power levels aboard the craft wavered erratically, as evidenced by flickering brownouts from time to time, accompanied by noises and stinks.

But there had ensued no visible breakthroughs, no spontaneous generation of a second Pellenera, for instance, and Ozzie, when he finally showed himself to his followers, radiated a stony sense of humiliation and defeat.

By the end of January, Tug and Sukey had something they felt worthy of submission to a publisher. Tug found the contact info for an editor at Drawn & Quarterly, an imprint of the global Harmsworth Publishing empire. After querying, he received permission to submit, and off the package went, Sukey's powerful black and white art deliberately left uncolored.

Nothing to do but wait, now.

Deep into the bowels of one February night, Tug was awakened by distant music from beyond the spheres. Blanket wrapped haphazardly around himself, he stumbled up onto the frosted deck, finding himself surprisingly alone, as if the rest of the ship had been ensorcelled into fairytale somnolence.

Moonlight silvered the whole world. Pellenera—piping, argent eidolon—loomed atop the bank of the feeder canal. Tug shivered. Did she herald the arrival of a new recruit? Where was the guy?

But no newcomer emerged from among the winter-bare branches. Pellenera seemed intent merely on bleeding out her heart through the ocarina, as if seeking to convey an urgent message to someone.

Tug's mind drowned in the music. He seemed to be seeing the world through Pellenera's eyes, gazing down at himself on the deck. Was *she* tapping *his* optic nerves, seeing herself on the shore? That music—

Tug had a sudden vision of the Nubian woman, dancing naked save for—

—a skirt fashioned of bananas?

The music stopped. Pellenera vanished.

What the hell had all *that* been about?

An o-mail response from Drawn & Quarterly came in March, just as spring arrived.

Tug rushed back to the *Tom Pudding* with an o-café printout of the message.

Sukey Damariscotta was playing a videogame with Janey Vogelsang when Tug tracked her down: *Spores of Myst*. He hustled her away from Janey, to a quiet corner, then bade her read the printout.

"Oh, Tug, this is wonderful! We've done it!"

"I can't believe it!"

"Me neither!"

Tug grabbed Sukey, hugged her close, kissed her passionately and wildly lips to lips.

Hands on Tug's chest, Sukey pushed back, broke his embrace.

"What are you doing?"

"Sukey, I—You've gotta know by now—"

"Know what?" Her face registered distaste, as if she had been handed a slimy slug. "Oh, no, Tug, you can't imagine us hooking up, can you? I like you, sure, a lot. I respect your talent. But you're way too old...."

Time must've crept along somehow in its monotonous, purpose-less, sempiternal fashion, although Tug couldn't have testified to that reality. All he knew was that in some manner he had crossed blocks of Carrollboro to stand outside The Wyandot. His old residence of thirty years' habitation was garlanded with scaffolding, its plastic-membraned windows so many blank, unseeing eyes, unbreachable passages to a vanished era, a lost youth.

In the end, he returned to the *Tom Pudding*.

What choice did he have in this fallen, inhospitable world?

Sukey acted friendly toward him, even somewhat intimate. But Tug knew that they would never relate the same way again, and that their collaboration was over, whatever the fate of their one and only book.

The voice of Ozzie Vasterling, when broadcast through the intercom system of the *Tom Pudding*—a system no one prior to this moment had even suspected was still active—resembled that of the Vizier of Cockaigne in the 1939 film version of that classic, as rendered by the imperious Charles Coburn.

"Attention, attention! Everyone report to my lab—on the double!"

Some folks were missing, ashore on their individual business. But Ozzie's lab soon filled up with two dozen souls, Tug among them.

Weeks ago, Tug might have been as excited as the others gathered here. But since Sukey's rebuff, life had lost its savor. What miracle could restore that burnish? None....

But yet—

Pellenera stood before the brane-buster, looking as out-of-place as a black panther in a taxi. Imagine a continent full of such creatures! Ozzie sat behind the keys of his harmonium. The brane-buster hummed and sparkled.

Ozzie could hardly speak. "Vibrations! It's all in the way the invisible strings vibrate! I only had to pay attention to her! Watch!"

He nodded to the Nubian, and she began to play her ocarina, as Ozzie pumped the harmonium attachment.

In the cabinet of the brane-buster, what could only be paradoxically described as a coruscating static vortex blossomed. Gasps from the watchers—even from sulky Tug.

With a joyous primal yawp, Pellenera hurled herself into the cabinet, still playing, and was no more.

The vortex lapsed into non-being as well.

Someone asked, "Is that the end?"

"Ha! Do you think I'm an idiot! I recorded every last note!"

Pellenera's looped song started up again, and the vortex resumed.
Everyone waited.

Time stretched like the silent heist scene in Hitchcock's *Rififi*.

Pellenera popped out of the cabinet, carrying something concealed
in the crook of her arm, but naked as water herself.

Even from the edge of the crowd, Tug noticed that her naked back
was inexplicably crisscrossed with a latticework of long antique gnarly
scars, and he winced.

Revealed, her burden was one perfect golden Cavendish banana.

She smiled, and took several steps forward, the spectators parting
before her like grasses beneath a breeze, until she came face to face
with Tug.

And she handed the banana to him.

MESOPOTAMIAN FIRE

JANE YOLEN & ADAM STEMPLE

lright, it isn't much of a dragon. I never said it was. More a lizard kind of thing. But if you lay down on your side and squint at it, you can see it's a dragon, as long as you're careful not to get too close.

Yeah—that's too close. Don't say I didn't warn you. That flame may be tiny but, like a match tip, it can really burn. I've got an ointment right here. *Johnson's 470.* I've tried others, but they all barely touch the pain. You should have seen what happened when I used the stuff in my kit. What a flare. Oh right. I do go on sometimes. Here it is. Just rub it in quickly. You'll hardly feel a thing by this afternoon.

You know, if I believed Jonathan Swift about the Lilliputians, I'd say that this is a dragon who could have terrorized them. Or the little people who stayed on the island in *Mistress Masham's Repose.* They'd surely have run screaming from it. Or it could have been the harrower of the Borrowers. Yeah—say that ten times fast. But those were in books, for God's sake. Not real. Not even faction. My girlfriend, Dana, the some-times editor, who used to go to this college, did you ever meet her? Dana Woodbridge. Though of course being an English lit major, she probably never took a science course. Oh the point? Sure. I was getting to that. You know, Emily Dickinson wrote "Success in circuit lies." Dana likes to quote that when we have our long discussions. Well, about faction, Dana told me that it's truth crossed with fiction. You know—made-up memoirs and that sort of thing. It's hot now she says.

Well, not as hot as dragon's breath, whatever the size. And mustache hairs, when they singe, smell godawful. As you've just found out.

I suppose I could have stamped on it when I first saw it. The dragon, not the mustache hairs I mean. Hard to stamp on them without hurting someone. Hahahahahaha. Oh, sorry. That's my sense of humor. Dana doesn't think I'm good at it either. But I'm working on it. But if I'd stamped on it at once… the dragon, not… Right you got that. I'll move on.

Well, if I had, I'd have gotten rid of the problem in a second. I mean, it wasn't a lizard and couldn't scurry away. It could fly a bit, but I think that whole flying dragon stuff was made up by people who didn't know a thing about flight muscles, and lift and birds having hollow bones. By *a bit* I mean it had the floating ability of a hot-air balloon, except with nothing to use as ballast or to throw overboard when it wanted to descend. It just stopped holding its hot breath, blew it out, and down it came.

Yeah, well, I wouldn't believe me either. And not because I have a reputation as a jokester. That was in high school. College, I'm all serious student. Geology major, anthropology minor. It's how I came upon the little dragon, on a geology field trip to the Mideast last summer.

Be specific? Right. I was in Egypt. But not the Egypt you think of now, all web cafes and big German cars. What? You don't think of big German cars? You haven't been to Cairo lately then. Well, not the Egypt *you* think of either. The Great Pyramids have been dug up so many times they're more gaping hole than grave marker now. No, I was in *real* ancient Egypt, exploring caves that were old before the first stone was placed at Giza.

I was deep underground, spelunking alone through a narrow tunnel. I love that word. Spelunking. Spelunking. Spelunking… oh, sorry. I didn't mind the tight fit, though the rest of the crew thought I was crazy to go off on my own. But you know me, sir, always the loner. Except with Dana of course, though being a loner is different than being alone. Dana showed me that. Oh right, that has nothing to do with what I'm trying to tell you, but she got that from one of the romance novels she was editing and it really struck me. She quotes me stuff all the time, broadens me a lot. Did I mention that she does freelance…?

Right. The tunnel.

The tunnel had just opened up into a sizeable chamber when the battery in my headlamp died. Let me tell you, you don't know darkness until you've experienced *underground* darkness. Your eyes don't adjust. Your mind either. You spend more than a few minutes in darkness that total, you're liable to turn into a gibbering idiot. Well, yes, but I had a touch of that before. Hahahaha. Oh sorry, sense of humor. None. I'll tell Dana. I bet she'll find *that* one funny.

That's why I always carry a spare battery for my light. But before I could get the battery changed—I'd practiced the maneuver in the spelunking class at the Y a dozen times or more because *Thorough* is my middle name. Well, actually it's Hyatt, but you get the picture. No, not those Hyatts, otherwise I would probably have majored in restaurant management and never found the little dragon. Oh, the point? Right. Sometimes I do wander a bit. I saw the tiny gout of flame that your mustache has so recently become acquainted with. It was plenty obvious in the blackness, but I can't say for sure if I would have noticed it if my light hadn't gone out at that exact moment. I find that's often the way with Great Discoveries.

Yes, this is my first and only Great Discovery, so perhaps I am being premature in saying that. But I bet if you ask other Great Discoverers about their Great Discoveries, they'd say they were just in the right place at the right time. As opposed to the right place but the wrong time. Or the wrong place at the wrong time. I wonder if there's a right time to be in the wrong place?

No matter. I scooped him up and headed for the surface. A number of specimen bags got burned before I figured out that if you wrapped him up tight and covered his head he'd go right to sleep. Must be some bat or bird DNA in him somewhere. They do that don't they? Anyway, that's a study for some other grad student, biology probably, or anthropology—though that's the study of man so maybe not. Either way, I'll want my name on the paper, too. You've taught me well, sir.

And lucky for me, despite how metallic those scales look, they aren't metal at all and so didn't set off the metal detector at the airport. His bones, being hollow, didn't ring any bells either. Must have looked like a painting or something to the x-ray machine. I was all ready for the questions, ready to be taken aside at customs, too, declaring the dragon a museum delivery. Had the papers and all. It's not so hard to fake those, you know. I got mine from a little man who was as brown and wrinkled as a walnut and I found him in Khan el-Khalili in Cairo, that's the big market. Oh right, you'd know that one well.

Well, his name was Achmed. The man, not the market of course. No last names. We were careful about that. I told him to call me Joe. Still, we'd better just keep that between us, sir. Don't want to get Achmed in trouble. But I needed those papers. I didn't know whether the Egyptian government would consider him their property under the Antiquities Act. The dragon, I mean, not Achmed. I certainly considered him mine. The dragon that is. And I was bringing him home. You know, that's why

Dana is the editor and not me. I prefer fiery dragons to pesky pronouns. No ointment for those. Hahahaha.

And of course I had to take the big chance bringing the dragon back. I mean—if I told my tale without this key bit of sulfurous proof, I knew no one would believe me. Especially not you, Dr. Puccini. And I'm real sorry about your mustache, but I did warn you. Really I did. You just had to get down so close to him. I didn't realize you were *that* nearsighted or I would have brought along a magnifying glass. Though a magnificent glass would have been more to the point. Yes, another joke. Well, maybe a *little* funny?

Now, to the business of my paper. You see, I can get down to the point when I have to. "The Mesopotamian Dragon: Fictions and Facts, A Transatlantic Case Study" and the D you gave me. You wrote in that green pen with the archaic flourishes: "We deal in truth in this class, or as near as we can come to it, Mr. Darnton, and not creatures out of myth."

I expect you understand your myth-stake now, sir. Hahahahaha. But seriously, my grade?

THE VISITED MAN

MOLLY GLOSS

In April after the death of his wife—her death coming only weeks after the death of his son—Marie-Lucien stopped going out of his apartment. It had been his habit to go out every morning to buy a newspaper, five bronze centimes for *Le Petit Journal*; but as he stopped caring to read about assassinations and political scandals, or anything else occurring in the world, so he stopped going out to buy the paper. Then he stopped going to the butcher, the tea shop, the fish market, the bakery. Every Wednesday and Saturday his landlord M. Queval brought a few groceries and sundries to him from lists he scribbled on scraps of old newsprint. He and M. Queval exchanged perhaps a dozen words while standing on the landing, words about frostbit spinach or the freshness of the fish, but otherwise Marie-Lucien saw no one, spoke to no one. Friends who came to the house went away after a few words passed through the cracked-open door, or perhaps without sight of him at all; and after the first weeks they stopped bothering to inquire of his well-being.

He had taken his pension from the service more than a year earlier, a pension barely sufficient to pay the rent and the groceries, and he had been working mornings for a trinket vendor in order to eke out a decent living for himself and his family. Now he stopped going out to work, which meant the matter of money would eventually become acute; but he ate very little, spent nothing on clothes, and the weather in April was warm enough to put off the question of coal. He slept in his clothes. In the morning he warmed up yesterday's bad coffee and drank it while looking out at the traffic in the street. Then he undressed slowly and performed the necessary morning ablutions, before dressing again in the same shabby clothes. Most of the hours of his days were spent turning over a deck of cards in slow games of Patience.

Late in May, after Marie-Lucien had spent the better part of two months alone with no expectation or wish for this to change, someone knocked at his door. He would not have bothered to answer, but the knocking became continuous and insistent and finally he felt forced to rise from his chair. The apartment directly below his, and just above M. Queval's street-side metal foundry, was occupied by an artist, a painter of poor reputation who people in the neighborhood said was either a clever joker or slightly mad, a precocious senile. It was this painter who now stood on the landing, wearing a tranquil expression as though he had not for the past many minutes been pounding vigorously on the door in a demand to be let in. He held in one arm a skeletal and filthy brown tabby, and announced matter-of-factly that the cat had followed him back from his morning walk through Montsouris Park, and that he could not take it into his own apartment because "as you know, there are the other cats." The two men had seldom met, seldom exchanged more than a remark about the weather as they passed each other going in or out of their apartments; and in the past two months they had not met or spoken at all. Now, as if they had already discussed the matter and reached some sort of agreement, he delivered the little tabby into Marie-Lucien's hands. "She is starving, you realize, and her stomach must first be calmed with tiny portions of oatmeal before she will be able to keep down cream and fish and begin to put on weight."

Marie-Lucien, who was startled out of words, managed only, "I cannot…" and the painter, who had already begun to descend the stairs, replied cheerfully without turning, "Oh my dear, none of us can."

Marie-Lucien put the cat on the floor of the landing and shut the door, but her continuous piteous crying was difficult to listen to. He finally opened the door again, but only to put out scraps of a lunch he had not eaten, which she ate and then immediately vomited. He was forced to boil up some oatmeal and feed it to her slowly until her starving stomach became calm. And of course by the time she began to put on weight from being fed little tidbits of fish and sips of cream, she had made herself at home in his apartment.

The arrival of the cat did little to change Marie-Lucien's habits. He continued to sleep in his clothes and to spend his days playing solitary card games. But now that his attention had been drawn to it, he frequently heard the voice of the painter rising up from the apartment below him, particularly at night, muttering to himself or perhaps speaking to his paintings; sometimes declaiming lines of poetry; sometimes singing badly or playing a few fragile notes on a violin, the refrains of humorous and nostalgic songs Marie-Lucien remembered from his own childhood and from the nursery days of his son. When the painter thumped heavily against the walls or the floor and woke him in the night, he complained aloud to the cat: "Do you hear him? The damn painter? He is stumbling drunk again." Presumably these sounds had been coming up through the floor during the entire year the painter had lived in the apartment below, and Marie-Lucien had simply been oblivious of them until now—preoccupied with watching over the illness and death of his son, and then his wife.

In June, after a string of unreasonably cold and rainy days, there was again a banging on the door and the painter held out a squat black dog whose wiry coat was muddy and matted. "Abused and abandoned," he said, with a brief, commiserating smile.

"I cannot," Marie-Lucien said, and shut the door.

The painter began beating on the jamb, calling and repeating "M. Pichon, M. Pichon."

Finally Marie-Lucien opened the door again. "I am not M. Pichon," he said unhappily. "Please go and find this man Pichon, give him the dog and leave me alone."

The painter shook his head, still smiling. "Ha ha, I am famous, among other things, for getting wrong the names even of my friends." He bowed slightly. "M. Guyard, I apologize." This was not Marie-Lucien's name any more than Pichon, but it seemed pointless to say so. "He likes tomatoes," the painter said, "and chicken," and for a confused moment Marie-Lucien thought he was speaking of Pichon, or Guyard; but then the painter placed the dog in his arms and turned for the stairs.

Hurriedly Marie-Lucien started after him, holding out the animal, which smelled of mud and oak leaves and the sewer. "This is impossible!" he protested. "M. Rousseau, take him back." He intended to sound strict and authoritative but he had been speechless for so long that his voice came out hoarse and thin; and even to his own ears, his urgent insistence that he could not keep the dog seemed as querulous as an old woman's whining. He was forced to trail the painter down the stairs, calling out ridiculously that he could not afford chicken even for himself, and as he followed the painter right into his apartment, repeating again his refusal to keep the dog, he was startled to find himself suddenly in a jungle—huge umbels, fans, rockets, cascades of intense greens, spangled with the enormous cups and corollas of unimaginably bright magenta and yellow flowers.

"Oh!" he said, and staggered back.

They were paintings, of course, many of them quite large paintings, standing along all the walls of the rooms, and Marie-Lucien blushed and straightened up when he realized it. In fact, they were not even very good paintings, having no more than a child's sense of perspective, and drawn entirely without shadow or relief. The tiger, which had seemed so ready to spring at Marie-Lucien from among the leaves, he now saw was flat and simple and unconvincing as a picture postcard. He frowned, and said the first thing that came into his mouth, which was, "The flowers are too large, I have never seen flowers in life this large."

"Haven't you?" the painter said, and gazed about at his own work, entirely unpersuaded.

Many of these jungle scenes were of death and dismemberment—jaguars and tigers and lions variously attacking Negroes, a white horse, a hunch-shouldered Indian buffalo. Yet there was something oddly innocent in all the expressions, as if the creatures were only playing at a game, and in a moment would scramble to their feet, laughing, their wounds nothing more than circus greasepaint. Now that Marie-Lucien had regained his composure, the feeling this summoned in him was odd as well: odd, that paintings of such violence and bloodshed conjured for him an ingenuous child's world, a world in which the lion lies down with the lamb.

After several moments the little black dog in his arms squirmed to be released, and woke him from the brief dream state he must have slipped into.

"M. Rousseau, I cannot keep this dog," he said hoarsely, unequivocally, and let the dog down onto the floor. The little thing immediately ran out the door and up the stairs, where his claws could be heard scrabbling across the floor of Marie-Lucien's apartment. This was followed shortly by the cat's yowl and then the dog's tortured yelp.

The painter laughed: "A dog is the emblem of fidelity," he said, as if pronouncing from a pulpit. Then he began rustling through cupboards, apparently in search of glasses or a bottle, for he said brightly, "We should first have a glass of wine," though he did not say what he meant by "first."

"I must…" Marie-Lucien tried to say, but Rousseau waved a hand and said, "All the more reason not to." He poured a few drops of vin blanc, the last from a dusty green bottle, into two paint-smeared cups and held out one of the cups to Marie-Lucien. "Santé!" he said, and downed the bit of wine in a single swallow. Marie-Lucien, because he could not readily think of a reason not to, drank his also. The wine was vinegary and tasted of the dust of the bottle; or perhaps there had been dust in the cups.

The painter then clapped him on the shoulder and began steering him from painting to painting in the two rooms of the apartment, declaiming before each one as if he were a docent in a museum. Not all of his work was of the jungle. There were a few commissioned portraits of children whose parents, Rousseau cheerfully admitted, had refused payment on grounds the painting did not resemble their child. Two were small portraits of the artist, painted not from mirrors but from "the image of my handsome self I carry in my own mind, ha ha!" One was a very strange painting of a man resembling Rousseau standing over an infant apparently abandoned beside a country road, though neither the child nor the man appeared the least frightened or disturbed by their circumstances. There were, as well, scenes from the Parisian countryside and the suburbs, and of Laval, where the artist had spent his childhood. In them, cows grazed in stiff profile, completely without perspective; roads ran between hedges and fences without any sense at all of a third dimension. It was evident to Marie-Lucien that Rousseau was a second-rate amateur; but at the same time he felt himself helplessly drawn into the world of the paintings, a world beyond everyday life, beyond time, a strange and dreamlike world in which childhood's careless days had deepened without abandoning their purity.

"The colors…" he said at one point, without any notion of how to finish the thought.

"Yes, yes. But it's my blacks that Gauguin admires: the perfection of my blacks."

Marie-Lucien did not for a moment consider the painter's boast to be true—Gauguin, after all, being a somewhat notorious artist—but he was more alert than most people to the color of hearse cloth, having recently watched the undertaker's mutes carry off first his only son and then his wife. Now that his attention had been brought to it, he became aware of the depth, the rich inkiness of the blacks in all the paintings; and he realized what it was he should have said about the colors: that their bold frankness must come from offsetting them with so much black.

When they finished their tour of the "Imaginary Museum," as Rousseau laughingly called it, Marie-Lucien went back up to his apartment where the black dog and striped cat had come to an uneasy détente; and he resumed his sequestered life, though the conditions were somewhat moderated from the need to bring a dog down to the street twice a day to relieve himself. He and the painter did not speak to each other again for more than a fortnight, or only on the handful of occasions when they passed on the front stoop as Marie-Lucien carried the dog out to the gutter. But one evening late in June Rousseau came to his door well after dark, banging on the jamb and calling out, "M. Bernier, M. Bernier." Then, as if they were old comrades, he took Marie-Lucien's arm and said, "*Jardin des Plantes!* Best seen at night, you know, leaning through the fence," and pulled him toward the stairs.

"I am not Bernier," Marie-Lucien said, but without expecting to accomplish anything by it.

"No, no, of course not, I have known Bernier for years and he is a vast pig of a man, lacking completely in charm, you are much superior in every way to Bernier." The painter spoke consolingly, as if Marie-Lucien had confided a terrible dissatisfaction with himself.

They walked along the streets in silence, Rousseau's arm looped through Marie-Lucien's. He was not an old man, the painter, not even as old as Marie-Lucien who was not yet seventy, but he strolled along at an old man's pace, limping slightly and facing straight ahead when he walked, turning his entire body on the frequent occasions when he paused to peer into shop windows with a concentrated frown. Marie-Lucien waited while the painter carried out these examinations, waited without interest but also without impatience. It had been three months since he had traveled farther than the sidewalk directly in front of M. Queval's foundry; he was astonished to find himself out and about so late at night, interested to find he was not afraid of the streets largely emptied of all but the unsavory and the wretched.

At the gates of the Botanical Gardens the painter clasped the iron bars with both hands and thrust his head as far into the closed park as his shoulders would permit. "Such a strange and mysterious world," he said very quietly. Marie-Lucien, standing behind him, peered into the darkness without seeing anything he considered strange or mysterious. But he became gradually aware that, away from street lamps as they were here, the trees and bushes were wrapped in fantastic black shadows. He pushed his own head between the iron bars and leaned into the fence; and after several moments he began to make out amongst the shrubbery the vivid yellow blossoms of a rose, magnified hugely against the blackness.

In the nights that followed, Marie-Lucien and the painter, after sharing a bowl of soup at one apartment or the other, shut the aggrieved cat and dog in the upstairs apartment and strolled through the Luxembourg Gardens and Montsouris Park and leaned into the fences of various private gardens. They explored not only the parks and woodlands and brushy clearings but traversed the bridges and aqueducts and watched the late-night goings-on at the quais and along the banks of the rivers and canals. They spoke little, which suited Marie-Lucien: he found Rousseau to be a strange sort, just as people had said, possibly a confidence trickster or a candid idiot. Once, while they were studying the statue of a lion in the darkness of the Luxembourg Gardens, the painter said matter-of-factly that the "other cats" he had spoken of, the ones that occupied his apartment, were in fact lions and jaguars and tigers that wandered in from the jungles to visit him at night and sit for their portraits. It was impossible to know if he was speaking figuratively, or if he was genuinely hallucinatory, or if he merely enjoyed playing the part of an eccentric artist. But Marie-Lucien, walking with him at night, looking into the dark corners of the city—coming suddenly upon the black statue of a lion in the midst of clipped hedges and graveled paths—often felt as he had when he had first walked into the painter's apartment and gazed on his strange canvases: a vivid awareness of how beautiful and dangerous the world was, both tender and cruel. And this was the closest he had come, since the deaths of his wife and his son, to discovering any sort of meaning in the world.

One night while they were standing on a viaduct watching the body of some sad unfortunate being fished out of the water, the painter said thoughtfully, "I have run into ghosts everywhere. One of them tormented me for more than a year when I was a customs inspector."

Marie-Lucien did not believe in ghosts. Belief in ghosts would have required him to believe in something beyond death, a world of the spirit. He had been, as a young man, at the battle of Sedan where thousands had died; and he had watched his wife and his son on their death beds; and he had never had the least inkling that any scrap or glimpse of the people he loved remained anywhere in the universe. He had come to the unshakable conclusion that death was unremitting and permanent; death, he believed, was death. He said to the painter, to turn him aside from his ghosts, "You were a *douanier?*"

Rousseau smiled modestly. "Nothing so grand. A mere inspector." But he was not put off the track. He said, "Whenever I was on duty this ghost would stand ten paces away, annoying me, poking fun." He turned to Marie-Lucien with a somewhat amused grimace. "Letting out smelly farts just to nauseate me."

Marie-Lucien smiled slightly.

"I shot at him, but a phantom apparently cannot die again. Whenever I tried to grab him, he vanished into the ground and reappeared somewhere else."

Marie-Lucien asked him uninterestedly—mere politeness—"Was he someone you knew? An old acquaintance?"

"Not at all. He was not haunting me, but the post, which was at the Gate of Arcueil. When I left that post, I never saw him again. I suppose something must have happened there, perhaps something in the way he was killed, that caused his soul to attach itself to the gate, or to the person guarding the gate."

At the muddy edge of the canal several men were now standing in the glare of gas lamps, surrounding the naked body of a young woman, a woman only recently dead, her body still lovely, unblemished, not sufflated, her long brown hair from this distance seeming to hang in a neat braid across one shoulder and breast. The painter's expression, looking down at the scene, slowly softened into satisfaction. "I don't like to read the big tabloids that talk a lot of politics, what I read is the *Magasin Pittoresque.*" He laughed. "The more drowned bodies in the river the greater my reading pleasure."

Marie-Lucien was taken aback. "That's a terrible thing to say."

"Is it?" Rousseau said, in a tone of complete sincerity, and might have been about to turn to Marie-Lucien to collect his answer, but suddenly swept his hand and his glance skyward. "There goes that poor woman's soul," he said, with surprised delight.

Marie-Lucien looked quickly where Rousseau had pointed but saw only the full moon hanging low and white on the night sky, as perfectly round as if it had been drawn with a compass. "What?" he said in frustration. He did not at all believe the painter had seen a drowned soul flying up to heaven but couldn't help his question, or its meaning: Not, *What did you say?* but *What did you see?*

"Ah, such peace!" the painter said quietly, which he may have meant as an answer.

In the early part of August, Rousseau came to Marie-Lucien's door unexpectedly—it was morning, and Marie-Lucien was still drinking his terrible coffee, still wearing the rumpled clothes he had slept in. The painter took hold of his arm and said, "*Le Ménagerie!* Best seen at night when the animals are at their most alert, but unfortunately open only in the daylight. Ten centimes and you're in." Marie-Lucien attempted to refuse. It was one thing, their nightly strolls, the two not-quite-old men leaning into fences, peering at trees and flowering shrubs in dark public parks and private gardens; but the daylight hours he intended still to keep for his own use, which was not grieving, as his friends had supposed, but a prolonged, expectant waiting for his own death.

Rousseau, of course, would not be put off. He had a long-established morning practice of strolling through one or another of his favorite amusement parks, and he had made up his mind to share that pleasure with Marie-Lucien. Shortly, they were out on the lively daytime streets, and Rousseau, brisk with morning energy, led the way to the Zoological Gardens, where he spent a good long while studying a mangy lion rocking restlessly in a space too small to accommodate pacing; and kinkajou monkeys and gibbon apes quietly pining in their cages. None of this was of much interest to Marie-Lucien, or only insofar as to strengthen his old opinion that he lived in a brutal, godless universe. He stood back from the animal pens, shifting his weight lionlike in anxious boredom.

When finally they left the zoo, Rousseau insisted they must visit the Palmarium, and the Orangerie, as well; and inside those hothouses, Marie-Lucien felt as if he had slipped once again into a dream. Confronted with a spectacle of perpetual novelty—huge Paulownia trees, tropical palms, mango and pineapple trees, thick-stalked grasses taller than any man—he seemed to recognize everything, to rediscover it all in his memories. It struck him suddenly that the foliage under the translucent glass vault was the most exalted green he had ever seen outside Rousseau's jungle canvases, and when he said this to the painter—a bit of mild praise coming rather late in their acquaintance—Rousseau replied offhandedly, "I don't seek and invent, my dear, I only find and discover."

"Well then, it seems to me, you find and discover strangeness above all," Marie-Lucien said, which the painter took as true praise and which provoked in him a pleased laugh.

In the weeks that followed, because Marie-Lucien had little interest in visiting the Zoo or the Monkey Palace again, they confined their morning walks to the Orangerie, the Palmarium and the Botanical Gardens, which Rousseau said was not an inconvenience. The animals in the menagerie were, after all, not suitable studies for his art—always either reclining or sitting in a torpor—and his genuine models (his expression guileless as a child's) were the wild ones who visited him at night.

One morning as the two men walked back through the streets from *le Jardin des Plantes* to the apartments, the painter wrapped an arm about

Marie-Lucien's shoulders and said, "Come into the studio, M. Bernal, see what strangeness I've been about in recent days. The woman has been posing for me, the woman we met on the quai."

Marie-Lucien had no recollection of meeting a woman on the quai, but this did not surprise him, as the painter had a practice of striking up conversation with virtually anybody they passed, even prostitutes and obvious villains; and Marie-Lucien the practice of not joining in. "I am not Bernal," he said mildly, but only from habit.

The painting Rousseau wished him to see was of a nude reclining on a Bordeaux-red chaise inexplicably set down in the midst of a jungle lush with impossibly huge Egyptian lotus blossoms. The work was far from completed—the foliage flourishing before the woman—but Marie-Lucien could already see that she was no one he recognized; or, given the painter's awkward draftsmanship, perhaps he would not have recognized her even if she had been someone he knew well. It was a very strange painting, of course, very much in line with the greater part of his work, and the sort of thing that caused Marie-Lucien to lose his foothold in the world: In the trees were exotic birds and monkeys, in the sky a perfectly round bone-white moon, in the foliage a glimpse of an elephant, as well as lurking lions and serpents; and oddest of all, a Negro snake charmer holding a musette to his lips. Even half-finished as it was, the painting gave an impression of stiff, stark peace, of Dantesque silence.

Marie-Lucien's wife had died slowly of consumption; for years before her death she had been unable to engage him in sexual congress, and it had been years since he had bothered to abuse himself. At the intersection of circumstance and advancing age, he had become celibate without taking a decision, and was somewhat interested in the fact that paintings and photographs of naked women no longer aroused him. In any case, this particular painting of a nude was not, to his eye, erotic. Her ankles were chastely crossed, her pubis neatly hidden behind the flesh of her thighs. One thick arm outstretched on the back of the chaise seemed in gesture toward the snake charmer or the lions, but whether this was to beckon or fend off, was difficult to know. She was dark-haired, dark-eyed, two twisted strands of her hair falling across one of her perfectly globular breasts. It seemed to Marie-Lucien that this was a woman not ashamed to be naked—not living in the world he knew, but in some universe absent the Biblical tale of sin.

"She is a Pole," the painter said, standing back in admiration of his own work. "A pious Polish girl, though I've drawn her as she is now, not pious at all but an innocent, an angel, restored to Genesis."

This was not quite what Marie-Lucien had been thinking, but near enough that he murmured, "Eve in Paradise."

The painter corrected him, in a tone of surprise, "Yadwigha, after death. Do you not recall how we watched her soul float up to the clouds?"

Marie-Lucien grappled through memory until he remembered the young woman lying dead on the bank of the canal, naked under the stares of half a dozen men. "It was only you who saw…" he began to say, but the painter was already going on, gesturing toward a Louis-Philippe sofa that was evidently the model for the chaise in his painting. "She has been posing for me here, every night. Her spirit has attached itself to me, which I suppose is due to my catching sight of her as she departed her body. Poor girl drowned herself out of grief."

Marie-Lucien said, smiling very faintly, "So not as pious as all that, if she killed herself. God condemns the suicide."

The painter brushed this away with a gesture. "God condemns no one, it's the priests who are always in a mood to condemn." He gazed at his painting in silence. "The girl had suffered greatly, her husband and child dead in an overturned taxi. How can we condemn her for finding this world unbearable? I should have found it unbearable myself, years ago, and ten times over, if I weren't a bit of a spiritist." He turned to Marie-Lucien with a smile. "Art is the confession of its maker. You shall have to look at my art, to know why sadness has not grabbed hold of me in its teeth."

It was Rousseau's nonchalance that offended Marie-Lucien, and caused him to remember suddenly a remark the painter had made, a remark about the pleasure he took from reading about drowned bodies hauled from the river. At the time, he had been distracted from it; but now, recalling the tone and the words, Marie-Lucien said bitterly, "What do you know of unbearable? of grief? of great suffering? When you have lost your wife and your son, as I have, then speak to me of unbearable."

The painter gave him a startled look. "Oh my dear M. Derain, I am sorry to hear of it. Sorry to hear of it. Your poor heart." He draped his arm across Marie-Lucien Derain's shoulders and drew him close.

But this was the beginning of the end of their friendship. Marie-Lucien took work soon afterward with a neighborhood pork butcher, and seldom found time to join Rousseau on his morning visits to the pleasure gardens. They carried on their evening explorations for a short while, but ended them after an argument: When Marie-Lucien objected to hearing another tale of ghosts, the painter said to him that people who had never dreamed when fully awake were loathe to admit the realness of dream; and Marie-Lucien took this badly. Afterward he merely nodded when he passed Rousseau going in or out of the apartments, and if the painter spoke to him, he replied in as few words as possible.

In January during a spell of cold, bright weather, Marie-Lucien began working very late helping the butcher render fat, and one night climbing the stairs after midnight carrying scraps of meat for the cat and the dog, he passed the painter's open door and saw a naked woman posing on the Louis-Phillipe sofa, her arm outstretched and beckoning, her pallid body clothed in moonlight. The woman, who may have heard his steps on the landing, turned to him a face not beautiful at all but transparent and luminous, lit from within; and then she resumed her pose, fixing her gaze perhaps on the moon that he could not see but which he imagined must be visible through the apartment window. Her expression in profile was difficult to interpret, her mouth seeming at the verge of amusement but her thick brows intent and straight. One long brown braid fell across her shoulder and one breast. The painter, too, turned and stood very poised and erect, one thumb pushed through the hold of his palette, his brush held down in the other hand. The look he gave Marie-Lucien was a questioning frown of expectancy and joy; but they did not speak, and Marie-Lucien continued up the stairs, his heart thudding. When he sat down inside his own apartment the animals came immediately into his lap, and he rested his trembling hands in their fur.

In March, Marie-Lucien heard from his landlord that the painter had hung a new canvas at the *Société des Peintres Indépendants*: a painting of a naked woman dreaming on a Louis-Phillipe couch. Word later went around the neighborhood that this new painting had brought Rousseau a flurry of minor attention, and the admiration even of other artists. When the pork butcher took his wife to the salon to view it, Marie-Lucien stayed behind and kept the shop open.

Often, during that winter, he heard the painter's voice in conversation with himself or with his paintings, and from time to time the voice of this or that visitor. Twice, Rousseau gave parties to which Marie-Lucien was invited, but which he did not attend, parties at which the host played his violin very badly, and Marie-Lucien heard rising up through the floor the sounds of people applauding and laughing at the same time.

After the second party, the painter knocked on Marie-Lucien's door to plead poverty and beg twenty-five francs. "I imagine if you had saved all the money spent on parties, you would not need to beg from your friends and acquaintances," Marie-Lucien said to him, after he had given over the twenty-five francs. He had not wished to be the man's friend or to be invited to his entertainments, so could not quite account for the sound of bitterness in these words. The painter was not at all taken aback. He kissed Marie-Lucien on both cheeks and said fondly, "My dear, you are like a brother to me," which Marie-Lucien felt to be a grandiose figure of speech.

In the months afterward, he seldom saw the painter. Once, through his window, he watched Rousseau limping up the street to the apartments, appearing so sickly and pale that Marie-Lucien was struck with a moment of remorse; but then, to M. Queval who was standing on the front stoop, the painter complained in an aggrieved voice that he "suffered greatly" from a phlegmon in his leg. These were the same words he had used, speaking of the drowned woman, the very words that had begun their estrangement—that she had "suffered greatly"—and when he heard them, Marie-Lucien turned away from the window.

In September he opened his newspaper and was startled to read that the painter had died. *Le Petit Journal* was famous for the brevity of its reporting, and spent only a few lines to say that the minor artist H. Rousseau had died of a blood clot after surgery to remove a gangrenous leg; and that he had belonged to the *Société des Peintres Indépendants*, where an artist paid twenty-five francs a year for the privilege of hanging his canvases.

It had been many months since Marie-Lucien had visited the Palmarium or the Orangerie. On the day of the painter's burial he walked through the hothouses slowly; and then went into the menagerie, which he and Rousseau had visited only once together. A jaguar trudged in circles, dazed and ill, in a narrow box where he bumped into all the corners; the lion reclined in a stupor. As Marie-Lucien was going out again, he turned to see if it was his friend he had glimpsed going in one of the other gates, though of course it was only an old man with a thick mustache, a sickly complexion, a slight limp.

He stopped at a newsstand to buy a copy of *Le Soleil* for the obituaries, and read as he was walking back to the apartments that Rousseau was "a painter without any of the notions required by art;" and that his friends had spoken of him as a man of generosity, credulity and good humor. His living relations were a daughter Julia, and granddaughter Jeanne; he had been preceded in death by two wives and six of his seven children. In the painter's last days, *Le Soleil* reported, he had become delirious: had spoken of seeing angels, and of hearing their celestial music.

When Marie-Lucien, climbing the stairs, passed the open door of the painter's apartment he saw a woman standing inside, a woman he remembered having seen twice before. She was gazing at a new, unfinished painting, standing before it as unclad as the figure in the painting, which was herself, Yadwigha. In the painting her dead body lay beside a stream, watched over by the wide eyes of lions and monkeys. In the painter's apartment, her ghost turned to Marie-Lucien with an expression innocent as a child's; a look of expectancy and of joy. In a moment a woman came out from the second room of the apartment, a women Marie-Lucien had never met nor heard the painter speak of, a woman in black crepe, the painter's daughter Julia. And in the unfinished painting, death's bright angel ascended through the impossibly blue sky.

GALÁPAGOS

CAITLÍN R. KIERNAN

MARCH 17, 2077 (WEDNESDAY)

Whenever I wake up screaming, the nurses kindly come in and give me the shiny yellow pills and the white pills flecked with gray; they prick my skin with hollow needles until I grow quiet and calm again. They speak in exquisitely gentle voices, reminding me that I'm home, that I've been home for many, many months. They remind me that if I open the blinds and look out the hospital window, I will see a parking lot, and cars, and a carefully tended lawn. I will only see California. I will see only Earth. If I look up, and it happens to be day, I'll see the sky, too, sprawled blue above me and peppered with dirty-white clouds and contrails. If it happens to be night, instead, I'll see the comforting pale orange skyglow that mercifully hides the stars from view. I'm home, not strapped into *Yastreb-4*'s taxi module. I can't crane my neck for a glance at the monitor screen displaying a tableaux of dusty volcanic wastelands as I speed by the Tharsis plateau, more than four hundred kilometers below me. I can't turn my head and gaze through the tiny docking windows at *Pilgrimage*'s glittering alabaster hull, quickly growing larger as I rush towards the aft docking port. These are merely memories, inaccurate and untrustworthy, and may only do me the harm that memories are capable of doing.

Then the nurses go away. They leave the light above my bed burning, and tell me if I need anything at all to press the intercom button. They're just down the hall, and they always come when I call. They're never anything except prompt, and do not fail to arrive bearing the chemical solace of pharmaceuticals, only half of which I know by name. I am not neglected. My needs are met as well as anyone alive can meet them. I'm too precious a commodity not to coddle. I'm the woman who was invited to the strangest, most terrible rendezvous in the history of space exploration. The one they dragged all the way to Mars after *Pilgrimage* abruptly, inexplicably, diverged from its mission parameters, when the crew went silent and the AI stopped responding. I'm the woman who stepped through an airlock hatch and into that alien Eden; I'm the one who spoke with a goddess. I'm the woman who was the goddess' lover, when she was still human and had a name and a consciousness that could be comprehended.

"Are you sleeping better?" the psychiatrist asks, and I tell him that I sleep just fine, thank you, seven to eight hours every night now. He nods and patiently smiles, but I know I haven't answered his question. He's actually asking me if I'm still having the nightmares about my time aboard *Pilgrimage*, if they've decreased in their frequency and/or severity. He doesn't want to know *if* I sleep, or how *long* I sleep, but if my sleep is still haunted. Though he'd never use that particular word, *haunted*.

He's a thin, balding man, with perfectly manicured nails and an unremarkable mid-Atlantic accent. He dutifully makes the commute down from Berkeley once a week, because those are his orders, and I'm too great a puzzle for his inquisitive mind to ignore. All in all, I find the psychiatrist far less helpful than the nurses and their dependable drugs. Whereas they've been assigned the task of watching over me, of soothing and steadying me and keeping me from harming myself, he's been given the unenviable responsibility of discovering what happened during the comms blackout, those seventeen interminable minutes after I boarded the derelict ship and promptly lost radio contact with *Yastreb-4* and Earth. Despite so many debriefings and interviews that I've lost count, NASA still thinks I'm holding out on them. And maybe I am. Honestly, it's hard for me to say. It's hard for me to keep it all straight anymore: what happened and what didn't, what I've said to them and what I've only thought about saying, what I genuinely remember and what I may have fabricated wholesale as a means of self-preservation.

The psychiatrist says it's to be expected, this sort of confusion from someone who's survived very traumatic events. *He* calls the events very traumatic, by the way. I don't; I'm not yet sure if I think of them that way. Regardless, he's diagnosed me as suffering from Survivor Syndrome, which he also calls K-Z Syndrome. There's a jack in my hospital room, filtered web access, but I was able to look up "K-Z Syndrome." It was named for a Nazi concentration camp survivor, an Israeli author named Yehiel De-Nur. De-Nur published under the pseudonym Ka-Tzetnik 135633. That was his designation or prisoner number or whatever at

Auschwitz, and K-Z Syndrome is named after him. In 1956, he published *House of Dolls*, describing the Nazi "Joy Division," a system that utilized Jewish women as sex slaves.

The psychiatrist is the one who asked if I would at least try to write it down, what happened, what I saw and heard (and smelled and felt) when I entered the *Pilgrimage* a year and a half ago. He knows, of course, that there have already been numerous written and vidded depositions and affidavits for NASA and the CSS/NSA, the WHO, the CDC and the CIA and, to tell the truth, I don't *know* who requested and read and then filed away all those reports. He knows about them, though, and that, by my own admission, they barely scratched the surface of whatever happened out there. He knows, but I reminded him, anyway.

"This will be different," he said. "This will be more subjective." And the psychiatrist explained that he wasn't looking for a blow-by-blow linear narrative of my experiences aboard *Pilgrimage*, and I told him that was good, because I seem to have forgotten how to think or relate events in a linear fashion, without a lot of switchbacks and digressions and meandering.

"Just write," he said. "Write what you can remember, and write until you don't want to write anymore."

"That would be now," I said, and he silently stared at me for a while. He didn't laugh, even though I'd thought it was pretty funny.

"I understand that the medication makes this sort of thing more difficult for you," he said, sometime later. "But the medication helps you reach back to those things you don't want to remember, those things you're trying to forget." I almost told him that he was starting to sound like a character in a Lewis Carroll story, but I didn't. Our hour was almost over, anyway.

So, after three days of stalling, I'm trying to write something that will make you happy, Dr. Ostrowski. I know you're trying to do your job, and I know a lot of people must be peering over your shoulder, expecting the sort of results they've failed to get themselves. I don't want to show up for our next session empty handed.

The taxi module was on autopilot during the approach. See, I'm not an astronaut or mission specialist or engineer or anything like that. I'm an anthropologist, and I mostly study the Middle Paleolithic of Europe and Asia Minor. I have a keen interest in tool use and manufacture by the Neanderthals. Or at least that's who I used to be. Right now, I'm a madwoman in a psych ward at a military hospital in San Jose, California. I'm a case number, and an eyewitness who has proven less than satisfactory.

But, what I'm *trying* to say, doctor, the module *was* on autopilot, and there was nothing for me to do but wait there inside my encounter suit and sweat and watch the round screen divided by the Y-shaped reticle as I approached the derelict's docking port, the taxi barreling forward at 0.06 meters per second. The ship grew so huge so quickly, looming up in the blackness, and that only made the whole thing seem that much more unreal.

I tried hard to focus, to breathe slowly, and follow the words being spoken between the painful, bright bursts of static in my ears, the babble of sound trapped inside the helmet with me. *Module approaching 50-meter threshold. On target and configuring KU-band from radar to comms mode. Slowing now to 0.045 meters per second. Decelerating for angular alignment, extending docking ring,* nine meters, three meters, a whole lot of noise and nonsense about latches and hooks and seals, capture and final position, and then it seemed like I wasn't moving anymore. Like the taxi wasn't moving anymore. We *were*, of course, the little module and I, only now we were riding piggyback on *Pilgrimage*, locked into geosynchronous orbit, with nothing but the instrument panel to remind me I wasn't sitting still in space. Then the Mission Commander was telling me I'd done a great job, congratulations, they were all proud of me, even though I hadn't done anything except sit and wait.

But all this is right there in the mission dossiers, doctor. You don't need me to tell you these things. You already know that *Pilgrimage*'s AI would allow no one but me to dock, and that MS Lowry's repeated attempts to hack the firewall failed. You know about the nurses and their pills, and Yehiel De-Nur and *House of Dolls*. You know about the affair I had with the Korean payload specialist during the long flight to Mars. You're probably skimming this part, hoping it gets better a little farther along.

So, I'll try to tell you something you don't know. Just one thing, for now.

Hanging there in my tiny, life-sustaining capsule, suspended two hundred and fifty miles above extinct Martian volcanoes and surrounded by near vacuum, I had two recurring thoughts, the only ones that I can now clearly recall having had. First, the grim hope that, when the hatch finally opened—*if* the hatch opened—they'd all be dead. All of them. Every single one of the men and women aboard *Pilgrimage*, and most especially her. And, secondly, I closed my eyes as tightly as I could and wished that I would soon discover there'd been some perfectly mundane accident or malfunction, and the bizarre, garbled transmissions that had sent us all the way to Mars to try and save the day meant nothing at all. But I *only* hoped and wished, mind you. I haven't prayed since I was fourteen years old.

MARCH 19, 2077 (FRIDAY)

Last night was worse than usual. The dreams, I mean. The nurses and my physicians don't exactly approve of what I've begun writing for you, Dr. Ostrowski. Of what you've asked me to do. I suspect they would say there's a conflict of interest at work. They're supposed to keep me sane and healthy, but here you are, the latest episode in the inquisition that's landed me in their ward. When I asked for the keypad this afternoon, they didn't want to give it to me. Maybe tomorrow, they said. Maybe the day *after* tomorrow. Right now, you need your rest. And sure, I know they're right. What you want, it's only making matters worse, for them *and* for me, but when I'd finally had enough and threatened to report the hospital staff for attempting to obstruct a federal investigation, they relented. But, just so you know, they've got me doped to the gills with an especially potent cocktail of tranquilizers and antipsychotics, so I'll be lucky if I can manage more than gibberish. Already, it's taken me half an hour to write (and repeatedly rewrite) this one paragraph, so who gets the final laugh?

Last night, I dreamed of the cloud again.

I dreamed I was back in Germany, in Darmstadt, only this time I wasn't sitting in that dingy hotel room near the Luisenplatz. This time it wasn't a phone call that brought me the news, or a courier. And I didn't look up to find *her* standing there in the room with me, which, you know, is how this one usually goes. I'll be sitting on the bed, or I'll walk out of the bathroom, or turn away from the window, and there she'll be. Even though *Pilgrimage* and its crew is all those hundreds of millions of kilometers away, finishing up their experiments at Ganymede and preparing to begin the long journey home, she's standing there in the room with me. Only not this time. Not last night.

The way it played out last night, I'd been cleared for access to the ESOC central control room. I have no idea why. But I was there, standing near one wall with a young French woman, younger than me by at least a decade. She was blonde, with green eyes, and she was pretty; her English was better than my French. I watched all those men and women, too occupied with their computer terminals to notice me. The pretty French woman (sorry, but I never learned her name), was pointing out different people, explaining their various roles: the ground operations manager, the director of flight operations, a visiting astrodynamics consultant, the software coordinator and so forth. The lights in the room were almost painfully bright, and when I looked up at the ceiling I saw it wasn't a ceiling at all, but the night sky, blazing with countless fluorescent stars.

And then that last transmission from *Pilgrimage* came in. We didn't realize it would be the last, but everything stopped, and everyone listened. Afterwards, no one panicked, as if they'd expected something of this sort all along. I understood that it had taken the message the better part of an hour to reach Earth, and that any reply would take just as long, but the French woman was explaining the communications delay, anyway.

"We can't know what that means," somebody said. "We can't *possibly* know, can we?"

"Run through the telemetry data again," someone else said, and I think it was the man the French woman had told me was the director of flight operations.

But it might have been someone else. I was still looking at the ceiling composed of starlight and planets, and the emptiness between starlight and planets, and I knew exactly what the transmission meant. It was a suicide note, of sorts, streamed across space at three hundred kilometers per second. I knew, because I plainly saw the mile-long silhouette of the ship sailing by overhead, only a silvery speck against the roiling backdrop of Jupiter. I saw that cloud, too, saw *Pilgrimage* enter it and exit a minute or so later (and I think I even paused to calculate the width of the cloud, based on the vessel's speed).

You know as well as me what was said that day, Dr. Ostrowski, the contents in that final broadcast. You've probably even committed it to memory, just like I have. I imagine you've listened to the tape more times than you could ever recollect, right? Well, what was said in my dream last night was almost verbatim what Commander Yun said in the actual transmission. There was only one difference. The part right at the end, when the Commander quotes from Chapter 13 of the Book of Revelation, that didn't happen. Instead, he said:

"Lead us from the unreal to real,
Lead us from darkness to light,
Lead us from death to immortality,
Om Shanti Shanti Shanti."

I admit I had to look that up online. It's from the Hindu Brihadaran-yaka Upanishad. I haven't studied Vedic literature since a seminar in grad school, and that was mostly an excuse to visit Bangalore. But the unconscious doesn't lose much, does it, doctor? And you never know what it's going to cough up, or when.

In my dream, I stood staring at the ceiling that was really no ceiling at all. If anyone else could see what I was seeing, they didn't act like it. The strange cloud near Ganymede made me think of an oil slick floating on water, and when *Pilgrimage* came out the far side, it was like those dying sea birds that wash up on beaches after tanker spills. That's exactly how it seemed to me, in the dream last night. I looked away, finally, looked down at the floor, and I was trying to explain what I'd seen to the French woman. I described the ruined plumage of ducks and gulls and cormorants, but I couldn't make her understand. And then I woke up. I woke up screaming, but you'll have guessed that part.

I need to stop now. The meds have made this almost impossible, and I should read back over everything I've written, do what I can to make myself clearer. I feel like I ought to say more about the cloud, because I've never seen it so clearly in any of the other dreams. It never before reminded me of an oil slick. I'll try to come back to this. Maybe later. Maybe not.

MARCH 20, 2077 (SATURDAY)

I don't have to scream for the nurses to know that I'm awake, of course. I don't have to scream, and I don't have to use the call button, either. They get everything relayed in realtime, directly from my cerebral cortex and hippocampus to their wrist tops, via the depth electrodes and subdural strips that were implanted in my head a few weeks after the crew of *Yastreb-4* was released from suborbital quarantine. They see it all, spelled out in the spikes and waves of electrocorticography, which is how I know *they* know that I'm awake right now, when I should be asleep. Tomorrow morning, I imagine there will be some sort of confab about adjusting the levels of my benzo and nonbenzo hypnotics to insure the insomnia doesn't return.

I'm not sure why I'm awake, really. There wasn't a nightmare, at least none I can recall. I woke up, and simply couldn't get back to sleep. After ten or fifteen minutes, I reached for the keypad. I find the soft cobalt-blue glow from the screen is oddly soothing, and it's nice to find comfort that isn't injected, something that I don't have to swallow or get from a jet spray or IV drip. And I want to have something more substantial to show the psychiatrist come Tuesday than dreams about Darmstadt, oil slicks, and pretty French women.

I keep expecting the vidcom beside my bed to buzz and wink to life, and there will be one of the nurses looking concerned and wanting to know if I'm all right, if I'd like a little extra coby to help me get back to sleep. But the box has been quiet and blank so far, which leaves me equal parts surprised and relieved.

"There are things you've yet to tell anyone," the psychiatrist said. "Those are the things I'm trying to help you talk about. If they've been repressed, they're the memories I'm trying to help you access." That is, they're what he's going to want to see when I give him the disk on Tuesday morning.

And if at first I don't succeed…

So, where was I? The handoff.

I'm sitting alone in the taxi, waiting, and below me Mars is a sullen, rusty cadaver of a planet. I have the distinct impression that it's watching as I'm handed off from one ship to the other. I imagine those countless craters and calderas have become eyes, and all those eyes are filled with jealousy and spite. The module's capture ring has successfully snagged *Pilgrimage*'s aft PMA, and it only takes a few seconds for the ring to achieve proper alignment. The module deploys twenty or so hooks, establishing an impermeable seal, and, a few seconds later, the taxi's hatch spirals open, and I enter the airlock. I feel dizzy, slightly nauseous, and I almost stumble, almost fall. I see a red light above the hatch go blue, and realize that the chamber has pressurized, which means I'm subject to the centripetal force that generates the ship's artificial gravity. I've been living in near zero g for more than eleven months, and nothing they told me in training or aboard the *Yastreb-4* could have prepared me for that sensation. The EVA suit's exoskeleton begins to compensate. It keeps me on my feet, keeps my atrophied muscles moving, keeps me breathing.

"You're doing great," Commander Yun assures me from the bridge of *Yastreb-4*, and that's when my comms cut out. I panic and try to return to the taxi module, but the hatchway has already sealed itself shut again. I have a go at the control panel, my gloved fingers fumbling clumsily at the unfamiliar switches, but can't get it to respond. The display on the inside of my visor tells me that my heart rate's jumped to 186 BPM, my blood pressure's in the red, and oxygen consumption has doubled. I'm hyperventilating, which has my CO_2 down and is beginning to affect blood oxygen levels. The medtab on my left wrist responds by secreting a relatively mild anxiolytic compound directly into the radial artery. Milder, I might add, than the shit they give me here.

And yes, Dr. Ostrowski, I know that you've read all this before. I know that I'm trying your patience, and you're probably disappointed. But I'm doing this the only way I know how. I was never any good at jumping into the deep end of the pool.

But we're almost there, I promise.

It took me a year and a half to find the words to describe what happened next, or to find the courage to say it aloud, or the resignation necessary to let it into the world. Whichever. They've been *my* secrets, and almost mine alone. And soon, now, they won't be anymore.

The soup from the medtab hits me, and I begin to relax. I give up on the airlock, and shut my eyes a moment, leaning forward, my helmet resting against the closed hatch. I'm almost certain my eyes are still shut when the *Pilgrimage*'s AI first speaks to me. And here, doctor, right *here*, pay attention, because this is where I'm going to come clean and tell you something I've never told another living soul. It's not a repressed memory that's suddenly found its way to the surface. It hasn't been coaxed from me by all those potent psychotropics. It's just something I've managed to keep to myself until now.

"Hello," the computer says. Only, I'd heard recordings of the mainframe's NLP, and this isn't the voice it was given. This is, unmistakably, *her* voice, only slightly distorted by the audio interface. My eyes are shut, and I don't open them right away. I just stand there, my head against the hatch, listening to that voice and to my heart. The sound of my breath is very loud inside the helmet.

"We were not certain our message had been received, or, if it had been, that it had been properly understood. We did not expect you would come so far."

"Then why did you call?" I asked, and opened my eyes.

"We were lonely," the voice replied. "We have not seen you in a very long time now."

I don't turn around. I keep my faceplate pressed to the airlock, some desperate, insensible part of me willing it to reopen and admit me once more to the sanctuary of the taxi. Whatever I should say next, of all the things I might say, what I *do* say was, simply, "Amery, I'm frightened."

There's a pause before her response, five or six or seven seconds, I don't know, and my fingers move futilely across the control pad again. I hear the inner hatch open behind me, though I'm fairly certain I'm not the one who opened it.

"We see that," she says. "But it wasn't our intent to make you afraid, Merrick. It was never our intent to frighten you."

"Amery, what's happened here?" I ask, speaking hardly above a whisper, but my voice is amplified and made clearer by the vocal modulator in my EVA helmet. "What happened to the ship, back at Jupiter? To the rest of the crew? What's happened to you?"

I expect another pause, but there isn't one.

"The most remarkable thing," she replies. And there's a sort of joy in her voice, even through the tinny flatness of the NLP relay. "You will hardly believe it."

"Are they dead, the others?" I ask her, and my eyes wander to the external atmo readout inside my visor. Argon's showing a little high, a few tenths of a percent off Earth normal, but not enough to act as an asphyxiant. Water vapor's twice what I'd have expected anywhere but the ship's hydroponics lab. Pressure's steady at 14.2 psi. Whatever happened aboard *Pilgrimage*, life support is still up and running. All the numbers are in the green.

"That's not a simple question to answer," she says, Amery or the AI or whatever it is I'm having this conversation with. "None of it is simple, Merrick. And yet, it is so elegant."

"Are they *dead?*" I ask again, resisting the urge to flip the release toggle beneath my chin and raise the visor. It stinks inside the suit, like sweat and plastic, urine and stale, recycled air.

"Yes," she says. "It couldn't be helped."

I lick my lips, Dr. Ostrowski, and my mouth has gone very, very dry. "Did you kill them, Amery?"

"You're asking the wrong questions," she says, and I stare down at my feet, at the shiny white toes of the EVA's overshoes.

"They're the questions we've come all the way out here to have answered," I tell her, or I tell it. "What questions would you have me ask, instead?"

"It may be, there is no longer any need for questions. It may be, Merrick, that you've been called to see, and seeing will be enough. The force that through the green fuse drives the flower, drives my green age, that blasts the roots of trees, is my destroyer."

"I've been summoned to Mars to listen to you quote Dylan Thomas?"

"You're *not* listening, Merrick. That's the thing. And that's why it will be so much easier if we show you what's happened. What's begun."

"And I am dumb to tell the lover's tomb," I say as softly as I can, but the suit adjusts the volume so it's just as loud as everything else I've said.

"We have not died," she replies. "You will find no tomb here," and, possibly, this voice that wants me to believe it is only Amery Domico has become defensive, and impatient, and somehow this seems the strangest thing so far. I imagine Amery speaking through clenched teeth. I imagine her rubbing her forehead like a headache's coming on, and it's my fault. "I am very much alive," she says, "and I need you to pay attention. You cannot stay here very long. It's not safe, and I will see no harm come to you."

"Why?" I ask her, only half-expecting a response. "Why isn't it safe for me to be here?"

"Turn around, Merrick," she says. "You've come so far, and there is so little time." I do as she says. I turn towards the voice, towards the airlock's open inner hatch.

It's almost morning. I mean, the sun will be rising soon. Here in California. Still no interruption from the nurses. But I can't keep this up. I can't do this all at once. The rest will have to wait.

MARCH 21, 2077 (SUNDAY)

Dr. Bernardyn Ostrowski is no longer handling my case. One of my physicians delivered the news this morning, bright and early. It came with no explanation attached. And I thought better of asking for one. That is, I thought better of wasting my breath asking for one. When I signed on for the *Yastreb-4* intercept, the waivers and NDAs and whatnot were all very, very clear about things like the principle of least privilege and mandatory access control. I'm told what they decide I need to know, which isn't much. I *did* ask if I should continue with the account of the mission that Dr. O asked me to write, and the physician (a hematologist named Prideaux) said he'd gotten no word to the contrary, and if there would be a change in the direction of my psychotherapy regimen, I'd find out about it when I meet with the new shrink Tuesday morning. Her name is Teasdale, by the way. Elenore Teasdale.

I thanked Dr. Prideaux for bringing me the news, and he only shrugged and scribbled something on my chart. I suppose that's fair, as it was hardly a sincere show of gratitude on my part. At any rate, I have no idea what to expect from this Teasdale woman, and I appear to have lost the stingy drab of momentum pushing me recklessly towards full disclosure. That in and of itself is enough to set me wondering what my keepers are up to now, if the shrink switch is some fresh skullduggery. It seems counterintuitive, given they were finally getting the results they've been asking for (and I'm not so naïve as to assume that this pad isn't outfitted with a direct patch to some agency goon or another). But then an awful lot of what they've done seems counterintuitive to me, and counterproductive.

Simply put, I don't know what to say next. No, strike that. I don't know what I'm *willing* to say next.

I've already mentioned my indiscretion with the South Korean pay-load specialist on the outbound half of the trip. Actually, *indiscretion* is hardly accurate, since Amery explicitly gave me her permission to take other lovers while she was gone, because, after all, there was a damned decent chance she wouldn't make it back alive. Or make it back at all. So, *indiscretion* is just my guilt talking. Anyway, her name was Bae Jin-ah—the *Yastreb-4* PS, I mean—though everyone called her Sam, which she seemed to prefer. She was born in Incheon, and was still a kid when the war started. A relative in the States helped her parents get Bae on one of the last transports out of Seoul before the bombs started raining down. But we didn't have many conversations about the past, mine or hers. She was a biochemist obsessed with the structure-function rela-tionships of peptides, and she liked to talk shop after we fucked. It was pretty dry stuff—the talk, not the sex—and I admit I only half-listened, and didn't understand all that much of what I heard. But I don't think that mattered to Sam. I have a feeling she was just grateful that I bothered to cover my mouth whenever I yawned.

She only asked about Amery once.

We were both crammed into the warm cocoon of her sleeping bag, or into mine; I can't recall which. Probably mine, since the micrograv restraints in my bunk kept popping loose. I was on the edge of doz-ing off, and Sam asked me how we met. I made up some half-assed romance about an academic conference in Manhattan, and a party, a formal affair at the American Museum of Natural History. It was love at first sight, I said (or something equally ridiculous), right there in the Roosevelt Rotunda, beneath the rearing *Barosaurus* skeleton. Sam thought it was sweet as hell, though, and I figured lies were fine, if they gave us a moment's respite from the crowded, day-to-day monotony of the ship, or from our (usually) unspoken dread of all that nothingness surrounding us and the uncertainty we were hurtling towards. I don't even know if she believed me, but it made her smile.

"You've read all the docs on the cloud?" she asked, and I told her yeah, I had, or at least all the ones I was given clearance to read. And then Sam watched me for a while without saying anything. I could feel her silently weighing options and consequences, duty and need and repercussion.

"So, you *know* it's some pretty spooky shit out there," she said, finally, and went back to watching me, as if waiting for some particular reaction.

And, here, I lied to her again.

"Relax, Sam," I whispered, then kissed her on the forehead. "I've read most of the spectroscopy and astrochem profiles. Discussing it with me, you're not in danger of compromising protocol or mission security or anything."

She nodded once and looked slightly relieved.

"I've never given much credence to the exogenesis crowd," she said, "but, Jesus…glycine, DHA, adenine, cytosine, etcetera and fucking etcetera. When—or, rather, *if* this gets out, the panspermia guys are going to go apeshit. And rightly so. No one saw this coming, Merrick. No one you'd ever take seriously."

I must have managed a fairly convincing job of acting like I knew what she was talking about, because she kept it up for the next ten or fifteen minutes. Her voice took on that same sort of jittery, excited edge Amery's used to get, when she'd start in on the role of Io in the Jovian magnetosphere, or any number of other phenomena I didn't quite understand, and how much the *Pilgrimage* experiments were going to change this or that model or theory. Only, Sam's excitement was tinged with fear.

"The inherent risks," she said, and then trailed off and wiped at her forehead before starting again. "When they first showed me the back-contamination safeguards for this run, I figured no way, right. No way are NASA and the ESA going to pony up the budget for that sort of overkill. But this was *before* I read Murchison's reports on the cloud's composition and behavior. And afterwards, the thought of intentionally sending a human crew anywhere near that thing, or anything that had been *exposed* to it, I couldn't believe they were really serious. It's fucking crazy. No, it's whatever comes *after* fucking crazy. They should have cut their losses…" and then she trailed off again and went back to staring at me.

"I had to come," I told her. "If there was any chance at all that Amery's still alive, I had to come."

"Of course. Yeah, of course you did," Sam said, looking away.

"When they asked, I couldn't very well say no."

"But do you honestly believe we're going to find any of them alive, that we'll be docking with anything but a ghost ship?"

"You're really not into pulling punches, are you?"

"You read the reports on the cloud."

"I *had* to come," I told her again.

Then we both let the subject drop, and neither of us ever brought it up again. Indeed, I think I probably would have forgotten most of it, especially after what I saw when I stepped through the airlock and into *Pilgrimage*. That whole conversation might have dissolved into the tedious gray blur of outbound, if Bae Jin-ah hadn't killed herself on the return trip, just five days before we made Earth orbit.

MARCH 23, 2077 (TUESDAY)

Tuesday night now, and the meds are making me sleepy and stupid, but I wanted to put some of this down, even if it isn't what they want me to be writing. I see how it's all connected, even if they never will, or, if seeing, they simply do not care. *They*, whomever, precisely, they may be.

This morning I had my first session with you, Dr. Elenore Teasdale. I never much liked that bastard Ostrowski, but at least I was moderately certain he was who and what he claimed to be. Between you and me, Elenore, I think you're an asset, sent in because someone somewhere is getting nervous. Nervous enough to swap an actual psychiatrist for a bug dressed up to pass for a psychiatrist. Fine, I'm flexible. If these are the new rules, I can play along. But it does leave me pondering what Dr. O was telling his superiors (whom I'll assume are also your superiors, Dr. T). It couldn't have been anything so simple as labeling me a suicide risk; they've known that since I stepped off *Pilgrimage*, probably before I even stepped on.

And yes, I've noticed that you bear more than a passing resemblance to Amery. That was a bold and wicked move, and I applaud these ruthless shock tactics. I do, sincerely. This merciless Blitzkrieg waltz we're dancing, coupled with the drugs, it shows you're in this game to win, and if you *can't* win, you'll settle for the pyrrhic victory of having driven the enemy to resort to a scorched-earth retreat. Yeah, the pills and injections, they don't mesh so well with extended metaphor and simile, so I'll drop it. But I can't have you thinking all the theater has been wasted on an inattentive audience. That's all. You wear that rough facsimile of her face, Dr. T. And that annoying habit you have of tap-tap-tapping the business end of a stylus against your lower incisors, that's hers, too. And half a dozen carefully planted turns of phrase. The smile that isn't quite a smile. The self-conscious laugh. You hardly missed a trick, you and the agency handlers who sculpted you and slotted you and packed you off to play havoc with a lunatic's fading will.

My mouth is so dry.

Elenore Teasdale watches me from the other side of her desk, and behind her, through the wide window twelve stories up, I can see the blue-brown sky, and, between the steel and glass and concrete towers, I can just make out the scrubby hills of the Diablo Range through the smog. She glances over her shoulder, following my gaze.

"Quite a view, isn't it?" she asks, and maybe I nod, and maybe I agree, and maybe I say nothing at all.

"When I was a little girl," she tells me, "my father used to take me on long hikes through the mountains. And we'd visit Lick Observatory, on the top of Mount Hamilton."

"I'm not from around here," I reply. But, then, I'd be willing to bet neither is she.

Elenore Teasdale turns back towards me, silhouetted against the murky light through that window, framed like a misplaced Catholic saint. She stares straight at me, and I do not detect even a trace of guile when she speaks.

"We all want you to get better, Miss Merrick. You know that, don't you?"

I look away, preferring the oatmeal-colored carpet to that mask she wears.

"It's easier if we don't play games," I say.

"Yes. Yes, it is. Obviously."

"What I saw. What it meant. What she *said* to me. What I *think* it means."

"Yes, and talking about those things, bringing them out into the open, it's an important part of you *getting* better, Miss Merrick. Don't you think that's true?"

"I think…" and I pause, choosing my words as carefully as I still am able. "I think you're afraid, all of you, of never knowing. None of this is about my getting better. I've understood that almost from the start." And my voice is calm, and there is no hint of bitterness for her to hear; my voice does not betray me.

Elenore Teasdale's smile wavers, but only a little, and for only an instant or two.

"Naturally, yes, these matters are interwoven," she replies. "Quite intricately so. Almost inextricably, and I don't believe anyone has ever tried to lie to you about that. What you witnessed out there, what you seem unable, or unwilling, to share with anyone else—"

I laugh, and she sits, watching me with Amery's pale blue eyes, tapping a keypad stylus against her teeth. Her teeth are much whiter and more even than Amery's were, and I draw some dim comfort from that.

"Share," I say, very softly, and there are other things I *want* to say to her, but I keep them to myself.

"I want you to think about that, Miss Merrick. Between now and our next session, I need you to consider, seriously, the price of your selfishness, both to your own well-being and to the rest of humanity."

"Fine," I say, because I don't feel like arguing. Besides, manipulative or not, she isn't entirely wrong. "And what I was writing for Dr. Ostrowski, do I keep that up?"

"Yes, please," she replies and glances at the clock on the wall, as if she expects me to believe she'll be seeing anyone else today, that she even has other patients. "It's a sound approach, and, reviewing what you've written so far, it feels to me like you're close to a breakthrough."

I nod my head, and also look at the clock.

"Our time's almost up," I say, and she agrees with me, then looks over her shoulder again at the green-brown hills beyond San Jose.

"I have a question," I say.

"That's why I'm here," Dr. Elenore Teasdale tells me, imbuing the words with all the false veracity of her craft. Having affected the role of the good patient, I pretend that she isn't lying, hoping the pretense lends weight to my question.

"Have they sent a retrieval team yet? To Mars, to the caverns on Arsia Mons?"

"I wouldn't know that," she says. "I'm not privileged to such information. However, if you'd like, I can file an inquiry on your behalf. Someone with the agency might contact you."

"No," I reply. "I was just curious if you knew," and I almost ask her another question, about Darwin's finches, and the tortoises and mockingbirds and iguanas that once populated the Galápagos Islands. But then the black minute hand on the clock ticks forward, deleting another sixty seconds from the future, converting it to past, and I decide we've both had enough for one morning.

Don't fret, Dr. T. You've done your bit for the cause, swept me off my feet, and now we're dancing. If you were here, in the hospital room with me, I'd even let you lead. I really don't care if the nurses mind or not. I'd turn up the jack, find just the right tune, and dance with the ghost you've let them make of you. I can never be too haunted, after all. Hush, hush. It's just, they give me these drugs, you see, so I need to sleep for a while, and then the waltz can continue. Your answers are coming.

MARCH 24, 2077 (WEDNESDAY)

It's raining. I asked one of the nurses to please raise the blinds in my room so I can watch the storm hammering the windowpane, pelting the glass, smudging my view of the diffident sky. I count off the moments between occasional flashes of lightning and the thunderclaps that follow. Storms number among the very few things remaining in all the world that can actually soothe my nerves. They certainly beat the synthetic opiates I'm given, beat them all the way to hell and back. I haven't ever bothered to tell any of my doctors or the nurses this. I don't know why; it simply hasn't occurred to me to do so. I doubt they'd care, anyway.

I've asked to please not be disturbed for a couple of hours, and I've been promised my request will be honored. That should give me the time I need to finish this.

Dr. Teasdale, I will readily confess that one of the reasons it's taken me so long to reach this point is the fact that words fail. It's an awful cliché, I know, but also a point I cannot stress strongly enough. There are sights and experiences to which the blunt and finite tool of human language are not equal. I know this, though I'm no poet. But I want that caveat understood. This is *not* what happened aboard *Pilgrimage*; this is the sky seen through a window blurred by driving rain. It's the best I can manage, and it's the best you'll ever get. I've said all along, if the technology existed to plug in and extract the memories from my brain, I wouldn't deign to call it rape. Most of the people who've spent so much time and energy and money trying to prise from me the truth about the fate of *Pilgrimage* and its crew, they're only scientists, after all. They have no other aphrodisiac *but* curiosity. As for the rest, the spooks and politicians, the bureaucrats and corporate shills, those guys are only along for the ride, and I figure most of them know they're in over their heads.

I could make of it a fairy tale. It might begin:

Once upon a time, there was a woman who lived in New York. She was an anthropologist, and shared a tiny apartment in downtown Brooklyn with her lover. And her lover was a woman named Amery Domico, who happened to be a molecular geneticist, exobiologist and also an astronaut. They had a cat and a tank of tropical fish. They'd always wanted a dog, but the apartment was too small. They could have afforded a better place to live, a loft in midtown Manhattan, perhaps, north and east of the flood zone, but the anthropologist was happy enough with Brooklyn, and her lover was usually on the road, anyway. Besides, walking a dog would have been a lot of trouble.

No. That's not working. I've never been much good with irony. And I'm better served by the immediacy of present tense. So, instead:

"Turn around, Merrick," she says. "You've come so far, and there is so little time."

And I do as she tells me. I turn towards the voice, towards the airlock's open inner hatch. There's no sign of Amery, or anyone else, for that matter. The first thing I notice, stepping from the brightly lit airlock, is that the narrow, heptagonal corridor beyond is mostly dark. The second thing I notice is the mist. I know at once that it *is* mist, not smoke. It fills the hallway from deck to ceiling, and, even with the blue in-floor path lighting, it's hard to see more than a few feet ahead. The mist swirls thickly around me, like Halloween phantoms, and I'm about to ask Amery where it's coming from, what it's doing here, when I notice the walls.

Or, rather, when I notice what's growing *on* the walls. I'm fairly confident I've never seen anything with precisely that texture before. It half reminds me (but only half) of the rubbery blades and stipes of kelp. It's almost the same color as kelp, too, some shade that's not quite brown, nor green, nor a very dark purple. It glimmers wetly, as though it's sweating, or secreting mucus. I stop and stare, simultaneously alarmed and amazed and revolted. It *is* revolting, extremely so, this clinging material covering over and obscuring almost everything. I look up and see that it's also growing on the ceiling. In places, long tendrils of it hang down like dripping vines. Dr. Teasdale, I *want* so badly to describe these things, this waking nightmare, in much greater detail. I want to describe it perfectly. But, as I've said, words fail. For that matter, memory fades. And there's so much more to come.

A few thick drops of the almost colorless mucus drip from the ceiling onto my visor, and I gag reflexively. The sensors in my EVA suit respond by administering a dose of some potent antiemetic. The nausea passes quickly, and I use my left hand to wipe the slime away as best I can.

I follow the corridor, going very slowly because the mist is only getting denser and, as I move farther away from the airlock, I discover that the stuff growing on the walls and ceiling is also sprouting from the deck plates. It's slippery, and squelches beneath my boots. Worse, most of the path lighting is now buried beneath it, and I switch on the magspots built into either side of my helmet. The beams reach only a short distance into the gloom.

"You're almost there," Amery says, Amery or the AI speaking with her stolen voice. "Ten yards ahead, the corridor forks. Take the right fork. It leads directly to the transhab module."

"You want to tell me what's waiting in there?" I ask, neither expecting, nor actually desiring, an answer.

"Nothing is waiting," Amery replies. "But there are many things we would have you see. There's not much time. You should hurry."

And I do try to walk faster, but, despite the suit's exoskeleton and gyros, almost lose my footing on the slick deck. Where the corridor forks, I go right, as instructed. The habitation module is open, the hatch fully dilated, as though I'm expected. Or maybe it's been left open for days or months or years. I linger a moment on the threshold. It's so very dark in there. I call out for Amery. I call out for anyone at all, but this time there's no answer. I try my comms again, and there's not even static. I fully comprehend that in all my life, I have never been so alone as I am at this moment, and, likely, I never will be again. I know, too, with a sudden and unwavering certainty, that Amery Domico is gone from me forever, and that I'm the only human being aboard *Pilgrimage*.

I take three or four steps into the transhab, but stop when something pale and big around as my forearm slithers lazily across the floor directly in front of me. If there was a head, I didn't see it. Watching as it slides past, I think of pythons, boas, anacondas, though, in truth, it bears only a passing similarity to a snake of any sort.

"You will not be harmed, Merrick," Amery says from a speaker somewhere in the darkness. The voice is almost reassuring. "You must trust that you will not be harmed."

"What was that?" I ask.

"Soon now, you will see," the voice replies. "We have ten million children. Soon, we will have ten million more. We are pleased that you have come to say goodbye."

"They want to know what's happened," I say, breathing too hard, much too fast, gasping despite the suit's ministrations. "At Jupiter, what happened to the ship? Where's the crew? Why is *Pilgrimage* in orbit around Mars?"

I turn my head to the left, and where there were once bunks, I can only make out a great swelling or clot of the kelp-like growth. Its surface swarms with what I, at first, briefly mistake for insects.

"I didn't *come* to say goodbye," I whisper. "This is a retrieval mission, Amery. We've come to take you…" and I trail off, unable to complete the sentence, too keenly aware of its irrelevance.

"Merrick, are you beginning to see?"

I look away from the swelling and the crawling things that aren't insects, and take another step into the habitation module.

"No, Amery. I'm not. Help me to see. Please."

"Close your eyes," she says, and I do. And when I open them again, I'm lying in bed with her. There's still an hour or so left before dawn, and we're lying in bed, naked together beneath the blankets, staring up through the apartment's skylight. It's snowing. This is the last night before Amery leaves for Cape Canaveral, the last time I see her, because I've refused to be present at the launch or even watch it online. She has her arms around me, and one of the big, ungainly hovers is passing low above our building. I do my best to pretend that its complex array of landing beacons is actually stars.

Amery kisses my right cheek, and then her lips brush lightly against my ear. "We could not understand, Merrick, because we were too far and could not remember," she says, quoting Joseph Conrad. The words roll from her tongue and palate like the spiraling snowflakes tumbling down from that tangerine sky. "We were traveling in the night of first ages, of those ages that are gone, leaving hardly a sign, and no memories."

Once, Dr. Teasdale, when Amery was sick with the flu, I read her most of *The Heart of Darkness*. She always liked when I read to her. When I came to that passage, she had me find a pencil and underline it, so that she could return to it later.

"The earth seemed unearthly," she says, and I blink, dismissing the illusion. I'm standing near the center of the transhab now, and in the stark white light from my helmet, I see what I've been brought here to see. Around me, the walls leak, and every inch of the module seems alive with organisms too alien for any earthborn vernacular. I've spent my adult life describing artifacts and fossil bones, but I will not even attempt to describe the myriad of forms that crawled and skittered and wriggled through the ruins of *Pilgrimage*. I would fail if I did, and I would fail utterly.

"We want you to know we had a choice," Amery says. "We want you to know that, Merrick. And what is about to happen, when you leave this ship, we want you to know that is also of our choosing."

I see her, then, all that's left of her, or all that she's become. The rough outline of her body, squatting near one of the lower bunks. Her damp skin shimmers, all but indistinguishable from the rubbery substance growing throughout the vessel. Only her skin is not so smooth, but pocked with countless oozing pores or lesions. Though the finer features of her face have been obliterated—there is no mouth remaining, no eyes, only a faint ridge that was her nose—I recognize her beyond any shadow of a doubt. She is rooted to that spot, her legs below the knees, her arms below the elbow, simply vanishing into the deck. There is constant, eager movement from inside her distended breasts and belly. And where the cleft of her sex once was…I don't have the language to describe what I saw there. But she bleeds life from that impossible wound, and I know that she has become a daughter of the oily black cloud that *Pilgrimage* encountered near Ganymede, just as she is mother and father to every living thing trapped within the crucible of that ship, every living thing but me.

"There isn't any time left," the voice from the AI says calmly, calmly but sternly. "You must leave now, Merrick. All available resources on this craft have been depleted, and we must seek sanctuary or perish."

I nod, and turn away from her, because I understand as much as I'm ever going to understand, and I've seen more than I can bear to remember. I move as fast as I dare across the transhab and along the corridor leading back to the airlock. In less than five minutes, I'm safely strapped into my seat on the taxi again, decoupling and falling back towards *Yastreb-4*. A few hours later, while I'm waiting out my time in decon, Commander Yun tells me that *Pilgrimage* has fired its main engines and broken orbit. In a few moments, it will enter the thin Martian atmosphere and begin to burn. Our AI has plotted a best-guess trajectory, placing the point of impact within the Tharsis Montes, along the flanks of Arsia Mons. He tells me that the exact coordinates, -5.636 ° N, 241.259 ° E, correspond to one of the collapsed cavern roofs dotting the flanks of the ancient volcano. The pit named Jeanne, discovered way back in 2007.

"There's not much chance of anything surviving the descent," he says. I don't reply, and I never tell him, nor anyone else aboard the *Yastreb-4*, what I saw during my seventeen minutes on *Pilgrimage*.

And there's no need, Dr. Teasdale, for me to tell *you* what you already know. Or what your handlers know. Which means, I think, that we've reached the end of this confession. Here's the feather in your cap. May you choke on it.

Outside my hospital window, the rain has stopped. I press the call button, and wait on the nurses with their shiny yellow pills and the white pills flecked with gray, their jet sprays and hollow needles filled with nightmares and, sometimes, when I'm very lucky, dreamless sleep.

DULCE DOMUM

ELLEN KUSHNER

Come see my band, he'd say, and they pretty much always did.

—Europe, huh? she asked languidly. They were lying in her bed, which was where he liked to be after the show, after they'd seen the band. Good sex, and the comfort of warm skin, and just enough talking to make it real.

—R&B goes over big there. And they love Todd's chops: authentic African-American. They don't need to know he went to Buckley with us and played lacrosse.

—Buckley, huh? She named some friends she said had gone there, and he knew one or two, but not well. A lot of those kids had gone away to boarding school after ninth grade, while he stayed in Manhattan with his family.

—So do you like it there, in Europe?

He stretched. —It's OK.

—So do you, like, spend a lot of time in any one city?

She wanted to know if he had a girlfriend there. Already she was trying to figure out if he was serious material. Oops, time to go. He kissed her, and she tasted very sweet. —Just here, he said, and kissed her again. —New York is home.

New York was home, but in New York the band was no big deal. So they played in a few bars here, and they had dinner with their families, and escorted a friend's sister to a fundraiser for art or literacy or wildlife, depending, and maybe took a niece or a cousin's kid to see "Nutcracker." Then the band went on the road again, the road across the sea, where playing the chords in tight jeans was enough, knowing home was always back here, waiting for him to take his place. His family was here, colorful and stable, in the stone castle with big windows on the Park. A window would always be open for him to fly back through, no matter how big he got, or how long he was away.

He fell asleep as soon as he'd come, and she didn't wake him, which was nice of her. His eyes snapped open at first light. It was an old East Village apartment with leaky venetian blinds. He was pulling on his jeans when he heard her say, Jet lag? and when he turned around she was spread out like a kid on the playground being an airplane, sleepily purring a sort of phlegmy *Vroom, vroom,* so he fell back onto her and improvised something about, *Be my jet plane, baby, ba-dum, ba-dum, Gonna make your engine scream,* so together they achieved one of those moments of intimacy that promise either a relationship's worth of in-jokes, or guaranteed embarrassment next time you meet.

He took her phone number, but he doubted he'd be back.

He called her late on Christmas Eve. She was home. She said, Come on up, which was good because he was standing at a payphone two blocks away, his cellphone deliberately run down, and it was raining.

She was wearing sweatpants and a fleece bathrobe with moons on it. The "I don't care if I'm attractive or not" gambit. He called her on it by falling to his knees before her, singing softly, "Oh, holy night, the stars are brightly shiiiiining…." So she took the cue and undid her sash.

In the castle where he grew up, two kings ruled. It was a brown stone fortress at the edge of Central Park; on rainy days their nanny would send his sister and him running up and down the back stairwell, to work off energy. That was their tower, the northeast corner of the big building. A famous musician lived on another floor, and sometimes in his tuxedo on his way to the Philharmonic he would use the back stairs, too, but they knew it was really their tower.

—You're not drunk, she said when she tasted his mouth. She seemed a little surprised. She must really like him.

He made an effort. —I'm sorry, he said. —I was just, you know, kind of wondering if, if you—

Her fingers were on his lips. —Shh. I know. I mean, I don't know, but I kind of do.

She let him fall on her, graceless and helpless. She was so warm, so alive.

He was allowed to think of them as kings. They were both golden, powerful men with strong wills and interesting work. When he was older, he'd made one joke about queens, and only one, and only once.

She wriggled around and took him in her mouth.
—Don't, he said. —Not now.
—Right. She came back up, and smooched his ear. —Full frontal?
He smiled in her hair. —Yeah.

And they were there right now, he thought, or tried not to think. There, in their castle, high above the Park, wondering when he was going to turn up to drink eggnog and light the fire and see the tree. If they were thinking of him at all. If they even had a tree this year.

He kept the last of his weight on his elbows, but he touched as much of her as he could, his front to hers, fitting her curves and pressing them down for the sense that there was something that could bear him, and she could.

They would ask his sister if she'd heard from him. They never pried, but when it came to something they both wanted, they didn't really care about privacy all that much. They didn't care that his phone was dead, or why.
"Kay doesn't let his battery run down."
"Not usually, no."
"Is he coming?"

He was. But not there.

—But we aren't *Oy Vey* Jews, she was explaining to him. He must have apologized for bothering her on Christmas Eve, and started her on her story: —My grandparents were, like, all Philharmonic subscription, Opera Guild, Metropolitan Museum members, and my mom went to Vassar… You know.
He knew. He hadn't cried, and that was good. He didn't, usually, but tonight he didn't trust himself. He smiled, and remembered to say, —So that's why you're home now? Waiting for stray lonely *goyim* to come in out of the rain?
She touched his hair. —It is my destiny. My spiritual practice, in return for killing your god. I feel I owe you something. Tomorrow I observe the

272 • ELLEN KUSHNER

ritual celebration of a movie and Chinese food, but for tonight... hot
sex with a hunky blond. What about you? Your folks out of town?

He waited too long to say No, and she kept going: —Went to Aspen
and forgot to book you a ticket? Gone to Vienna for the winter balls and
left you to take care of the Shih Tzu?

—Nuh uh. He nuzzled her hair again. Her scalp smelt like herbs, and
the ends of her hair a little like popcorn. He wasn't ready to leave, even
though they were getting to the talky bit, and he should. Soon.

—It's OK, she went on; —I'm used to spending Christmas Eve with
people who are depressed about their families. It's kind of a specialty. In
college I had all these divorced friends —I mean, their parents were—and
they were all upset, you know, spending Christmas Eve with one parent,
and the Day with the other... so I'd make them come over and we'd do
stupid kid stuff like painting on clown faces—you don't hate clowns,
do you? Some people are really weirded out by them.

—My sister hates clowns. But I don't care. What else did you do?

—Well, we made french fries from scratch. She scrunched up her
face. —Boring, huh?

—Not really. Not if the point is to get someone to feel happy and
normal. Food is good that way. My dad is, like, the king of comfort food.
If you like whole steamed sea bass.

—Is your dad, um, Asian?

(And a second husband? Because he himself was blond? She was so
obvious.)

—Naw, he's just a foodie. When he's jetlagged, he used to go to the Ful-
ton Fish Market to get the first catch, back when it came in there at dawn.
Makes his own duck confit. You know, like that. My other dad—

—Stepfather?

—No. Two dads, no mother.

—Oh, Peter! she chortled, and rather sharply he said, —*What*?

—Sorry. She ran a fingertip down his arm in apology. —Peter Pan.
"Haven't got a mother."

—Lost boys, he said. —That's us, all right.

—Except for your sister.

She lay waiting to listen, but he could feel her quivering with another
quote.

—Spit it out, he said, and she chortled, —"Girls are far too clever to
fall out of their prams."

He pinned her deliciously down. —Better stop reminding me of my
sister, or things could get weird.

—How weird? she purred.

He pulled back slightly and she gasped, —God, I'm an idiot. You're not there for a reason, and I—I'm sorry, I'm just an idiot. She bunched her fingers in his curls —Sorry— and kissed him.

He had kissed his sister exactly once. They were both fifteen, and both a little drunk, and she said, OK, let's just get it over with, so they puckered up, but at the first sign of moist inner membrane they broke apart, going *Eew*! like six-year-olds, and Eloise said, OK, so now can we stop worrying?

And he said something blindingly original like, Yeah, I guess.

He'd still been a little scared, then, that he'd like his sister the way her dad liked his dad. It was a huge relief, so huge they never spoke of it again. He was sure his sister was back home with them tonight. Eloise got along with both of them so well. Her own dad didn't scare her, even now.

This kiss was enthralling, deep and thoughtful. He always liked the kisses that happened after, building their way back to urgency, but not there yet, not urgent, just deep. He liked the way she assumed there would be an after, too. She wouldn't kick him out before he was ready to go.

—So it's just us, she murmured into his cheek. —Just you and me, and a city full of people full of their own crazy business out there, who don't know we're even here.

—With no idea what we're up to.

—Not a clue.

Was he talking too much? She seemed to want it, but did he?

Mouths licked and pinched and sucked between words. Words dropped in between their busy lips and teeth. She said, That's nice… and he occupied her mouth with his to keep words out, to keep words in.

—Not thinking of your sister now, huh? she asked him, and he moaned, No— and so, of course, then he was.

His sister said he couldn't possibly remember the first time; they were too young. But that was her, not him. He was five whole months older. He remembered, really well.

They were in the living room high above the city, with all the glittering lights, the fire in the fireplace, the huge tree, the spread of cakes and fruit and decorated Christmas cookies—some the gifts of clients, the best ones baked by his dad—the spiced wine they each got a sip of… he could have been remembering any year, sure. The tree never seemed to get less huge, no matter how much he grew. Maybe their dads kept buying bigger ones. He wouldn't put it past them to think of that.

But he remembered seeing the book for the very first time that night. Eloise was on her own father's lap on the sofa, he was sitting on the floor next to them, and Linton reached one arm out around his little girl to show Kay the pictures. The book was little, with pale blue cloth and animals stamped on the front in gold, and the smell of the old paper rose up even through the pine and spices.

"He's going to get chocolate on it," his own dad said, but Linton just kept holding the book out to him.

"It's OK, Graham," Linton said. "They won't know it's not hundred-year-old chocolate by the time it goes to auction next."

"What about carbon dating?" muttered Eloise.

"That's just for dinosaurs and fossils," Kay said. "Gimme."

"'Give it to me,'" Linton corrected.

"Please," added Graham.

He held the book carefully. There were line drawings of animals, almost on every page. They all wore clothes. You could tell the animals were still little, though, because of their being next to leaves and grass and things. There were colored pages, too, pretty and pale, of animals rowing boats. "Read," Kay said.

Linton opened the book, began reading something about spring-cleaning. Then he said, "No. Not tonight. I think it should be more…." He flipped through the pages, and began again:

> *Home! The call was clear, the summons was plain.*
> *"Ratty!" Mole called, "hold on! It's my home, my old home! I've just come across the smell of it, and it's close by here, really quite close. And I must go to it, I must, I must!"*

Kay had barely understood it, the first time, but it was the voice that mattered.

> *Home! Why, it must be quite close by him at that moment, his old home that he had hurriedly forsaken, that day when he first found the river.*

The voice, warm and flexible and fluid like the river, taking him somewhere he'd never been before, introducing the two animals who were such good friends, and looked after each other when they were lost in the snow, and found the pathway to the Mole's little house in the ground, and Ratty made the fire and cooked some snacks, and then—and then—

—He's a musician, he said, —my other dad.
—What kind?
—Piano, mostly.
It was the harpsichord, really, but there was always one thing he changed or left out whenever he talked about them. He just did.
—Jazz?
—No. Classical. And new music. Downtown stuff.
—Is that where you get it from, the music?
—He's not my bio dad.
She pulled both his arms around her, flattening her breasts against him. —Sorry.
—He hates what I do, my band, anyway.
—Music snob?
—No. He thinks I've got no technique. And know what? He's right.
—Ohhhh, you've got technique, all right. I love your technique.

Every year after that, Linton read from the book on Christmas Eve. The same chapter, *Dulce Domum*, where they're trudging through the snow on their way back to Rat's cozy River Bank digs, but Mole suddenly catches the scent of his old underground home, and they go and find it but then it's all cold and there's no food and then they build up a fire and then Rat finds some biscuits and sardines and then they light candles and then – and then they hear voices, and Mole says, "I think it must be the field-mice. They go round carol-singing this time of year," and then they open the door to the field-mice with lanterns and mittens and little red scarves and then—and then—

> We others, who have long lost the more subtle of the physical senses, have not even proper terms to express an animal's intercommunications with his surroundings…and have only the word "smell," for instance, to include the whole range of delicate thrills which murmur in the nose of the animal night and day….

—Enjoying yourself?
He was giving her all he could, holding back carefully, holding back to observe her giving in to him, to observe how she enjoyed it, to admire

his own skill and selfless self-restraint.

—Mrrrrrph….

—Is that a Yes? It is, isn't it? Cat got your tongue?

—You're evil.

—No I'm not. I'm good.…

Linton tried reading Dickens once instead, and Eloise nearly had a meltdown. They were very young. Funny how, now that things were surreally bad, his sister was acting like nothing was wrong, and he was the one who couldn't stand it. Especially since it was her dad who was so messed up.

—Wait, she said. She pushed her tangled hair back from her eyes with the back of her wrist.

—What?

—My turn.

He tried to say No, but he shivered with delight as she did things, delicious things with him on Christmas Eve.

—Cat got your tongue? she purred.

> He stopped dead in his tracks, his nose searching hither and thither… A moment, and he had caught it again; and with it this time came recollection in fullest flood.

He lost it. She was giving him everything he wanted, and it was a terrible thing. All that physical pleasure, tricking him into feeling on top of the world, feeling powerful and invulnerable and joyous. And then—And then—

He heard the music.

> Villagers all, this frosty tide,
> Let your doors swing open wide

Linton at the harpsichord, the book in front of him so he could improvise right there as the little mice came to the door in the snow, and the lamps were held high, and they sang their carol:

> Though wind may follow, and snow beside,
> Yet draw us in by your fire to bide;
> Joy shall be yours in the morning!

The very first year, Linton just spoke the words, fiddling around with underscoring as he read. The second year, though, he had composed a tune, secretly, to surprise them, and when he got to the field-mice he put the book down and went to his instrument, and rattled it off on the keyboard, singing with gusto.

> *Here we stand in the cold and the sleet,*
> *Blowing fingers and stamping feet,*
> *Come from far away you to greet—*
> *You by the fire and we in the street—*
> *Bidding you joy in the morning!*

They made him sing it again, in falsetto, to sound like mice. And after that they copied him, learned the tune, made harmonies. Every year since then, as Kay changed from treble to baritone, and Eloise's soprano grew from piping to rich, it was the song they sang on Christmas Eve.

Were they singing it now? He doubted it. He doubted it very much. If they were, he would be there. He would be there, singing, instead of right here, howling, as his pleasure refused to be staved off another measure.

> *"Oh, Ratty!" he cried dismally, "why ever did I do it? Why did I bring you to this poor, cold little place, on a night like this, when you might have been at River Bank by this time, toasting your toes before a blazing fire, with all your own nice things about you!"*

Oh, and he knew he should be there now. He should be there with them. Even if they weren't singing. *Especially* if they weren't singing.

Omne animal triste post coitum.

All animals are sad after sex.

She nuzzled his neck. They were stuck together, the sheet wrapped around their legs, soaking up sweat and come. He started to shake.

He didn't know which he hated more, the idea that they weren't, despite what had happened, or the idea that they were: that somehow Linton was sitting gamely at the keyboard, pale and shaky—unless he was flushed, yeah, maybe he was flushed with a recent feeding from the bags in the fridge, for which Graham had called in every favor that years on the Board of the Sloan-Kettering could bring him—Linton sitting at the keyboard, eyes glittering with pleasure, young and strong and sure of himself for a few hours, until the daylight rolled around again and he had to go back in the—oh, no, it wasn't funny, but you had to laugh—the dark little place with the door where no light entered, where the bad kids were shut up in Victorian novels, the place where old coats were stored, fur coats that parted to reveal another kingdom, the dark place where hungry young men hid the truth until we all got enlightened and everything changed... and now his dad was back in there again because the light was so bad for him he cried and he burned when it touched him—

—What is it? she said. —You're shaking. What's the matter?

—Nothing, he said. —I'm OK.

She rubbed some of the wet off him with an edge of the sheet, and reached down for a quilt, and pulled it over them both.

—I don't think you're feverish, she said. She felt his forehead with her wrist, and he couldn't help smiling, it was such a Wendy thing to do. —You're kind of cold, really.

—*Omne animal triste post coitum.* Only in my case, it's *chilly*, not *sad*.

—You're chilly *and* sad.

—It'll pass.

—OK.

She didn't say anything, just held him.

I want you to be here, his father had said. *I want to see you. We both do.*

I don't want to see him. He didn't say that. He'd never say that. He just wouldn't show up. It wasn't even that he didn't want to see him. He didn't want to hear the voice.

—Did you ever have a tree? he asked. —Or a Chanukah Bush or something?

She squeezed him in mild protest. —Tacky. If you want a tree, have a tree, I say. Don't try to whitewash it. Don't, like, frigging lie about it.

—So you wanted one.

—Well, yeah. Of course. A *tree* in your *house?* Come on.

—I like that you don't have one.

—Good. I'm glad. She stroked his hair. —But you know what? For you... for you, Kay, I might get one. If you wanted it.

—You would?

—And when my mother visited, I'd say that it was all your fault.

—You would?

—I would. You'd back me up, though, wouldn't you?

—I would. For you, I'd lie to a nice old lady who probably marched against the Pentagon and won't drink coffee that isn't Fair Trade certified.

—Hey, when did you meet my mom?

—So how is she?

—Fine. But I was just kidding.

—I know, he said. —But your family. Are they all right?

—Yeah. Sure. I just saw them last week. We always have this Chanukah party. With big piles of *latkes*. Is there something—

—No. It's just… you never know. You never know when something's going to happen. I mean, one day you're all fine, and the next—the next —you just can't believe it. It's literally incredible. Like something you read in a book. Not something that could really happen. Not to anyone real. Not to anyone at all. Let alone someone you know. You see it, you know it, but you just cannot believe it. She told me, she even showed me, and I didn't believe her.

—Is she OK? Your sister, I mean.

—Eloise? She's fine.

—What about your dad?

—Graham's a busy man. A very busy man, these days. Calling in favors. Calling up doctors. Calling on one-eyed gypsies from Transylvania…. No, they're fine. They're both fine. They don't know what happened, but they're sure it isn't catching.

She understood, at last, or thought she did. —Your other dad, she said. —Is he… sick?

He made a little noise into her breast.

—Like, really, really sick? And you just can't face it?

He thought of the syringes on the table, the plastic bags in the fridge and in the microwave, heating to 98.6.

—You couldn't either, believe me.

—I know, she said. —I know. I hear about stuff, and I—I feel so lucky, sometimes.

—It's like—I can't go home. Home isn't even there anymore.

—I know. She tightened her hold. She waited, then said, —Is he all… different?

—Yeah. He used to be so—well, civilized. Disciplined. Controlled. And now—Now I wouldn't trust him with anything. Not the book, not anything. You can't turn your back on him. He's hungry all the time.

—He is?

—He'll eat anyone if he doesn't stop himself. He'd eat the fucking field-mice if he could!

—I thought it was supposed to make you not eat much, she said gently.

—He *doesn't* eat much. He doesn't eat anything. He used to like broccoli rabe and anchovies and crème caramel. He can't take real food at all, now.

She touched his wrist. —I'm really, really sorry.

—Yeah, well.

—I'm glad you're here.

—Yeah.

Her warm fingers slipped around his wrist, soft against his pulse, like life holding onto life. She'd know if anything happened to him. She'd know….

The radiator clanked, and, on the edge of sleep, he jumped.

"*Sii-lent night…*"

The sound drifted up from the radiator, no, from the window it was under, which rattled in a gust of wind, covering for a moment the words, the silly happy people out there singing in the street, and then it was, "*Allllll is calm… Alllll is bright….*"

> "*Yes, come along, field-mice,*" cried the Mole eagerly. "*This is quite like old times! Shut the door after you. Pull up that settle to the fire.*"

She said, —I'll be your home, tonight.

—*Dulce Domum*, Kay said quietly.

—*Dulce?* Is that, like, ice cream?

—It's the chapter in the book, stupid. Latin for "Home, sweet home."

—I've got half a jar of *dulce de leche* from the corner bodega. When's the last time you ate?

—Breakfast, I guess.

—Get up, she said. —In my home, we make fried eggs and toast in the middle of the night when we're especially happy. It's a tradition.

> *And they braced themselves for the last long stretch, the home stretch, the stretch that we know is bound to end, some time, in the rattle of the door-latch, the sudden firelight, and the sight*

of familiar things greeting us as long-absent travellers from far overseas.

ABOUT THE AUTHORS

Daniel Abraham was born in Albuquerque, New Mexico, earned a biology degree from the University of New Mexico, and spent ten years working in tech support. He sold his first short story in 1996, and followed it with six novels, including fantasy series "The Long Price Quartet," **Hunter's Run** (an SF novel written with George R. R. Martin and Gardner Dozois), dark fantasy **Unclean Spirits** (as M. L. N. Hanover), and more than twenty short stories, including International Horror Guild Award-winner "Flat Diane" and Hugo and World Fantasy award nominee "The Cambist and Lord Iron: a Fairytale of Economics." His most recent book is **The Price of Spring**.

Peter S. Beagle was born in Manhattan on the same night that Billie Holiday was recording "Strange Fruit" and "I Gotta Right to Sing the Blues," just a few blocks away. Raised in the Bronx, Peter originally proclaimed he would be a writer when he was ten years old. Today he is acknowledged as an American fantasy icon, and to the delight of his millions of fans around the world is now publishing more than ever. He is the author of the beloved classic **The Last Unicorn**, as well as the novels **A Fine and Private Place**, **The Innkeeper's Song**, and **Tamsin**. He has won the Hugo, Nebula, Locus, and Mythopoeic awards. His most recent book is collection **We Never Talk about My Brother**. Upcoming are new novels **I'm Afraid You've Got Dragons** and **Summerlong**, and new collection **Mirror Kingdoms: The Best of Peter S. Beagle**.

Elizabeth Bear was born in Hartford, Connecticut, on the same day as Frodo and Bilbo Baggins, but in a different year. She lives in Manchester, Connecticut, with a presumptuous cat, a giant ridiculous dog, the best roommate ever, and a selection of struggling houseplants. Her first short fiction appeared in 1996, and was followed after a nearly decade-long gap by fifteen novels, two short story collections, and more than fifty short stories. Her most recent books are novels **Chill**, **By The Mountain Bound**, and novella **Bone & Jewel Creatures**. Bear's "Jenny Casey" trilogy won the Locus Award for Best First Novel, and she won the John W. Campbell Award for Best New Writer in 2005. Her short story "Tideline" won the Hugo and Sturgeon awards, and her novelette "Shoggoths in Bloom" was a Hugo nominee.

Pat Cadigan was born in Schenectady, New York, and grew up in Fitchburg, Massachusetts. She studied at the University of Massachusetts and University of Kansas, edited small press magazines *Shayol* and *Chacal*, and published her first story in 1980. One of the most important writers of the cyberpunk movement, she is the author of sixteen books, including debut novel **Mindplayers**, which was nominated for the Philip K. Dick Award, and Arthur C. Clarke Award-winners **Synners** and **Fools**, as well as two nonfiction movie books on the making of *The Mummy* and *Lost in Space*, five media tie-ins, and one young adult novel, **Avatars**. Her short fiction is collected in Locus Award-winner **Patterns**, **Dirty Work**, **Home by the Sea**, and **Letters from Home**. She currently lives in London with her husband, the Original Chris Fowler.

Paul Di Filippo sold his first story in 1977. Since then he's had several hundred short stories published, the majority of them collected in his dozen short story collections. He has written nine novels, including **Fuzzy Dice** and **Spondulix**. His most recent books are novel **Roadside Bodhisattva**, collection **Harsh Oases**, and short illustrated novel **Cosmocopia**. He is currently working, at last (!), on **A Princess of the Linear Jungle**, a sequel to his multiple award-nominated novella **A Year in the Linear City**. He lives in his native state, Rhode Island, amidst eldritch Lovecraftian surroundings, with his mate of thirty years, Deborah Newton, a chocolate cocker spaniel named Brownie, and a three-colored cat named Penny Century.

Jeffrey Ford was born in West Islip, New York. He worked as a machinist and as a clammer before studying English with John Gardner at the State University of New York. He is the author of seven novels, including **The Physiognomy, Memoranda, The Beyond, The Portrait of Mrs. Charbuque, The Girl in the Glass,** and **The Shadow Year**. His short fiction collections are **The Fantasy Writer's Assistant and Other Stories, The Empire of Ice Cream,** and **The Drowned Life**. His fiction has won the World Fantasy Award, Nebula, Edgar Allan Poe Award, Fountain Award, Grand Prix de l'Imaginaire, and the Shirley Jackson Award. Ford lives in southern New Jersey where he teaches writing and literature at Brookdale Community College.

Karen Joy Fowler was born in Bloomington, Indiana and attended the University of California at Berkeley between 1968 and 1972, graduating with a BA in Political Science, and then earning an MA at UC Davis in 1974. She published her first science fiction story, "Praxis," in 1985 and has won the Nebula Award for stories "What I Didn't See" and "Always." Her short fiction has been collected in **Artificial Things** and World Fantasy Award-winner **Black Glass**. Fowler is also the author of five novels, including debut **Sarah Canary** (described by critic John Clute as one of the finest First Contact novels ever written), **Sister Noon, The Sweetheart Season,** and **Wit's End**. She is probably best known, though, for her novel **The Jane Austen Book Club**, which was adapted into a successful film. She lives in Santa Cruz, California, with husband Hugh Sterling Fowler II. They have two grown children.

Molly Gloss was born in Portland, Oregon, and studied at Portland State College (now University). She worked as a schoolteacher and a correspondence clerk for a freight company before becoming a full-time writer in 1980. In 1981, she took a course in science fiction writing from Ursula K. Le Guin at Portland State University. Her first short story, "The Doe," was published that same year, and was followed by a dozen more, including Hugo and Nebula Award-nominee "Lambing Season." Her first novel **Outside the Gates** appeared in 1986, and was followed by **The Jump-Off Creek, The Dazzle of Day, Wild Life,** and **The Hearts of Horses. Wild Life** was a James Tiptree Jr. Award-winner. In addition, she has won the 1990 Ken Kesey Award for the Novel, the 1996 Whiting

Writers Award, as well as the PEN Center West Fiction Prize. Gloss has also written book reviews, essays, an appreciation of Ursula K. Le Guin, and an introduction to the memoir of a woman homesteader. Molly Gloss lives and writes in the Pacific Northwest.

Nicola Griffith is a native of Yorkshire, England, where she earned her beer money teaching women's self-defense, fronting a band, and arm-wrestling in bars, before discovering writing and moving to the U.S. Her immigration case was a fight and ended up making new law: the State Department declared it to be "in the National Interest" for her to live and work in this country. This didn't thrill the more conservative powerbrokers, and she ended up on the front page of the **Wall Street Journal**, where her case was used as an example of the country's declining moral standards. In 1993 a diagnosis of multiple sclerosis slowed her down a bit, and she concentrated on writing. Her novels are **Ammonite** (1993), **Slow River** (1995), **The Blue Place**, (1998), **Stay** (2002), and **Always** (2007). She is the co-editor of the **Bending the Landscape** series of original short fiction published by Overlook. Her non-fiction has appeared in a variety of print and web journals, including **Out**, **Nature**, and **The Huffington Post**. Her awards include the Tiptree Award, the Nebula Award, the World Fantasy Award, and the Lambda Literary Award (six times). Her latest book is a memoir, **And Now We Are Going to Have a Party: Liner Notes to a Writer's Early Life**. She lives in Seattle with her partner, writer Kelley Eskridge, and takes enormous delight in everything.

Caitlín R. Kiernan was born in Dublin, Ireland, but grew up in rural Alabama. She studied vertebrate paleontology, geology, and biology at the University of Alabama at Birmingham and the University of Colorado at Boulder. She then taught evolutionary biology in Birmingham for about a year. Her first short story, "Persephone," appeared in 1995. Since then, her fiction has been collected in nine volumes, including **Tales of Pain and Wonder; To Charles Fort, With Love; Alabaster**; and, most recently, **A Is for Alien**. Her stories include International Horror Guild Award-winners "Onion" and "La Peau Verte," SF novella **The Dry Salvages**, and IHG finalists "The Road of Pins" and "Bainbridge." Kiernan's first novel, IHG Award winner and Stoker finalist **Silk**, was followed by **Threshold**, **The Five of Cups**, **Low Red Moon**, **Murder of Angels**, and **Daughter of Hounds**. Upcoming is major new novel **The**

Red Tree and short story collection **The Ammonite Violin & Others**. Kiernan now lives in Providence, Rhode Island.

Ellen Klages was born in Columbus, Ohio, and attended the University of California at Berkeley, but left in her sophomore year, spending time as a camp counselor and working at a book factory, then returned to college, graduating from the University of Michigan with a philosophy degree. She wrote for San Francisco science museum Exploratorium, collaborating with Pat Murphy and others on a series of science books for children, beginning with **The Science Explorer**. Klages's first story, "Time Gypsy," appeared in 1998 and was nominated for the Hugo and Nebula awards. It was followed by a dozen more, including Nebula nominee "Flying Over Water," and Nebula winner "Basement Magic" (2003), most of which were collected in World Fantasy Award-finalist **Portable Childhoods**. She was a finalist for the Campbell Award for Best New Writer in 2000. Klages is the author of two novels, **The Green Glass Sea**, which won the Scott O'Dell Award for Best American Historical Fiction, and sequel, **White Sands, Red Menace**, which won the California Book Award for YA Fiction.

Ellen Kushner was born in Washington, D.C., and raised in Cleveland, Ohio. She attended Bryn Mawr College and graduated from Barnard College. After graduating, she found a job in publishing at Ace Books as a fantasy editor, and then went on to edit fiction at Pocket Books/Simon & Schuster. Her first novel, **Swordspoint: A Melodrama of Manners**, introduced the fantasy world Riverside, to which she has since returned in **The Fall of the Kings** (written with Delia Sherman), **The Privilege of the Sword**, and several short stories. Her second novel, **Thomas the Rhymer**, won the Mythopoeic Award and the World Fantasy Award. Kushner is also the editor of **Basilisk** and **The Horns of Elfland** (co-edited with Don Keller and Delia Sherman), and has taught writing at the Clarion and Odyssey workshops. Upcoming is an anthology of "Bordertown" stories co-edited with Holly Black. Kushner is perhaps best known in the U.S. as the host of the national public radio show *Sound & Spirit*, a musical exploration of world myth, spirituality and the human experience, and as the creator of *The Golden Dreydl*, which uses music from Pyotr Tchaikovsky's "The Nutcracker" to tell a Hanukkah story, in collaboration with the Shirim Klezmer Orchestra. Kushner lives in Manhattan, on Riverside Drive, with her partner, the author and editor Delia Sherman.

Maureen F. McHugh was born in Loveland, Ohio. She received a B.A. from Ohio University in 1981, where she took a creative writing course from Daniel Keyes in her senior year. After several years as a part-time college instructor, she spent a year teaching in Shijiazhuang, China. It was during this period she sold her first story, "All in a Day's Work," which appeared in *Twilight Zone*. She has written four novels, including Tiptree Award-winner and Hugo and Nebula Award nominee **China Mountain Zhang, Half the Day Is Night, Mission Child,** and **Nekropolis.** Her short fiction, including Hugo Award-winner "The Lincoln Train," was collected in **Mothers and Other Monsters,** which was a finalist for the Story Prize. She is currently a partner at No Mimes Media, an Alternate Reality Game company, and was a writer and/or managing editor for numerous projects, including *Year Zero* and *I Love Bees*.

Nnedi Okorafor was born in Cincinnati, Ohio. She earned a BA in rhetoric at the University of Illinois, C-U in 1996 and an MA in journalism from Michigan State University in 1999. She attended the University of Illinois in Chicago, getting her MA in English in 2002 and completing her PhD in 2007. She is the author of the novels **The Shadow Speaker** and **Zahrah the Windseeker**, winner of the Wole Soyinka Prize for Literature in Africa. **Zahrah the Windseeker** was also shortlisted for the 2005 Carl Brandon Parallax and Kindred awards and a finalist for the Garden State Teen Book Award and the Golden Duck Award. **The Shadow Speaker** was a Booksense Pick for Winter 2007/08, a Tiptree Honor Book, a finalist for the Essence Magazine Literary Award, the Andre Norton Award, and the Golden Duck Award and an NAACP Image Award nominee. Her children's book, **Long Juju Man**, won the 2007/08 Macmillan Writer's Prize for Africa. Forthcoming are her young adult novel **Akata Witch** and her adult fantasy **Who Fears Death**. She is a professor of creative writing at Chicago State University and lives with her family in Illinois.

Jane Yolen is the award-winning author of more than 300 books, mostly written for children. She is also a professional storyteller on the stage, has been an editor, and is the mother of three grown children, and the grandmother of six. Her best-known work, the critically acclaimed **Owl Moon** (illustrated by John Schoenherr) won the prestigious Caldecott Medal in 1988. Her fiction has won the Christopher Medal (twice) the Nebula (twice), World Fantasy Award, Society of Children's Book Writers (twice), Mythopoeic Society's Aslan (three times), Boys' Clubs of America Junior Book Award, and she had a National Book Award finalist. Six colleges have given her honorary doctorates. Her works for adults include the powerful holocaust fantasy **Briar Rose**, and the "Great Alta" trilogy. Some of her short fiction has been collected in **Once upon a Time (She Said)**. She lives in Hatfield, Massachusetts, and St Andrews, Scotland.

Adam Stemple was born in Minneapolis, Minnesota. The son of Jane Yolen and her late husband David Stemple, he is a writer and professional musician. A member of Irish band Tim Malloys, he has written four novels, including **Pay the Piper** (written with Jane Yolen), and a number of short stories.

Night Shade Books Is an Independent Publisher of Quality SF, Fantasy and Horror

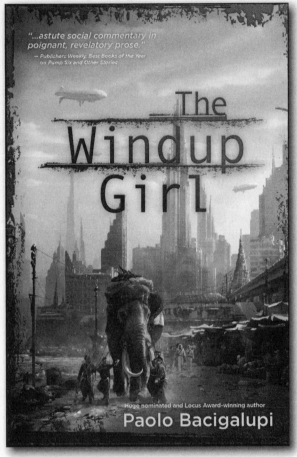

ISBN 978-1-59780-157-7, Trade Hardcover; $24.95

Anderson Lake is a company man, AgriGen's Calorie Man in Thailand. Under cover as a factory manager, Anderson combs Bangkok's street markets in search of foodstuffs thought to be extinct, hoping to reap the bounty of history's lost calories. There, he encounters Emiko...

Emiko is the Windup Girl, a strange and beautiful creature. One of the New People, Emiko is not human; instead, she is an engineered being, créche-grown and programmed to satisfy the decadent whims of a Kyoto businessman, but now abandoned to the streets of Bangkok. Regarded as soulless beings by some, devils by others, New People are slaves, soldiers, and toys of the rich in a chilling near future in which calorie companies rule the world, the oil age has passed, and the side effects of bio-engineered plagues run rampant across the globe.

Night Shade Books Is an Independent Publisher of Quality SF, Fantasy and Horror

ISBN 978-1-59780-133-1, Trade Hardcover; $24.95

Paolo Bacigalupi's debut collection demonstrates the power and reach of the science fiction short story. Social criticism, political parable, and environmental advocacy lie at the center of Paolo's work. His fiction has been collected in various best of the year anthologies, has been nominated for the Nebula and Hugo awards, and has won the Theodore Sturgeon Memorial Award for best SF short story of the year.

The eleven stories in *Pump Six* represent the best of Paolo's work, including the Hugo nominee "Yellow Card Man," the Nebula- and Hugo-nominated story "The People of Sand and Slag," and the Sturgeon Award-winning story "The Calorie Man." The title story is original to this collection. With this book, Paolo Bacigalupi takes his place alongside SF short fiction masters Ted Chiang, Kelly Link, and others, as an important young writer that directly and unabashedly tackles today's most important issues.

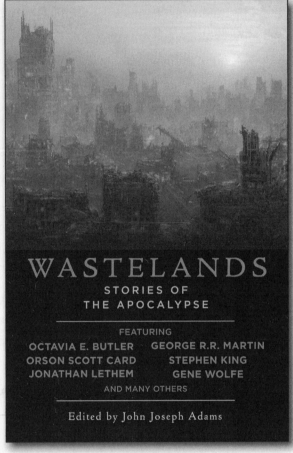

Night Shade Books Is an Independent Publisher of Quality SF, Fantasy and Horror

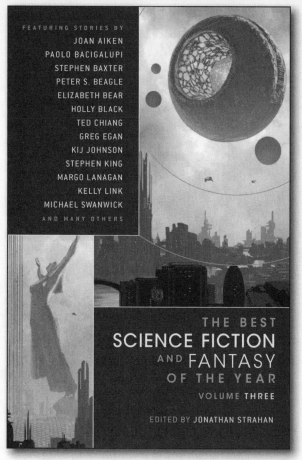

FEATURING STORIES BY
JOAN AIKEN
PAOLO BACIGALUPI
STEPHEN BAXTER
PETER S. BEAGLE
ELIZABETH BEAR
HOLLY BLACK
TED CHIANG
GREG EGAN
KIJ JOHNSON
STEPHEN KING
MARGO LANAGAN
KELLY LINK
MICHAEL SWANWICK
AND MANY OTHERS

THE BEST
SCIENCE FICTION
AND FANTASY
OF THE YEAR
VOLUME THREE

EDITED BY JONATHAN STRAHAN

ISBN 978-1-59780-149-2, Trade Paperback; $19.95

An alien world with an argon atmosphere serves as the stage for the ultimate self-examination; an African-American scientist dissects a Lovecraftian slave race while fascism rears its head on the other side of the world; an elderly Jewish artist attracts a celestial muse; a doomed village of scavengers discovers the scattered pieces of a metal man; a stalwart reporter gambles on an interview with the power to alter the world; a steel monkey defends a young girl from a rival family's assassins; two girls discover that the cruel social rituals of adolescence apply differently in fact than in fiction...

The depth and breadth of science fiction and fantasy fiction continues to change with every passing year. The twenty-eight stories chosen for this book by award-winning anthologist Jonathan Strahan carefully map this evolution, giving readers a captivating and always-entertaining look at the very best the genre has to offer.

Night Shade Books Is an Independent Publisher of Quality SF, Fantasy and Horror

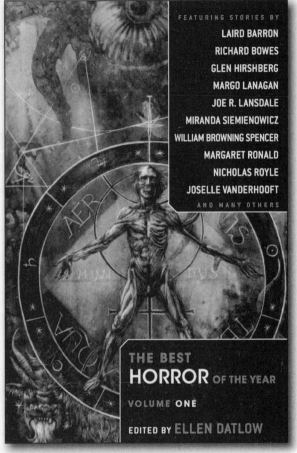

FEATURING STORIES BY

LAIRD BARRON

RICHARD BOWES

GLEN HIRSHBERG

MARGO LANAGAN

JOE R. LANSDALE

MIRANDA SIEMIENOWICZ

WILLIAM BROWNING SPENCER

MARGARET RONALD

NICHOLAS ROYLE

JOSELLE VANDERHOOFT

AND MANY OTHERS

THE BEST
HORROR OF THE YEAR
VOLUME **ONE**
EDITED BY ELLEN DATLOW

ISBN 978-1-59780-161-4, Trade Paperback; $15.95

An Air Force Loadmaster is menaced by strange sounds within his cargo; a man is asked to track down a childhood friend... who died years earlier; urban explorers delve into a ruined book depository, finding more than they anticipated; residents of a rural Wisconsin town defend against a legendary monster; an orphan returns to a wicked witch's candy house; an unanticipated guest brings doom to a high-class party; a teacher attempts to lead his students to safety as the world comes to an end around them...

What frightens us, what unnerves us? What causes that delicious shiver of fear to travel the lengths of our spines? It seems the answer changes every year. Every year the bar is raised; the screw is tightened. Ellen Datlow knows what scares us. The twenty-one stories and poems included in this anthology were chosen from magazines, webzines, anthologies, literary journals, and single author collections to represent the best horror of the year.